Praise for Manda Collins's delightful debut . . .
How to Dance with a Duke

"Warmth, wit, and delicious chemistry shine through every page . . . With a heroine to root for and a hero to die for, *How to Dance with a Duke* is a romance to remember."
—Bestselling author Julie Anne Long

"Sexy, thrilling, and romantic—whether she's writing of the mysteries of the heart or of the shady underworld of Egyptian relic smuggling, Manda Collins makes her Regency world a place any reader would want to dwell."
—*New York Times* bestselling author Kieran Kramer

"Manda Collins writes sexy and smart historical romance, with a big dash of fun. Romance readers will adore *How to Dance with a Duke*!" —Vanessa Kelly, named one of *Booklist*'s "New Stars of Historical Romance"

"Regency lovers have a new author to add to their dance cards! Manda Collins heats up the ballroom and writes romance to melt even the frostiest duke's heart. With sparkling Regency wit, a dash of mystery, and just the right amount of steam, *How to Dance with a Duke* is an enchanting debut, sure to sweep readers off their feet!"
—Tessa Dare, named one of *Booklist*'s "New Stars of Historical Romance"

Also by Manda Collins

How to Dance with a Duke

How to Romance a Rake

Manda Collins

St. Martin's Paperbacks

This is a work of fiction. All of the characters, organizations, and events portrayed in this novel are either products of the author's imagination or are used fictitiously.

HOW TO ROMANCE A RAKE

Copyright © 2012 by Manda Collins.
Excerpt from *How to Entice an Earl* copyright © 2012 by Manda Collins.

All rights reserved.

For information address St. Martin's Press, 175 Fifth Avenue, New York, NY 10010.

ISBN: 978-0-312-54925-1

Printed in the United States of America

St. Martin's Paperbacks edition / August 2012

St. Martin's Paperbacks are published by St. Martin's Press, 175 Fifth Avenue, New York, NY 10010.

10 9 8 7 6 5 4 3 2 1

For all the doctors, nurses, prosthetists, and countless other medical professionals who have taken care of me over the years. I literally would not be here without you.

Acknowledgments

Once again, I have about a million people to thank, but I'll stop before then. I promise.

Thanks to my wonderful editor Holly Blanck, and everyone at St. Martin's who works behind the scenes to bring my books to the shelves, both virtual and actual. Thank you for allowing me the freedom to write a story about someone like me.

To my always-upbeat, always-on agent, the fabulous Holly Root, who is always there when I've got a question or a crazytime freak-out, and tells me the truth without crushing my spirit.

To the Vanettes, for shared squees and laments, and never calling my questions dumb.

To Lindsey, for always-sound opinions and for sharing my opinions about oh-so-many things. You, madam, rock!

To Julianne and Santa, for always having my back and for being your hilarious, talented selves. Love you guys!

To Janga, for reading this book in its earliest, most flawed form, and loving Juliet unabashedly.

To Cindy and Katie for preserving my sanity on more than one occasion and for always responding to my distress calls with speed and support.

To my family for not whining (too much) when I drop off the radar to write and my sister Jessie for rallying the local troops and reminding me to eat when I was on deadline.

To Toni Blake, Vanessa Kelly, Julie Anne Long, Tessa Dare, Kieran Kramer, and so many others for continued support. You guys are not only gifted writers, but also generous, gifted people. You guys make me proud to call myself a romance writer.

One

From his close-cropped golden curls to his gleaming dancing shoes, Lord Deveril was a man envied by men and adored by women.

And he was bloody tired of it.

A leader of the fashionable set, he was dressed tonight for his family's annual ball in a style slavish young fops had dubbed "Deverilish," which was marked by a blend of Brummell's simplicity and a hint of dash. His pristine neck cloth was skillfully tied in a knot called—what else—the Deveril, and was anchored by a ruby stickpin that could keep a young buck in hats for a century or more. The cut of his black coat was looser than in Brummell's day but the tailoring was exquisite. And at his wrists he wore just a hint of lace.

It was not, he reflected, as he kissed the elderly Lady Sophronia Singleton's gloved hand and complimented her horrific scarlet turban, that he minded his popularity so much. Given the snubs he'd endured from the hypocritical *ton* when his father had still been drinking and whoring his way through London, the *ton*'s approval had been a welcome change at first.

It hadn't happened overnight, of course. He had been ruthless in his social campaign for those first few years. He'd worked hard to establish himself as a man of substance as well as style. He gambled, but only enough to prove himself honest. He had his share of liaisons with willing widows and even kept a few mistresses. But though he'd enjoyed the affairs while they lasted, always in the back of his mind was the memory that he was proving to the world just how different he was from his father.

And eventually, his diligence had paid off. Whereas he'd left university still in the shadow of his father's notoriety, now he was considered a good 'un by the gentlemen, and a catch by marriage-minded mamas.

Given what his social status might have been, then, Alec knew just how ungrateful it was for him to admit he was less than satisfied with it. His ennui sprang, he supposed, from the knowledge that if he so chose, this same pattern could continue on into his dotage. Breakfast at White's, horseflesh at Tattersall's, seeing and being seen in the park, followed up by some evening entertainment or other. The same people, the same food, the same conversation.

"Why so gloomy, Deveril?" Colonel Lord Christian Monteith asked from his usual post, one shoulder propped against a marble column. "Trouble with the old cravat? Champagne not shining your Hessians as bright as you'd like? Stickpin poking you in the . . . ?"

"Don't be an ass, Monteith." Alec raised his quizzing glass and a dark blond brow, channeling his annoyance through the eyepiece.

"Sorry, chap, that thingummy doesn't work on me," Monteith said apologetically. "My head's too thick. Its powers cannot penetrate to my brain."

With a sigh, Alec tucked the glass away. "Should have known you'd ignore it."

Taking up a position on the other side of Monteith's pillar, he nodded toward the ballroom floor. "Why aren't you dancing?" he asked.

"Already did."

"What, you danced once and having done your duty, retired here to this pillar?" It was unfair for Monteith to shirk his duty when Alec knew full well that there were plenty of ladies who would be without a partner. Ladies like his sisters. He ignored the fact that his own failure to marry someone who could serve as a chaperone for them might also impact their social success or lack thereof.

"For your information, Lord Hauteur," Monteith returned, "I danced with at least five ladies and now I am resting my tired bones, rather than sprinting to the card room as my less noble spirit would have me do."

Oh. "Where's Winterson?"

The Duke and Duchess of Winterson had become good friends with Alec earlier in the season through their investigation of the Egyptian Club, of which Alec had been a member. Theirs had been a rather hasty marriage, but to his delight they seemed blissfully happy together. Winterson and Monteith had served in the campaign against Napoleon together and were often to be seen surveying the crowds at these *ton* entertainments.

"Keeping watch over his lady wife," Monteith said with a frown, "and intimidating young swells into paying court to her cousins."

Alec felt an unfamiliar pang of jealousy. He'd been considering the possibility of marriage as a means of curing his ennui, and the Duchess of Winterson's cousin Lady Madeline Essex was high on his list of potential candidates. Curvy, blond, and quiet, Madeline would make an excellent viscountess. And her easy manners would endear her to his sisters. But if Monteith beat him to the punch, it wouldn't matter whether his sisters liked her or not.

"How is that working?" he asked, careful to keep his tone neutral.

"Not too well." The taller man grinned. "I don't think Miss Shelby or Lady Madeline care for being managed by their cousin's husband. Took quite a bit of convincing to get Lady Madeline to dance with me, and that was only grudgingly done. I do not think the lady cares for me."

Something in Alec's gut unknotted. He had come to admire both ladies over the past few weeks. But he had no wish to compete with his friend as a rival for Lady Madeline's hand. He was quite sure he could hold his own, but Monteith could be charming when he set his mind to it. Things would be much better if Monteith set his sights on Miss Juliet Shelby, the Duchess of Winterson's other cousin.

Slim and fair of complexion with deep auburn hair, Miss Shelby could have been the toast of the *ton* were it not for an accident during her teens that had left her with a pronounced limp. Alec had been partnered with her at a card party some weeks ago and found her to be a sensible and witty young woman. She was not one to suffer fools gladly, and he could only imagine her annoyance at Winterson's interference. If he guessed right, she'd much rather have spent the evening at home working on one of her compositions for the pianoforte.

"On the other hand," Monteith continued, "Miss Shelby and I had a delightful conversation speculating over the identity of the artist everyone is chattering about. She thinks he's probably some unknown trying to gain the spotlight. I think it's probably some chap with a flagging career who wishes to raise speculation about his work."

"*Il Maestro,* you mean?"

All of London had been engrossed with learning the identity of the mysterious artist who had begun showing his controversial paintings a little over a month ago. The gallery owner claimed not to know, as did the few who had purchased pieces from the show. And it was generally agreed that the longer he kept his identity a secret the more intrigued the public would become.

"Who else?" Monteith said with something like disgust. "I blame Byron for all of this ado. He swans about with his dark looks, spouting poetry and seducing women, and now every other fellow with the least bit of artistic inclination thinks a foreign sobriquet and risqué art are the shortcut to celebrity."

"Yes," Alec reasoned, "but Byron didn't keep his identity a secret. He makes sure everyone knows it's himself he's writing about."

The other man grimaced. "Just wait. *Il Maestro* will have a grand unmasking as soon as he's whipped the ladies into a sufficient frenzy of curiosity." He smiled. "All except for Miss Shelby, that is. I think a surfeit of chatter about that blighter is what sent her over the edge."

"What do you mean?" Alec asked, his brow furrowed. "Is she unwell?"

He did not like to think of Juliet ill. And it was the duty of a good host to ensure the comfort of all his guests, of course.

Monteith's glib tone turned serious. "I think her leg might be paining her a bit," he said. "And of course her harridan of a mother refused to allow her to take the carriage home."

On that point, Deveril and Monteith were in firm agreement. Lady Shelby was one of the most beautiful women to grace the *ton*. She and her two sisters had taken society by storm when they'd made their debuts some two and a half decades earlier. The daughters of an undistinguished Dorset squire, they'd been introduced to the *ton* by a distant cousin and within months married three of the most eligible bachelors in town. Of the three, Rose was the least admired. Not because of her looks, which had only improved with age, but because of her unpleasant nature.

"It would have surprised me to hear she had done so," he remarked. "Lady Shelby loves no one but herself. And even those feelings come with conditions."

The other man made a snort of agreement.

His respite from his guests over, Deveril took leave of his friend and wandered over to the line of chairs that had been set out for the matrons and those young ladies who either did not care to dance, or had not been asked. An empty seat next to Lady Madeline Essex beckoned, but as he glanced up he saw a familiar figure slipping through the doors leading to a hallway off the family rooms. Changing direction, he threaded his way through chattering guests, and finally made his way to the exit.

When he reached the corridor, it was deserted except for a few wandering pairs taking advantage of the less crowded room for quiet conversation. Or perhaps for assignations. He was hardly one to judge.

Turning into a side hallway, he saw what he was looking for. A familiar man was turning a key in the door of Alec's office.

"Uncle," he said, making no effort to hush his approach. "Is there something I can help you with?"

Roderick Devenish gave a start at being caught, but quickly regained his composure.

"Nephew." He nodded, revealing the extent to which his graying hair had begun its slow retreat toward the back of his scalp. "I was just wondering if you had any of those Spanish cheroots you like so much."

Bollocks. But Alec did not challenge him.

"Were you, indeed?" he asked blandly, letting his eyes convey what he really thought of that falsehood. "I would have offered one if I knew you wanted one. Of course I didn't realize you had a key."

A pregnant silence fell between the two men. Alec marveled at his uncle's audacity. He was just like Alec's late father.

"A legacy of my youth, I'm afraid," Roderick said, fingering the key in his hand. "And I thank you for the offer, but I've decided I don't wish to indulge after all."

"Then I'll have to ask you to return to the ballroom," Deveril said, his voice still calm. "If the other guests find you wandering about in the family quarters then they'll think we're actually family."

At the cut, Roderick let his urbane mask slip.

"You know as well as I do that the same poisonous blood runs in us both."

His sneer made him look every one of his fifty years.

Unwilling to be led down that path tonight, Alec shook his head. "Get out," he said simply. The steel in his tone was sharp and cold. "But first give me the key."

The naked hatred on his uncle's face was nothing new. It was akin to the look his own father had turned on him so many years ago. Grudgingly, he slapped the key into Alec's outstretched hand. Turning, he stalked back down the hallway in the direction from which Deveril had come, his displeasure evident in every step.

When he was sure Roderick was gone, Alec let himself into the study to ensure that nothing had been disturbed. To his relief nothing had. He did find, however, a collar—the same sort worn by the housemaids. He had no illusions that it had been dropped in the course of her regular duties. Roderick, it seemed, was as ever, just like his late brother.

The same blood might run in both of them, but Deveril was determined to ensure no woman he encountered would ever find herself a victim of it. He'd built his entire adult life upon that principle.

When he stepped back into the hall, he saw that the door to the music room three doors down was slightly ajar, and strode down the hall. Tonight, it seemed, the ballroom might be the least crowded room in Deveril House.

Hiding behind a screen was not how Miss Shelby had intended to spend the bulk of the Deveril ball.

When she'd arrived an hour earlier, she and her cousin Madeline had dutifully made their way to the side of the ballroom, where chairs had been set up for the chaperones and wallflowers. Though their other cousin, Cecily, had recently wed the Duke of Winterson, Juliet and Maddie had no illusions that they were now to be accepted among the elite of London society.

After an hour or so of chatting with Maddie, and later Colonel Lord Monteith, a friend of Winterson's, she'd felt the familiar sting of pain in her left leg. But it was the note in her reticule that made her less than eager to socialize. Pleading a headache, which showed every indication of becoming a real complaint, she excused herself to pore over the cryptic message in private.

Limping through the darkened corridors of Deveril House, she finally found the music room, which was, thankfully, deserted. She'd always admired the room, and had even played the magnificent pianoforte a time or two for the small musical evenings Viscount Deveril's sisters sometimes held. Though much younger than Juliet and her cousins, Lydia and Katherine Devenish were personable young ladies, and among the few friends the cousins could name among the more fashionable crowds of the *ton*.

She'd no sooner stepped into the music room than she heard familiar voices approaching in the hall. Cursing fate, she hurried as quickly as her painful leg would allow behind an elaborately decorated chinoiserie screen, where she lowered herself onto a tufted stool and waited for her unwelcome visitors to leave.

"I cannot account for it, Felicia," Miss Snowe complained. "It is bad enough that Cecily Hurston has stolen a march on every eligible female in London by marrying Winterson, but now she thinks to foist her ridiculous cousins on the *ton*. I had thought that Lydia and Katherine had more discernment than to allow such unfashionable people free rein in their ballroom. Or Lord Deveril for that matter. I am sorely disappointed in the Devenish family at the moment."

"Oh, I agree wholeheartedly," Amelia's bosom friend, Lady Felicia Downes, said.

What a surprise. Juliet rolled her eyes.

"It's insulting to anyone of taste," Lady Felicia continued. "As if we've forgotten how the Ugly Ducklings languished with the rest of the ineligibles these past three years. Does Cecily Hurston really believe that her lucky marriage will erase Lady Madeline's plumpness or Miss Shelby's unfortunate limp?"

Juliet could hardly be surprised at Felicia's unkind words, but hearing them aloud stung. For the three years since their debut, when Amelia had dubbed the unfashionable cousins "the Ugly Ducklings," they'd been subjected to one unkindness or another from the blond beauty and her friend. Though she had hoped that Cecily's marriage to the Duke of Winterson would give the cousins a much needed social boost, it would appear with Amelia and Felicia the change in status for Cecily had barely registered. And it most certainly hadn't erased their derision for Madeline and Juliet.

"Cecily Hurston may have trapped Winterson into marriage," Amelia said, "but there is no way that Lady Madeline or Miss Shelby can possibly expect to make comparable matches. Why, the idea is preposterous."

"While it is certainly within the realm of possibility that Madeline will go on a strict reducing regimen," Amelia continued, warming to her topic, "there is certainly nothing that Juliet can do about her unfortunate limp. I had supposed that one such as she would be confined to her home and not be thrust upon genteel society. I wonder what her parents were thinking to bring her out as if she were any normal girl."

Juliet felt her cheeks redden with anger. It wasn't as if she had never heard such sentiments expressed before. Indeed, her own mother had at times said similar things, though she had had the decency to keep her thoughts out of hearing of the public. So long as Juliet kept the true nature of her unfortunate injury secret, Lady Shelby had agreed that her daughter might attend as many society events as she wished. But to hear Amelia Snowe, who had fooled the gentlemen of the *ton* into believing her to be a sweet and nurturing angel, express such sentiments was infuriating.

"I daresay," Felicia responded, "they are hoping to marry her off to some aged lord who has already sired an heir. The idea of anyone else wishing to marry such an antidote is laughable. What man would possibly wish for the mother of his children to drag herself around with a walking stick?"

As she listened to the two girls share their mirth at her expense, Juliet vowed to "accidentally" trip Amelia at the first opportunity.

"You don't suppose they've already chosen someone, do you?" Amelia asked, once her giggles had subsided. "Because I would dearly love to be present at that wedding! How does one stumble down the aisle, do you think?"

"At least we would not be forced to see her dance at her own wedding! Imagine what a spectacle that would be! Carroty hair mixed with a halting gait. She will be as amusing as a performer at the circus." This came from Lady Felicia.

The laughing fit brought on by that bit of mean-spiritedness was interrupted by a cough. A gentleman's cough.

"Miss Snowe, Lady Felicia," she heard a deep voice say. "How is it that you are not on the dance floor?"

Juliet could all but hear Amelia's simpering smile slide back into place.

"Your lordship," she cooed, "what a delightful entertainment you've hosted this evening. Felicia and I were just taking a bit of a rest in between sets."

"I thank you for the compliment," Viscount Deveril said smoothly, though was that a hint of annoyance Juliet heard in his voice? "I must ask you to return to the festivities," he continued, his voice definitely cool. "This room is for family use only."

And you two are not family, his voice implied. Juliet bit back a cheer.

"We will leave at once," Amelia said her voice thick with apology. Of course she would not wish to insult an eligible like Deveril, Juliet thought cynically.

"We apologize for the intrusion, my lord," Felicia cooed.

Juliet bit her lip to keep from laughing at the insincerity.

"There is no harm done, ladies," Deveril assured them with more generosity than they deserved. "And I pray you," he added, "try not to stumble down the hall. One would hate to see the two of you make a spectacle of yourselves. This isn't the circus, you know."

Behind the screen, Julie's mouth fell open in astonishment. Had the Viscount Deveril, leader of the fashionable set, just delivered a set down on her behalf? It was not to be believed!

In the room at large, an awkward silence fell, no doubt while Amelia tried to come up with a suitable response. Apparently she was unable to do so, because Juliet soon heard both ladies thank his lordship again for the warning and hurry away in a rustle of silk skirts and the firm click of the closing door.

Waiting a few minutes more to ensure the room really was empty, Juliet was making to rise from her seat behind the screen when she heard the viscount's now familiar voice.

"You may come out now, Miss Shelby. Your detractors have gone back to the ballroom."

Juliet dropped her head into her hands in frustration.

He had known she was there the whole time.

Damn. And double damn.

Schooling her features, she rose awkwardly from her seat and stepped out from behind the screen.

When he'd overheard Miss Snowe and Lady Felicia mocking the ducklings, Alec had been surprised by the jolt of anger he felt on their behalf. Especially when Amelia made her degrading remarks about Miss Shelby. There was no other young lady of the *ton* who had both red hair and a limp. That her hair was a rich auburn, rather than the hue of carrots as the two spiteful ladies had implied, was, he supposed, beside the point.

"Come now, Miss Shelby, you are not going to ignore me, are you?"

Alec stepped farther into the room, and feeling the chill in the air, crouched before the fireplace to stoke it a bit. And to give his companion another moment to emerge from her hiding place. He was rewarded after a minute or so with the sound of a gown rustling and an uneven gait sliding along the thick Aubusson carpet.

"Here I am, my lord," she said from behind him. "I had best leave now. I too am sorry for intruding in the family rooms."

Alec rose easily from his crouching position before the fire. It was clear from her expression that Miss Shelby wished to be quit of his company. And he could hardly blame her. But, coming upon her here had given him an idea.

"I'm afraid that was a bit of a fib I told Lady Felicia and Miss Snowe in order to hasten their departure. This is one of the family rooms but you are more than welcome to stay."

He watched a series of mixed emotions flicker over her face. Chief among them confusion. As her green eyes narrowed he realized that she was really quite pretty when one stopped to actually see her. He supposed he was as guilty as anyone of defining her by her injured leg.

"Indeed?" she asked, regaining her composure. "I thank you for the compliment, but I will leave as well. I feel sure my cousins will have missed me by now."

As she turned to go, walking stick in hand, Alec reached out a hand to stay her. But the touch must have startled her, for she gasped and the sheet of foolscap she clutched floated to the floor.

"My apologies," he said, releasing her immediately, then bent to retrieve the paper for her. "I only meant to request you to stay for a moment and talk with me. I have something I wish to discuss with you."

He handed the note to her, and saw wariness in her green eyes as their gloved hands brushed.

"What do you want of me?" she asked, distrust oozing from every pore as she tucked the note into the reticule hanging from her wrist.

What was this? Alec wondered. She suddenly behaved as if he were some kind of lecher.

"I mean you no harm, Miss Shelby," he assured her. "Truly." She must have found something trustworthy in his disclaimer, for she nodded once and allowed him to direct her to a chair near the enormous harp his sister Lydia played from time to time.

"What was that about?" he asked before he thought better of it. He knew it was smart for a young lady to look out for herself, but there had been something else there in her eyes when she'd watched him.

A faint blush suffused Juliet's cheeks, and Alec was struck by her prettiness. Her features were sharp, with a pointed chin and a narrow nose, and a creamy smooth complexion, but it was her expressive green eyes that made her so attractive.

"My apologies, my lord," she said. "I'm afraid I was overset and I took out my pique on you."

"Bad news?" he asked, his gaze dropping to her reticule.

"Indeed," she said. "I . . . that is, my friend has been called away on personal business." Her eyes clouded. "I would not be so worried, but she has, in the past, been stricken with melancholy to such a degree that . . ."

"You fear she might harm herself," Alec said, understanding at once why she would be upset. He knew from personal experience what melancholy might make a woman do.

"Yes," Juliet said, her expression relaxing at his words. "My friend—I dare not say her name, because she has told me of her struggles in confidence—says that she is going to visit family in the north, but I was given to believe that she had no family. So I am worried that her tale might be just that. A tale to stop me from worrying."

Alec took this in. While he did not discount Juliet's assessment of the situation, he also knew the degree to which friends and family of those who suffered from melancholia tended to see every expression of sadness as a sign of impending relapse.

"Is there anything I can do to help?" he asked. "Perhaps I could have someone check into her whereabouts?"

She gave a sad smile. "I thank you for your kind offer, my lord," she said, "but I feel sure that my friend would see such an act as a violation of her privacy."

Alec gave a nod. He'd suspected as much, but seeing this young woman who clearly had her own struggles to endure had prompted him to make the offer. He mentally cursed Amelia and Lady Felicia for causing her even more distress.

"But you wished to speak to me of something else?" his companion prompted. "I can hardly think what it might be, given the chasm that gapes between us."

Her words stung. Perhaps because there was some truth to them. Still he could not fail to ask, "Because it is so unthinkable for 'someone like me' to wish to speak with 'someone like you'?"

"Well, you must admit that you are considerably more socially successful than I am," she defended herself. "Only consider how Miss Snowe and Lady Felicia mocked me. And they are hardly the only members of the *ton* who say such things."

"Speaking of those two," Alec said, "whatever have you and your cousins done to incur the wrath of Miss Snowe?"

Juliet stiffened. "I hardly think that we are to blame for

Miss Snowe's incivility," she said with a frown. "However," she conceded, "I believe she is currently annoyed with Cecily for stealing the Duke of Winterson from her. Of course, she does not account for the fact that Winterson had no intention of marrying her in the first place, but then Miss Snowe is not known for her ability to perform logical deductions."

"I do apologize," Alec said quickly, "I did not mean to imply that you brought on her enmity." His brows furrowed. "But she did seem particularly harsh about you, I think. Did you perhaps steal one of her beaux as well?"

He meant the last line to be teasing, but Miss Shelby's laugh was mirthless. "Hardly, my lord.

"I believe," she went on, "that Miss Snowe singles out my cousins and me because she failed to bring my elder brother up to scratch several years ago in Bath. When Matthew chose to marry someone else, Miss Snowe decided to take out her disappointment on us."

"Three years is a long time to nurse a grudge," Alec said, leaning his shoulders against the Adam fireplace.

"Well, I daresay if she had managed to marry someone else in the interim—Winterson, perhaps—she might have given up," Juliet said. "But since she has as yet been unsuccessful on the marriage mart, she still has anger enough to fuel her spite."

"It must be unpleasant for you." Which was an understatement, he knew.

"In truth, it does not bother me," Juliet assured him. "I am accustomed to being singled out. I dislike it when she vents her spleen on my cousins, however. They are not as skilled at deflecting such venom as I am."

"That being the case, however," he said, "I dislike hearing her mock your . . ."

Juliet looked up, one dark red brow raised in good humor. "My injury, shall we call it?"

At his mute nod, she went on. "I wish you would not let

it concern you, my lord. I have been subjected to worse."
She smiled wryly. "And at least in one respect, Amelia is
perfectly correct. I cannot dance."

What the devil was she doing enclosed in an antechamber
conversing with Lord Deveril of all people? Juliet wondered.

She'd been pleased to have him rout Miss Snowe and her
henchwoman Lady Felicia, but now she needed to make
her escape before someone saw them together. But to her
dismay, her host showed no signs of allowing her to leave.

"Have you ever tried to dance, Miss Shelby?" he asked,
his angelic countenance contorted into a frown. For a moment, Juliet imagined him as an avenging angel rushing to
her defense. It was a heady thought.

"Though I imagine her situation is quite different from
yours," Deveril continued, "I know that my great-aunt
Augusta, who suffers from a similar problem, found that
while she cannot walk without a limp, she was rather good at
dancing. Something to do with having a compensatory sense
of balance."

Though she knew he meant well, Juliet rather doubted
that Lord Deveril's Great-aunt Augusta's ailment was quite
as severe as her own. Still, it was kind of him to suggest it.

"I have not tried to dance, my lord," she said, "but I can
assure you that there is little chance of my being able to do
so. I'm afraid my—"

"I beg your pardon, Miss Shelby," he interrupted, "but if
you haven't tried, then how can you possibly know?"

His audacity surprised her. For as long as she'd known
him, or more accurately known of him, Lord Alec Deveril
had been held up as a pillar of good breeding and elegant
manners. He was hardly the sort of man one would expect
to interrupt a lady. Still, his question gave her pause.

How could she know without having tried? She thought

of the dance card that her cousin Cecily had given to her a week ago.

Earlier that season, when Amelia Snowe had left her reusable ivory and filigree dance card in the ladies' retiring room at the Bewle ball, Cecily, then Miss Hurston, had snatched it up in hopes of using it herself. After all, it had been signed by the most eligible gentlemen of the *ton* and Amelia had just proven herself once more to be the most unpleasant and hateful young lady of the cousins' acquaintance. But now that Cecily was happily married, she had passed it on, as a sort of good luck token, to Juliet. She was not bold enough to trick the gentlemen into thinking they had signed up for dancing with her rather than Amelia, as Cecily had done, but she would like to put the dance card to use on her own. Perhaps have the gentlemen of the beau monde scrawl their names on the ivory slats of the dance card in hopes of taking a turn about the room with *her* for a change.

But since it had come into her possession, Juliet had been wondering just how she could make that happen. It was perfectly acceptable for young ladies who were unable to dance to sit out the set with a gentleman. But what if Lord Deveril was right? What if she could actually dance? The very idea was revolutionary. It could change everything.

"I suppose you are right," she conceded at last. "I cannot know, never having tried. But I would hardly wish to try it in a ballroom full of spectators. If my mama was worried that my playing the pianoforte would create a spectacle, she would have an apoplectic fit if she knew I was considering dancing."

"Which," his lordship said with a grin, "is why you should have a select group of people teach you. Perhaps just your cousins and a few other ladies and gentlemen."

He looked so pleased with himself that Juliet nearly laughed aloud. "And I suppose you would wish to be a member of the party?" she asked.

"Well, it was my idea," he said guilelessly.

Juliet found herself smiling. "I have no doubt that Cecily will be happy to host such a party at Winterson House."

"What sort of hostess duties are you committing me to, Juliet?" the Duchess of Winterson demanded from the doorway. "And what on earth are you doing closeted with Lord Deveril? I know you have no care for your reputation, but if your mama were to know she'd have the two of you married before morning."

Apparently unfazed by the duchess's warning, Lord Deveril merely grinned, and bowed to her cousin. "I shall leave you to explain your plan to the duchess, Miss Shelby. I enjoyed our conversation very much."

When he had gone, Cecily looked speculatively at her cousin.

"Yes, Juliet, explain your plan to your cousin," she said. "And please include the part that involves the gorgeous man who just left the room."

Cursing the blush she felt rising on her fair skin, Juliet did just that.

Two

Three nights later, Juliet stood nervously as Cecily and Winterson demonstrated the movements of the polonaise, their hands clasped as they stepped and spun. Since Winterson still felt the effects of a war injury to his leg, it was useful for Juliet to see how the steps of the dance might be modified to accommodate him.

"You can see, Juliet," Cecily said, suiting her actions to her words, "that you take a sliding step, like this, and then bend the knee every third step."

"You have to follow the steps of the lead couple, of course," Winterson said, turning with Cecily's left hand in his right and her right in his left. "It's more of a promenade than anything else."

"I've attended my share of balls," Juliet reminded them, "I believe I know the steps. It's just a matter of performing them."

"Then let's get started," Cecily said with a firm nod. She gestured to Lydia, Deveril's sister, who was their accompanist for the evening. "Everyone take your partners."

At her words, Juliet felt her heart pound. It was the moment of reckoning and she suddenly wished that she hadn't been so firm in her assertion that all she wanted was practice to learn the steps. What if she failed miserably? What if she fell? What if she . . .

"Shall we, Miss Shelby?" Lord Deveril said, stepping

out from behind her as the rest of the couples formed and went to stand in promenade position. "I promise not to lead you astray."

She'd, of course, fretted over who would be burdened with partnering her, but in her imaginings she had never dreamed that Deveril would be the one. She rather thought that Monteith would be the one. She felt none of the unease with him that she felt with Deveril. Whereas Monteith made her laugh, Deveril made her nervous.

"Well, Miss Shelby?" he repeated. "Shall we?"

And without waiting for her to agree to it, he simply took her hand in his and led her to stand up beside the other couples. Other couples who had stood waiting, watching while she dithered.

"Deep breath," Deveril said, squeezing her hand. "We are your friends, so there's no need to be nervous. Besides, if you are nervous, then I am nervous. And you do not wish to see me when I'm nervous."

"What happens?" Juliet asked, keeping her voice low as they waited for the music to start.

"I bite," he whispered.

There was no time for Juliet to react, for the music commenced and she spent the next little while trying to maintain her balance and mastering the sliding steps of the dance. It wasn't particularly vigorous. And because she could not point her right foot, she had to rely more on her partner than she would have liked. Even so, once they'd gone through a few figures, Juliet felt much more confident in her ability not to embarrass herself should she ever attempt to dance in public.

"I really must thank you for suggesting I try it, my lord," she told Lord Deveril as they waltzed. He'd proved to be a patient teacher. And despite that provocative remark earlier, he had been the perfect gentleman. "I find that I enjoy dancing a great deal more than I could have guessed."

If she were completely honest with herself, it wasn't

only the dancing that she enjoyed. Being held in the arms of London's most eligible bachelor was something to anticipate, no matter how she tried to suppress her reaction.

"I would never have had the audacity to even consider the idea if you hadn't suggested it," she continued, trying desperately not to notice how he smelled of cloves and sandalwood.

"The pleasure is all mine, Miss Shelby." If Lord Deveril noticed that she was melting in his arms, he gave no indication of it. Instead, he smiled down at her in that agreeable way of his that made her breathless and comfortable all at once.

"I am pleased to see that my suspicions were correct," he continued. "Otherwise I would have missed the opportunity to dance with such a delightful partner."

"Can't say I expected such forward thinking from you, Deveril," Monteith interrupted, gliding past with Cecily in his arms. "Thought you spent all your time coming up with new ways to tie your cravat. Or new receipts to bring your boots to the brightest shine."

If they were ladies, Juliet would have described the reaction of the gentlemen to this salvo as giggles. But from her own experiences with her brother, Juliet knew that gentlemen never giggled.

"I fear, Monteith," Deveril retorted, "you are mistaking my interests with those of my valet. Indeed, if I have any standing as a man of fashion at all, I owe it to him. Perhaps you've considered retaining one for yourself? Or perhaps you mean for your neck cloth to look as if it has been crushed by an elephant?"

"He's got you there, Monteith," Winterson snorted. "Told you that cravat wouldn't pass muster with Deveril. Though I don't think Phillips is going to like having his handiwork disparaged like that."

"Gentlemen, pray remember that you are supposed to be on your best, most charming behavior!" Cecily chided the men. "One's partners at a ball do not generally call out to one another across the room."

"Well, not at *ton* balls anyway," Lord Fortenbury, who was dancing with Winterson's cousin Serena, said. "There are certain other entertainments where the social rules are a bit more . . . flexible."

"Yes, well, we do not discuss those in mixed company, do we, Fort?" There was a hint of steel in Winterson's tone.

"Really, darling," Cecily said. "How are ladies supposed to know anything of the real world if gentlemen are forever protecting them from fast talk? If you treat us like children to be sheltered from every little hint of scandal, how will we deal with real scandal when we run across it?"

"Madam, I pray you, desist from requesting fast talk until you have gone home for the evening," Monteith objected. "I have no wish to meet your husband over pistols at dawn. He's a better shot than I am."

"And what are your feelings on the matter, Miss Shelby?" Deveril asked, diverting Juliet's attention from the other dancers. "Do you share your cousin's attitude toward the edification of ladies?"

"I can hardly admit otherwise in her hearing, can I?" Juliet asked with a laugh. "Cecily can be quite persuasive on the matter, so I definitely share some of her more liberal leanings. However, I'm not sure I wish to know precisely what real scandal entails. Or rather, I do not wish to experience it for myself."

"Ah, you are cautious, then."

Juliet refused to look up into his face for fear she'd reveal just how captivating she found him. Besides, he was only doing her a kindness. It hardly implied the man was ready to throw himself at her feet.

"Indeed," she answered primly. "I would not wish to become the subject of talk. Or rather, no moreso than usual."

"I'm afraid that when you reveal your newfound dancing skills at the next ball you attend you will inevitably become the subject of talk," Deveril told her, dipping his head a bit to look her in the face.

"But only of the best sort," he assured her with a warm smile. "Society loves nothing better than a triumph."

Juliet nodded, unable to voice her appreciation for his kind words.

They danced along in companionable silence while the easy chatter of their friends sounded around them. Juliet reveled in the feel of his hands, one at her waist and the other clasping hers tightly. She had very few moments of this sort, when she could hide away in the deep recesses of her mind, to bring out in times of trouble as a salve to combat loneliness. But she knew, with a certainty born of experience, that she would always remember this waltz.

For too long she'd allowed herself to be pushed to the side, like a broken bit of furniture that was no longer of use. She hadn't been completely repaired, but she now knew that she was not so damaged as she'd once thought. And the knowledge filled her with hope—for the first time in years.

No one, she vowed to herself, would rob her of such opportunities again.

"Juliet! What on earth are you doing?"

Like an unskilled bow on a violin, the sound of Viscountess Shelby's voice brought all activity in the room to a halt.

Just like her mother to spoil things. Juliet closed her eyes in an effort to steel her emotions. She had hoped that Lady Shelby would remain ignorant of her dance lessons until after she'd been able to demonstrate them in public. Her mother was much more likely to acquiesce to the change in her daughter's social status if it were presented as a fait accompli. She had her own reasons for wishing Juliet to remain in her current position at the edges of the *ton* and none of them involved her offspring's well-being. Juliet had learned that the hard way years ago.

When Juliet made to pull away from Deveril, she felt his arms tighten about her for a flash before he let her go.

"I am dancing, Mama," she said to her mother, who stood in the doorway, her hand at her breast as if she'd discovered her daughter in an orgy rather than a simple dancing party."It's quite harmless."

"I am so sorry, Your Grace," the butler said from behind Lady Shelby. "She slipped past me as I came to give you her card."

Perhaps sensing that her histrionics would not be best received by the present company, Lady Shelby visibly composed herself. "But, I am family, so I knew you would not wish to stand on ceremony, my dear Cecily," she crooned, assuming a more solicitous mien. "And I did so wish to see my dear daughter dance. I hate to think of what effect it might have on her injury."

"She is perfectly all right, as you can see, Aunt," Cecily informed her as she stepped forward to offer a supporting arm to Juliet. "I daresay it's even good for her."

"Indeed, Lady Shelby," Deveril said, flanking Juliet's other side, "she is a natural dancer. It was I who suggested it in the first place, if you must know. I've an aunt who suffers from—"

But before he could complete his thought, Lady Shelby interrupted the viscount. "I am sure your aunt is quite able to do as she wishes, my lord. But you do not understand the fragile nature of my daughter's health. I will thank you to let me know how best to take care of my own flesh and blood."

"Mama," Juliet objected, mortified at her mother's rudeness.

"Juliet, my dear," Lady Shelby said, turning her head in that way that signified she was about to issue a towering scold. "Might I speak with you in the hall for a moment? The rest of you will excuse us, of course."

* * *

Alec watched as Juliet followed her mother from the sitting room, her limp more pronounced than it had been all evening.

"What was that about?" he demanded. "One would think that Lady Shelby disapproved of Miss Shelby dancing at all."

The pall cast over the room by Lady Shelby's arrival hovered over the erstwhile revelers like a dark cloud.

"Come, my lord," Cecily said to him, linking her arm through Deveril's and pulling him toward the table where refreshments had been laid out earlier. "Let me pour you a cup of tea."

"It's a da . . . er, dashed shame," Winterson said, leading Lady Madeline to the refreshments as well. "It's as plain as a pikestaff Lady Shelby resents Juliet enjoying herself."

Though he was in agreement with his friend, Alec didn't say so. He knew that he should be taking this opportunity to sit beside Lady Madeline and chat with her about some inconsequential frivolity, but he found himself reluctant to chat lightly of this and that while all the work he'd done to bring Miss Shelby out of her shell was being undone in another room.

"Here, Lord Deveril," Cecily said from his elbow, offering him a cup of tea. "Do not let my aunt's scolding bother you. I can assure you we have endured far worse from her over the years. Indeed, I believe she was much calmer than she would normally have been since she would dislike having you gentlemen know how difficult she can be. You will not believe it but you probably saved Juliet a public scold by your mere presence."

"But why would she be so angry because Miss Shelby tried dancing?" he asked. "How can she possibly object to having her daughter participate more actively in society? I have seen mothers of debutantes before. And they do not make a habit of preventing their daughters from making good matches!"

Winterson choked on his tea. "I should say not! If only they did, the lot of us might have slept more easily these past few years."

Madeline, who had been looking on with a frown, spoke up. "I do not know the reason behind it, but Aunt Rose has always been hard on her children. And you are right that it's odd for her to sabotage Juliet's chances at making a good match. But she's been this way ever since Juliet's accident."

"What actually happened?" Deveril asked. He knew it was perhaps rude of him to ask such a question, but he sensed the circumstances surrounding the incident that had left Juliet crippled lay at the heart of Lady Shelby's censure.

"We are not even exactly sure ourselves," Cecily said, sipping from her own cup of tea. "The year Juliet was fourteen her father was posted with the Foreign Office to the Congress of Vienna. And while they were there something happened. Whether it was an accident or a deliberate injury we don't know. But whatever occurred, it was grave indeed. I know that at one point they were unsure whether Juliet would even survive the injury, so it cannot have been minor. They remained abroad for two more years, and when they returned, Juliet was completely changed."

"How so?" Monteith asked, stretching his long legs out before him as he reclined in an armchair.

"You will not believe it, but before they left," Madeline said, "Juliet was the most animated of us three cousins."

Alec felt his jaw drop a little.

"You're joking," Winterson said, his brow furrowed. "Juliet? Quiet Juliet?"

"I've seen it happen to soldiers," Monteith said, his face serious. "You have too, Winterson. We all have. A young fellow full of his own importance goes off to war and comes home a changed man."

"Yes," Deveril said, "but a gently bred young lady living in polite society abroad is hardly exposed to the same sort of atrocities as a hardened soldier. No matter how close Vienna was to the battle of Waterloo."

"Whatever happened, it must have been very difficult indeed," Cecily said. "Because the Juliet who left and the Juliet who returned were like night and day. And of course there was the injury."

"Which was . . . ?" Monteith asked from his perch before the fireplace.

"We don't know." Madeline's blue eyes were serious. "We have never known. Cecily and I agreed that we would wait for Juliet to tell us about it, thinking that for us to bring up the subject ourselves would perhaps be too intrusive. And there was a certain amount of . . ."—she paused, as if searching for the right word—"hesitation, I suppose, in her manner every time our conversation even approached talk of her time abroad, that we simply became accustomed to avoiding the subject altogether."

"As a result," Cecily continued, "we never did learn what happened to her. Or why. All we know is that something definitely occurred that left Juliet with a bad limp, and that our aunt has tried her hardest to make sure that Juliet does nothing to draw attention to herself."

"Why allow her to debut, then?" Alec asked. This whole business made no sense. He'd never particularly liked Lady Shelby but he'd never considered that Juliet's unpopularity actually sprang from a concerted effort on her mother's part to prevent her from being accepted. "One would expect her to simply forbid Juliet from going out in society at all."

"Oh, Lord Shelby wouldn't allow it," Madeline said. "I think Juliet would have been just as happy not to make her come out at all. But her father insisted that she do so along with us."

"I overheard Lord and Lady Shelby arguing once at a house party. She was demanding that he give up his ridiculous insistence that Juliet be treated like any other young lady." Cecily scowled at the memory. "I will never forget the scorn in her voice when she spoke of Juliet. As if she were an embarrassment. That was not terribly long after Juliet made her debut. She had gone for a walk on the terrace with Lord Filton and she'd slipped on a stone. You would have thought she'd fallen headfirst into the Serpentine at Hyde Park for the way Lady Shelby carried on about it."

Deveril shook his head. He'd had no idea that any of this had been going on. He certainly hadn't done anything to ensure that any of the Ugly Ducklings, as Amelia Snowe had dubbed them, were sheltered from the unkind members of the *haut ton*. A pang of shame washed over him at the knowledge. He'd been so busy worrying about himself, he'd not even noticed the dramas going on beyond the fringes of his more fashionable set of friends.

"You didn't know," Madeline said softly.

Deveril looked up to find the curvy blonde's gaze on him. She saw more than she let on, he'd wager. He was startled to remember that she was the one he'd originally intended to woo. Certainly he felt none of the dizzying array of emotions that Juliet inspired in him when he looked upon her. No, Madeline was a nice enough young lady, but he was not drawn to her in the same way as he was to Juliet. And perhaps that was all to the better. He had learned from his father's example just what hardships could arise from a match based on passion. Much better to marry someone he liked, but felt no passion for.

"No," he said at last. "I didn't know, but I cannot help but feel responsible somehow. If I had been more alert to her situation—"

"You could have done nothing," Cecily said baldly. "Only Lord Shelby has ever been able to sway Aunt Rose and even then he is not always successful. I daresay you weren't even introduced to us until last year. One can hardly blame you for failing to intuit that Juliet was being held back."

A sharp cry from the hallway startled them all. Alec, his

senses attuned from years spent with his brute of a father, knew all too well what damage a parent could visit upon a child. Even an adult. Incensed, he stalked toward the pocket doors.

He was arrested by a hand on his arm.

"My lord, perhaps you should wait," Cecily said quietly.

He pulled out of her grasp and continued to the door.

Behind him he heard Winterson bidding his wife to let him go.

Ignoring the talk behind him, he stepped into the hallway, his dancing slippers echoing on the marble floor.

He scanned the richly appointed room, and saw the door to an adjoining chamber ajar, the warm glow of lamplight spilling into the hall.

He could hear the sound of weeping and, for the first time, stopped. What right did he have to intrude upon Juliet's pain? But something stronger than common sense made him press on, an urge he hardly understood leading him to seek her out.

Carefully, he walked to the door, and peered inside, so as not to startle her. To his relief, she was alone. And at first glance he saw no sign that she had been mishandled physically.

She sat in a small chair before the fire, a handkerchief in one hand and what appeared to be a note in the other.

"Miss Shelby," he asked, trying not to let his anger for her current state infuse his voice. "Are you well?"

She looked up, her eyes bright with tears. Stricken, she dabbed at her eyes with the handkerchief, made to stand.

"Lord Deveril, I did not hear you come in," she said, her voice shaking, but strong. "If you will give me but a moment I will be back to finish our lesson."

"Do not trouble yourself, Miss Shelby," he said, moving closer, wishing he could take her into his arms to offer comfort. But even the Duchess of Winterson, with her liberal ideas, would frown upon that, he suspected.

He settled for a comforting hand on Juliet's shoulder.

"Is there something I may assist you with?" he asked. "Shall I bring your cousin to you?"

She closed her eyes, as if to give herself strength, then shook her head.

"No," she said softly. "No, I will be all right in a moment. I just needed a bit of time to myself."

Her words implied that she wished him to leave, and he could not blame her. But he also knew that such situations, if left to be handled on their own, could lead to dire consequences.

"Miss Shelby," he said. "Was your mother very angry about the dancing, then?"

She stared at him blankly for a moment. As if she didn't understand his question. Perhaps she had been struck by her mother? He didn't see any signs of it on her person, but clothing could hide bruises. He knew as well as anyone.

But her words suggested otherwise. "Yes, my lord, she was quite angry, but that's not why I am overset."

She sighed, and looked into the fire, as if choosing her words carefully. He gave her the space she needed.

Finally, she spoke.

"My mother is fearful that my injury will bring shame on the Shelby name," she said. Her tears had gone now, leaving only resignation in their wake. "But I am accustomed to her histrionics now. The only real power she has over me is that of public embarrassment."

Her lips curved upward in a wry smile.

"I find it ironic that in her efforts to save herself from scandal, she creates them all on her own."

She held up the note between her slim fingers. "It is this which caused my outburst," she said. "I am sorry to have given you the wrong impression."

He pulled the chair opposite hers closer and took a seat. "Is it your friend? The one you spoke of the other evening?"

"Yes." She tucked her handkerchief into the sleeve of her gown, and smoothed the silk of her skirts. Then, as if she had decided something, she handed him the note. "You can read it if you like."

He took it from her, his gloved fingers brushing hers as he clasped the missive.

The paper was inexpensive. The sort that could be had at any common stationers'. On the outside Juliet's name was written in a neat, curving hand. The direction of her father's London town house beneath.

> *My dear Juliet,*
>
> *I am afraid that circumstances have come to a head, and I am no longer able to remain in London. I know this will mean an end to our lessons, but I am confident that you will find someone to take my place. Your talents are such that any musician of sense will take you on without hesitation.*
>
> *I beg that you will not try to contact me. Your mother will not care to have our acquaintance furthered. Especially given my altered situation. I have seen to it that Alice is well cared for. I will not give you my direction, lest you be tempted to follow me.*
>
> *Take care of yourself, dear friend, and know that I will always remember your friendship in my time of need.*
>
> *Anna Turner*

Juliet watched as Deveril scanned Anna's brief note. His expression revealed nothing of his reaction to it. In the firelight, his dark blond hair, fashionably tousled, sparked with hints of gold. He really was a breathtakingly beautiful man. It was not difficult to understand why he had risen to such prominence in the fashionable set. One with such looks and charm would find it easy to win the favor of those who crossed his path.

"She is your music teacher?" he asked, finally looking up. If he noted that her gaze had lingered on him for overlong, he gave no sign of it.

"Yes," she replied, looking down at her hands, as if searching out spots of dust on her gloves. "She is also a dear friend."

She did not say that Anna was also the closest thing to a mother she had ever had. Without her, Juliet would never have found the strength to recover from the injuries she sustained to both her body and her spirit on that long-ago spring day.

"What are the circumstances she speaks of? Your worries the other night seemed to hinge on her melancholia. But this sounds as if she is running away from something. Or someone. And why does your mother disapprove of her?"

Juliet wondered how much to tell him. And gave herself a mental shake for telling him anything of Anna's note at all. He could care nothing for the plight of an impoverished clergyman's daughter. And yet, there was something about him that told her he did care. He was interested. And having kept Anna's secret for so long, she found herself wishing to unburden herself of the whole sordid story. A story she had kept even from Cecily and Madeline.

"After my . . . accident," she said, looking up from her hands to find his blue eyes fixed upon her face, his gaze unnerving but at the same time exhilarating. "After my accident, my father hired Anna to instruct me on the pianoforte. I had played as a small child, and upon our return to England, I found myself restless. Needing some activity to fill the endless days, and sometimes nights. I could not ride. I could not walk about the countryside, which had once been my greatest joy. And with music, I could find some . . ."

She struggled to find the right word. "Some release for the emotions that haunted me."

She looked up to find him still watching her. "It was very bad, you see. The accident. And Anna was a godsend. She was kind, and what I needed more, a taskmaster. She insisted I give all my attention to my music. And it worked. Before long, I was playing constantly. Day and night."

"Which kept you from brooding," he said quietly. "A smart woman, your Mrs. Turner."

"The cleverest," Juliet agreed. "She lived with us and even came to London with us when I was to make my come-out. But the month before I was to make my debut, my mama announced that Anna had been dismissed and that I was to have no more contact with her."

Deveril leaned forward in his chair. "Why?"

"Mama had accused Anna of casting out lures to Papa. Which was ridiculous. Only later did I learn that one of his friends had importuned her. And . . ." She blushed. "Anna was in a delicate condition. I was not surprised that Mama would put the entire blame on Anna. And with no family to turn to, and no reference, she was at her wit's end. I had enough pin money saved up that I was able to care for her until the child was born. Mama didn't know about that of course. And though Anna objected, she acquiesced for the sake of the child."

"These are very complicated issues for a young lady to handle on her own," Deveril said, a frown wrinkling his brow. "What happened to the child?"

"Oh, Anna kept her," Juliet said, her remembered joy at her ability to help her friend denting her earlier sorrow. "She was able to rent a small house in Hans Town where she teaches the pianoforte to the daughters of tradesmen who wish them to marry into the upper classes. We put it about that she was a widow, whose husband had died in the war."

"What of the child's father?" Deveril demanded, standing to lean one shoulder against the fireplace, his fists clenching in anger. "If he importuned her against her will, he deserves to be thrashed."

"I could not agree with you more," Juliet returned. "But Anna refused to name the man. Only that he was a friend of Papa's who had stumbled into her chambers one evening in his cups. I suppose he was looking for a willing chambermaid. Or unwilling as the case may be."

It was infuriating to know that women, especially those without male relatives to protect them, were so powerless against men with bad intentions. And, like it or not, it was always society's insistence that the woman was at fault. No matter how dishonorable the man who had forced her was.

Alec was silent. His anger was evident in every inch of his person. Juliet wished that he'd been there when Anna had first confessed her secret. She had little doubt that the man before her would have been able to persuade her music teacher to tell just who had raped her.

"So, now your Miss Turner . . . or Mrs. Turner," he said, "is leaving London. Without explanation. Could it be that she consented to this unknown fellow and is running off with him?"

Juliet shook her head. "There is no way she would do such a thing. She was too upset over the whole incident to have been lying. I believe that somehow Mama found out her location and threatened her with exposure if she did not leave town at once."

"Your mother did bring you the note," he agreed. "But what of the one the other night?"

"That was brought to me from Anna's maid, so I know it came directly from her," she said. "And as for Mama's bringing the one tonight, I suppose it's possible that she forced Anna to write it. But I really think Mama's coming here with the note was just an excuse for her to see what Cecily and I were up to. Mama is nothing if not curious. And she is vigilant about ensuring I draw no attention to myself. The seal on the note was intact, so she cannot have read it."

"Why is she so determined to keep you from marrying?" Deveril asked suddenly. "I mean to cause no offense but one would think if she is concerned about you bringing shame upon the family that she would wish you married off and away from her as soon as possible."

He did not mince words, did he?

"She wishes me to marry," she said. "But the man of her choosing. And since I refuse, she retaliates by ensuring that I do not draw the attention of any other gentleman."

"Who is the man of her choosing?"

She paused, reluctant to even say the man's name aloud.

"Turlington," she admitted.

Deveril's eyes widened in shock. "I see why you would refuse."

Lord Philip Turlington was a man of some thirty-five to forty years old, who was well known throughout the *ton* for his artistic endeavors. While handsome enough, there was something about the man that made Juliet's skin crawl.

"Yes, and do not ask me why she chose him of all people, but for some reason she is determined that I will wed him. If it were not for Papa I would have been married to the man months ago. But as Papa cannot stomach the man, he refuses to grant his consent to the match."

Alec shook his head. What a coil. He had known Juliet's situation was difficult, but he was beginning to believe it was nigh impossible.

"And I can guess that Mrs. Turner disliked the idea of your marrying Turlington as well?"

He could not help but think that it was in Mrs. Turner's best interest for Juliet to remain unmarried as well. After all, if she were no longer able to control her own purse strings then she would no longer be able to supplement Mrs. Turner's income.

But Juliet got there before him. "Yes, but not because she would lose my pin money, if that's what you are thinking. Mrs. Turner has earned enough income from her teaching to pay her own way for some months now. Truly she is not the grasping harlot my mother would have the rest of society believe."

"And now she's gone—and left her child with someone else."

Her expression sobered. "Yes. That is what concerns me most," she admitted. "It is inconceivable to me that Anna would leave her daughter in someone else's care while she fled the city. Some mothers, yes, but not Anna. This is what disturbed me most about the letter. You see, Anna told me last week that she felt as if she were being watched."

"How so?"

"Well, she saw the same man—a man who did not belong to her neighborhood—standing at the end of her street. And then she saw him again when she took Alice to the park. She said she felt unsettled. Uneasy. It is not at all like her to imagine such things, my lord. She is prone to overwhelming sadness, it's true, but never has she imagined things. I believed her about being watched."

She frowned. "What troubles me most about all of this is that I am powerless to do anything about any of her problems. Now that Mama has found out about the dance lessons she will never let me out of her sight. The only reason she did not demand that I return home this evening is that she was too afraid to cause a to-do before you and the other gentlemen."

If Lady Shelby's stunt earlier were what she considered discreet, he shuddered to imagine her in unfettered rage.

Gazing at Juliet, he considered his options. If he offered to assist her, that would mean spending more time with her, which would not be a hardship. Still, he had made it a practice to refrain from spending more time than was necessary with any woman to whom he felt drawn. And he definitely felt drawn to Juliet. For her own safety he should keep as far from her as possible. But it would take a stronger man than he to say no to her in her present state.

But even if he were not worried about his own potential to hurt Juliet, he had to help her for another reason. He suspected that his uncle might have something to do with her friend's predicament. Not only was the man friends with Juliet's father, he was also notorious for a propensity to take what he wanted, whether the lady was willing or not. He had no knowledge about his uncle's whereabouts during the time that Mrs. Turner was accosted, but something about the whole situation made him uneasy.

"Miss Shelby," he said aloud, "I hope that you will allow me to investigate your friend's disappeance further. Indeed, I insist upon it."

"But why on earth should you wish to help me?" Juliet asked, a furrow between her brows. "You have been very kind, of course, but I feel sure you have other obligations that must take up your time."

He waved off her protestation. "I have a most efficient private secretary to see to my correspondence, and a more than able bailiff to oversee my country house. You will be doing me a kindness to offer an occupation to cure my boredom."

When she still seemed about to protest again, he took her hand. "Please, Juliet," he said. "Let me help you."

"I suppose if you must," she said, her cheeks pink, "then you must. But I hope that you will not hold me accountable should Mrs. Turner prove to have simply gone to visit friends in the country. I wonder now at my own worries. I am doubtless allowing my imagination to get the better of me."

"I do not think you are imagining things at all," Alec said. "In fact, I have come to believe over time that when one experiences feelings of unease there is often a very good reason for it."

She frowned. "I should think you would have little reason to worry. You are a leader of the fashionable set. You have two lovely sisters who are adored by everyone they meet. And you are a man and therefore have perfect autonomy."

Taking her hand to lead her from the room, Alec gave a wry smile. "You might be surprised to know what a man such as I may worry over."

Three

"Why are we searching this ladybird's flat again?" Monteith asked the next morning as he and Deveril alighted from a hackney outside Number 25 Hans Place.

After spending a sleepless night arguing with himself over the wisdom of becoming involved in Juliet's search for her music teacher, Alec had arisen at dawn to the realization that no matter how inconvenient his attraction to Miss Shelby, he had a familial responsibility to discover if his uncle were indeed involved in her friend's disappearance.

"For the tenth time, Monteith," he growled as they climbed the stairs to the door, "she is not a ladybird. She is a gently bred music teacher and we are doing it as a favor to a friend."

"A lady friend?" Monteith persisted. "Because, Dev, I really cannot see you doing this for another chap. Not that I think you're disloyal, but the whole *ton* knows about your charm with the fairer sex. Winterson and I were speaking of it just the other evening. You converse with them as if they are reasonable, rational beings. It's fascinating."

"God's teeth, Christian, you'd best not let the Duchess of Winterson hear you speaking like that. She'll have your guts for garters. And Winterson's as well."

"Bah. Cecily does not frighten me," the ex-cavalryman said, waving away Deveril's warning. "Though I will admit that she can be a tartar when she's got the bit between her teeth, she and I have an understanding. I promise not to drag Winterson into trouble, and she allows me to live."

If he'd been in a better mood, Deveril might have laughed, but his conversation last evening with Juliet hung like a pall over him on this blustery May day. He tried to remember that it was Lady Madeline he was meant to be wooing, but it was difficult when the scent of orange blossoms kept intruding.

"You are serious about this, aren't you?" Beneath his sunny disposition, Alec suspected that Monteith saw more than he let on. "I can think of only one woman who could persuade you to go out and about before your toilette was completed."

Deveril stopped; an involuntary hand went to his bristly jaw. "What are you talking about?"

"Don't try to cozen me, man. It's been obvious to me for this age that you've got a sweet spot for Juliet Shelby."

Dammit. "Don't be absurd, Monteith. I'm not nursing a *tendre* for anyone. In fact, I've had my eye on Lady Sylvia Randall of late. She's just broken things off with Nash and—"

Christian made a rude noise. "It won't wash, old fellow. Whenever she enters a room you practically light up like a lucifer match."

Double dammit.

"Monteith, I beg of you, keep silent on this matter or I will be forced to silence you physically, which will ruin my neck cloth." He ignored for the moment that his neck cloth had been hastily tied this morning due to his preoccupation with one Miss Shelby.

"Aha! So I am correct! You do have a *tendre* for Miss Shelby! Only true love would make you risk your cravat."

Deveril turned to face the other man, his expression deadly serious. "Listen to me well, Colonel Lord Monteith. If you whisper this nonsense to anyone—and I mean any living being on this planet—I will see to it that the patronesses of Almack's are all informed that you wish to marry one of this season's debutantes. Not only that but that you wish their assistance in the matter."

Monteith blanched. "You wouldn't."

"Try me."

"It was just a jest, Deveril. I wouldn't actually tell anyone. Well, Winterson, of course, but he already knows. In fact, he was the one who pointed it out to me last night."

Deveril sighed, resisting the urge to thrust a hand through his hair. "I have agreed to visit Mrs. Turner's flat as a favor to Miss Shelby, but all that exists between us is friendship. If you must know, I have decided that I will be making an offer for Lady Madeline Essex soon."

"You are serious?" Monteith gaped. "I mean, Lady Madeline is a sweet chit, but she's hardly who one would expect you to—"

"To what? Marry?"

"Well, no," Monteith stated baldly. "And why the devil would you put yourself in that position?"

"What position?"

"Come on, Deveril. If you marry Juliet Shelby's cousin you will spend the rest of your days being forced to interact with Juliet at every family gathering until the end of time. You are setting yourself up for a lifetime of misery. Unless . . ."

Deveril did not like the look in Monteith's eye.

"Unless what?" he asked, his voice deceptively calm.

"Can it be that you are so fastidious that you would give her up because of her infirmity?"

It was a reflex. That was all Alec could think later to account for what happened next.

One minute he was standing on the steps of Mrs. Turner's flat having a civil, if uncomfortable conversation with Monteith, and the next he was plowing his fist into Montieth's jaw. Caught off guard, Monteith fell backward down the three steps leading to the walk below.

"Here now!" shouted a gray-garbed woman from the doorway, which had opened shortly after Monteith's shocked shout. "This is a respectable house! Don't you fribbles bring your mischief onto my doorstep. I'll call the constable. See if I don't."

Surprised by his own actions, Deveril stepped down to offer Monteith a hand up. Which Monteith took warily, then set to brushing his breeches off and settling his hat back atop his head.

"You've got a strong right, there, friend," he told Deveril, grasping his jaw between thumb and forefinger to test its soundness. "You've been working with Jackson, haven't you?"

"Sorry," Alec told him, a bit sheepish. "I didn't mean to—"

"Oh, you meant to," Christian said with a knowing smile. "Which tells me more than an admission would have."

Deveril's strong reaction to Monteith's taunt had shocked even him. He'd always prided himself on the difference between his father and himself. Especially when it came to physical violence. What sort of man struck one of his best friends simply because he disliked something he'd said?

"That's no excuse," he told Monteith. "Even if I did find your accusation abhorrent, I shouldn't have done it."

"Away with ye," the housekeeper shouted down to them again. "I've sent the footman for the watch. Respectable folk don't hold with brawling in the streets."

Deveril mounted the steps to stand before the woman, his most charming smile at the ready. "I do apologize, ma'am, but my friend lost his footing."

"Hmmph," she grumbled. "That's not what it looked like to me."

Christian stepped up beside Deveril, sweeping his hat from his head in a formal bow. "I assure you, ma'am, we would not be so crass as to engage in fisticuffs like common street thugs. I'm afraid I have a lamentable sense of balance. The war, you know."

At that last, the housekeeper's features softened slightly. "Well, I suppose there's no harm done."

She turned to go back inside, but Deveril raised a staying hand. "Ma'am, we were just on our way to beg your assistance. I believe you recently had a tenant called Mrs. Turner living here?"

At the name, the woman scowled. "What if I did?"

"We would like to see her rooms, if that would be all right with you?" Alec said, exuding charm for all he was worth. "I loaned her a favorite book and she was unable to return it before her departure. I thought perhaps she would have left it behind here."

The woman made a disgusted sound. "If you can find it in that mess you're welcome to it," she said. "I thought she was a respectable widow lady and I let her stay on account of the child. But she just up and left without a word three days ago and left the flat in shambles. And left that fancy piano and all. What's a poor old woman to do with such a contraption, I ask ye? I asked Mr. Kimber in Sloane Street to come get the lot and sell it for what Mrs. Turner owed on account of the child, you see?"

"What about the child?" Alec asked, a tickle on the back of his neck telling him that something was terribly wrong here.

"Why, she left it here with me, didn't she?" the old woman said, her mouth pursed. "And not a penny did she leave me for the child's care. I would never have guessed that a genteel sort like that would just up and abandon her child. I know the quality has some strange ways, but if'n you'd seen her with the babe you'd be just as surprised as I am. I never would ha' guessed she had it in her to leave her child. And for a man too."

"Where is the child now, Mrs. . . . ?" Monteith asked, all levity erased from his manner.

"Parks, yer lordship," the old woman said, then her gaze sharpening she looked from one to the other of them. "See here, you aren't the man who took her away? Because I warn you now that I will not let that little girl leave this respectable house to live in a house of sin. I don't care if she is the child's mother. I can make do."

"No, no," Deveril assured her. "We are friends of Mrs. Turner's former pupil. And we've come at her behest. The young lady is afraid something untoward has happened to Mrs. Turner and we agreed to come investigate."

This seemed to satisfy Mrs. Parks. "That nice Miss Shelby, I reckon," she told them. "She is here every Monday without fail. And a proper young lady, make no mistake. It was her who convinced me to let Mrs. Turner let the flat in the first place. It's a shame her trust was so misplaced."

Not willing to discuss Juliet with the woman, Alec indicated that he and Monteith wished to come inside, and the woman shrugged and opened the door for them to follow her in.

While it was not a lavish establishment by any means, the house itself was clean and tidy. At least the entry hall was. As they followed her up the narrow staircase, Alec tried to imagine Juliet spending time here. He was so accustomed to seeing her in the fashionable haunts of London—even if she did manage to avoid the more lively circles—it was difficult to see her in this mean little house, with its sparse furnishings. He wondered if she came unaccompanied or brought a footman along. He disliked thinking of her encountering the other inhabitants of Hans Town unprotected.

"Here it is," Mrs. Parks said, fitting the key into the lock. "I've got work to do in the kitchen and the child will need to be fed. I'll leave the two of you here to yourselves. Just come and let me know when you leave so I can lock the door back."

The two men stepped into the room, their boots echoing

on the carpetless floor, and set to work, Deveril taking the small bedchamber and Monteith the parlor/sitting room.

With only a small bureau and an ancient bedstead, the tiny room seemed even smaller thanks to the clothes and belongings scattered across the floor. A plain cotton night-rail draped haphazardly over the washbasin, and one of the pillows had been sliced open, its feathers coating the bed and floor like a downy snowfall.

When the obvious places to hide things, like the bureau, turned out to contain nothing more interesting than a sachet and a bedraggled ribbon, Alec began to search the less obvious locations. Thinking back to his schooldays when secrecy had sometimes been necessary, he felt the undersides of the bureau drawers, in hopes that Mrs. Turner had affixed something there. And sure enough, he discovered a letter beneath the second drawer from the bottom.

It had been franked by the Earl of Mounthaven, though the letter itself was from that gentleman's personal secretary, one Alistair MacEwan. Since the notion of reading a lady's personal correspondence did not sit right with him, he tucked the letter into his coat to give to Juliet later.

From the next room, Monteith called out. "Do you get the impression that someone has already been here before us?"

Having moved over to search between the bed ropes and the mattress, Deveril had to shout from his supine position beneath the bed. "Yes, I do. In fact, it almost feels as if someone purposely ransacked the room to make it appear as if Mrs. Turner left in a hurry."

"What the devil are you doing on the floor, man?" Monteith had wandered into the bedchamber. "This is no time for a nap."

"Ha, ha, bloody, ha," Deveril said, then finding what he'd been searching for, he slid out from beneath the bed.

Holding his find up for Monteith to see, he stood and brushed off his coat and breeches, knowing he'd be raked over the coals later by his valet.

"A diary?" Monteith asked. "Not a very convenient location for it. Let's have a look."

"I'd rather wait and let Ju . . . Miss Shelby look at it first. There might be personal information here."

Though he shook his head, Monteith didn't object.

"Nothing in the parlor?" Deveril asked, giving the room one last glance before the two men stepped into the other room.

"Nothing," Monteith affirmed. "With the exception of the baby's things, it looks as if Mrs. Turner took everything with her. Either that or she simply didn't have very much to begin with."

They closed the door and stepped back into the narrow hallway, taking the stairs two at a time until they reached the apartments below. From the kitchens they could hear the baby crying loudly, but the sound of a loud smack silenced her momentarily. Then, the wailing came again, this time louder.

"Be quiet or I'll give you another!" they heard Mrs. Parks say menacingly.

Deveril and Monteith exchanged a look. With silent agreement, they walked into the kitchen.

At the sight of the two men, Mrs. Parks was all smiles, saying over the baby's cries, "My lords, I hope you were able to find some clue as to where this poor mite's mother has gone off to."

"Indeed," Alec said, taking in the sight of little Alice, whose face bore the bright red mark of a palm print. "What's happened here?"

Looking from the baby to Alec, Mrs. Parks gushed. "Oh, the poor little thing needs her nap. Pay her no mind. All babies cry."

"I believe I should cry too if someone biffed me in the face," Monteith said with deceptive calm. "Wouldn't you, Deveril?"

"Indeed I should," Deveril said. "In fact, I believe if I

were a small child at the mercy of a grown woman who took advantage of my helplessness I'd cry quite loudly."

The mask of civility vanished from the woman's face and was replaced by a hard look. "Since the child's mother left her in my care, I don't see what business it is of yours how I discipline the child. The money that slut left won't last the week and then I'm stuck with another mouth to feed."

"I hardly think such a small child requires discipline, madam," Deveril said coldly. "As to your guardianship of the child, you may safely conclude that that arrangement is at an end now. We'll be taking Alice with us."

"Yes, we'll be taking Alice with—" Monteith echoed, then stopped. "Wait? We're taking Alice with us?"

"Yes we are," Alec said firmly. "Kindly gather together the child's belongings and we'll take her now."

Not one to miss an opportunity for exploitation, Mrs. Parks moved closer to the child, but thought better of it when Alec made a threatening sound. "And what of my expenses? I've taken good care of the babe for two weeks now."

"You'll be compensated, have no fear," Alec said, his disgust evident in his voice.

With a satisfied nod, the woman stepped out of the room to get Alice's things.

"What the devil are you playing at?" Monteith said in a low voice. "We can't just take this baby away from here. Where will we take her? It's not as if your sisters or my mother are going to welcome some bast—"

"My sisters will not object," Alec interrupted. "It's not as if my family is unfamiliar with children from the wrong side of the blanket. And I have reason to believe this one might belong to my uncle. Though I'd prefer it if you kept that speculation to yourself."

"You have my word," Monteith said. "And if you think your sisters won't mind, I suppose your house is as good a place as any to shelter her. Anything is better than this place. I don't spend much time around children, but I don't think they cry like that without good reason."

"They don't," Alec said grimly, remembering his own childhood and how his father's tempers had affected him. He could still remember the sting of an open palm across his cheeks. If he had any say in it, Alice would never feel that sting again.

With the promise of compensation, Mrs. Parks's attitude changed dramatically. She had gathered the baby's things and changed and dressed her while Monteith went to alert the coachman that they'd be leaving shortly.

Finally, some ten pounds poorer, Alec carried Alice from the dingy rooming house, Monteith following with Alice's things.

As if she knew she were being rescued, Alice clung tightly to Deveril, wrapping her little arms round his neck.

If the coachman thought it irregular for his master to be accompanied by a baby, he kept his thoughts to himself.

Ensconced in the carriage, Alice now fingered the simple ebony stickpin adorning Alec's cravat, while the two men stared bemused at one another.

"This will make an excellent story for Winterson's delectation," Monteith said finally. "Only one thing remains to be seen."

"What's that?" Alec asked, removing a small hand from poking him in the eye.

"Whether little Alice gets carriage sick."

Deveril's response was not fit for a child's ears, though Alice didn't seem to mind.

While Deveril was searching Mrs. Turner's flat, Juliet was trying to listen politely to Lord Turlington's comments about the paintings they observed in the new Southerton Gallery.

She had planned on asking Madeline to accompany her

to see if Mrs. Turner had perhaps gone to visit her sister in Richmond, but when she'd reached the breakfast table that morning, her mother informed her that they were to attend the gallery opening with Lord Turlington.

"Wear the new peach sarcenet," Lady Shelby told her. "And ask Weston to arrange your hair in something more elaborate than your usual chignon."

As usual, Lady Shelby herself was exquisite. Her dark, glossy tresses were artfully arranged to reveal her elegant neckline. And her deep russet-colored gown fit her to perfection. Juliet wondered, not for the first time, if it were possible for such a plebian specimen as herself to be birthed by such a paragon.

"I had hoped to visit Madeline today," she said, hoping that the mention of her cousin would remind Lady Shelby that she was not the only one of the Ugly Ducklings who had yet to snare a husband. But it was of no avail.

"I'm afraid that is impossible, Juliet." Her mother's rosy lips pursed in a pouty frown. "Lord Turlington has requested your company in particular. I believe if you handle him carefully he might be brought up to scratch."

Juliet stirred a spoonful of sugar into her tea and said nothing. Her mother had begun pushing her toward Turlington at the beginning of the season. Even before Cecily had married Winterson. It had come as a surprise because until this year her mother had openly scoffed at the notion Juliet would ever marry at all because of her injury.

Never one to balk at speaking her mind, Lady Shelby had lamented the consequences of Juliet's accident almost from the moment it happened. Not so much the fact that Juliet would find ambulation difficult, but that she would not be able to take her rightful position in society.

But this season, even before the family made the journey from their estate in Kent, Lady Shelby had begun to sing a different tune. She'd praised the virtues of married life to her daughter. She'd taken a renewed interest in Juliet's fashion choices, even going so far as to insist that she wear colors that for most debutantes would be verboten.

Accustomed to blending in with the other young unmarried ladies of society, Juliet had braced herself for taking a more active role in *ton* activities, but to her shock, she soon learned that her mother's hopes for her centered on one gentleman alone: Lord Turlington.

A widower in his late thirties, Turlington was known for his passionate interest in art. A painter himself, he could often be found discussing his interest with anyone who would listen. And he had written several well-received pieces of criticism for various serial publications. As an expert in his field, he was impressive. As a marriage prospect for an unassuming young lady, however, he left much to be desired.

Though she had often chafed at her mother's lack of optimism regarding her marriageability, Juliet found her sudden insistence that Lord Turlington could be hers for the taking odd in the extreme. His title was not particularly old, or prestigious. And he was viewed by many, including Juliet's own father, as a grasping social climber.

Then there was her own opinion of the man. Not only did she find Turlington's constant discussion of his own accomplishments tedious, she also thought that his assessment of his own skill as an artist was dead wrong. Since her mother had developed an interest in him as a possible suitor for Juliet, she had paraded her daughter through the various galleries of London that had Turlington's works on display. And if she were being completely honest, Juliet found them . . . disturbing.

Like most artists of his generation, Turlington liked to paint scenes from great historical or literary events. But Turlington's always seemed to depict women in some sort of dire situation. Having gone through a dire situation of her own, she did not care to see such raw emotions depicted on canvas. And though she knew the models themselves were merely acting, she could not help but sense that

Turlington, with his brush and paints, brought life to such emotions because he enjoyed them.

"Juliet, are you attending to me?" Lady Shelby demanded. "I said that Turlington might be brought up to scratch. I should think you would be grateful considering that only recently you had no hopes for making a marriage at all."

Ah, yes, Mama, do not mince words.

"I am not sure that I should find Lord Turlington to my liking as a husband," she said aloud. "I know he is your friend, but I was hoping that I might be able to find someone a bit closer to me in age . . ."

"For what, pray?" Lady Shelby asked. "For dancing, as you were attempting at Winterson House last evening? My dear Juliet, you know that I wish more than anything that you were like other young ladies, but you are not. A young husband would only find you tedious because you would not be able to keep up with him . . . physically, I mean."

She raised one perfectly arched brow. "Do you know what I refer to?"

Juliet felt a blush rise in her cheeks. "I . . . I . . . think so."

"I do not mean to be unkind, my dear, truly I don't. But husbands require certain . . . duties of their wives. Duties that require a certain degree of . . . physicality. I simply do not believe your injury would allow you to participate in such activities. At least not with the regularity that a young man would require."

Juliet kept her eyes on her toast, suddenly not as hungry as she was when she entered the room.

"An older husband," Lady Shelby said briskly, "would be much more willing to overlook your frailty. Indeed, I believe he might even be willing to let you continue with your study of the pianoforte. After all, you will need some way to occupy your time."

Stunned, but unsurprised, at her mother's tactlessness,

Juliet didn't bother to reply. It would do no good to argue with her, she knew. And upon the subject of Lord Turlington, she was not to be gainsaid.

"Come, finish your breakfast and we'll be off. Turlington has a new painting at Southerton's. It is of Desdemona, I believe. One of his new series based on the heroines of Shakespeare. I will try to persuade him to take us to Gunter's afterward. You will like that, won't you?"

Lady Shelby rose and glided from the room, her smooth gait everything that Juliet's was not.

Was this really what things had come to? she wondered. Was she to be forced into marriage with a man who repulsed her simply because her mother willed it? For the millionth time she wondered what had persuaded her mother to become so hell-bent on marrying her daughter off to Lord Turlington. To go from disbelieving that her daughter could marry at all to attempting almost daily to press her into marrying Turlington was strange indeed.

She wished Anna were here to discuss the matter with her, or that she were somewhere that Juliet knew she was safe. Her letter of last evening had left her uneasy and worried. She wondered if Lord Deveril had been able to learn anything new during his visit to Hans Town.

Unbidden, the memory of how she had felt in Lord Deveril's arms sent a little thrill down her spine. She had a suspicion that marital duties with the viscount would be just as energetic and frequent as her mother had described. And despite her injury, she had a feeling that she would adapt to the situation if her husband were someone like Deveril, someone she could respect and care for. As opposed to the older, and unsettling, Lord Turlington. She tried and failed to imagine the older man investigating the disappearance of her former music teacher as Deveril was doing. Turlington would dismiss the matter as beneath his notice, she had little doubt. Which was another point in Deveril's favor.

Not that Juliet was keeping a tally.

What was most surprising with regard to Lord Turlington was her mother's sudden championing of the man as the ideal suitor. Something, Juliet was convinced, had made Lady Shelby change her mind regarding her daughter's marriageability. And Juliet wanted to know what that something had been.

With a sigh for her wasted breakfast, she rose from the table, leaning on her elegantly carved walking stick, and made her way to fetch her bonnet and pelisse.

When they arrived at the Southerton Gallery it was to find the entrance teeming with curious visitors.

"Never say this is all for your painting, Turlington," Lady Shelby cooed, making Juliet feel slightly ill. She'd been complimenting the gentleman lavishly from the moment he handed them into his carriage. And somehow managed to make it seem as if Juliet were the one making the compliments.

"I'm afraid not, Lady Shelby, Miss Shelby," he said, ushering them through the crowd. "I believe this is for the latest work by *Il Maestro*."

Juliet had read about the mysterious painter in the *Times*. His identity was unknown, and the subject matter he depicted was shocking in the extreme. While Juliet found Turlington's paintings disturbing, those of *Il Maestro* were outright frightening. Drawing from the gothic tradition made popular by the novelists Walpole and Radcliffe, *Il Maestro*'s paintings were bone-chilling, depicting all manner of unspeakable acts. And in a city where hangings were still viewed by some as jolly good entertainment, works like these were considered tame by most.

"Mama, please do not let us go inside," Juliet asked, her distress such that she actually clutched her mother's arm, something she had not done since a small child, when she'd been scolded severely for wrinkling her mother's sleeve.

"Do not fear, Miss Shelby," Lord Turlington chided, chucking her under the chin as if she were a child. "It is merely artistic expression. It cannot harm you. Though I approve of your diffidence. A lady can never be too careful about what she allows herself to be exposed to."

And against her will, Juliet was ushered into the busy gallery, where the line snaking around the room led into a side room, where presumably *Il Maestro*'s latest monstrosity was on display.

When the line had moved but a little, Juliet took advantage of her mother and Lord Turlington's distraction as they discussed some esoteric art technique with an acquaintance to slip back into the crowd. Making her way past small groups of people, she finally reached the side entrance to the gallery, where she slipped into a small courtyard that had been set up for visitors to rest their weary feet. Taking advantage of a bench, Juliet gingerly lowered herself to sit, and plied her fan in an effort to cool her overheated cheeks.

"Ah, here you are," she heard from the doorway. She turned to see Lord Deveril, resplendent even in day wear of buckskin breeches and highly polished boots, with a bottle-green coat, snowy white shirt, and neck cloth.

"Lord Deveril." She smiled, feeling a little breathless to see him again. Especially in light of the aforementioned duties. "I did not expect to see you again so soon."

"But Miss Shelby," he chided, bowing over her hand, "I did tell you that I would report as soon as I'd learned something."

"Oh, of course. Mrs. Turner." She blushed to have forgotten her friend so quickly. "You are so kind. I had not expected you to learn anything so soon."

"Well, the news isn't much, I fear," he told her, his expression serious as the gentle May breeze ruffled his golden hair. "May I?" he asked, indicating the seat beside her.

She really shouldn't, but Juliet found it impossible to refuse him. She gave a small nod and he sat beside her.

Quickly he outlined his and Monteith's experience that morning at Mrs. Parks's establishment.

"We found little to indicate whether or not Mrs. Turner's flight was voluntary or by force, though it did not appear that she'd packed a bag," he said. "And I found something that I thought would be of interest to you."

Reaching into his pocket, he removed a small blue bound book.

"Oh," she cried, taking it from him. "It is her teaching notebook. I bought this for her last Christmas when she complained of running out of space in her old one."

"I have only made a cursory examination," Deveril explained, his expression serious, "Not having been a friend, I did not feel quite right about invading her privacy in such a manner. But I thought that perhaps you would be the most appropriate person to read over it."

"Thank you," she told him, her eyes filling with moisture. "You cannot know how much this means to me."

"I think I do," he told her, taking her gloved hand in his. "I also wanted to let you know that Mrs. Turner left something else behind. Something not quite so easy to carry in my pocket."

She frowned. "Her piano?" she asked.

"No," he said, his brow furrowed in a frown. "I'm afraid that Mrs. Turner left her daughter behind with Mrs. Parks."

Juliet's heart sank. If Mrs. Turner had left Baby Alice behind then something was definitely wrong. Though Mrs. Turner was fond of Parks, she was not comfortable with leaving Alice there for extended periods.

"Where is she?" Juliet asked, rising from her seat, her need to be doing something, anything, urging her to action. She gripped her walking stick in frustration. "She cannot stay with Mrs. Parks. What if whoever has taken Anna comes for Alice as well?"

Alec stood too, staying her with a comforting hand on her arm. "I have brought her to my house in Berkeley Square," he said, attempting to calm her agitation. "I thought it best, given your mother's dislike of Mrs. Turner and the circumstances of Alice's parentage."

Juliet nodded. He watched as she took a deep breath, and reined in her emotions. He suspected, given her past difficulties, that this was a skill she'd been forced to learn on her own, in order to survive in her parents' household.

"That is for the best," she said, her emotions once more under control. "I know Mama would not agree to let Alice stay with us, no matter my wishes. But what of your own family? Will your sisters object?"

He smiled. "They are used to my quixotic temper and will not be bothered in the slightest. In fact, I suspect they both will sneak up to the nursery every chance they get. I will have my man of business hire an appropriate nurse-maid for the babe. And you are, of course, welcome to visit the child whenever you wish."

"I am grateful for your willingness to upset your household in such a manner," Juliet told him, "You behave as if it is nothing, but taking in a child, especially one with the stigma of illegitimacy, is no small thing."

He took her hand. "There is a special place in Hades for those who hold the sins of a child's parents against them." He gave a bitter laugh, "I should know. And given what Monteith and I found in Mrs. Turner's flat this morning, your friend had no notion that she'd be gone for more than a few hours. I am well able to care for her until her mother's return. If anyone asks, I shall put it about that she's the child of a distant cousin who was called away suddenly . . ."

He did not add that he suspected that tale might be close to the truth if she was, as he suspected, his uncle's by-blow.

"I cannot thank you enough, my lord." Her worry was evident in the shadows beneath her eyes. Still, she seemed to draw from some inner reserve of strength, straightening her spine and returning to the subject at hand. "So, if you believe Anna had no idea she'd be leaving, was her note coerced?"

* * *

Alec longed to set her fears for her friend at rest, but he could not bring himself to lie. "I think it likely."

Her resignation made his gut ache, still he knew she would not wish him to lie to her.

"Given your knowledge of her habits, and her affection for her child, I find it difficult to believe that your friend left her home voluntarily. There was no visible sign of struggle in her rooms, but Mrs. Parks heard an altercation. She assumed it was the couple in the house next door, but I believe that it must have been Mrs. Turner and the man who took her away."

"But why?" Juliet demanded, her worry turning to anger. "Anna never divulged the name of the man who attacked her. She lived a quiet and unassuming life far removed from the society she was born into. She was a threat to no one."

"We will not know the answer to that until we find out who took her," he said, "and where." He suppressed a pang of guilt at the thought of his uncle's possible involvement in the matter. Juliet would not be so grateful for his assistance when she learned the truth.

"I would like to come see Alice," she told him. "Would that be agreeable? Once she's settled?"

"Of course, you are most welcome to come visit the child," he said. "Perhaps you would like to bring one of your cousins along."

He was about to issue an invitation for her to come that very afternoon, but was interrupted by the arrival of Lady Shelby and Lord Turlington, who rushed forward as if they had spent hours searching for her, rather than the quarter hour Juliet had likely been outside.

"Where on earth have you been, Juliet?" Lady Shelby demanded, her frown directed at both Juliet and Deveril. "It is highly improper for you to be here alone with Lord

Deveril. I would think a gel of your age would know better.
And you, Lord Deveril, you should know better as well."

Alec stepped closer to Juliet, offering her his physical
support if she had need of it.

"Lady Shelby." He bowed. "A conversation between
friends in broad daylight can hardly be considered improper.
I found Miss Shelby resting here and we kept one another
company. You do your daughter a disservice to suggest
otherwise."

Turlington stepped forward and offered Juliet his arm,
which she had no choice but to accept.

"Miss Shelby, I hope you are recovered," he said, his gaze
never leaving Deveril's. Alec noted with annoyance Turlington's possessive posture. "Come, let me show you Rickarby's
new work. It is dedicated to the Regent, you know."

That left Alec alone with Lady Shelby. He found himself inwardly amused. For all of his father's and uncle's bad
behavior, he himself had never been warned off from any
particular young lady. Quite the contrary, he often found
himself being pursued by matchmaking mamas with designs on his title.

"I do not know what sort of game you are playing with
my daughter, my lord," Lady Shelby said coolly. Her eyes,
although the same color green as Juliet's, were infinitely
more calculating. "I thought at first that you must be using
her as some sort of amusement. A man must grow weary of
being fawned over constantly. I imagine her clumsy attentions must be refreshing when compared to more skilled
compliments."

He said nothing, though his distaste for Juliet's mother
grew by multiple degrees.

"But now," she said, her expression speculative, "now, I
believe you are up to something altogether more . . . sweet."

"I don't know what you mean."

"I think you've developed some sort of *tendre* for her,"
she said baldly. "And I dislike telling you, as I realize how

unlikely it is to have any gentleman show an interest in her given her . . . flaw, but I'm afraid Lord Shelby and I have already promised Juliet's hand to someone else."

If this were true, Alec surmised, then no one had told Juliet about it.

"I suppose you mean Turlington?" Alec felt a muscle in his jaw flex at the idea of Juliet being manhandled by one such as Turlington.

"Of course." Lady Shelby nodded. "I haven't informed my daughter yet, of course. But she will do her duty. If nothing else Juliet is a biddable girl. And given the fact that she has little other chance at marriage, I believe she will be persuaded to accept him. That is, so long as you maintain a safe distance from her."

"And what makes you believe that I pose any danger to your plot?" He gazed intently at a speck of dust on his coat sleeve, refusing to let his adversary know how attuned he was to her response.

"Oh, come now, Lord Deveril. I know the signs. At least when it comes to my daughter. She all but bursts into flames when you enter a room."

Though he was careful not to show it in any way, Alec inwardly cheered.

But Lady Shelby's next words dampened his triumph. "Do not think that I do not appreciate your condescension. She is far too plain for a high stickler like you. Why, you've got waistcoats that are prettier than my Juliet. But I must ask that you curtail these little tête-à-têtes with her. Because while he is handsome enough, I know perfectly well that Turlington cannot hold a candle to you when it comes to looks and charm. And make no mistake, Juliet will marry him eventually. It only remains to be seen whether she does so willingly or through coercion. It will be a kindness on your part if you will allow her the illusion of making the decision for herself."

And, thinking she'd made her point, Lady Shelby

sashayed back through the side door and into the gallery within.

Stunned into silence, Alec watched her go with a mixture of astonishment and contempt. If he were honest, he did feel a surge of triumph at Lady Shelby's revelation that Juliet showed a preference for him. But that happiness was tempered by outrage on Juliet's behalf.

Did she really have so little respect for Juliet's wishes that she would force her into marriage with Turlington? Even if she were as plain as Lady Shelby said, and he was in definite disagreement with her views on the matter, there seemed little need to force Juliet into marriage. Unless, of course, Lady Shelby had some other motive for backing the match. Which, doubtless, she did.

It was the only explanation for her pains to warn Deveril off.

Any other mother of an unmarried daughter would eat Prinny's pocket watch if it meant securing a viscount as a son-in-law. The fact that Lady Shelby was against the very idea meant that she had some other scheme up her elegant sleeve.

Alec ran a weary hand over the back of his neck. He'd best visit his uncle sooner rather than later. The more he learned about his family's responsibilities toward Mrs. Turner and little Alice, the sooner he would be able to set Juliet's mind at rest. At least on that score.

He'd consider how to prevent her mother from marrying her off to the loathsome Turlington later. For that he'd need assistance from Monteith and Winterson. He had little doubt that Cecily would find her aunt's plans regarding Juliet's matrimonial status objectionable. And Cecily with an objection was a force to be reckoned with.

Four

Alec ran his uncle to ground in his bachelor rooms at the Albany where he was looking much the worse for wear after a night spent at the gaming tables.

"Come to ring a peal over my head, have you?" Roderick asked, his eyes narrowed against the anemic sunlight peeking through a chink in the drapes. Casually attired in a dressing gown and hunched over the small breakfast table, the older man scowled into his tea.

Waving away the offer of refreshment from his uncle's valet, who hovered nearby, and indicating that he should leave them alone, Alec surveyed his father's youngest brother. "It is nothing to me if you wish to spend what little income you have in the pursuit of winnings that will never exceed your losses," he said baldly.

It was a mark of Roderick's fatigue that he did not object to his nephew's assessment of his nocturnal activities, merely shrugged.

"But I did not come here to offer my opinion on your dissolution," Alec said, crossing his arms over his chest. "I came because I want you to tell me what role you played in the dismissal of Miss Anna Turner from Viscount Shelby's household."

"What makes you think I had anything to do with that?" Roderick asked, his expression shuttered.

"Oh, come now," Alec said impatiently, "I realize that

the rumor mill is often wrong, but in this case, I know there was more fire than smoke. You were an intimate of Lord Shelby at the time, and I know your penchant for seducing innocents. You are distressingly like my father in that."

"I was hardly the only friend of Shelby's with an eye for the tasty Miss Turner, nephew," Roderick said. At Alec's harsh stare, he shrugged and threw up his hands. "But if you must know the truth of it, I never touched the chit."

"I find that hard to believe," Alec said. "What stopped you?"

Embarrassment crossed the older man's face. "If you must know, she did. Or rather, some other chap did. I sneaked up to her rooms to . . . ah . . . press my suit, and someone was there before me."

Alec unfolded his arms and leaned forward. "Did you see who it was?"

"Of course not!" Roderick actually looked offended. "As soon as I heard the unmistakable sounds of shagging I left."

At least his uncle had *some* standards, Alec thought grimly.

"Surely you had some guess as to who it might be," he pressed. If his uncle weren't Baby Alice's father, then whoever was might be responsible for the music teacher's disappearance.

But Roderick shook his head. "I went back to the billiard room and every other man at the house party, with the exception of the servants and secretaries of course, was there. If the man I heard was one of the guests, he was damned quick about it."

Alec bit back a curse. He had hoped that his uncle would give him some information that would lead to Mrs. Turner's whereabouts. But as so often happened with the man, he had only added to Alec's frustrations.

Pushing back from the table, Alec rose. "Thank you for the information," he said grudgingly.

"Not as if I have any use for it," the older man said. "I presume you're helping the Shelby chit in her search for the Turner woman."

At Alec's nod, his uncle tilted his head and said with more sincerity than he'd offered in some years, "Watch out for that one, nephew. She won't settle for less than a happy marriage. And the men in our family are simply not made for happiness."

Alec didn't bother informing Roderick that he was safe from Miss Shelby given the arrangement her mother had already made for her with Turlington. Even so, the warning echoed behind him as he took his leave.

"What an appalling situation." Cecily shook her head, concern shadowing her dark eyes. "I had no notion you were dealing with all of this, darling. You should have told us."

"I know you have your own worries, what with your father and Winterson being so overprotective these days. But since it appears that Anna is not simply away for a brief jaunt, I decided I had to tell someone. Aside from Deveril, that is."

Juliet had arrived at Winterson House early that morning to request her cousin's company. She could hardly go to Deveril's town house unchaperoned. And Cecily was very interested in babies now that she was expecting one of her own.

They were now comfortably ensconced in the well-sprung Winterson town carriage for the painfully short drive through Mayfair from Winterson House to Deveril House.

"Yes," Cecily said, her mouth pursed. "I have been waiting for you to tell me about this new association between yourself and Lord Deveril. He was positively ready to challenge your mama to a duel at our little dance party."

Juliet felt herself redden, an unfortunate consequence of her fair complexion and red hair. "You exaggerate, surely. He is simply a friend. And when he came upon me that evening when he suggested the party, he found me reading the note from Anna. I'm afraid I blurted out my worries and he had no choice but to assist me."

"I wonder if you are correct about that." Cecily snorted. "I cannot imagine Lord Turlington would offer his assistance so readily."

It was Juliet's turn to snort. "That is because he sees Anna and other women like her as entirely beneath his notice. He expends more concern for the care and upkeep of his art collection." She shook her head in disgust before returning to Cecily's original concern. "There is nothing between myself and Lord Deveril but friendship, and a very slight one at that. He is far too eligible for the likes of me."

"I will not even dignify your last statement with a response," Cecily said with a chiding glance. "As for friendship, there are far less stable foundations upon which to build a marriage."

Alarm coursed through Juliet. "Cecily, you must stop this at once. Lord Deveril is a friend and that is all. Besides which, Mama is determined to marry me to Turlington. So, it is fruitless to speak of my marriage to anyone else." And, she did not add, she would be mortified if Deveril suspected any hint of partiality for him on her part. Not only was he far above her touch, he did not know the whole story of what had happened to her in Vienna.

Cecily looked as if she'd like to argue, but said simply, "I think you are wrong, but I won't mention the matter again. At least not until you're ready to talk sense. As for Lord Turlington, I think your mama should be horsewhipped for even considering Turlington for your hand. And I hold out every hope that we can find someone—even if he is not Lord Deveril—to save you from that terrible fate."

Reaching out her gloved hand, Juliet took Cecily's and squeezed it. "Thank you," she said. "I would, of course, not be opposed to finding someone besides Turlington to take me from my parents' care. If Papa were more willing to involve himself in matters not having to do with diplomacy, perhaps it would be tolerable, but as things stand now, I am at her mercy."

"I have an idea of how to combat the situation, if you'll let me," Cecily said with a smile. "It involves a trip to Madame Celeste's"

Though shopping was not her favorite pastime, Juliet could see the wisdom in ensuring she looked her best if she were going to attract someone besides Turlington.

"I don't know that Mama will be amenable to such a plan, however," she said aloud. "I might be able to convince her it is for Lord Turlington's benefit, though."

"I will do my best to convince her of the same," Cecily said. "Though she does not care for me in general, I think she is unable to stop herself from toadying now that I outrank her. I shall use my rank against her."

At last, the coach drew to a halt, and in a few moments, Juliet and Cecily were being admitted by a very proper-looking butler, who informed them that his master had left instructions for them to be admitted to the nursery.

"I will inform his lordship that you are here," he said, showing them into an elegant front parlor, decorated in a style from a generation before. But rather than dated, the room seemed comfortable, homey, in a way that her parents' town house, decorated and redecorated whenever the mood struck her mother, was not.

"Please do not disturb his lordship," she protested as the butler made to leave them. "I am sure he is quite busy." After her assurances to Cecily that there was nothing between herself and Deveril but friendship, she did not wish to expose herself to her cousin's scrutiny lest she betray in some unconscious way her admiration for the man. Which Cecily would misinterpret as romantic attachment.

"His lordship specifically requested that he be informed if you were to come visit the child, miss," the butler said. With that, he was gone.

"I hardly think it odd that your *friend* would wish to see you when you come to visit," Cecily said guilelessly. "After all, that is what *friends* do."

"Sometimes, Cecily," Juliet said crossly, "you are too cunning by half."

Her cousin laughed. "That is just what Winterson says. If it is any consolation, he also says that I am a pain in the—"

"Good morning, ladies," Deveril interrupted, stepping into the little parlor and immediately filling the room with his presence. "I am so glad you decided to come see our young visitor."

"We do not mean to intrude," Juliet said quickly. "I am quite sure you are busy. If you'll just direct us to the nursery we can go find Alice ourselves."

Rather than clutching the lifeline she'd just tossed him, Lord Deveril waved away her suggestion. "Nonsense, I could use a break from the tedium of estate business. I will take you upstairs myself."

Studiously avoiding her cousin's eye, Juliet allowed him to usher them into the main hallway and up the stairs to the third-floor nursery.

Facing the back garden, the rooms were quite large and airy, the windows situated to capture as much of the meager sunlight as London would allow.

The nurse Alec had arranged for the child, Mrs. Pennyfeather, greeted them with a curtsy, though all eyes were on her charge.

In a clean and serviceable dress, little Alice clapped her hands with glee to see her visitors. Seated atop a rocking horse, she raised her arms in the universal baby gesture that said "pick me up!" and kicked the horse into motion as she pressed her arms up.

"Good morning to you too, Miss Alice," Deveril said, lifting her from the horse, and carrying her over to meet her visitors. He dismissed the maid as he walked forward.

"I'm afraid she's taken a bit of a liking to me," he told

Juliet and Cecily, gesturing for them to take seats on the small settee situated on the other side of the room. "She was less than happy where her mother left her, and sees me as a sort of liberator from there."

Bemused to see the fashionable Lord Deveril allowing his cravat to be ruthlessly wrinkled by the child in his arms, Juliet wished suddenly that he were not quite so perfect. Surely it was too much to ask that he was unkind to animals or made a habit of tripping old women. The notion was just as absurd as Cecily's earlier hopes that Juliet could catch the man's eye. He was simply a decent gentleman. But he wasn't the only decent gentleman in the world. She'd find another if she could.

"I don't blame her a bit," Cecily said with a smile. "All the smart girls recognize a handsome gentleman when they see one."

Juliet studiously avoided the speaking glance her cousin gave her. "She seems quite happy here. I am relieved to know Anna's child is being well taken care of."

"Of course, Miss Shelby," he said, disengaging the baby's hand from his ear. "As I said before, I am glad to be of any assistance I can. She is welcome to stay here as long as she wishes. My sisters are already making mad plans for the child's come-out ball and have married her off to a German princeling in their minds. Though I believe Katherine would prefer a royal duke for her."

"Perish the thought," Juliet said with a laugh. "I shouldn't wish a royal duke on my worst enemy. Though I suppose the status would be nice."

"As I told them too," Deveril said with a grin. Then, his expression turning serious, and he said soberly, "She is welcome here, Miss Shelby. And I will do whatever I can to assist you to find her mother."

"I appreciate your assistance," Juliet said. "More than you can know. I cannot think what has happened to Anna, but I intend to find out. In fact, I plan to visit her musical mentor this afternoon. I simply wished to check in on Alice before I did so."

At the mention of Anna's mentor, Deveril's gaze sharpened. "Is the fellow in a location where it would be safe for you to visit him? I hope you plan to take the duchess with you. If not, I would be happy to—"

Juliet and Cecily spoke at once.

"There's no need—"

"Oh, that would be perfect!"

The cousins turned to look at one another, silently arguing the point. Which Cecily won.

"That would be lovely of you, Lord Deveril," she said after cowing Juliet's protest with a speaking look composed primarily of raised eyebrows and determined eyes. "I must admit that I'm not feeling quite the thing. Though I had promised Juliet to accompany her to this musician fellow's establishment, and I do so hate disappointing her."

"Not as much as I hate being disappointed," Juliet said under her breath.

Aloud she said, "I would greatly appreciate your escort, my lord. But please, if you have another engagement do not hesitate to tell me so. I can take a maid with me, if necessary."

"Not a bit of it, Miss Shelby," he said. "I would be honored to escort you. I have a fondness for music myself so it will be an entertainment for me to come with you."

The matter settled, they lapsed into the stilted conversation of adults watching a baby as a means of entertainment. Some quarter of an hour later, Juliet and Cecily bid their farewells, and Deveril promised to call upon Juliet that afternoon at her father's house.

"Perhaps it would be best for us to meet at Winterson House," Juliet said quickly. She did not want her mother to assume she was setting her cap for Deveril, after all.

"Very well, Miss Shelby," he said, "I shall see you this afternoon."

"There now," Cecily said, once they were safely back in the Winterson carriage. "That wasn't so difficult, was it?"

"What?" Juliet demanded. "Cornering Lord Deveril into accompanying me on a visit you'd already promised to do yourself?"

"Oh, don't be a spoilsport, Juliet," her cousin replied. "It's as plain as the nose on your face that he wishes to assist you in this matter. Whether it's because he has a *tendre* for you—which is what I suspect—or it's because he has some other reason for wishing to find Mrs. Turner, it doesn't matter. It can do you no harm to spend time in the company of a handsome gentleman. If nothing else he will be an excellent practice-gentleman for you."

"What on earth is a practice-gentleman?" Juliet asked, curious despite her annoyance.

"A practice-gentleman is one upon whom one tests one's flirtation skills while waiting for the permanent-gentleman to come along."

"Have you been listening in on Amelia Snowe's conversations with Lady Felicia again?"

"You might laugh now, miss," Cecily said with an arch look, "but you won't be so glib when you are working your wiles on your permanent-gentleman and luring him into matrimony."

But Juliet was very much afraid that if her mother had her way, there would be no flirtation, practice or otherwise. And certainly not with Lord Deveril.

Deveril called for Juliet at Winterson House that afternoon at two o'clock. Juliet had changed into a serviceable wool gown, though her pelisse was a deep green color that flattered her coloring. He longed to see her dressed in such flattering colors more often. Despite her infirmity he had a suspicion that her position at the fringes of the *ton* could easily be circumvented if she were properly outfitted in a manner befitting her social standing.

"Good afternoon, Miss Shelby," he said with a slight bow. "Shall we depart?"

"Of course," she responded with a smile. "Thank you again for agreeing to accompany me to Signor Boccardo's studio. I cannot tell you how much it will relieve my mind if he has news of Anna."

Once the formalities were out of the way, Alec offered Juliet his elbow and made to lead her down the front steps of Winterson House.

She stared at his arm for a moment, as if she were unfamiliar with such simple gestures. Still, she slipped her arm through his and allowed him to assist her without comment. It was such a simple courtesy, and yet Alec had the feeling that Juliet had become accustomed to fending for herself in such matters.

Her arm, where it held his, was strong, and he was pleased to note that she trusted him to ensure her safety. And, he noted to himself with a wry smile, he was behaving like a damned halfling. No doubt Juliet received every sort of courtesy and he was imagining himself into a white knight role out of simple vanity. Still, he didn't imagine her shiver when he lifted her into the curricle. So perhaps she felt the frisson of attraction between them as well.

Even so, he made sure to keep an inch or so between them on the seat of his equipage—no mean feat in such a sporty vehicle.

"What do you know of Signor Boccardo?" he asked once they were under way. "I believe you said he was Mrs. Turner's musical mentor?"

"Yes," she replied, watching avidly as they passed through the familiar streets of Mayfair. "He was engaged to teach music to the local squire's children in the village where Anna grew up. Her father was the local vicar and she was allowed to take lessons along with the squire's children."

"And she turned out to be more talented than the squire's children?" he guessed, steering his horses within an inch of a passing cart.

"Indeed," Juliet responded, reaching up to hold on to her bonnet as a breeze tried to catch it. "I'm afraid the squire's children weren't very nice about it either. Though I suppose they were jealous of her talent as well. Still, when Anna's father died unexpectedly, Signor Boccardo and the squire were quite helpful in securing a position for Anna with a family in the county as their music instructor."

They fell silent for a moment, and Alec had the distinct impression that Miss Shelby was gathering the courage to ask him something. When she cleared her throat, he knew he was correct.

"My lord," she said tentatively, "I do not wish to pry into your private business. But there is something I need to ask you. Of course, if you do not wish to answer you are perfectly at liberty to tell me so. And I do not like to—"

"Miss Shelby," Alec said, cutting short her preemptive apologies. "You are perfectly welcome to ask me anything."

He gave her a sidelong wink. "Within reason of course."

Her cheeks reddened. "Of course," she replied. He felt her bracing to blurt out her question, and he, in turn, braced to have it asked of him. Probably it would be something having to do with the rumors she'd heard about his father. It disappointed him that she would be intrigued by such gossip, but he supposed it was not unusual for young ladies to find scandal intriguing.

"My lord, do you have a . . . a . . . *particular* interest in finding Anna?" she asked, keeping her gaze firmly ahead of her. "That is to say, are you perhaps, her *special* friend? I couldn't help but notice how concerned you are for little Alice's well-being, and I can think of no other reason why you would be so concerned about finding her. And you were so ready and willing to assist me in my search for her."

Before he could respond, she kept on, "I wouldn't be

shocked or surprised if it were true. I mean, it is not un-usual for gentlemen to . . . that is to say, I know gentleman have their intrigues, and I have guessed for some time that Anna was supplementing the income I gave her in some manner. And knowing how little she charges for her lessons, I know she has to be getting more funds from somewhere. And—"

Alec had to put a stop to this before the poor girl talked herself into a swoon.

"Stop!" he said before she could go on. "Do stop, Miss Shelby. I will respond to your questions just as soon as I am able to find a . . . a . . . stopping place."

Though she was in mid-sentence, she stopped obediently and he made a mental note to tell her how grateful he was for it. He turned his attention to the road and was relieved to see that they were nearing Green Park. It would make as good a place as any to have their little chat.

He waited until the curricle stopped moving before he turned to her. She stared studiously at her gloved hands, which were clasped together tightly. He wished he could ignore propriety and take her hand in his, but that would hardly make her more comfortable. And she was already uncomfortable enough.

"Miss Shelby," he said finally, watching her intently. "Please be assured that I have never even met your Mrs. Turner, let alone conducted a liaison with her."

She let out a sigh—whether it was of relief, he did not know. He doubted she would continue to be relieved once she heard his reasons for wishing to assist her.

"There is, however," he went on, hoping she would not be too angry with him, "a member of my family whom I believe is . . . ehem . . . intimately acquainted with your friend."

At this, she lifted her head to look fully at him. "Your uncle," she said with a moue of distaste.

He could hardly blame her for the sentiment since he disapproved of the man too.

"Yes," he said. "I suspected him at first of being the father of your friend's child. He is, after all, not known for always being a gentleman when it comes to women who are in a position to be exploited. And I believe he was spending a great deal of time with your father during Mrs. Turner's time in your household."

"He was indeed," Juliet said with a sigh. She suddenly looked weary, as if she'd been bearing more than her fair share of this burden for too long. He wished there were some way he could help her, aside from simply driving her around town.

"Well, I suppose I cannot blame you for thinking the worst of your uncle," she continued. "Though I can tell you that Anna has refused again and again to tell who Alice's father is. And believe me, I've tried repeatedly to make her name the man who attacked her. But she was firm about that. Even though I did try to persuade her to tell us simply for safety's sake. I dislike thinking that such a man is free to prey upon unprotected young women with impunity."

"As do I," Alec said, his mouth twisting with anger. He knew there were certain so-called gentlemen who enjoyed exerting their power over those women who should be off-limits, and it sickened him to think that his own uncle might be one of them. But he knew well enough what the men in his family were capable of. "But I have since spoken to Roderick and he swears that he has never been involved with Mrs. Turner. And though I do not trust the man as far as I could lift him, I do believe he is telling the truth in this instance."

Juliet's brow furrowed, still, however. "Then why have you continued to assist me?" she asked, puzzled. "You are under no obligation to help me, I assure you."

"My dear Miss Shelby," Alec said, assuming his social mask once more, "cannot a fellow offer his assistance to a damsel in distress for no other reason than to enjoy her company?"

She gave him a winsome half smile. "I think a fellow

can talk a great deal of nonsense," she said with a laugh. "Now, do be serious. I can just as easily ask Cecily or Winterson to help me find Miss . . . Mrs. Turner. I do not wish to take advantage of your good humor."

"Miss Shelby," he said, damning propriety, and taking her gloved hand in his, "Juliet, I wish to assist you in this matter for your own sake. Because I wish to help you find your friend. And perhaps a bit because I wish when it was needed, that someone had lent their assistance to my mama, who also found herself involved in a situation that was more than she could handle alone."

If she was taken aback, she did not show it. Instead, Juliet looked down at their joined hands. When she glanced up, he saw that there was a suspicious moisture in her eyes.

"Well, whatever your reasoning, my lord," she told him, "I thank you. And I feel quite sure that your mama would be enormously proud of you."

Pulling her hand away, she untied and retied the ribbons of her bonnet and turned to him. "Now that we've got all that out of the way, let's get to Signor Boccardo's before the afternoon gets away from us. Alice needs her mama."

Resisting the urge to kiss her on the nose, Alec simply nodded, and giving his horses the signal to set off, he steered them back onto the pavement and toward Bloomsbury, where Boccardo's studio was located.

The silence as they drove to Signor Boccardo's studio allowed Juliet to marvel at her own temerity. Had she really accused Lord Deveril of keeping Mrs. Turner as his mistress? Not in so many words, but that's what she'd done.

She wasn't sure when the idea had first occurred to her, but the more she considered his continued offers of assistance, the more she'd begun to see the possibility as a likelihood. As soon as he'd mentioned his uncle, however, it had all become clear to her. Of course Deveril had suspected his uncle of being Alice's father. And if Alice were his uncle's by-blow it would make a great deal of sense that Lord Deveril would wish to take the child under his protection. That Alice was not, indeed, his cousin, made little difference now. He had agreed to take care of the child, and as a gentleman he would do so whether the child was a relative or not.

Juliet was still in a bit of a brown study when the curricle came to a halt before an unassuming house on a quiet Bloomsbury street. She felt a little thrill when Alec took her by the waist and lifted her to the ground beside the curricle. Did she imagine the flash of fire in his eyes when he looked at her? She had no way of knowing, but felt the telltale flush in her own cheeks with a mixture of exasperation and embarrassment. Most days she enjoyed her fair skin and auburn hair, but it did become tiresome to have her every emotion displayed upon her cheeks.

"Shall we?" Lord Deveril asked, offering her his left arm so that she might use her walking stick in her left.

They were shown by a footman into a small but lavishly furnished sitting room, where the signore's origins in Italy were evident in the continental décor. Thick carpets covered the floor, and various sculptures, paintings, and bric-a-brac filled every available surface in the little room. Even so it was a comfortable, well-lived-in sort of chamber. One that had obviously seen a woman's hand, Juliet thought as she noticed the needlework stretched out upon a wooden frame just next to a comfortable-looking chair.

"My dear Lord Deveril, to what does La Fortunata owe the pleasure?" asked a striking woman of middle years without preamble as she swept into the chamber.

Juliet was startled by the woman's entry, but not particularly surprised to know such a creature was already acquainted with Alec. She was gorgeous and had doubtlessly enjoyed a career in the opera before marrying the signore. And though he was discreet, Alec did have a bit of a rakish reputation. Unless, of course, this woman was a pupil of the signore and she and Alec knew one another from elsewhere.

Seemingly unfazed by the beauty's entrance, Lord Deveril bowed over her outstretched hand. "Fortunata," he said with a smile, "it's been some time. I did not expect to find you in Bloomsbury of all places."

La Fortunata gave an exquisite shrug. "It is where my Pietro has his studio and so long as he must be here, then so too must I."

She turned her gaze upon Juliet, a speaking brow raised as she looked her up and down. "This is your wife, my lord? She is not in your usual way, I think."

Before he could correct her, Juliet took the bull—or the diva as it were—by the horns and broke in. "Goodness me, no! I am merely his lordship's acquaintance. We've come to see your husband about my friend, who is missing."

The beauty looked as if she wished to inquire why his lordship was paying calls with someone who was a mere acquaintance, but Alec cut in. "Miss Shelby is a friend, Fortunata, and I have agreed to escort her here today. I had no idea you'd be here—"

"Or you would not have come," Fortunata said, laughing heartily. "No, do not deny it. It is, how do you say, written all over your face."

She turned to Juliet. "Have no fear, Miss Shelby, your lord and Fortunata were never lovers. He knows me only because of my friendship with his friend Fortenbury who—"

"Yes, well, we don't wish to bore Miss Shelby with that tale," Deveril interrupted, his own countenance reddening. "Perhaps you might inform your husband we're here, Signora Boccardo?"

Giving him a wink, the singer bade them be seated while she went to tell her husband that he had guests. Juliet watched bemused as the woman sashayed from the room.

"What interesting friends you have," she said wryly as the door closed behind the other woman.

"If I'd had any notion Fortunata had married this Boccardo fellow there's no way I'd have accompanied you here," he said, giving in to impulse and thrusting his hands through his hair. "I'd heard Fortunata had married, but I had no idea the fellow would turn out to be your Signor Boccardo."

"Yes, well, I'm glad to have met her," Juliet said with a laugh. "I shall have to ask Lord Fortenbury about his acquaintance with—"

"You will do no such thing," he said, interrupting her. "Good Lord, Fort would swoon if you asked him about—"

He was forestalled from continuing by the entrance of a man Juliet presumed to be Signor Boccardo.

"My lord," the man greeted Alec, before turning to Juliet. "And Miss Shelby!" His expression softened on seeing her, and he hurried forward to take both of her hands in his and kiss her in Continental fashion on both cheeks.

"I have heard so many good things of you from Anna. She says your skill on the pianoforte is unparalleled to any of her other students."

He was good-looking in an exotic sort of way. She could tell that he was a passionate man, simply from the exuberance of his manner of speaking. At his praise, Juliet felt herself blush with pleasure. "Thank you so much, signor," she said. "I know that Anna values your opinion so I am pleased to know she's spoken to you of me."

"Anna is the reason we are here," Alec said firmly, and Juliet was glad of the prompt.

"Yes, signor," she said, "I'm afraid Anna has disappeared and I wondered if you might have some idea of where she's gone."

Gesturing that his guests should take seats, the musician took the chair before the fire, rather incongruous given his height, but he didn't seem to mind.

"Tell me all," he said, leaning forward to place his elbows on his knees.

Quickly, Juliet told him about Anna's strange missives and the arrangements she'd made for Alice. She also told him of her suspicions that Anna's notes might have been coerced in some way.

When she was finished, Signor Boccardo shook his head in bafflement and Juliet felt her heart sink.

"I had hoped that this was all behind her," he said, his expressive face creased with worry. "She has the child. And her fiancé, Mr. MacEwan. I thought she was beyond all that."

He leaned back. "I don't know how much Anna told you about her life growing up. In the village."

Juliet frowned. She was beginning to realize just how little she knew about her friend. She'd had no notion that Anna was engaged to be married. The idea that her mentor would make such a decision without telling her was worrying. It made Juliet wonder what other secrets Anna had been keeping from her. It was hardly Signor Boccardo's fault, however, so she kept her own counsel on the matter. Aloud, she said, "She told me about her father's strictness if that is what you mean."

The pianist frowned, his expressive hands clenched. "When I came to Little Wittington, there seemed to me a . . . how do you say . . . a curse upon the place. Always there were smiles and happiness, but I could see at once that it was all a lie. The Reverend Turner, he was a hard man. Strict. He disapproved of Anna's passion for music. Oh, it was all well for her to play like the other young ladies. For show. But he saw the way the squire's sons looked at her as she played. The way they watched her, the intensity . . ." He shrugged. "The reverend forbade her from playing. He refused to let her go to the manor house. I am no horseman but even I can see he is like the farmer who shuts the barn after the horse has already escaped."

"What happened?" Alec asked.

"One night, Anna, she sneaks out of her father's house and goes to the manor house." Signor Boccardo shook his head at the memory. "I lived there, which is why I know so much. I am awakened by a scream in the night. The whole house was awakened, and there is Anna in the music room. Her gown is torn, and the squire's eldest son, he has a red mark on his face."

Juliet gasped. "He assaulted her? Oh, poor Anna."

She didn't say that something similar had happened to her friend in her own father's household as well. It was just too terrible to speak aloud.

"He said he did not," the signore said sadly. "I admit I found it hard to believe. He was a good boy. But even good boys can fall prey to temptation. The vicar, though, he believed the boy. And condemned Anna for teasing the young man."

"Of course he did," Alec said, disgusted. "That type always does."

"He cast her out, didn't he?" Juliet guessed.

"He did," Signor Boccardo said, nodding. "Even though Squire Ramsey and his family had no reason to spread the tale, the Reverend Turner would not stand for a hint of gossip. I could not let her fend for herself. And she was the most talented of my pupils there. So I brought her with me to London and saw to it that she got a position with a wealthy family."

"Mine," Juliet said.

"Yes, Miss Shelby," the Italian said with a sad smile. "I had hoped that Anna would prosper with your family. But it seems that she is always to be taken advantage of."

"What happened to her family?" Alec asked. Juliet looked at him. Of course! Perhaps Anna had finally relented and gone to her family for help, just as Juliet had suggested.

But Signor Boccardo's next words killed that notion. "They died in a fire not long after we left the village," he said. "Everyone—the vicar, his wife, her sister—they all died."

Five

Juliet was quiet as Alec led her back out to his curricle. It wasn't until they were once more driving through the streets of Bloomsbury that she spoke.

"Could Anna have been pursued by the squire's son?" she asked.

Alec pondered the notion. It was possible, he supposed. Being accused of attempted ravishment would certainly rankle with a young man. Even if the accusation were true.

"It is possible that he feared she would carry the tale with her to London," he said. "And it doesn't sound as if Signor Boccardo took any great pains to hide his direction."

"I wonder if Anna left of her own accord because of some threat from Ramsey or if he came for her and made her write those notes to me to throw me off her trail."

Alec glanced over and was startled by the determination in Juliet's face. "Let's not jump to conclusions," he cautioned. "We don't know that this Ramsey fellow has anything to do with Anna's disappearance. Why don't you let me send an investigator to Little Wittington to visit the squire's house? He can determine if Ramsey is even in a position to threaten Anna. For all we know the fellow has moved to the colonies and become a blacksmith."

"I suppose I can hardly go traipsing about the countryside searching for clues," she said, "can I?"

"No," he said with a half grin, awed once more by her

pluck. "You really can't. It isn't the thing for young ladies to traipse. At least not unmarried ones."

That seemed to sober her. Dammit, he hadn't meant to remind her of Turlington. She had enough to worry about.

"I promise that as soon as I hear something from my man I will let you know," he told her, glancing over to let her see that he was sincere.

That seemed to placate her. "Thank you, my lord, for bringing me to see Signor Boccardo today. And thank you for helping me look for Anna. I know you are doing it because you feel some sort of obligation on your uncle's behalf, but whatever the reason I'm grateful."

That his uncle had ceased to be a factor in his continued assistance, he didn't bother telling her. Letting her think of him as a self-interested party was better for both their sakes.

"Perhaps you could show us something a bit more daring, Madame Celeste?" Cecily asked the modiste in what her cousins were coming to know as her "duchess tone." "I realize that Miss Shelby is yet a debutante, but surely she can wear something with a bit of dash that won't be too terribly scandalous."

Juliet watched in amazement as the older woman, who purported to have come to England from France during the terror, but who most people speculated had been born somewhere much closer to her new home—like Bermondsey—hurried to do the new Duchess of Winterson's bidding. It was difficult still to see Cecily as anything other than the scholarly bluestocking she had been before her marriage to Winterson earlier in the year. And yet, it would seem that those who depended on the custom of one of the most highly placed ladies of the *ton,* like Madame Celeste, had no trouble at all remembering her cousin's leap in status.

"Thank you again, Cecily," she said in a low voice as they waited for the modiste to fetch another bolt of fabric.

"If you hadn't insisted upon accompanying me here, I have little doubt that Mama would have brought Turlington along. It's difficult enough to make decisions about what sort of gowns to purchase, but between Mama and her criticisms and Turlington's oily compliments I feel sure I'd have succumbed to the headache before three minutes of our session had passed."

After her clandestine visit to Signor Boccardo's with Deveril the day before, Juliet had returned home in a somber mood. She spent the evening ruminating over the day's events, and pondering how what Signor Boccardo had told them affected her understanding of Anna's situation. A good night's sleep hadn't given her any more insight into the problem.

When she received a note from Cecily the next morning summoning her to the modiste's, Juliet had thought about sending her regrets, but she knew that Cecily would have no compunction about hunting her down and dragging her to the dressmakers'. And she did need some new gowns if she were to escape Lord Turlington's clutches. So when her cousins called shortly after breakfast to collect her, Juliet had done the sensible thing and gone with them.

"We are going to Madame Celeste's to buy you some shockingly expensive new gowns and there is nothing you can say that will change my mind," her cousin had told her. And soon Juliet was doing the thing she loathed most in the world. Being fitted for new gowns. It had once been on Cecily's most-hated list as well, but somewhere between meeting Winterson and becoming his duchess, her cousin had learned to enjoy shopping. Juliet blamed Winterson.

"I still cannot believe that your father has allowed Aunt Rose to coerce you into an engagement with Turlington." Cecily's mouth pursed as if she tasted something sour. "Has she that little confidence in your ability to find a husband on your own?"

"Well, I can hardly blame her on that account. I have been out for three years now with no offers." Juliet sighed. "Not to mention the fact that I am one of the notorious Ugly Ducklings thanks to Amelia Snowe."

The duchess waved her hand. "Amelia Snowe is a spiteful cat, and well you know it. Indeed, I believe most of the *ton* knows it as well, though they are so frightened of becoming her next target for scorn that they allow her to continue on unfettered."

"Speaking of Amelia," Madeline, who was seated on the other side of the settee from Juliet, interjected, "when do you plan on using the dance card, Juliet? You can no longer use your leg as an excuse. Especially since your successful lessons the other evening."

If only her cousins knew the truth about her leg injury, Juliet mused, perhaps then they would understand just how frightened she was to practice her newfound dance skills in public. Yet, she did know that if she were going to find a husband for herself—someone besides Lord Turlington or anyone else her mother might decide would suit—then she would need to make more of an effort to gain the *ton*'s notice. A flash to that moment earlier yesterday when Lord Deveril had lifted her into his curricle gave her pause, but she dismissed the memory. A man like Deveril would not need to settle for a limping pianist with a gorgon for a mother. If she wished to find a husband she would need to cast her net as wide as possible. Hence the trip to Madame Celeste's establishment to choose a new wardrobe.

Her mother might once have objected to such attempts at improving her appearance, but she had recently decided that Juliet owed it to Turlington to be at her very best, even if it meant drawing heretofore undesired attention to herself. And if Juliet could use her mother's own machinations against her, so much the better.

Before she could respond aloud to her cousins, the

modiste returned with two assistants in tow, each holding one end of a large bolt of green silk.

"Zis shade, I zink," Madame hissed in her faux-French accent, "eet is zee perfect color for zee young lady's eyes, yes?"

Juliet removed her glove, so that she might feel the softness of the silk against her fingers. It was indeed a lovely color. And rather close to the color of her eyes.

"Yes." Cecily nodded. "It is perfect. And I also would like to see something in a deep rose hue."

"Are you sure it won't clash with my hair?" Juliet asked. "Mama has always warned me against pinks."

"It must be the right sort of pink, darling," her cousin soothed. "Trust me. I won't send you out before the lions in anything that doesn't suit you."

"Lions," a male voice sounded from behind them. "I did tell you she's grown bloodthirsty, didn't I, Deveril?"

The three cousins turned to see the Duke of Winterson, carelessly elegant in buff breeches and a blue coat of superfine, followed by Lord Deveril, enter the room. Juliet felt her cheeks heat, and dared not let herself catch Deveril's eye. Her cousins knew, of course, about their errand yesterday, but she did not wish them to guess for a moment just how drawn she was to the man.

"Dearest." Cecily sounded cross. "I thought I told you that I would see you this evening." Since discovering that she was expecting a happy event, the young duchess had found her spouse to be a trifle overbearing in his efforts to ensure her health and safety.

"Sheathe your sword, my dear," he said mildly, leaning down to kiss her cheek. "I have come to collect you at your stepmama's request. She says that your father needs your assistance with some sort of documents and refuses to be calmed until he sees you." Turning to Juliet and Madeline, he bowed. "Ladies, a pleasure as always."

Since Cecily's father had only recently begun to recover

from a life-threatening apoplexy, he had to rely on her for assistance with his scholarly work. Juliet could see that Cecily was torn.

Before her cousin could respond, Juliet squeezed Cecily's hand.

"Go," she said, smiling. "Maddie and I will be fine here on our own. Madame Celeste will not steer me wrong lest she risk your wrath, as you well know. And you know as well as I do that your father would not have asked for you if he did not consider the matter to be urgent."

"Are you sure?" Cecily still looked torn, but it was clear to anyone who knew her as well as her cousins did that she felt compelled to go to her father..

"Perhaps I might be of assistance?" Lord Deveril bowed to the three women. "I have often helped my sisters choose their gowns for the season," he said. "And I am quite conversant with the fashions making the rounds just now."

Which, to Juliet's mind, was akin to saying that Mr. Wordsworth knew a bit about poetry.

"Oh, would you mind terribly?" Cecily asked, her gaze lighting on the man who had set the fashion among London gentlemen since he'd come up from Oxford. "Not to suggest that Juliet and Madeline don't have exquisite taste, you understand." Her quick glance her cousins' way rather suggested the opposite. "But I would feel so much more comfortable knowing they had someone to act as a guide to them."

Juliet and Madeline exchanged a look, but forbore from pointing out that until recently their cousin had been just as clueless as they were about fashion. One didn't wish to upset an *enceinte* lady after all.

"It would be my pleasure," Deveril said with a grin, suggesting that he knew just what the Duchess of Winterson's cousins were thinking. "Never fear, Your Grace," he assured her, "I will make quite sure that Miss Shelby does not choose anything that will endanger her reputation."

"Oh la." Cecily laughed, rising from her seat and tucking her hand into the crook of Winterson's arm. "I have no worries on that score. If it were up to Juliet she'd have Madame Celeste construct a cloak of invisibility that would shield her from all notice altogether. You must make sure that she chooses something that will make her stand out, Lord Deveril. Something that will show the *ton* just what an exquisitely beautiful lady she is."

No pressure, Alec thought to himself, watching Winterson and his lady leave the shop. Turning, he saw both Miss Shelby and Lady Madeline watching him expectantly.

When Winterson had mentioned he was on his way to Madame Celeste's establishment, he'd agreed to go along to keep his friend company, though if he were completely honest, he had jumped at the chance to ensure Juliet was all right after their meeting with Signor Boccardo yesterday.

Before he could say anything, however, Madame Celeste caught sight of him and hurried over.

"My lord," she gushed. "How wonderful eet is to see you. How can I be of service?"

"My thanks, madame," he told the modiste. "I am here to assist Miss Shelby. I understand you have been helping her with color choices?"

"Ah yes, my lord," she said. "But we need to take measurements and to choose patterns."

"Excellent," he said with a smile. "Please bring the ladies some tea, and the pattern books. Lady Madeline and I will go over the patterns while you take Miss Shelby's measurements."

Though Juliet frowned, she didn't object as she was led into the back where Deveril knew she would be poked and prodded to within an inch of her life. It was the way of fitting rooms the world over. Or so he surmised, never having been the world over.

When she was gone, he found himself startled to realize that he was alone with Lady Madeline. She was a nice enough girl, he supposed, but he had never really had occasion to speak with her much before.

"You are growing fond of her," Lady Madeline said once Juliet had left the room. It was a statement, not a question.

What the devil was it with the women in this family? Deveril wondered. Only yesterday he'd been accused of basically the same thing by Juliet's mother. Unlike Lady Shelby, however, he sensed that Lady Madeline's interest was out of concern for Juliet.

Alec turned to look at her. "I don't know what you mean," he said. He liked Juliet, Miss Shelby, a great deal. But that was a far cry from fondness. They were friends, that was all.

"I've seen you watch her," she said, taking a sip of the tea one of the seamstresses had brought them. "Have no fear. Your secret is safe with me."

He made a noncommittal noise. It could hardly be called a secret given the number of people who had informed him of the so-called fact in the past few days. And, he reminded himself, his connection to Juliet was strictly one of obligation. Obligation and friendship. He had agreed to help her find her missing friend, and until they learned something definitive about Mrs. Turner's whereabouts that was how their connection would remain. Though he was horrified at the notion of Juliet being married off to a snake like Turlington, there was little he could do to stop such a thing from happening. Especially given his own family history.

"She dislikes him," Madeline continued conversationally, "Turlington, that is. If you are worried at all about his having a prior claim or some nonsense like that."

"Are you always this forthright, my lady?" he asked, torn between shock at the blonde's frankness and admiration for her boldness. "I admit that I doubted there could be another young lady as demanding as your cousin, the Duchess of Winterson, but I find I was mistaken."

She smiled, the expression transforming her from merely pretty to lovely. "Cecily possesses enough brass for the three of us," she said, grinning. "But yes, I do find that more often than not a bit of plain speaking saves misunderstandings. Don't you?"

While he agreed to the concept, he couldn't help but imagine how different the world might be if everyone were given to that kind of plain speaking. The mind boggled.

"At times," he said cautiously, wondering whether agreeing with the chit would lead her into more dangerous waters. "However, I do wonder if your cousin, Juliet I mean, would like knowing you were speaking about such a private matter while she isn't here."

"Well, you can hardly expect me to ask you if you're in love with her while she's sitting here with us. For one thing, it would cause her to inflict some sort of bodily harm upon my person. And I'm not at all fond of such things. For another, I can hardly expect you to give me a truthful answer when the object of my question is in the room. Common decency would dictate that you keep from saying anything that would wound her feelings. So I thought I'd ask you while she was being measured so that I could know which way the wind blows and plan accordingly."

He stared. "Plan? Accordingly?" Did Wellington know about this girl, he wondered, and if so had she sat in on the strategy sessions for Waterloo? If she hadn't been still in the schoolroom at the time, he would have little difficulty believing it were true.

"Yes," she explained patiently, as if she were talking to a child. "If you do have some sort of finer feelings for my cousin, then it would behoove you to act on them sooner rather than later. Her mother is trying to marry her off to Lord Turlington, of all people—do you know him? A more cloying fop I've never met! The mere idea of him makes my toes twitch. At any rate, with her mama scheming with Turlington, and Lord Shelby away on diplomatic business, it is up to Cecily and me to make sure that Juliet is saved from her mama's nefarious plot."

"And how might you plan to prevent this, Lady Madeline?"

Really, she was quite fascinating. Utterly mad, of course, but still interesting.

"Well, you'll have to compromise her, of course."

It was a good thing, Alec reflected, that he had chosen not to take tea, for as his luck was currently running, he would assuredly have been taking a drink when Lady Madeline announced the first portion of her plan, which would have caused him to send a shower of tea out over his breeches.

"I beg your pardon," he said, "but I thought you just said that I should compromise your cousin."

"It's the only way," she said calmly, taking her own tea without danger of stray showers. "Aunt Rose is a hard woman, my lord. She is as ruthless as the meanest lord of the underworld when it comes to her own wishes. And she wishes for Juliet to marry Lord Turlington. Lord knows why, of course. One never knows with Aunt Rose. She undoubtedly owes him a gambling debt or some other such nonsense. It doesn't matter, really, since whatever the reason for her debt to him, she will sacrifice Juliet to pay it."

"How do you know?" he asked.

"Oh, dear." Lady Madeline frowned. "I had hoped that you were one of the gentlemen who understood that ladies aren't always as silly as they seem. Pray, do not disabuse me of the notion, for if you are it will quite upset me."

He started to respond, but she cut him off.

"As I was saying," she continued, "you need to compromise Juliet. And the sooner, the better. It's quite easy to get into her bedchamber from the trellis at the back of her father's town house. We've gotten in and out of there half a dozen times in the past few years."

"Wait!" Alec held up a staying hand. "Lady Madeline, I know you mean well, but really, I cannot simply go about compromising young ladies just because it has been asked of me."

"No one has made mention of young ladies, my lord," she snapped. "Only one young lady needs compromising, and I must assure you that it will be the easiest thing in the world . . ."

Alec felt his eyes goggle.

"Oh, don't be a goose," Madeline chided. "Of course I don't mean that Juliet is of easy virtue. Goodness, you men can be so old-womanish at times. I simply mean that getting into her bedchamber will be quite easy. And once you are found out—and really, all you'll need to do is ring for a servant and the word will spread like wildfire—then Lord and Lady Shelby will be at great pains to cover the whole thing up. Which they will do, by marrying Juliet off to you posthaste."

She smiled at him and took another sip of tea, as if she had just told him about a new scheme to provide food to the starving. He was starving, but it was for a large glass of brandy to soothe his nerves.

"Lady Madeline," he began, only to be interrupted by the arrival of Madame Celeste with an armful of fashion plates. "Ah, yes, excellent. Madame Celeste."

As if she'd not just encouraged him to creep into her cousin's bedchamber and ruin her, Lady Madeline brightened at Madame Celeste and began to thumb through the sketches.

"Oh, this is lovely," she said, pointing to a simply styled morning gown. "I believe this would suit Juliet admirably."

Still slightly stunned, Alec nodded, and turned his attention to the fashion plates. But all he could think of was Miss Shelby, flushed with sleep, and laid out on her bed as if she were his for the taking. Which was utterly ridiculous, he firmly told himself. He had no such designs on Miss Shelby and the sooner he realized it, the better.

Even so, it was going to be a long, long afternoon.

Six

*I*n the back of Madame Celeste's establishment, Juliet was trying her best to keep from disrobing in front of the seamstresses.

"Can you not simply take my measurements while I remain clothed?" she asked the modiste, whom the frustrated first assistant had summoned. "I am not comfortable with removing my garments for an audience."

Juliet knew it was odd of her to be so adamant, but she knew how gossip was spread, and if anyone at Madame Celeste's guessed her secret all her years of maintaining the fiction that her accident had merely left her with a mangled foot would have been in vain.

For her own part, she cared little of what the *ton* thought. She had long ago come to the realization that the loss of her foot had been a small price to pay when compared with what might have happened that day in Vienna. Since returning to England she had become aware of just how many people died from simple blood loss when physicians removed their mangled limbs. The only embarrassment, to her mind, came from the knowledge that she had survived not because of any divine providence, but simply because of an accident of birth. If she'd been born to a poorer family, it was doubtful that she would have received such excellent care.

Expecting the modiste to be impatient with her request, Juliet was instead surprised to see compassion in the woman's eyes.

"You do not wish to show the scars, eh?" Madame Celeste gestured to her feet.

At Juliet's nod, the older woman nodded. "All right, then. You will go into the little room and remove your clothing. We take the measurements from those."

Relieved that she would not be forced to defend herself further, Juliet followed the first assistant to the fitting room.

"Take off everything but your shift," the assistant told her, as she unfastened Juliet's gown at the back. "I will wait just outside so that you may hand them to me. It will take longer this way, you know."

But Juliet didn't care about the time, so long as her secret remained secret.

She undressed quickly and, clothes in hand, she opened the door, giving the assistant her stays, corset, and gown.

Now, shivering in her shift, she lowered herself to the overstuffed chair situated in the corner of the tiny room. Wishing all this might have been accomplished without her being separated from Madeline and Deveril, she wondered what the two of them were discussing while they examined fashion plates.

She had noticed the way Deveril watched her cousin. Had even been made jealous by it. It was ridiculous for her to mistake his interest in helping her find Anna for an interest in her, but when she felt the intensity of his gaze, she had a difficult time remembering just why the notion was so foolish.

There were a number of reasons why it made more sense for a man like him to set his sights on Madeline rather than Juliet. For one thing, Madeline was healthy and hale. In fact, she was ridiculously robust and enjoyed nothing more than a vigorous ride in the park, or a country ramble. For another, Madeline, with her fashionable blond crop and short stature, was to Juliet's mind the epitome of a pocket Venus.

Yes, she might be lumped in with Juliet and Cecily—well, just Juliet now really—as an Ugly Duckling, but there was nothing remotely ugly about Lady Madeline Essex. She might have a tendency to speak her mind overmuch, and had at times entered into discussions that made her less than comfortable company, but overall, Juliet thought that with the exception of the highest sticklers, Madeline had far more chance of marrying well and overcoming her less than stellar social status than she did.

Which was, of course, why Juliet spent her time waiting in the back of Madame Celeste's shop imagining her cousin and Lord Deveril, their angelic blond heads together, getting along famously and planning to elope to Gretna Green as soon as the opportunity presented itself. He would declare himself on bended knee, a beam of sunlight shining down from the heavens to denote their approval of the match, while Madeline, a light wind ruffling her golden curls, smiled her acceptance of his proposal. And they would live happily ever after in connubial bliss while Juliet grew older and, having refused her mother's insistence that she marry Turlington, lived as an unpaid servant with her brother Matthew and his unpleasant bride, the former Miss Snowe.

It was on these unhappy thoughts that Juliet dwelled as she heard an exclamation from the other side of the door, and the murmur of voices.

"She can't be gone!" hissed the first assistant. "She promised me that she would be back today at the latest."

"Well, according to her note she won't be coming back," said a second, harder voice.

"Let me see it," the first assistant demanded.

The rustle of paper indicated that the note had exchanged hands.

"Why would she do this?" asked another voice, doubtless one of the seamstresses. "Jane needs this position if she wants to get her daughter back. And why would she go off with such a one as him? She said she'd never trust a man again."

"For enough money I'd go off with old baggy eyes. At least he's got the blunt to pay for nice clothes and a fancy house. It's a sight better than being ordered about by Madame and her hoity-toity customers."

"That's because you're no better than you should be, Hetty," said the other girl. "Jane ain't like you. She don't want a man's money. She wants an honest wage and a way to get her baby back. I don't believe it. She wouldn't leave London again. Not when she's so close to having enough money to bring her little girl back."

"I don't like it," the first assistant said, her voice clipped. "I don't think she would leave on her own either. And didn't she say she thought she'd been followed last week?"

"Aye," said Hetty. "She said some gent she didn't know was following her from her rooms to here and back again."

Juliet shivered. She remembered Jane from a previous visit to Madame Celeste's with her mother. She had seemed a gentle, well-mannered young woman. Not at all the sort who would leave behind her child for a frivolous reason. And, unfortunately, Jane's plight sounded quite similar to Anna's. From the mysterious note, to the man following her, to the existence of a child.

"Right," she heard the first assistant say sharply. "No more about Jane. We'll lose our own positions if we don't get back to work."

"But Meggie, what if whoever took Jane takes a fancy to me or Hetty? What then?"

The first assistant, Meggie, made an impatient noise that sounded much like Madame Celeste. "Just stay together. Don't go anywhere alone."

"Are you going to tell Madame?" Hetty demanded. "Maybe she'll hire another footman to watch out for us."

The silence was deafening. So much for Madame, Juliet thought wryly.

"Just be careful," Meggie repeated. "Now, Hetty, take these back to Miss Shelby and escort her to the front."

Juliet heard the rustle of fabric as the first assistant handed her clothing back to Hetty.

At the brisk knock on the door, she opened it to peek out.

"Here are your clothes, miss," Hetty, who was rather unfortunate-looking, said quietly. "Let me know and I'll do up your back. You're ready to leave, I think."

"Thank you," Juliet told her, closing the door again to keep her curious eyes from looking at her feet.

Quickly, she got dressed and a moment later, her walking stick in hand, she was following the seamstress back to the front of the shop.

"I heard your conversation about your friend," she told the girl as they walked. "Can you tell me where she lived?"

Hetty stopped and turned to look at her. "Begging your pardon, miss," she said, "but what can you care about a shopgirl going missing?"

If she'd asked such a question of Lady Shelby, Juliet guessed that her mother would report the insolence to her mistress at once. Since she was hardly her mother, she simply shrugged. "I have a friend who disappeared under similar circumstances and wondered if the two might be connected."

This seemed to satisfy Hetty, for she gave a brisk nod and told her Jane's address. Which happened to be one street over from Mrs. Turner's flat.

"It's not like her, miss," Hetty said. "She's a good girl. She wouldn't just leave her babe for some man."

"I believe you," she replied.

When they reached the sitting room where she'd left Madeline and Deveril, Juliet was surprised to see only Deveril there.

"Miss Shelby," he said, bowing over her hand, "I hope your fittings were not too tedious."

"They were fine, my lord," she said briskly. "But what has happened to my cousin?"

"Ah." Deveril smiled. "She recalled a previous appointment and begged me to ask your forgiveness for deserting you."

"But we came in her carriage," Juliet said, her panic at being left behind with Deveril rising, even as a small part of her rejoiced to know that they hadn't been out here this whole time making calf eyes at one another. "I suppose I can have Madame call for a hansom."

"No need," he told her, "I brought my curricle. We'll be perfectly respectable."

"Oh, but I couldn't," Juliet protested, though the idea of riding beside him in such a small conveyance had its appeal. "I couldn't put you out like that. You must have other things to occupy you, surely."

"Nothing at all," he assured her. "And I can have Madame deliver your gowns to your house."

"But there has been no time to—"

"She very kindly offered to send along a few gowns she had made up for another customer who was delinquent in paying for them, after they are altered to fit you of course."

Juliet was surprised at his temerity to make such a decision for her. As if reading her mind, he smiled at her. "Your cousin gave her permission, I assure you, Miss Shelby. I can be a bit overbearing, but I do have my limits."

She blushed at being so easily caught out. "I apologize, my lord, for doubting you."

"Shall we go?" he asked, offering her his elbow.

As Hetty handed her the pelisse she'd worn in earlier, Juliet remembered the seamstresses's conversation about their friend Jane.

"My lord." She pressed a staying hand to his arm. "I wish you to listen to a story for a moment."

She nodded to Hetty, who related the story of the missing Jane, elaborating a bit more on her friend's situation.

It seemed that Jane had fallen in love with a scoundrel who had promised to marry her but then refused when she discovered she was with child. She had gone to stay with her sister in Bath for the birth, and upon her recovery had returned to London and attained a position with Madame Celeste.

"It makes no sense for her to just go off with some man again, my lord," Hetty said. "It's a lie and we all know it. Something has happened to Jane. Either some abbess has stolen her and put her to work, or worse. But there's no way Jane would leave her babe behind."

"Thank you for sharing your story with us, Hetty," Deveril told the little seamstress. "I promise you that we'll look into the matter. And in the meantime, you girls look out for yourselves."

He did not speak until they were seated in his curricle, his hands expertly steering the horses from Bond Street toward Mayfair.

"It does seem suspicious," he told Juliet, taking them within an inch of a lumbering apple cart. "Not only the fact that there is a child involved again, but also the note. With Mrs. Turner, the note makes sense, seeing as how you were her closest friend. But with Jane Pettigrew, there is risk involved with leaving a note. After all, very few women of her class are even able to read. As an explanation, the note in her case leaves much to be desired."

Juliet considered. "True. But there is generally someone in their lives who can read a note to them. And the more people who know the note's contents and hear the explanation, the faster the lies spread. I suspect before the day ended that the news Jane had left town with a man was all over London. Even if she were to return today her reputation would already be ruined."

"Excellent point," he said, flicking the leader's ear with his whip as the horse tried to nip his comrade in the harness. "I wonder . . ."

"What?" Juliet demanded, trying not to pay attention to the feel of his warm thigh pressed against her own.

"Do you suppose that their reputations have something to do with why they have been taken?"

"What do you mean?"

"Well, it occurs to me that both Mrs. Turner and Miss Pettigrew were able to rehabilitate themselves after one bout with notoriety. Mrs. Turner was dismissed from your parents' home for an indiscretion with a gentleman. And Miss Pettigrew lost her position with a milliner for the same thing. And they both were able to leave, have their children, and make lives for themselves again."

"Are you suggesting that this villain is taking them as punishment for their past sins?" Juliet was horrified at the notion.

"Or"—he frowned—"he is ensuring that this time they are well and truly ruined."

Either way, the notion was monstrous. But enough to give her grave concern for Anna.

"Come," he said, "let us speak of something less troublesome. How goes your dancing?"

"That is hardly a subject without trouble for me, your lordship," she said. "But I believe it is going well enough. I may even be good enough to try my new skills in public soon."

"Excellent," he said. "You must save a dance for me."

"Drat," Juliet said, remembering that his name was on Amelia's dance card. She could hardly pass it off as her own with Deveril, since he knew very well that she had not danced before he taught her. For that matter, her former aversion to dancing would make it impossible to bluster through convincing a passel of gentlemen in their cups that they'd already asked her. "Double drat."

"What?" Deveril asked. "Am I so awful a dance partner?"

"No, it's not that," she said, wondering if she should tell him about her dance card problem. He was so influential that he might even be able to smooth things over with the other gentlemen.

Deciding that he was trustworthy, she explained to him how she and Madeline had made it possible for Cecily to use Amelia's dance card at the Bewle ball.

"I knew that wasn't her card!" he exclaimed. Turning to glance at her, his eyes lit with mischief. "I'll tell you a secret as well. We all were just so pleased that Amelia had left for the evening that dancing with Cecily was a relief."

"She will be pleased to hear it, my lord," Juliet said with a laugh. "And now that Cecily has passed the card on to me . . ."

"Ahh, so now we have the real reason for your learning to dance. I thought I was simply so persuasive you couldn't say no."

"Well, you are persuasive," she said, "but yes. This was my reason."

Something seemed to click in his mind, because he asked, "So, why did Cecily pass the dance card on to you? Are you supposed to use it to find a husband as well?"

Juliet felt her ears turn scarlet, wondered if she'd said too much.

"Yes," she admitted, trying not to pay too much attention to the way his arm brushed against her as he handled the reins. "Though Mama's wishes for me to marry Turlington and Mrs. Turner's disappearance have made the whole thing seem trivial and silly."

"And I haven't been helping, have I?" he asked, his expression so penitent that she could no more scold him than she could drown a puppy. "With my teasing and questions."

"Your offer to help me find her has been one of the kindest things anyone has ever done for me," she told him truthfully. "I know you probably offer your assistance to all sorts of damsels in distress, but honestly, you have been a great help." Especially considering that I haven't told you the whole truth, she thought.

He stole a glance at her before turning his attention back to the horses. She wasn't sure what emotions it was she saw in his eyes. But it made her heart beat faster.

"No," he said, a little grin curving his lips. "You are my only damsel in distress at the moment."

She said nothing as she tried to interpret his words.

"Do you know, Juliet?" he asked, adding, "I think we are good enough friends that we may address one another by our Christian names in private."

The idea of sharing privacy with the handsomest man in London was certainly nothing she'd ever considered before. Much.

"I believe," he continued, "Juliet, that you may be the first female ever to admit having done wrong. I think we'd better keep this between us lest the rest of your sex learn of your treachery."

"They can hardly shun me for being sensible," she said. "And besides that, there is little enough reason for them to fear me. I am no threat."

She hated the note of resignation in her voice, but she only spoke the truth. It was clear to anyone with eyes that she wasn't as pretty as her mother and aunts. Or even Cecily and Madeline. With her red hair and pale skin, she was as unfashionable as could be. Add in her limp and she was far outside the range of even passable.

"Fishing for compliments, Juliet?" He did not look at her, but she heard the chiding note in his voice.

Unwilling to discuss the matter further, she was saved answering by their arrival at her family's town house.

"Will I see you at the Hargreave musicale this evening?" Alec asked as he lifted her from the carriage. She tried and failed not to feel the exhilaration of being held, even briefly, in his arms. Something about him just seemed to make her body thrum with awareness.

"I believe so," Juliet answered as he handed down her walking stick. It was amazing, she reflected, how little she noticed her infirmity when she was in his company.

"Wear the blue silk, Juliet," he told her, a puckish glint in his eye as he said her name again. "I believe it will go nicely with your hair."

As she made her way into the house and up to her room, Juliet sent up a small prayer to the fashion gods that the blue would be one of the gowns Madame Celeste finished altering today.

And that her mother chose not to attend the musicale. Because if she saw Juliet's reaction to Alec, Lady Shelby would waste no time ensuring that Turlington secured her hand for good.

"Where is your cousin this evening?" Alec asked Lady Madeline and the Duchess of Winterson, after they'd exchanged greetings at the Hargreave musicale that evening.

He'd tried not to make his inquiry about Juliet the first thing he said to her cousins, but it was clear from the way the two ladies exchanged a knowing look that his subterfuge had done nothing to disguise his interest. *Dammit.* Could not a man inquire about a lady's whereabouts without being suspected of nursing a *tendre*?

"I had a note from her," Cecily said, her expression deceptively bland. "I believe she decided to remain home this evening with a headache. Though between us, I think her leg is bothering her. She tends not to admit to it most of the time."

Alec frowned. She'd seemed perfectly well when they'd parted that afternoon. In fact, she'd seemed eager to attend the function in her new gown. But the fittings had gone on for some time. He should have ensured that the modiste didn't overtax her injury. Thinking back to their encounter during his ball he cursed himself for not thinking of it sooner.

"Does she often have a great deal of pain?" he asked. He disliked the thought, though she doubtless was accustomed to it at this point. Even so, being accustomed to something did not mean it was any easier to deal with.

"Occasionally," Lady Madeline said, her brow furrowed. "I don't believe her ankle pains her quite so much as it once did, but there are most certainly times when it becomes a problem."

It was a credit to Lady Madeline that she showed such concern for her cousin. The more time he spent with her, the more he liked her. And she inspired none of the troubling tempestuous emotions that assailed him when he was in Juliet's company. But any idea he might once have had about marrying Lady Madeline had been put to rest at Madame Celeste's when she urged him to seduce her cousin.

"You know," Madeline said, her brown eyes thoughtful. "I believe on nights such as this, Juliet can often be found resting in the back garden of her father's town house."

Cecily nodded. "She does enjoy the night breezes, doesn't she? And if she cannot be found in the garden, she may sometimes be playing the pianoforte in the little sitting room. It has the prettiest French doors opening out into the garden."

Alec looked from one of the women to the other. Coupled with Madeline's scandalous suggestion of the afternoon that he climb the trellis outside Juliet's bedchamber to her rooms, he was beginning to feel like a heroic pawn in the cousins' version of a Shakespearean drama.

"But I would make haste to get there before Lord and Lady Shelby return from whatever engagement they have attended this evening. I believe they planned to attend the opera with my stepmama," Cecily continued. "If I were going to go meet with Juliet, I mean."

"Which we certainly will not be doing." Madeline nodded. "Why would we when we are here at the musicale, and it is about to start. But if I were leaving I would do so now before anyone realized I had even come."

"You really think that I would be mad enough to intrude upon your cousin at home? Knowing that her parents are out?" Alec looked from one to the other. Neither seemed the least bit put out by his distress.

"Well, we can hardly control what you do, Lord Deveril," Cecily said with a cat-in-the-cream-pot smile. "We simply wish what's best for our cousin."

"Definitely," Madeline said. "In fact, I would argue that time is of the essence, considering that Lady Shelby seems determined to marry Juliet to the loathsome Lord Turlington."

"Who," Cecily said, "by the way, is here. I just saw him speaking with Lord Fortenbury."

It was a sign of Deveril's agitation that he gave in to the urge to run his fingers through his artfully disordered hair.

Telling himself that his valet's ire was the least of his worries, he excused himself and hurried from the music room and out into the night.

When Juliet had arrived home that afternoon, it was to find her mother waiting for her.

"My dear daughter," Lady Shelby breathed, pulling Juliet close in an unexpected embrace, enveloping her in the heavy rose scent she wore in deference to her own name. "You will never guess what has happened. At long last."

A knot of anxiety formed in Juliet's belly. There were very few things that moved her mother to actual emotion, and so far, the only things that Juliet had been a part of had been very bad indeed.

"I do not know, Mama," she said carefully, untying her bonnet so that she had something to do with her shaking fingers.

"Silly chit," Lady Shelby chided with unaccustomed

cheer. "It is the best news imaginable! Lord Turlington has spoken to your father."

It took a moment for the news to sink in. "Spoken to Papa about what?" she asked, hoping that she had simply misunderstood her mother's announcement.

"Don't be obtuse, child." Lady Shelby's good cheer was beginning to flag a bit in the face of her daughter's lack of enthusiasm. "He asked your father for your hand and Lord Shelby has accepted."

The silence in the entry hall was deafening.

"Come, Juliet, do not be missish." Juliet's mother changed her tone. "You cannot have expected some fairy-tale nonsense or the like. When you lost your foot in that ridiculous accident, I thought there was no chance you'd ever find someone willing to marry you. And here not only has someone offered, but he is a handsome lord with no qualms about your injury. Surely even you can see how providential this is."

"And the fact that I have no wish to marry Lord Turlington?" Juliet demanded. "Has that no bearing on the situation?"

"That is unfortunate," Lady Shelby said, following Juliet into her bedchamber, "but it will not deter your father or me from approving the match."

All traces of good humor were gone now from Lady Shelby's angelic visage. Even as she approached her middle forties she was a stunning woman. And if Juliet had been graced with but a fraction of her mother's beauty she would not now be having this argument.

"I will apply to Papa," Juliet said, limping to the window in her agitation. "He will not allow you to force me into a marriage I have no interest in."

"He will tell you to do your duty," Lady Shelby snapped. "I have tried to make this as easy as possible for you, but you have spent your time mooning over Deveril instead of becoming better acquainted with Turlington."

"I do not wish to become better acquainted with Turlington," Juliet said fiercely. "Mama, he makes me uncomfortable. Surely even you can understand that there is something not quite right about the man."

"I understand no such thing," her mother snapped. "He is a handsome and fine gentleman who has been the soul of patience with your mississhness. The time has come for you to stop this childish nonsense and accept his suit."

"It is not childish for me to wish for a husband who has some real affection for me," Juliet retorted, desperation making her voice shake. "Mama, why are you doing this? What hold does Turlington have over you?"

At her question, Lady Shelby's face paled.

"You have no idea what you are speaking of," she hissed. "Now, I suggest you lie down for a while before we depart for the opera."

"But I have promised Cecily and Madeline that I would attend the Hargreave musicale this evening," Juliet protested. Though when compared to the news that she was engaged to Turlington without her consent, the knowledge that she would be unable to attend the musicale was a minor inconvenience.

"Well, they will have to live with disappointment," Lady Shelby said, her voice cold. "As will you, daughter. In fact, I will instruct Turlington to procure a special license so that you may be married as soon as possible. I believe next week will give me enough time to plan a celebration."

Not if I have anything to do with it, Juliet thought, watching her mother exit the room.

If someone had asked him what he expected to find when he entered the back garden of Shelby House, Alec would not have guessed he'd find Miss Shelby backing out of the French doors leading from the house onto the terrace.

The sky was dark with clouds, and the only illumination

to the area was from the kitchens. The rest of the house, with its other inhabitants out for the evening, was dark.

He watched in fascination as Juliet continued walking backward, presumably watching for some authority figure, who would arrest her escape.

Not wishing to startle her, he hissed her name as he came up behind her. "Juliet."

Even so, his quarry jarred with surprise, and turned to face him.

"What are you doing here?" she demanded, a hint of desperation in her voice. "Deveril, you must leave here at once."

To his surprise, she made as if to push him away. Could she be expecting someone else? Or worse, was she running off to meet some other man? The very idea made his jaw clench.

"What are *you* doing?" he asked, not giving an inch. "Who are you sneaking off to meet?"

"None of your business," she hissed. "Now kindly leave so that no one hears you."

"You've already been detected," he said in a low voice, "so go back inside and rest your leg as you told your cousins you were doing."

She frowned at the mention of Cecily and Madeline. Perhaps her lie was bothering her conscience.

"How do you know what I told them?" she asked. "And it is highly improper for you to mention legs in my company," she added, her mouth pursing in annoyance.

"They told me," he said, pointing her toward the French doors, but finding her surprisingly strong in her resistance. "And you are hardly in a position to preach propriety, madam."

"And you are not my father, my brother, or my husband and have no authority to tell me where to go or what to do," she snapped, her voice a low hiss in the night air, her green eyes reflecting fire in the moonlight.

"As your friend," he growled, "I have every right to prevent you from behaving rashly."

"If you were my friend you would—"

Stopping mid-sentence at the sound of one of the kitchen maids giggling from inside, Juliet made a "follow me" gesture and led him into a small area of the garden that was enclosed on three sides by climbing vines. Nestled within the bower was an iron bench just large enough to seat two.

The hitch in her stride was more pronounced, Alec noticed as he walked behind her. So perhaps she had not been lying about her reasons for remaining at home. Still, there was something more that agitated her.

"Tell me what has happened to cause you such distress," he said when they were far enough from the house for privacy, struggling to keep his tone gentle. The sight of her in such pain made him want to smash something, and he regretted his sharp words to her earlier.

For one of the most celebrated flirts in London he certainly had difficulty behaving like a gentleman in this lady's company.

Seven

*J*uliet shifted from one foot to the other, leaning heavily on her walking stick, and it was impossible not to notice her wince.

"Sit down, for God's sake," he ordered. Part of him expected her to tell him to go jump in the Thames, but to Alec's surprise, she kept silent, lowered herself to the bench.

"There is no shame in admitting to human frailty, Juliet," he said quietly. "Even battle-scarred soldiers must bow to their body's wishes from time to time."

"That's easy for you to say," she grumbled. "You've never—"

"What? Fought in a battle?" he asked wryly. He was well aware that his position as the heir to a peerage had given him a handy excuse to remain in England during the wars with Napoleon. But he was not ashamed of the fact. There were plenty of small services that could be helpful to the crown here at home, many of which he had undertaken.

But Juliet was talking of something else.

"No," she said with impatience. "I've never fought in a battle either. What I was going to say is that you've never had to confront the fact that your own body is failing you. You're a young man. You're fit. You're handsome. You're in the prime of health and, with a few exceptions, your body will do whatever you tell it to do."

Thinking of one particular part of him that seemed to

have a mind of its own, he disagreed, but did not say so aloud.

"And mine," she continued with obvious annoyance, "does not even allow me to stand without assistance. It is maddening sometimes."

Knowing some of what Winterson had gone through with his war injury, Alec was surprised to realize that Juliet might have some of the same complaints. Ladies, after all, were not expected to be active and participate in all manner of sporting activities. There had been her issue with dancing, but that had seemed different to him at the time. Perhaps because that was an activity which required a partner.

Which reminded him again of other activities requiring two people. He was a cad and ruffian to think of such things while she was telling him of her struggles.

"So, it is the state of your health that has you in such a fit of pique?" he asked, firmly returning his mind to the subject at hand.

"Not my health," she admitted, with a frown, twisting the silver ring she wore on her right hand. Around and around and around. "Well, not only my health."

He lowered himself to the bench beside her, the vulnerability in her voice and mien making it impossible to deny her some human contact. He wanted to take her in his arms and offer her reassurance, but contented himself with taking her hand in his. Though she gave a small gasp, she did not pull away.

"I don't know how much you have heard about my mother's attempts to make a match between Lord Turlington and me," she continued, staring out into the darkened garden.

What he knew was that Lady Shelby was dead set on marrying Juliet off to Turlington whether Juliet liked it or not. But he only said, "Enough."

"She informed me this evening," she said, her voice laced

with contempt, "that my father has already given him his consent and that she is pushing Lord Turlington to apply for a special license so that we may be married as quickly as possible."

"What?" Deveril turned to face her and knew from her expression that she was serious. He had known Lady Shelby was determined but he was under the impression that her plans would not be put into motion for some months. "Why is she rushing this?"

Unable to sit still, he stood and paced the small area of the bower, thrusting a hand through his hair. What he wanted to do was get his hands round Turlington's neck, but as the man was not there with them, he had to content himself with a string of oaths.

Juliet watched him, her expression resigned.

"I think you know that my mama was not best pleased about my dancing lessons. I thought it was because . . ." She paused, making Alec wonder what she wasn't telling him.

"Well, for another reason," she finished. "But I think she was planning all along to make me marry Turlington. And calling attention to myself by dancing increased the likelihood that someone else would make an offer. She needs me to remain an ugly duckling."

He frowned. "Do not call yourself that. Amelia is a spiteful cat and only said that because she feared you three would eclipse her."

"Oh, I know very well that I am not nearly as beautiful as Mama," Juliet said wryly. "She has told me so herself for many years now."

There was a special place in Hades for spiteful parents, and Alec was quite sure that his father was there warming a seat for Lady Shelby.

"You are lovely. Take it from a man who knows."

The compliment pleased her, he saw it in the upward curve of her full red lips.

"Thank you, my lord," she murmured softly. If he hadn't known she was untutored in the art of seduction, the downward cast of her dark lashes, and the smile as ancient as Eve would have fooled him. But Juliet Shelby was as innocent as she was beautiful. And the sight of her resting in a moonlit bower of roses was as tempting a sight as Alec had ever seen.

As if pulled by a web of her creation, he stepped forward and knelt before her, like a knight swearing fealty to his lady.

"May I kiss you, Juliet?" he asked, even as his mouth took hers.

The contact sent an immediate rush of desire through him. Everything was Juliet. The scent of blossoms, her soft lips, the little moan of surprise she made as he opened his mouth to suck at her bottom lip. Unable to stop himself, he tasted the seam of her lips, pressing with his tongue until she let him in.

He took her shoulders in his arms, and felt a surge of triumph as she lifted her arms to twine about his neck, one hand stroking into his hair.

Her kiss was passive, untutored, and even that gave him a thrill of excitement. The knowledge that he was the first to hold her like this aroused a primitive possessiveness in him that he hadn't known he was capable of.

But she was not to be a passive partner for long. Just as she'd taken quickly to dancing, Juliet learned to mimic his movements, sliding her own tongue along his, even as her firm breasts thrust against his chest.

He pulled her closer. Lifting one hand to stroke the underside of her breast, he stroked upward, caressing the hardness of her nipple with the palm of his hand.

Juliet gasped as she felt Alec's hand brush the bud of her nipple, the contact sending another wave of sensation downward to the ache that had been building between her legs. She knew it was dangerous to engage in such licentious behavior, but her mind was drugged with desire and the need for more.

Before tonight she'd barely ever touched a man, with the exception of taking their arms to walk into dinner and the like. But that was so commonplace, it hardly registered.

This, however, this maelstrom of scent and touch and sensation, had her heady with excitement. From the moment his lips touched hers, the tentative softness of his kiss making her chest tight with longing, she'd known that this man had the power to lead her places she'd never imagined.

Every touch, from the scrape of his teeth over her lower lip, to the solid strength of his arms pulling her closer, sent her nearer to a precipice, but she had no idea what lay on the other side.

She murmured soft words, his name, inarticulate sounds of pleasure that in her right mind she'd blush to remember. But here in this garden bower away from every worry, every problem, she felt removed from the rest of the world. Alec's strong arms and skilled caresses cocooned her from the darkness of everyday life.

The sharp clang of the watchman's bell broke the spell.

Juliet felt Alec still, then with a sigh, and one quick kiss on her lips, he leaned back from her and stood, quickly turning his back to her while he took several deep breaths.

She took a moment to catch her own breath, the rush of sensations slowly subsiding into a low, nameless ache.

His long legs, lean in the evening breeches that were de rigueur for *ton* entertainments, led up to muscular thighs and buttocks tapering into a lean waist. His broad shoulders were unbowed by life, though now she suspected that he might have had his own share of troubles to weigh them down.

There was no denying that the Viscount Deveril was a breathtakingly beautiful man.

A man who had just spent a quarter of an hour kissing her senseless.

"I should apologize for that," Alec said, his back still turned to her. "But I find I cannot."

"Good," Juliet said. "Because if you apologized I would be forced to apologize too. But I find I cannot."

He turned, a wry smile at his mouth. "A fine pair of unrepentants we are," he said. His eyes turned serious. "Juliet, I—"

"Don't," she said quietly. "Let's not speak of it further. I don't expect anything from you other than friendship. I can be content with that."

Before he could speak, she continued, "As for Lord Turlington, I will figure out a way to convince my father of his unsuitability. Father has proven himself to be a reasonable man the few times I've gone to him with issues over which my mother was prepared to fight me. I simply hope that he will do so again this time."

"But you must have a care about how you handle the situation, Juliet," Alec protested. "You do not wish to be branded a jilt."

Juliet laughed at that. "I would much rather be called a jilt than Lady Turlington, my lord."

When he did not join her in her amusement, she soothed him. "Come now, my lord. Something must be worked out. If nothing else, then I will follow my earlier plan and run away."

"Where would you go?" he asked. "You can hardly disappear into the night. It's not safe."

She was touched by his worry. Truly, for she could think of no one but her cousins, and Anna, who had given her much thought these last several years. "I appreciate your concern. But I do have some connections I can call on should this scheme of my mother's go much further."

He stepped closer, his eyes deadly serious. "Do not make any decisions until you hear from me. Will you promise me that, at least? I know things seem desperate right now, but I may be able to come up with a solution that does not require you to disappear."

"But I—" she began before he stopped her with a gloved finger against her lips.

"You trusted me to investigate the disappearance of your Mrs. Turner," he said, his voice husky with some emotion she could not name. "Will you not also trust me with yourself?"

She did not bother to point out that trusting him with Anna's disappearance was infinitely less terrifying. She had that much self-respect, at least.

"All right," she told him. "All right, I'll wait to hear from you."

He didn't speak, just nodded and turned to stalk back through the back garden into the mews beyond.

She watched him disappear into the night, her fingers against her lips as she remembered his kiss.

After a restless night of tossing and turning, reliving the encounter with Alec in the garden, Juliet spent the next day at the pianoforte attempting to banish the nervous energy plaguing her. Even though her mind was consumed by thoughts of Alec, she had little choice but to agree with her mother's suggestion that they spend the evening attending a musicale at the home of Lord Turlington's mother.

Lady Wilhelmina Turlington was a renowned *ton* hostess with a fondness for European-style salons and her musical evenings were gatherings where conversation and spirits flowed freely. It was just the sort of entertainment Lady Shelby would have disparaged before she decided Juliet should marry Lord Turlington, but Juliet was not about to draw attention to her mother's hypocrisy on the issue. She feared that her indiscretion with Alec of the previous evening was writ large upon her face.

The kisses aside, and that was with some difficulty, she had felt better after unburdening herself to him last night. His attentiveness was intoxicating. He listened to her—really listened—in a way that no one, even her cousins, had ever done.

As for the kisses, and other intimacies, wonderful as they had been, they could never be repeated. Not only did she believe that he had simply been dazzled by the moonlight, but she knew her place in the pecking order of the *ton,* and she was painfully aware that Lord Deveril was so far beyond her reach as to make even contemplating a match with him absurd in the extreme. He was a leader of the *ton* and one of the most sought-after bachelors in society. He attracted attention wherever he went, and even had a following among young men who wished to ape his fashionable attire and mannerisms. Whereas she was relegated to the fringes of polite society, and despite Cecily's recent spectacular match with the Duke of Winterson, she was a member of the most ridiculed trio of young ladies in London.

Once daylight had descended upon the city, she had no doubt he'd come to his senses. Or, at the very least, he must have realized that he was destined for someone of better looks and fortune than Miss Shelby, who was not only a wallflower, but also harbored a secret that made it impossible for her to make anyone a proper wife. Except, according to her mother, Lord Turlington. But that owed more to her mother's odd relationship with the gentleman than to any attractiveness on Juliet's part.

But before she had to face that gentleman again, she had a brief errand to run.

In the first few weeks of Mrs. Turner's absence from Shelby House, she and Juliet had been unable to communicate via conventional means, and had frequently left notes for one another with a trusted print shopkeeper whom both ladies patronized for their sheet music needs. Because they'd not needed to use Mr. Frampton as a go-between since Lady Shelby sanctioned their continued acquaintance once more, Juliet hadn't considered that Anna might have left her a note there once again until late last night as she tossed and turned. It was unlikely, of course, but worth a try.

When she descended from the carriage in Cheapside, she was struck as always by the bustle of people going about their business. Compared with the languid movement of the *haut ton,* the industry of the merchants and their customers was jarring indeed.

"Weston," she told her maid, who had accompanied her, "you may visit the stationers' next door if you wish. I know how dull you find Frampton's."

"I will, miss." The maid didn't hide her relief, but she made a token protest nevertheless. "But you know I don't like to leave you alone."

"Oh, fie, Weston," Juliet returned. "You are bursting at the seams to get away from here. Do not worry. I'll be fine. Mr. Frampton will look after me."

With a slight shrug the other woman turned and hurried toward the other shop. Juliet opened the door to Frampton's, and gripping her walking stick lest anyone should accost her, she stepped inside, pausing a moment to appreciate the scent of ink on paper.

The proprietor hurried forward, his eyes lit with pleasure. "Miss Shelby, what a pleasant surprise. It's been too long."

A musician himself, Frampton had left the itinerant life of an orchestra player when he married the daughter of a prosperous merchant, who set his son-in-law up in business for himself. But his knowledge about music and his understanding of what both the public and musicians looked for in a song made him second to none in his collection of sheet music. He carried not only songs from little-known and popular English composers, but also imported the best compositions from the Continent. But while Juliet appreciated all of this, she valued Mr. Frampton for his easy manner and generosity of spirit most of all.

She offered him her hand and a wide smile. "It has been too long, Mr. Frampton. I've been busy with the social whirl, I'm afraid. And you know how much I'd rather have been here searching out some intriguing bit of new music."

"I do, indeed, Miss Shelby." He seemed about to say something else, but must have thought better of it, for he turned and said, "Let me show you some of the newest arrivals from Paris. I know you like something that will challenge your finger skills."

They spent the next few minutes discussing the merits of Beethoven, versus some of the newer composers emerging on the scene. At last, however, Juliet broached the subject that had brought her to her old friend. She explained briefly that Mrs. Turner had left town abruptly and that her friends were concerned that she might be in some sort of trouble.

"And I wondered," she concluded, "if she might have visited here before she left. Perhaps left a note here for me like we used to do in the old days?"

It was unlikely, Juliet knew, but Mr. Frampton's nod had her heart beating faster.

"I have seen her," he said, his brow knitted with concern, "but she left nothing here apart from the compositions I bought from her."

"Compositions?" To Juliet's knowledge, Anna hadn't composed anything in years. She always said that a truly skilled musician had no need of writing her own tunes. That coming to the piece fresh, without any preconceived notions about just what had influenced the composition, was the best way to reach the true meaning of a song.

"Indeed." Mr. Frampton stepped behind the counter where he displayed new sheet music, and removed a sheaf of pages.

The sound of the bells at the entrance to the store caused him to look up at the new customer. Handing the music to Juliet, he excused himself and left her to stare down at the precisely marked notes that began to sound in her head as she read them, playing the tune they spelled out as surely as if a pianoforte were there in the shop.

She knew the song well. She'd even played it herself, working to master the particularly tricky fingering at the end of the fourth measure. Anna hadn't broken her rule about composing, however. For these weren't her compositions.

They were Juliet's. Anna had stolen her pupil's original compositions and sold them. The sense of betrayal was like nothing she'd known before. She tried to think of rational explanations for Anna's deception. It was entirely possible that she'd needed to leave London in a hurry and Juliet's compositions had been the fastest way to get funds. But it was still a blow to know that rather than simply coming to her and asking, Anna had taken advantage of their friendship and taken something so personal and sold it.

She was so lost in her thoughts, that she didn't hear the footsteps behind her until she felt a tentative hand on her arm.

"Juliet."

Closing her eyes, she took a deep breath and turned.

There stood Alec. Looking unaccountably thunderous.

The sound of his voice sent immediate warmth straight to her stomach and lower, as she remembered last night's interlude in the back garden.

Turning, she saw that Alec was just as well turned out as ever. And her own expression must have been forlorn indeed, for he immediately frowned.

"What's wrong?" The way he stood at attention, as if he were ready to go slay dragons for her, made her heart squeeze in her chest.

* * *

"What's wrong, she asks." Alec asked the question aloud, but it was clearly rhetorical. "Perhaps you might tell me why you are alone in a print shop with no proper chaperone?"

His harassed tone immediately set her back up. "I'm not sure what business it is of yours. I am not a child and you are neither my father nor my brother."

Something almost feral flickered in his blue eyes, and Juliet realized her mistake. A sensation that was not alleviated when he stepped closer. "No, I am neither your father nor your brother. But that does not mean I have no interest in keeping you safe."

Juliet's heart pounded in her chest as she looked up at him. She inhaled the scent of sandalwood mixed with warm male, and she found herself remembering in excruciating detail what it had felt like to be wrapped in his arms.

Fighting her response, she lifted her chin. "I am perfectly capable of taking care of myself. Simply because I am not like other ladies—"

He interrupted her before she could complete the thought. "No, you are not like other ladies," he said firmly. "You are more—" He stopped before he could complete the thought.

"You are as vulnerable as any other unchaperoned lady," he finished. "And as such, you should not expose yourself to danger by shopping unattended in this part of town. Have you any idea how much some enterprising fellow might ask your father for in ransom? Or how much a canny abbess might charge a man for the privilege of deflowering you?"

At his crudity, she recoiled.

Seeing he'd shocked her, as he'd intended, Alec relented. When he'd spied the Shelby coat of arms gracing the carriage in the narrow lane, he'd at first thought Lord Shelby must be visiting a mistress. But since that gentleman was addressing Parliament today, that explanation was out. Then he recognized the sign marking the shop as a purveyor of sheet music and he knew it must be Juliet inside.

"You must take more care, Juliet," he said now. "Especially given the fact that your mentor has more than likely been taken against her will."

The reminder of Mrs. Turner's disappearance seemed to bring Juliet back to her senses, and she glanced down at the papers in her hand, as if trying to decide something.

Before she could speak, however, the proprietor of the shop stepped out from the back room and proffered more pages. Seeing Alec, he bowed.

"My lord," the old man said, "what might I do for you this fine day? Perhaps the latest from Mr. Beethoven? I know how your sister enjoys him."

"Nothing today, Frampton," Alec said. "Though perhaps I will bring Katherine back later this week. She is, as you say, fond of Mr. Beethoven."

Continuing, he watched as Juliet scanned the sheet music Frampton had brought her. "I am a friend of Miss Shelby's family and wished to assure myself that she was not here unescorted."

If Frampton read more into the situation than was warranted, Alec was not going to disabuse him of the notion. He was perfectly content to let the man, and anyone else who might happen by, know Juliet was not without friends.

Turning his attention to Juliet, he asked, "Do you wish to purchase those?"

She looked up, pain evident in her eyes, but she quickly shuttered the emotion. "Yes, Mr. Frampton, please wrap these and any others by the same composer." Giving him her card, she continued, "If you should get any others in please contact me as soon as you can."

At her speaking glance, Alec swallowed the question on his tongue, and stood silently with Juliet as they waited for Frampton to prepare her package.

They were haggling over who would be paying for the

purchases when a blowsy young woman whom Alec took to be Juliet's maid entered the shop.

At the sight of Alec, the maid's eyes grew round. "Miss," she said quickly, "I asked if they had any more of the green ribbon but they did not. I hope I didn't keep you waiting for too long."

Juliet's lips twitched, though whether it was from her maid's poor acting skills, or for another reason Alec couldn't say. "It's all right, Weston," she said, "Lord Deveril is a friend."

At that, Weston nodded. "Shall I have John bring the coach around?"

Before she could respond, Alec intervened. "That won't be necessary, Weston. I shall take Miss Shelby up in my curricle with me."

He met Juliet's gasp of protest with a quelling look, and apparently reading the message there, she remained silent. After bidding Mr. Frampton good day, they made their way out into the street, where Alec handed her into the curricle.

It was some few minutes, while he navigated the narrow lane and they set off for Mayfair, before he spoke.

"I realize that you are accustomed to a certain degree of latitude given your mother's lack of propriety herself," he said. "But you must promise me that until we figure out what happened to Mrs. Turner you will not go anywhere unescorted."

"Don't you wish to know why I was there?" Juliet asked, skirting his question.

Really, the woman was maddening, Alec thought, staring out over the horses' heads.

"I'm listening."

Quickly she explained how she and Anna had used Mr. Frampton's shop as a means of exchanging letters.

"So, what did you discover?" Alec asked, admitting to a grudging respect for her ingenuity, if only to himself.

"I discovered," Juliet said with a hard edge to her voice, "that my friend—or rather the woman I thought was my friend—has been taking compositions that I wrote for myself and no one else, and selling them to Mr. Frampton for publication."

He wasn't sure what he'd expected, but it hadn't been that.

"Are you sure?" he asked, hoping for her sake that there had been a mistake of some sort.

Her laugh was far too cynical for one so young. "I'm quite sure. Though I suppose I can take some comfort in the knowledge that she didn't attach her own name to them, but instead invented a pseudonym for Mr. Frampton to attach to them."

He was silent as he negotiated the curricle past an erratically driven apple cart. Finally, when they were nearing a less congested stretch of road, he spoke. "Can there have been some reason for Mrs. Turner to do something like this? Perhaps she needed more funds than she was able to earn on her own?" Thinking to Winterson and his lady's use of codes to unravel a mystery earlier that season, Alec said, "Could she have been sending some sort of message through them? Something only you could understand?"

Sighing, Juliet allowed her shoulders to bow in weariness. "I don't know. I suppose it's possible. I hadn't time to read through all of them. Just a cursory glance to assure myself that they were indeed my compositions."

"And they were?"

Again the bitter laugh. "Yes, they're mine. I didn't even know that my own copies were missing. I suppose Anna must have taken them by mistake after a lesson and then simply saw a means to earn some money. I only wish she'd come to me if she needed more funds. Didn't she know I'd give her more if I could?"

For Juliet's sake, he said, "Perhaps she knew you were dealing with your own problems and didn't wish to ask for more. It cannot have been easy for her to take your charity after her child was born."

"No," she said, sighing, "it wasn't. I had to appeal to her love of the babe to get her to take as much as she did." She straightened in her seat. "So why would she stoop to outright theft now? It makes no logical sense. She must have had another reason to do it. She needed funds for something she couldn't tell me about."

Alec considered this. "What would she be unable to tell you about?"

"I don't know," she said thoughtfully. "Her expenses were minimal. And Alice wasn't ill so it can't have been a physician."

"What about blackmail?"

Juliet gripped his arm, and he felt the touch straight through his coat.

"That's it!" She nearly vibrated with excitement. "It has to be. Nothing else makes sense. She was an unwed mother with a need for discretion because if parents of her pupils were to learn the true circumstances of Alice's birth they'd turn her into a social pariah at once. Someone must have figured out that there was no Mr. Turner and decided to earn some extra money."

Her relief at finding a plausible reason for her friend's betrayal was palpable. Alec only hoped that her theory was right and that they weren't expending all this energy to find a woman who might be better left unfound.

"I wouldn't be surprised to learn that her landlady was attempting to extort some extra funds from Mrs. Turner," he said aloud. "Perhaps she overheard you and Mrs. Turner discussing her situation?"

She thought about it. "A definite possibility. I shouldn't think her above that sort of thing. Especially after what you told me of her treatment of little Alice. Anyone who would mistreat a child wouldn't balk at blackmail."

"There is also another possibility," Alec said. "What if

someone with knowledge of the happenings at Squire Ramsey's has decided to blackmail her?"

"To what end?" Juliet asked. "I should think what happened in Little Wittington would have long since ceased to be of interest."

"But knowledge of either scandal could ruin her reputation with the wealthy cits whose children she teaches."

They fell silent for a moment as they entered the traffic of more fashionable London streets.

Finally, Alec spoke. "I must ask you to make me a promise, Miss Shelby."

He could feel her gaze on him. Saw her raised brows from the corner of his eye.

"I had thought we'd dispensed with titles last evening," she said quietly. It was a bold statement for her, and he liked to think that her comfort in his presence made her able to speak her mind.

Glancing around to ensure they were not under scrutiny, he pulled the curricle down a relatively quiet street, and drew the horses to a halt. Keeping the reins firmly in his left hand, he turned to her, dipping his head a little to see beneath her bonnet brim.

"Juliet," he said seriously, meeting her frank gaze with one of his own. "I will not endanger your reputation by addressing you by your given name in public. And I won't apologize for what happened last night. Though I suppose I should if I were a true gentleman."

"I can think of no one who is more qualified to call himself a gentleman than you," she said. "And if you apologized for last night I would draw your cork."

Her use of the cant phrase startled from him a laugh.

"So, what is this promise you wish to coax from me?" she asked, her expression impish. Really, if the rest of the *ton* were aware of this side of her personality Amelia Snowe would find herself with serious competition for her position as reigning toast.

"You cannot go out searching for clues to Mrs. Turner's disappearance on your own. It is too dangerous. At this point we have no way of knowing whether your friend left of her own volition or was spirited off by someone up to no good. I won't allow you to risk your safety."

At the mention of Mrs. Turner, Juliet's expression fell, and she grew serious. Alec despised himself for breaking her good mood, but he could not stand by while she put herself in harm's way.

"If you must go out in search of your friend," he said seriously, "then at least take Cecily or Madeline with you. I won't suggest that you contact me, because that would endanger your reputation. But I will be sure to seek you out at social occasions so that we can compare notes and determine what our safest course of action might be."

"Then you won't call on me yourself?" Her question was offhand, as if she were wondering aloud whether it would rain later, but he was not fooled by her studied indifference.

He reached out a gloved finger and tipped her chin back so that he could look into her eyes. "Juliet," he said softly, "I am the last man you wish to become involved with. The men in my family . . . my father . . ."

A quick nod told him that she was not unaware of his father's and uncle's reputations. "Last night was . . ." He searched for a way to describe their encounter in the darkness of the garden. "It was sweeter than anything I've known in a long while," he said finally. "But it cannot happen again. For your sake. You deserve a man who can give you a lifetime of happiness. And I'm afraid I am incapable of doing that."

"If you don't mind, my lord," she said curtly, "I would like to return home now. I have an engagement this evening and Mama will be looking for me."

He supposed he was asking too much for her to acknowledge his clumsy attempt to warn her off. Perhaps she hadn't been as affected by their kiss as he'd been. And besides, what sort of self-important bastard demanded to be forgiven for protecting a woman from an entanglement?

Their drive was silent until they reached Shelby House. A footman stepped forward to assist Juliet from the carriage, and Alec accepted her cool thanks and farewell with good grace.

"If you wish to visit Alice," he said, unable to stop himself, before she turned away, "I am gone most mornings. I will leave word with my staff that you are to be allowed in whether I or my sisters are there or not."

She nodded her acknowledgment, then turned, and for a woman with such a severe leg injury she managed to mount the steps in a remarkably speedy fashion.

Cursing himself for a ham-handed fool, Alec turned his attention to his horses and drove away.

Still clutching her compositions, Juliet navigated the steps to the door of Shelby House with Weston close behind her. As she divested herself of her pelisse, the butler informed her that her cousin Madeline was waiting for her in her sitting room. Her sitting room that had an excellent view of the front entrance.

Cursing her ill luck, and feeling perilously close to tears, Juliet made her way upstairs and prepared herself for an interrogation. Ah well, at least it was Maddie and not her mama who awaited her.

"Never say you've been out driving with Lord Deveril, Juliet!" her cousin greeted her without preamble. "He has shown a marked partiality for you ever since our dance lessons."

"Well, I do not think anything will come of it," Juliet said, gratefully accepting a cup of tea as she lowered herself to the settee. "Even if Mama wasn't determined to see me marry Turlington, Alec . . . that is, Lord Deveril, just informed me that he is incapable of giving me the 'lifetime of happiness' I deserve."

Madeline's mouth dropped open. "Incapable? You don't suppose he means that he cannot . . ."

Juliet gave a startled laugh despite herself. "No, I don't think that's what he meant. He was speaking about the men in his family in general."

"Oh, that." Maddie waved away the notion. "He is just being noble, then. This happens all the time in novels. The hero is drawn to the heroine despite himself, and then ruins everything by pushing her away."

"Yes, well, this isn't a novel. It's my very real life and I do think he has some serious concerns. His father was Devil Deveril, after all. Perhaps the sins of the father—"

"Except that Lord Deveril has never shown the least propensity to behave like his father. Indeed, quite the opposite. He does have a bit of a rakish reputation, but nothing so troubling as his father, or his uncle for that matter."

Juliet knew Maddie was right. Alec was as far from his father's type of man as a son could be. He was a gentleman through and through, and would no more seduce and abandon her than he would leave little Alice in the care of an abusive woman.

"I fear you are right," she said aloud. "But that doesn't mean he'll change his mind. So, I will put him from my mind and concentrate on finding Anna. I doubt Mama would approve Lord Deveril's suit if he were to ask anyway, so the whole matter is moot."

Maddie looked as if she'd like to argue, but refrained from doing so. Instead she asked, "What are those pages? New sheet music?"

Remembering the reason she'd been in Deveril's company in the first place, Juliet told Maddie what she'd learned at Mr. Frampton's shop.

"So, Anna has been stealing your compositions?" Maddie whole being trembled with outrage at the teacher's betrayal.

"After all you've done for her! What a wicked thing for her to do."

"I must admit that I was shocked," Juliet said. "But after I thought of it a bit, I wondered if she needed funds for some reason she couldn't tell me about."

"You think she was being blackmailed?" the other girl asked. That they'd both leaped to the same conclusion said something about how their minds worked, but Juliet wasn't overly concerned about that. Between Juliet's dealings with her mother, and Maddie's extensive reading they were both acquainted with the darker side of human nature. Even if Maddie's was fictional, that didn't mean she was incorrect.

"I do," Juliet said. "After all, she was in an even more precarious social position than she was in as a member of our household. At least here she was somewhat protected by my father. Out on her own, her reputation was her life. One blemish could mean ostracism. And therefore a loss of the only means she had to make a living."

"Who knew the real circumstances of little Alice's birth?" Maddie asked. "You don't suppose your mama told anyone, do you?"

"No," Juliet assured her. "She knows that if she reveals any of Anna's secrets, Anna and I will reveal hers. I never thought that I'd be in a position where I'd have to blackmail my own mother, but I suppose given who my mother is, this is a small enough price to pay."

"Is there anyone Anna might have confided in?" Maddie bit into a macaroon. "Someone besides you, I mean?"

"The only person I can think of is her mentor, Signor Boccardo, but he made no mention of it when Alec and I met with him."

She sighed, staring into the murky depths of her tea. "Between this business with Mrs. Turner and my mother's championing of Lord Turlington's suit, I begin to think you and Cecily are the only ladies in my life I can trust. I cannot believe I was so wrong about Anna."

"Dearest, you mustn't punish yourself for trusting her. She was your friend, after all. And we do not know yet why she did the things she did. Yes, she did steal your compositions, but what if, as you have suggested, she needed the funds? Who knows what any of us might stoop to given the right circumstances. And she has always supported you in your dislike of Turlington, has she not?"

"Indeed," Juliet said thoughtfully. "She warned me against him even before my mother began to propose him as a possible suitor. When he practically ran tame in our house—back before she was dismissed—Anna warned me that he was not to be trusted. She even cautioned me to lock my door when he was in the house."

"You see?" Maddie reassured her. "Mrs. Turner had your best interest at heart. I feel sure that there is some rational explanation for her betrayals. At least I hope so. For your sake. And for little Alice's sake as well. Surely she would not have left the baby behind without some serious inducement."

Juliet considered her cousin's words. Perhaps if she hadn't been so estranged from her mother, she would not have placed so much faith in Anna. Even so, despite all of her current misgivings, she still feared for Anna's safety. Maddie was correct. Anna would not have left Alice behind without very good reason.

Alice. It all came back to Alice.

Eight

$\mathcal{N}$ow, my dear," Lady Shelby said, pulling on her gloves as they rode through the streets of Mayfair in the Shelby carriage, "you must make sure that you speak only when spoken to, and that you pay special attention to anything Lord Turlington or his mother says to you. I want you to make a good impression on the family. And none of that slipping off to brood on your own like you did at the gallery. I mean for you to show them that you are more than capable of being the sort of wife an artist like Turlington needs."

Perhaps having realized that she'd crossed a line last night, Lady Shelby, while still pushing her into an unwanted match, had been kinder today. Juliet was not so naïve as to think that it had anything to do with her protests of last evening, but suspected that her mother had remembered the old adage about flies and honey. Whatever the case, she was thankful for the softening of her mother's demands, if only because it would make their time spent together a bit less fraught. With all she'd learned this afternoon, and her decision that she might be forced to ruin her own reputation in an effort to escape marriage to Turlington, she felt a strange sense of calm and empowerment.

"Yes, Mama," she told her mother, in what she hoped was a meek tone.

"Good girl," Lady Shelby praised her. "I do like that

ensemble on you. It hides your infirmity quite nicely. And the color is pleasing."

It was a silk gown of cerulean, one of the pieces Deveril had chosen for her from Madame Celeste's. Juliet had worn it especially for her visit to the Turlington household because knowing she looked particularly well in it—or that Deveril thought she did—made her feel capable, no matter that he'd warned her off thinking of him in a romantic way that afternoon. The gown made her feel strong, and able to handle whatever sort of problems the Turlingtons sent her way. When they arrived at the Turlington residence, they were ushered into a drawing room decorated in dark, bold colors. The walls were draped in a russet-colored fabric and the furniture was a mix of dark woods and intricately patterned upholstery.

"Ah, Lady Shelby," crooned a woman in a feathered turban from her position perched on the edge of a settee, "I am so glad you were able to attend."

Juliet followed her mother to the circle of people already gathered around the woman she presumed to be Lady Turlington. The room itself was full to bursting with guests, who were clustered in small groups throughout the chamber. The conversations ranged from heated arguments to desultory chats and everything in between.

When she and her mother reached Lady Turlington's group, a few of the gentlemen on the edge of the group stepped back so that they might pay their respects to their hostess.

"May I present my daughter, Miss Shelby?" Lady Shelby asked, pushing Juliet forward to make her curtsy to the other woman.

Up close, Juliet saw that Lady Turlington was older than she had at first seemed. Her hair was an unnatural shade of yellow and the lines around her eyes and mouth had been softened, if Juliet was not mistaken, by a judicious use of cosmetics. She knew that women from earlier generations had not balked at using paints and powders to augment their looks, so it was less surprising than it might have been. But knowing how her mother abhorred the use of such unnatural enhancements, she was reminded once more of just how low her mother had come to push her only daughter into marrying the son of a woman she might otherwise have shunned.

"Lady Turlington," Juliet said, rising from her obeisance. "It is a pleasure to make your acquaintance."

"Well, child," the countess said, looking her over with such intensity that Juliet almost offered her teeth for inspection, "you are a pretty enough little thing, aren't you? I suppose you'll do."

As there was no polite way to reply to such an observation, Juliet said nothing.

Seeming disappointed, Lady Turlington shrugged and said, "There are some young ladies over there. I suppose you'd rather go have a chat with them. We're discussing Elgin's Marbles, and even I know that's no fit topic for an unwed chit's conversation."

Dismissed, Juliet glanced to her mother, who nodded her acquiescence.

When she approached the circle of younger ladies, Juliet felt her heart sink when she saw that among them was Miss Snowe. What on earth was she doing at an artistic salon? Unable to turn away without causing offense, she stepped forward, her limp feeling more conspicuous than usual.

"So I told Lord Spencer that he could either dance with me or retire to the card room in peace," Amelia was saying, her china-doll blue eyes alight with merriment. "Of course he chose me."

"Naturally, my dear Miss Snowe," said young Lord Lymington. "Any man would prefer you to a game of cards."

Juliet fought to keep her eyes from rolling at the young baron's gallantry. Perhaps if she were quiet she could go chat with the circle of young matrons near the doorway.

A hand on her arm diverted her attention from Amelia and her coterie. Her heart sinking at being recognized and therefore unable to slip away on her own, Juliet turned to see Miss Katherine Devenish, Lord Deveril's younger sister.

"My apologies for intruding," the blond-haired young lady, who bore a strong resemblance to her brother, said. "I am so pleased to see you here, however. My brother has talked of no one else of late."

Juliet felt the eyes of everyone in the group on her. "You must have mistaken me for my cousin Lady Madeline Essex," she said with a self-conscious laugh. Surely Deveril had not been so indiscreet as to mention their kiss last night to his baby sister.

But Katherine shook her head. "No, I am quite sure it was you he spoke of," she said. "I have met Lady Madeline as well, of course, but I believe it was you he referred to when he spoke of the gifted pianist."

Since Madeline could barely play scales, it did seem that Lord Deveril had been speaking of Juliet. She was somewhat stunned at the notion though she supposed it was unremarkable enough.

Her eyes narrowed as she listened to this exchange, Amelia spoke up. "I was unaware that you played, Miss Shelby. In fact, I recall you declining to do so once at Lady Lymington's musicale."

"But declining to play does not necessarily mean that one cannot play, Miss Snowe. I simply did not care to do so that evening." Juliet wished that someone would change the topic of conversation. Fervently.

"Ah, well," Amelia responded, her voice studiously languid. She sometimes affected an air of ennui that Juliet supposed was meant to convey sophistication. What it conveyed to Juliet was pretension. "I suppose I should not be surprised that one so unaccustomed to moving about in society would have a fear of playing before an audience."

Since Juliet had been out in society longer than Amelia, the insult was clear. Aloud, she said coolly, "Again I must correct you, Miss Snowe. Fear has nothing to do with it. It is more a case of not wishing to be the center of attention."

"Well, I for one would love to hear Miss Shelby play," Lymington said nervously. It was clear he was unsure what dark undercurrents passed between the two women, but wished to quiet the waters.

"So would I," Amelia chimed in. "If, of course, Miss Shelby is willing to break her rule against being the center of attention. Though honestly, I think it is a bit . . ." She paused, as if searching for just the right word.

An inward tug of competition rose in Juliet's chest. She had long wished for some way to put Amelia in her place. Or to show her that there were other young ladies besides her small fashionable circle in the *ton*. Yes, she had helped Madeline arrange for Cecily to use Miss Snowe's dance card earlier in the season, but this was a chance to best Amelia all on her own. And, she thought with satisfaction, to show just how superior an instructor Mrs. Turner really was.

"I think it's a splendid notion," said Lord Turlington as he strode across the room to Juliet's side. She had not seen him since that day at the gallery and the time and distance had done nothing to improve her opinion. She felt the hairs on the back of her neck rise as he touched her arm. Cursing her sharp tongue for drawing their group to his attention, she pretended a civility toward him that she did not feel.

"Come, Miss Shelby," he said, offering her his arm, which she had no choice but to accept, "I will show you and the others to the music room, where you may play and entertain us."

Her stomach knotted—her desire to put Amelia in her place was at war with her dislike of drawing attention to herself. And what would Mama say when she found out?

Calling upon the reserve of inner strength that she had long used to steel herself to the scorn of her peers, Juliet took Lord Turlington's arm and allowed him to lead her toward the music room.

Alec arrived at the Turlington town house in Half-Moon Street later than he had planned. As he handed his hat and gloves to the butler, he was informed that the guests had moved to the music room.

Despite his warning to Juliet that afternoon, he had been unable to resist the urge to see her tonight. And to protect her from both her mother and Turlington.

He heard the piano music before he reached the room. If he wasn't mistaken it was a sonata by Beethoven. The one he and Juliet had discussed at Frampton's. He'd heard the same piece mangled terribly by a pastel-gowned debutante only last week. But this. This was different. Whereas the debutante's rendering had made him want to cover his ears in anguish, this pianist prompted another kind of anguish. That sweet, sad feeling that only a well-crafted bit of poetry or music or prose could evoke.

When he entered the music room, the assembled company was quiet, all eyes were on the figure at the piano, whose deft fingers flew over the keyboard.

If her auburn hair, escaping from its tidy chignon, were not clue enough, Alec would have known it was Juliet by the tilt of her head. Could he really have become so attuned to her every mannerism that it took only that to identify her? He shook off the notion, deciding to consider that Pandora's box later.

Leaning his shoulders against the doorjamb, he watched

entranced as she bent low over the keyboard. As if she were coaxing the music from it. If this was the result of her training at Mrs. Turner's hands then that lady was indeed a gifted instructor. He was not pleased to see that it was Turlington who stood behind her turning the pages as she played. Though it put him in the position of dog in the manger, he would do whatever it took to make sure the man stayed as far away from Juliet as possible. Especially given what he'd learned of the other man that afternoon at White's. Turlington, it seemed, had a reputation for deep play. So deep in fact that it was a not-so-very-well-kept secret that his estates were mortgaged to the hilt. He had just the other evening lost so much at the tables that he'd been forced to offer up his brandnew curricle as payment for the debt. Which had, doubtless, been bought on credit in the first place.

Though many fashionable gentlemen of the *ton* thought there was no shame in refusing to pay the tradesmen who kept them in fine style, Alec had seen the results of such excess on his father's estate growing up. The elder Lord Deveril had thought it no great matter to refuse wages to his staff, who had had little choice but to remain in his employ. Most of their families had lived on the estate for generations. While he had tried to right many of his father's wrongs since his accession to the title, Alec knew that it would take years to repair the damage done to the estate and the village under his father's tenure.

But the most damning detail he'd unearthed about Turlington that morning had not to do with what that gentleman owed, but what was owed him. Lady Shelby, it would seem, was also addicted to deep play. And Alec had learned— after paying handsomely for the information—that Lady Shelby was deeply indebted to the man. So much in debt that she was willing to pay the fellow with the hand of her daughter? That remained to be seen. But since Lord Shelby was known to have refused to pay his wife's debts in the past, it was likely that he had also refused to repay Turlington from the Shelby coffers. And so Lady Shelby had come to an agreement with Lord Turlington.

Alec would not hesitate to inform Lord Shelby of just what his wife was up to, but that gentleman was currently in Paris on diplomatic business. And by the time he returned, it might just be too late to rescue Juliet from her mother's machinations.

Now, he watched Turlington carefully to ensure that the blackguard took no liberties as he leaned over Juliet's shoulder to turn her pages. He saw her flinch away from him a couple of times, but for the most part she was so lost in her playing that he doubted she was even aware she had an audience.

What a talent she'd been hiding, he mused. He had suffered through enough poetry readings and musical evenings to know that the majority of young ladies were not all that proficient at the talents they professed to possess. Anything that would set them apart from the sea of other pastel-wearing young ladies—anything short of scandal, that was—was to be grasped with both hands and paraded before the assembled army of eligible males again and again until one unsuspecting fellow fell into the trap. But Lady Shelby had her own plans for Juliet, and so this asset had been hidden just as her others had been.

Alec burned with indignation on Juliet's behalf. The notion of this vibrant woman at the pianoforte being married off to the lecher currently standing behind her sickened him. Even if he could not marry her himself, he might be able to use his influence to introduce her to some eligibles. There were any number of decent fellows he counted as friends who would make decent enough husbands for Juliet. He suppressed the twinge of jealousy he felt at the idea of her married to someone else. It was for the best, he told himself. She'd be much better off with a steady chap. Someone who could take care of her as she deserved. Someone without the blood of Devil Deveril running through his veins.

If he suddenly felt disheartened by the notion, he told himself it was simply the music. He would do the right thing by Juliet.

Seeing her happy would be worth the discomfort to himself.

The sound of applause ringing in her ears, Juliet lifted her head to see genuine appreciation in the eyes of Lord Turlington's guests.

Eschewing that gentleman's arm, she rose from the piano herself, using her walking stick to bolster her strength.

"Miss Shelby, you play marvelously," Lord Fortenbury said from the small crowd of well-wishers who had gathered around her. She was surprised to see that the group consisted primarily of gentlemen. Wasn't that a change?

"You must promise to let me accompany you to the opera next week," one young buck, whose shirt points threatened serious damage to his eyes, gushed.

"I know my mama sent an invitation to her rout next week, but I'll make sure that she sends another, just in case the first was misdirected."

"Would you care for a trip to the park tomorrow in my new curricle, Miss Shelby? I should like to speak to you about Mr. Schubert's latest composition."

It was almost too much, and Juliet found herself in the novel position of being overpopular.

Before she could respond to any of the questions, however, her mother stepped into the room, casting a pall over the erstwhile happy chatter.

"You will excuse us, won't you?" Lady Shelby said through a frigid smile. "I am afraid there is something my daughter and I must discuss."

Juliet nearly fell as her mother pulled her, with little care for her stability or her injured limb, into an antechamber.

"What do you think you're doing, Juliet?" her mother demanded once they were out of earshot of the rest of the gathering. "You are not to attract the attention of anyone but Lord Turlington. I thought I'd made myself clear on that matter."

So vehement was her mother's wrath that Juliet stepped back from her. "Mama, you knew Lord Turlington was going to have me play. You were there when he suggested it. I thought that if you had some objection you would say so then."

"Well, I thought perhaps he would be pleased to see that you have some talent after all, but he seemed unimpressed. And he did not like to see you as the center of all that gentlemanly attention. If you think to give him a disgust of you that will keep him from marrying you, then I warn you that with or without the benefit of matrimony the man will have you. Make no mistake on the matter."

"You cannot be serious!" Juliet cried. "You are no better than a Covent Garden abbess if you threaten such things."

As soon as the words were out of her mouth, Juliet knew she'd made a mistake. Her mother's hand, even encased as it was in a glove, struck with such force against her cheek that Juliet felt her neck snap with the force of the blow.

"Get away from her." Lord Deveril, his eyes blazing with cold fury, stepped into the room and pushed Lady Shelby away from her daughter.

When she did not move as quickly as he would have liked, he pulled Juliet back away from her. She stumbled, but Deveril's arm was strong and she appreciated the uncommon sensation of being able to trust someone else to prop her up.

"I said get away, madam," Deveril continued. "You will not lay another hand on her as long as there is breath in my body."

Stunned at being so spoken to, Lady Shelby gaped. Then her eyes narrowed on the pair. "So, I was not mistaken, then," she said silkily. "I would never have guessed that you would be one to succumb to such low desires, Lord Deveril, but then I suppose a bit of novelty would be difficult for one like you to come by. And I suppose you *are* your father's son."

"Lady Shelby," he said, his voice taut with anger, "you would do well to be quiet before I forget that you are a lady. You are not fit to call yourself a mother, much less to someone of Juliet's worth. If you continue in this manner I will have no choice but to let the rest of the *ton* know just how low you've sunk."

"Your concern for my daughter is touching, my lord," Lady Shelby said nastily, "but you forget yourself. You are nothing to my daughter. And until she is of age, she is mine and her father's to do with as we please."

She stepped closer, and boldly ran a finger down Deveril's cheek. "Come, my lord, surely you would prefer to be entertained by a woman of some experience rather than a trembling innocent like Juliet."

Bile rose in Juliet's throat as she watched her mother trying to seduce Alec.

"Thank you, no, madam," he told her, stepping back and away from her touch. "I would sooner bed a venomous snake."

Anger flashed in Lady Shelby's eyes, then she flicked her gaze to Juliet. As if she hadn't just been rebuffed, she said, "Come along, Juliet. I find myself weary of the company tonight."

Not pausing to see if her daughter would follow, Lady Shelby left the room.

When Juliet made as if to follow, Alec refused to let her go. "We're getting out of here."

"What do you mean?" Juliet demanded. She'd never seen anyone as angry as Lord Deveril had been when he saw her mother strike her. Her cheeks flamed with shame at the memory. It was humiliating to have him witness her mother's ill-treatment of her. Almost as humiliating as seeing her mother attempt to seduce him. She closed her eyes against the memory.

"Come," he said simply, careful to make sure that she had her footing before hurrying her through the kitchens to the mews beyond.

Nine

Alec led Juliet up the steps of Winterson House, and to his credit, the ancient butler didn't raise an eyebrow at the appearance of two unexpected visitors at this hour of the evening.

He was still too angry to speak in anything but mono-syllables when Winterson and Cecily entered the room—Winterson in shirtsleeves and hastily donned breeches and boots, and Cecily in a robe that was more modest than many evening gowns.

"Deveril, you'd better have a damn good reason for pull-ing us out of bed at this hour," growled the duke.

"We did not go out tonight for a reason," he added with a speaking glare.

But Alec didn't much care why the duke and duchess had remained home.

"Cecily, perhaps you can take Juliet to your sitting room for some tea?" he asked, not missing the way her eyes wid-ened at his use of her cousin's given name.

With a brisk nod, Cecily moved to her cousin's side.

"Come, dearest," she said, wrapping an arm about Juliet's shoulders. "We'll go and let these two have their gentle-men's talk."

But Juliet was not to be pawned off so easily. She re-fused to be moved from her position near the window.

"I have a right to be involved in my own fate, Alec," she said, resentment flashing in her green eyes. "I am not an imbecile."

"No one is saying that you are," Alec said, his gut tightening at her bravado. Most young ladies of his acquaintance would have dissolved into a puddle of tears by now. But not his Juliet.

"Please," he continued. "Go with Cecily and let me talk things out with Winterson. I won't make any decisions without consulting you first. All right?"

Her turmoil was evident in her porcelain features, which were just now beginning to regain some color after her earlier upset. Finally, she gave a short nod and let Cecily take her from the room.

He did not miss the sharp look the duchess gave her husband as they passed. Nor did Winterson, who squeezed her shoulder.

They had barely left when Winterson moved to the sideboard.

"So," he asked, pouring them both a glass of brandy, "what happened? Did that bitch of a mother finally go too far?"

Alec took the glass and lowered himself wearily into an oversized armchair.

"Your question implies that you are already aware of how Juliet has been treated by her mother," he said, stretching his long legs out before him. "If that is the case then I would like to know why you've done nothing about it."

Winterson raised a brow at the younger man's leashed fury.

"I have done nothing about it," he told Alec, sitting in the chair opposite, "because while it is disgusting to see the sort of trauma a parent can inflict on a child, there is nothing illegal about it. I could hardly kidnap Juliet and force her to move in with us. She is, for the next few months, a minor."

Alec grunted. "In answer to your question, yes, she has

gone too bloody far. She's all but pimped the girl to that bastard Turlington. And she has threatened to—"

He paused, not wanting to tell secrets that were not his to begin with.

"Let's just say that she has made Juliet's life a living hell for the past few weeks and promises to continue unless something can be done about it."

"Well, what do you suggest?" Winterson asked. "I can offer to let her come here, but there's nothing I can do if Lord and Lady Shelby demand to take her back."

"A solution has occurred to me," Alec said, staring into the dark liquid in his glass, "but I'm not sure that Juliet will agree to it."

"So," Winterson said carefully, "the wind blows in that direction, does it? I must admit, I thought you were moving toward a match with Madeline, but I do think you are better suited for Juliet."

Alec stood, stalking over to stand before the fire.

"I did," he said, "at one time consider asking for Madeline's hand. She would be a much . . . safer choice for me, I think. We are friendly and I think we would get along well enough together."

"But?"

"But Juliet needs me more," he said. "And there is the small matter of the fact that I have all but compromised her already."

Winterson's smile turned to a frown.

"Perhaps you'd care to tell me what the hell that means," he said with deceptive calm. "Did you compromise her a little? Or a lot?"

Alec turned from gazing into the fire.

"It depends, I think, upon what your definition of the term entails. Did I take her virginity? No. But I certainly have done more with her than is allowed by convention. Enough so that I was considering marrying the girl even before tonight's incident."

Since Winterson himself had been forced to marry Cecily by special license under much more scandalous circumstances—well, discounting tonight's midnight escape—Alec hardly thought the duke was in a position to judge.

But apparently, Winterson did not see the matter that way.

"You were 'considering' marrying her before tonight? Are you saying that you compromised her and were thinking about not marrying her?"

"Well, when you put it like that it sounds dishonorable," Alec protested.

"If the shoe fits," Winterson ground out. "I should thrash you. The only thing saving you is the fact that it would upset Cecily. And I do not wish to upset her."

"There is no reason for you to thrash me, or for Cecily to be upset. I did not compromise Juliet . . ."

At Winterson's glare, Alec conceded, "All right, I compromised her, but I'm going to marry her."

"Only if she'll have you, old son," Winterson said, his blue eyes like steel.

"Of course," Alec said. He wasn't a monster, after all. If Juliet wouldn't have him, then he wouldn't force her. Which was a damned sight more than her parents could say.

"So, what exactly happened tonight to make you make a run for it with her?"

Alec explained about the scene he'd witnessed between Lady Shelby and Juliet earlier that evening. And what he'd heard Juliet's mother threaten her with. Even now his hands curled into fists thinking of it.

"Damn," Winterson said with an answering frown. "I've never liked Lady Shelby much just on her own merits, but if what you say is true she's even worse than Cecily and I thought."

"Oh, it's true," Alec said, his jaw clenching in anger at Juliet's ill-treatment. "If she were a man she'd be meeting me at Hampstead tomorrow."

He did not elaborate on his own history of abuse at his father's hand or how he'd failed to protect his mother from a similar fate. It was enough to know that he could help Juliet escape now.

"So, the fact remains," Winterson said, "that Juliet is still a minor. I take it you're making a trip to Scotland?"

Alec nodded. "I'm not going to let her remain here and be forced into marriage with Turlington. I would like to hope that Lady Shelby hasn't heard the talk about just what sorts of pleasures he indulges in Covent Garden, but it hardly seems possible. She runs in a fast set herself so I have little doubt she knows something of his reputation."

"Agreed," Winterson said. "Cecily has been worried about Juliet of late, especially since Lady Shelby has pressed more strongly for the match with Turlington. It's one of the reasons she and Madeline have been pushing for her to make herself more visible in the *ton*."

Alec nodded. "I suspected as much. I know Juliet has been grateful for their support."

"Well," the duke said, rising from his chair. "All that remains is for you to ask Juliet for her consent, and you can be off for Gretna."

"What do you mean?" Alec asked, the idea that Juliet might refuse him stopping him in his tracks. "Of course she'll consent."

Winterson shook his head in disappointment.

"A word of advice, old fellow," he said, slipping a companionable arm round Alec's shoulders, "do not ever take a woman's response to a question for granted. They are a wise and wonderful sex, but predictable, they are not."

And mulling over those words of advice, Alec followed Winterson up the stairs to Cecily's sitting room.

"Tell me what's happened," Cecily said, handing her cousin a cup of tea.

Juliet closed her eyes in appreciation of the warm, sweet drink. Calmed by the ritual of it, she felt better able to face Cecily's questions.

"Mama all but ordered me to marry Turlington," she said bitterly. "And when I refused she threatened to give me to him without benefit of marriage."

Cecily put down the creamer with a thud, rattling the china spread out over the table.

"And what did you say?" she asked, her voice hot with anger. "I hope you told her to go to the devil!"

"Well, I told her she was little better than a procuress. That was when Alec came in." She did not tell of the blow her mother had delivered to her face. It was probably evident, but she could not speak of such a thing, even with Cecily.

"And what was his response? I could wish he'd drawn her cork, but of course as a gentleman he could never do such a thing."

"Oh, I think he wished to," Juliet said with a rueful smile, remembering her relief at seeing him standing there in the doorway looking ready to commit murder on her behalf. "But he settled for telling her that she was unfit to be a mother to anyone, and that if she went through with her plans he would see to it that the whole *ton* learned of it and she'd be shunned from good society forever."

"Ah." Cecily nodded. "A perfect threat. If there's anything Aunt Rose fears more than being ostracized, then I don't know what it is."

"Yes, that's just what I thought," Juliet said, "but I think she underestimated how much Alec had overheard. She actually tried to seduce him into dropping his threat. Which he resisted, of course. One only had to look at his face to know he'd sooner bed an asp."

"Juliet!" Cecily's eyes widened in shock at her cousin's words. But then she let out a reluctant giggle. "Though you are right. She does bear much resemblance to a poisonous snake."

"She realized soon enough that no amount of flattery or coercion on her part would change his mind. Then she told me to follow her, which I ignored. A few moments later Turlington's footman came saying she'd given orders that neither one of us was to leave the room."

"Oh, dear. I feel sure Lord Deveril didn't like that."

"No." Juliet grinned. "Lord Deveril did not. He told the fellow that if he knew what was good for him he'd let us go at once. And then he gave the man his card and said that if Lord Turlington gave him the sack, he should get in touch with the butler at Deveril's town house to see about another position."

"Ah, smart man," Cecily said with approval. "In these times good positions are hard to come by and unless Turlington is kinder to his servants than he is to his prospective fiancées then no servant with two thoughts to rub together would agree to stay on for less wages."

Juliet nodded. "So, Alec led me into the hallway and we slipped out through the back garden and waited for his carriage."

"I cannot help but notice that you call him Alec," Cecily said, looking at Juliet over the rim of her cup as she sipped her own tea.

"Yes," she said carefully, feeling her cheeks burn. "We are friends, I think."

"You think?"

"Well . . . I mean to say . . . we are . . . um . . ."

"I am sorry, my dear, but I don't recall ever being moved to blush over a friendship," Cecily said gently.

Juliet looked down under her cousin's knowing gaze, but said nothing.

"You love him, don't you?"

"What?" Juliet demanded. "Don't be absurd! It's as I said, we are just—"

"Oh, cut line, Juliet. You haven't been able to keep your eyes off him all season."

"Well, maybe I have a bit of a *tendre*," she admitted. "But I am not so foolish as to have formed a serious attachment. I mean, look at him!"

She gestured downward toward the sitting room where Winterson and Deveril were talking.

"And look at me," she continued, waving a hand from her head to her toes. "I am well aware that I am no prize. And add in my limp and I'm positively doomed to spinsterhood."

"Oh, do not be so dramatic. You are doomed to no such thing."

"Right," Juliet said bitterly, resting her head against the back of the chair. "I do have one man who would love to marry me. Or bed me, at least. I musn't discount Lord Turlington."

"My," Cecily said with surprise, "I never thought you to be maudlin or have a propensity to feel sorry for yourself."

Juliet sighed and passed a weary hand over her eyes. "I am having a trying time of it just now. My apologies."

"There is nothing to apologize for," her cousin said, touching her lightly on the shoulder. "I am a beast to tease you. But I really do hate to hear you say those things about yourself. It is nothing more than what your mother wishes you to think. Because she is a spiteful, jealous cat who cannot endure the idea that her own daughter might be more appealing than she is."

Smiling ruefully, Juliet reached up to cover her cousin's hand with her own. "I wish you were right, but I have seen myself in the glass. And I am nowhere near as beautiful as she is. Though I will admit that I am certainly a much more pleasant person."

"Darling, you are far and away more pleasant than any of the Fabulous Featherstones. And that includes my own dear stepmama."

Juliet was saved a response by the sound of Winterson

opening the door. He stepped into the room, followed closely by Alec.

"Come, Your Grace," the duke said, leaning down to take Cecily's hand. "Let's go have a drink in the other room."

The duchess frowned. "What do you mean? We have tea right here. And weren't you and . . ."

Then, catching her husband's meaningful glare, her eyes widened.

"Oh! Yes, of course, we keep the special wine in your study, don't we? I for one could use some. It's been a very eventful evening."

She paused before Deveril, but Juliet couldn't see what passed between them, just that he gave her a nod that seemed . . . reassuring. What on earth was going on?

The air seemed to vacate the room along with Winterson and Cecily, but as Alec watched Juliet, her green eyes glistening in the firelight, he realized that he wasn't the only one suffering an attack of nerves.

"Are you well?" he asked, stepping closer to where she perched on the edge of a chintz-covered chair. He noted with a hint of annoyance that she'd torn her gown in their haste to exit Turlington's house. The reminder of just what she'd run away from tonight solidified his resolve to ensure she was never so mistreated again. "You did not hurt your leg, did you? In our haste to leave?"

Wiping her gloveless palms on the skirt of her gown, Juliet shook her head. "No," she said, "I am fine." Though she was clearly not at ease, she was also not cowering from him. That was something, at least.

Stopping before her chair, he went down on his haunches before her so that they were eye to eye. This close, he could see the tiny freckles that dusted her cheeks and nose, and the darkness of her lashes against her pale skin. Her face, though pretty enough, boasted something that most ladies of the *ton* wanted but could never have: character. It shone in her intelligent eyes, and her expressive mouth.

"You know why I am here, do you not?" he asked softly.

She was not stupid, his Juliet. She knew what he meant to ask.

"But," she said quietly, "you need not do it. I am sure that Winterson and Cecily would be able to find somewhere . . ."

His eyes dropped to where her hand twisted nervously in the fabric of her skirt. She was not entirely composed, it would seem. He covered her hand with his, stopping its motion.

"No," he said firmly, his voice harsher than he'd intended. "You should not have to spend the rest of your days running from them."

She kept her eyes downcast. He lifted her chin with a finger so that he could gauge her emotions.

"I don't think you wish that either," he said softly. "Do you?"

"No," she said, turning her gaze from his, as if the intimacy of it was too much. "But neither do I wish for you to sacrifice yourself simply because you happened to be the one to rescue me tonight. That hardly seems fair. Especially given what you told me this afternoon. You can hardly have changed your mind in the space of a few hours."

"The situation has changed in the space of a few hours," he said simply. He moved his head so that she had no choice but to see him. "And so have my thoughts on the subject."

"Well, perhaps they have, but you shouldn't have to marry me for it. You did nothing wrong. And it's not as if we . . ." She paused, her silence implying what she would not say aloud.

"No," he said with a wry smile. "We did not . . ." He indicated her silence with a wave of his hand. "And yet, we came very near last night. And unless I am mistaken, ladies have been compromised over far less than that."

"I won't have you marrying me out of some misguided sense of obligation, Alec," she said, resolve causing her nervousness to ebb away. "If the choice is between you and Turlington, then of course I would choose you. But there is a third option. I can marry neither of you and live on my own. Indeed, I had all but decided as much this afternoon."

"After our discussion, you mean?

"Don't flatter yourself," Juliet snapped. "You aren't the only man in London, you know. I only meant that this afternoon I came upon the notion of ruining my reputation all on my own, so there is no need for you to marry me. I can simply use tonight's fracas as the means for it. Indeed, I count tonight's events as a blessing."

"What of the damage to *my* reputation?" Alec demanded. "I can hardly find suitable matches for my sisters if I'm under the cloud of scandal for compromising you and then refusing to marry you."

Juliet blanched.

"I've spent the better part of my life trying to remove the taint of being heir to Devil Deveril. And to some degree I've succeeded. But ruining your reputation will also ruin mine. And by association those of my sisters."

"So, your protests about not being able to give me the sort of marriage I deserved were only valid until your reputation was threatened?" she demanded.

"Of course not," Alec said, thrusting a hand through his carefully coiffed curls. "I still think you deserve a lifetime of happiness. Tonight's circumstances haven't changed that. I shall simply have to ensure your happiness myself."

Juliet stared at him. Of all the expectations she'd harbored for this evening, receiving a proposal from Alec had not been chief among them.

"I cannot ask it of you," she said, reaching out to grasp his hand in spite of her determination to keep him at a distance. "I will simply retire to one of Winterson's estate properties in the country. And you will find someone more suitable to wed. Someone who will bring consequence to your sisters."

"But what if I don't want someone more suitable ?" Alec asked, his gaze unwavering. Despite his earlier determination to push her away, he now found himself wanting more than anything for her to agree to wed him. He still thought she deserved better. But at some point, he'd gone from trying to protect her from him, to wishing to protect her from the rest of the world. At least he knew *his* intentions were honorable. Which was more than he could say for Lady Shelby or Turlington.

Juliet had not actually confessed yet to not wishing to marry him, he noted, allowing a sliver of hope to work its way into his chest. "What if I want you?

"Juliet." He felt her hand, still gripped in his, tremble slightly. "I could wrap this up in all sorts of romantic folderol, or confess myself to be madly in love with you or compose an ode to your freckles. But we would both know it was false. I wish for us to start things out with sincerity. And I like you far too much to lie to you."

She did not reply, just nodded for him to continue.

"It is true that I have been considering marriage this season. And perhaps I might, if left to my own devices, have chosen someone else. Someone I liked less. Someone I could keep at arm's length. But that's beside the point. You are the one I kissed quite thoroughly in your parents' back garden. You are the one I whisked away from Turlington's house tonight. I might have tried to warn you off this afternoon, but you're the one I went to see at Turlington's. You're the one I'm asking to marry me, now. It's you. I am asking you."

He took both her hands in his now and squeezed. He wasn't sure if it was to reassure her or himself.

"Will you?" he asked. "Will you marry me?"

Ten

*S*he had to be dreaming.

That was the only explanation for the fact that she was sitting in Cecily's sitting room receiving a proposal from Lord Alec Deveril, one of London's most handsome, fashionable gentlemen. But even in her dreams she wouldn't have entertained what could only be an unattainable fantasy. Her ability to dream had disappeared along with her childhood in a Vienna street years ago.

And yet, it seemed real enough. She felt his strong hands grasping hers. She felt the heat of his body as he knelt before her, gazing expectantly at her as if awaiting a reply.

Just in case it was not a dream, she decided to reply, but found that her voice had left her. So, she simply nodded, and the very next minute found herself being thoroughly kissed.

"Excellent," he said, drawing back from her. Was it her imagination or was he not a little bit breathless? Perhaps she wasn't the only one who would benefit from a match between them.

At least that is what she promised herself as she watched him stand, then go to the door to call for Winterson and Cecily.

He needn't have bothered. They were standing just outside the door.

Cecily rushed forward and gave Juliet a fierce hug.

"Darling, I am so pleased for you!" she said, pulling back to gaze into her eyes. Whatever she saw there must have reassured her for she nodded in approval, then tugged Juliet to her feet and gestured for her to follow.

"We will go raid my closet so that you will have gowns enough for the trip."

"What trip?" Juliet asked, balking. Alec had said nothing about a trip.

"You'll have to go to Gretna, of course," Cecily told her as if it were a mere detail. "You are not yet of age and there is no way your parents will consent for you to marry Lord Deveril now. Especially given tonight's little episode."

"It will be all right," Alec told her, reaching out to squeeze her hand reassuringly. "And on the way back I think we can make a stop at the Mounthaven estate to speak with Mr. MacEwan about your Mrs. Turner."

At the mention of her missing friend, Juliet felt a stab of guilt. Here she'd spent the entire evening worrying about her own troubles and she had not given any thought to Anna's disappearance.

"But what about my things?" Juliet asked, thinking not only of her clothes, but also of all those things she would need to take care of her injured leg, like binding cloth and the special salve she used to reduce the worst of the chafing. And for that matter, how would she manage to keep the extent of her injuries hidden from Alec? "And my maid? I cannot travel without her."

"There's no time," Alec said, though he seemed apologetic about it. "And we dare not return to your parents' house to retrieve your things anyway. Perhaps Cecily can lend you some things to take with you. And I'm sure we can ask one of the maids where we stop for the night to serve you for a night or two."

Suddenly it all felt incredibly complicated, and Juliet was swept with a sense of just how much this journey she was about to undertake would change the course of her life. She would leave London Miss Shelby and return the Viscountess Deveril. And in the meantime she would somehow have to tell Alec the truth about what had happened to her in Vienna. Could she marry him without doing so? She supposed she could, but the idea of keeping such a secret from him was unimaginable.

And, even so, what choice did she have? If she remained in London one day longer she would find herself married to Turlington, with his overeager smiles, and the gaze that made her feel contaminated in some way.

No, she would go with Alec and marry him. Perhaps he would be angry at her failure to reveal her secret beforehand, but she would do whatever it took to ensure their life together was a comfortable one. She had already made excellent progress in becoming more outgoing in social situations, so she would be able to attend to her duties in her capacity as the viscountess. And as far as she knew her leg injury had no effect on her effort to conceive or bear children, and that was what a titled gentleman needed most from a wife.

Wasn't it?

It was a little less than two hours later that Alec finally climbed into the carriage with Juliet and rapped on the ceiling to signal the coachman to depart.

Though he was sanguine with his decision to marry her, Alec found himself at a loss for words now that he and Juliet were alone together. He hoped it was not an ill portent for their married years to come.

There had been a moment back in Winterson's drawing room, when he had wondered if Juliet might not change her mind about the whole affair and return to her parents' house. It might have only been a case of nerves, or perhaps she had some special belongings she feared would be destroyed by her mother if she did not retrieve them now.

Whatever the reason had been, she must have realized the danger lurking for her if she did not leave London with him tonight, for she had consented the next moment to go along with the scheme.

She looked now out the carriage window, watching the great houses of Mayfair pass by them as they slowly made their way through London for the journey north. Her finely wrought features were limned in moonlight, giving her face an ethereal quality that reminded him just how close she had once come to leaving this world altogether. For one fierce moment, he allowed himself to imagine how that might have changed his own world, and was suddenly grateful to the foreign physicians who had saved her.

"You should probably try to sleep while you can," he told her, fighting the urge to invite her to pillow her head on his shoulder. He didn't wish to rush his fences, after all. The journey was just starting.

"I will, thank you," Juliet said, not turning from her position at the window. "Though I doubt I will be able to sleep. I am still too overset from the fracas with Mama and Lord Turlington, I think."

He would not have thought so from her attitude at the time. Her calm had been one of the reasons he'd wondered whether or not she needed rescuing at all. He knew, of course, from their discussion the other evening that she had no wish to marry Turlington. And her mother could hardly be said to hold her daughter's undying affection. Yet, tonight—or last night, he supposed—she had stood up for herself with a strength of mind he'd often wished to possess himself in his earlier interactions with his father.

There had been no tearful pleading, no histrionics, no dramatics. Those had come not from Juliet but from Lady Shelby herself. And all the while, Juliet had stated again and again that she would not do as her mother wished and consent to marry Turlington. He had been willing to let Juliet fight her own battle until Lady Shelby had crossed the line and threatened to give her daughter to Turlington without marriage. And then there had been the blow. That had been when he made his presence known and stepped in to offer her his support. Only then had Juliet seemed to break.

What sort of trauma must she have dealt with in her young life that it was an act of kindness that brought her to tears, rather than an act of aggression?

She gave a slight shudder as a gust of wind rattled the windows of the coach, and abandoning his earlier circumspection, he wordlessly transferred himself to sit beside her and gather her into the warmth of his greatcoat.

"Rest," he told her, tucking her head into the crook of his neck.

At first she held herself away from him, only allowing her head and shoulders to touch him. But gradually she began to relax and before five minutes had passed she had let down her guard completely and drifted off to sleep.

Closing his own eyes, Alec tried not to consider just how right it felt to have her soft body pressed snugly against him. A more prudent man would have resisted the urge to offer her comfort, thus risking his own ability to remain emotionally untangled from her. But it was nearly three o'clock in the morning, it was cold, and he was damned if he'd make her sit alone, pillowing her head upon the carriage window, when he had a perfectly good shoulder to offer.

If he also reveled in the sweet, clean scent of rose water on her skin, and the way that her body seemed to fit perfectly against his? Well, he would set about making the terms of their relationship plain as soon as she was out of harm's way. Until then, it would be best to ensure her comfort so that she did not risk going back to her mother and Turlington.

His head pressed against the soft silk of her hair, he slept.

* * *

They made the journey in six days' time, stopping only to change horses and for meals. By the time they arrived in Longtown near the Scottish border, Juliet felt as if every bone in her body had been struck with a hammer. While the coach was fast and well sprung for its kind, it was still no substitute for the large, elegant traveling coaches she was accustomed to traveling in.

As the miles passed behind them, Juliet and Alec discussed any number of topics from music to literature (Juliet was a fan of poetry while Alec preferred histories). Their opinions upon the current political climate, and the state of the Continent now that Napoleon had been defeated, led to spirited arguments, and Juliet was pleased to note that he did not discount her opinions on such matters simply because she'd been born female.

What they did not talk about, however, was Alec's childhood and Juliet's life during and after her accident. Juliet told some amusing stories about her family's travels abroad at her father's various postings with the Foreign Office, but she was always careful not to brush upon that fateful day in Vienna that had changed her life forever. If Alec found her omission odd or particularly revealing, he didn't say so. And as if by mutual consent, Juliet did not press him about what it had been like growing up as the only son of Devil Deveril.

She was relating the tale of the day she and her brother had smuggled a puppy into the nursery when the carriage came to an abrupt halt.

Frowning, Alec said, "You know where the pistol is. Take it out and wait for me to get back."

Opening the carriage door, he jumped down and Juliet, her heart pounding, felt her heart rise in her throat. So far there had been no hint that her parents had discovered her destination, but she knew her mother would not like being thwarted. The thought of what she might do to retaliate for

Juliet's defection gave her a chill that had nothing to do with the weather.

She and Alec had been careful to introduce themselves as Mr. Thomas Gidney, solicitor, and his sister, Miss Annabel Gidney, at each of the inns where they had stopped along the way. As such, they slept in separate chambers, much to Juliet's relief.

There had been more than enough opportunities to reveal the true nature of her injury to him, but the more time passed the more difficult it became to broach the subject. Though she did not care to admit such a thing to herself, a small part of her greatly feared that should Alec learn that she was not only crippled, but maimed as well, he would find some way to escape marrying her. Nothing he had said or done up to this point had led her to believe that he would be so cruel, but knowing as she did that there were very few options for her now if she did not marry him, she kept silent. Careful not to reveal her leg to the maids who assisted her at the inns where they stopped for the night, she also refused for Alec to tuck hot bricks beneath her feet, even though the coach grew colder and colder as they moved farther north. Telling him that the heat pained her injured leg, she did warm her hands when she could, and managed to keep her secret.

After that first night, when she had fallen asleep on his shoulder, whenever he sensed that she was growing tired, Alec reached for her, and though she had never thought herself a particularly touch-friendly person, she found herself becoming more and more addicted to hearing his steady heartbeat beneath her ear while she slept. So much so that she had difficulty falling asleep once she was tucked into her solitary bed when they reached the inn.

Now, hoping that a slight mishap was what had caused the carriage to stop so abruptly, she listened carefully for sounds of shouting or any sort of fracas that might explain why it was taking Alec so long to return. All was quiet, however, and she was just about to retrieve the volume of Shelley's poetry she'd been reading before the stop when the carriage door wrenched open and she was staring into Turlington's watery blue eyes. She gave a little cry of dismay.

"Well, well, well," he said, his gaze raking over her with a possessiveness that made her skin crawl. "If it isn't the little bird who flew from the nest. Come, pet, it's time to come home."

Gone was the civilized veneer that marked Turlington as a leading member of the *ton*. His usual sangfroid had been replaced by the dirt and dishevelment of days filled with hard travel and too little sleep. And the intensity of his gaze frightened her.

Shrinking back against the squabs, Juliet fought to hide her fear, knowing instinctively that Turlington would enjoy it. "There is absolutely no inducement that will make me go with you willingly, my lord. If you want me, you'll have to take me by force."

She realized her mistake at once. A man like him would enjoy her protests. "I will," Turlington said with a leer, "have no fear of that. But there is the matter of dispatching your young Galahad before we go. It was really quite convenient that we caught up to you so close to Gretna. We can be married this evening and enjoy our wedding night in one of the elegant little inns that populate the town. God knows there are enough of them."

Thinking to lull him into a false sense of security, Juliet schooled her features to hide her disgust and real fear for Alec's safety. "I knew you would find us," she said, careful to sound defeated. "I should have known escape was too much to hope for."

"Well, you were up against myself and your mama." Turlington preened, patting her on the cheek. Juliet fought hard not to flinch."Your young Deveril is hardly cunning enough to thwart us. The good news for you is that you need have no fear of bumping into him in town. Where we're sending him he will be gone for a long, long time."

Juliet blanched, trying to determine if Turlington was merely trying to frighten her, or if he told the truth. Ultimately, she decided, the man could not be trusted and she would not be at all surprised if he hid the truth about Alec's whereabouts. So, biding her time, she made a great show of appearing to acquiesce and then secretly planned her escape.

Eleven

*A*lec knew something was not right as soon as he stepped out of the carriage. For one thing it was too quiet on the road and there was no sign of his coachman or outriders. For another, an unfamiliar coach was stopped in the middle of the thruway, blocking the road.

"No sudden moves, guv," a raspy voice said in his ear, just as he felt the muzzle of a pistol at the back of his neck. "Or I might lose my grip on this here gun."

"Where is my coachman?" he asked, raising his hands to indicate that he had no intention of struggling. "And my outriders?"

"They're all tied up snug on the other side of the carriage," the voice said. "No need to worry about them. Or the little lady. She's going right back to the hospital where she belongs."

Hospital?

"I don't understand you," he said, his mind working to figure out a way to extricate himself and Juliet before the man behind him made good his threat.

"Oh, her mam told us all about it," the man said, pushing him forward to the front of the carriage. "Takes a cold-blooded fellow to steal a girl away from them that's got her best interests at heart just for the sake of a fortune. Not that I wouldn't be tempted meself, o'course. A fortune would make things a bit easier, I can't lie. But this gel's not in her right mind and that's why I agreed to help."

"Wait," Alec begged. "What do you mean 'not in her right mind'?"

Obviously Turlington and Lady Shelby had concocted some sort of story to convince this man to help them kidnap Juliet.

"Lor' don't tell me you don' know about 'er problems. You would know, wouldn't ye, since ye stole her right out of the 'ospital where she was being kept."

"My good man, you obviously haven't had a chance to speak with the lady. If you had you would know that she's quite capable of speaking on her own behalf. Come, let's go and I'll show you."

He felt the man behind him pause, hoped that he'd made some inroads with him. But the pistol pressed harder into the back of his head.

"They said ye'd deny it," the man holding him said.

Deciding that argument would not be the means by which he effected their escape, he threw back his elbow into the man's midsection and ducked as the gun discharged in a cascade of powder. Catching the man's shoulders behind him, he flipped him over his head and onto his back. The wind knocked out of him, his attacker lay stunned while Alec searched him for a weapon. He found only a knife, which he took from the protesting man. Unwinding his neck cloth, he used the knife to cut it in half and used each piece to bind the man's hands and feet.

"When you learn the truth of the matter, you'll be glad I stopped you before you harmed me," he told the fellow. "It's a hanging offense to murder a peer."

Shouting from the other side of the carriage drew his attention.

"Alec!" he heard Juliet shout from the other side of the carriage. Not wanting to alert Turlington and Lady Shelby to the fact that he was free, he made his way to the edge of the carriage and peered around it. He saw Turlington and Lady Shelby each with an arm locked onto Juliet's arms, marching her toward their parked carriage. Aside from the coachman, he could see one outrider waiting for them.

"Be quiet," Lady Shelby said through clenched teeth. "Deveril is not going to help you. If you had simply listened to me and accepted your fate none of this would have happened. Turlington will make you an excellent husband."

"Yes, if I wish to be overcome by revulsion night and day," Juliet responded, still trying to break away from them. "Alec!"

"You will keep a civil tongue in your head, miss," Turlington snapped. "Do not forget your mama's offer to give you to me without benefit of marriage. It is only through my good will that you are getting a ring on your hand at all. I might yet change my mind if you continue to insult me."

Since they had their backs to him, Alec crept around his carriage, keeping close to the vehicle. He found his own driver slumped over the box, and to his relief, still alive. Careful not to make noise, he searched the cubby where he knew the fellow kept an extra pistol and was rewarded to find their attackers hadn't checked for it themselves.

Ensuring that it was loaded, he made his way to the other vehicle, and was able to hear the heated discussion going on inside.

"Really, Juliet," Lady Shelby was saying harshly, "it is bad *ton* for you to be so missish about this. Any other young lady would be pleased beyond measure at the prospect of marrying Lord Turlington."

"Be that as it may, Lady Shelby," Alec said, opening the coach door, "she will not be marrying him, bad *ton* or no."

* * *

Juliet's relief on hearing Alec's voice was unparalleled. He stood in the carriage door looking disheveled and angry and more handsome than she could have imagined.

"Despite my family's reputation, madam," he continued to Lady Shelby, "I've never struck a woman, but in your case I might be pressed to make an exception."

Wrenching herself away from Turlington and her mother, Juliet hurled herself out of the carriage, and was relieved to feel Alec's free arm pull her close.

"Now," he said to her erstwhile kidnappers, "I want you both to remain here in your carriage. I will retrieve your cohort, and give him into your tender care. Then you are to return to London. At once."

Turlington huffed, his already pink cheeks growing redder. "I will not be ordered about by a—"

"At once," Alec said, his hand holding the pistol unwavering, his voice as sharp as a gunshot.

"This is preposterous," Turlington said with a snarl. "You have no authority here, Deveril."

"I have no qualms about killing you, Turlington," Alec said coldly. "The only thing preventing me from doing so now is the presence of Juliet. I would challenge you to a duel, but since you have shown yourself again and again to be anything but a gentleman, I do not feel the need to adhere to the rules of gentlemanly conduct where you are concerned."

The raw hatred in Turlington's eyes terrified Juliet on Alec's behalf. She had little doubt that the man would do his best to harm Deveril at the earliest opportunity. Still, she was grateful to be out of the villain's clutches for now.

"I hope you're pleased with yourself, Juliet," Lady Shelby said, making her disgust apparent. "Do not expect to be welcomed back into the family with open arms."

Whereas at one time Juliet might have been cowed by her mother's words, in Alec's arms she felt none of the old fear as she faced her now. "The only family I need," she said firmly, "knows of your cruelty and has assured me that they will support me. I have no fear of losing them and they are all that matter now. As for Father, I doubt he'll even notice I've gone."

Which was little more than the truth. Though she did love her father, Juliet had long ago realized that he was far too concerned with matters of state to trouble himself over his wife's misdeeds.

Before her mother could protest, Alec said to her, "I would not recommend your recounting this misadventure to your cronies back in London, Lady Shelby. If any word of this gets out I will see to it that your own scheme to marry your daughter off to your lover is known to every gossip-monger in the beau monde. You will be unable to show your face in polite society ever again."

Lady Shelby glowered at him, but did not speak.

With a short nod, Alec closed the carriage door on Lady Shelby and Lord Turlington, and led Juliet back to their coach. Their coachman had regained consciousness and had found and untied their outriders, and before long they were under way.

Ensconced once more in their own carriage, Alec eyed Juliet. "Are you all right?" he asked, brushing his hands down her arms as if to reassure himself of her safety. "Did they hurt you?"

"They had no time to hurt me," she responded truthfully. "They had barely got me away from the carriage when you returned. How on earth did you escape so quickly?"

"I grew up with Devil Deveril," he said with a slight smile. "I am quite adept at defending myself."

There was something he wasn't saying but Juliet didn't push him. They'd gone through quite enough already this morning.

"Now," he said with a grin, "let's go to Gretna and get married."

Gretna Green was a town very much aware of its most precious resource. And it wasn't the scones in the ramshackle tea room at the edge of town.

Rather than retire to the inn to refresh themselves, Alec and Juliet went at once to the blacksmith's shop which dealt almost exclusively with young couples crossing the border from England to marry. The man who presided over their wedding was, to Juliet's surprise, not a blacksmith at all, but Robert Elliot, grandson by marriage to the original Gretna blacksmith, Joseph Paisley.

"Now," the man said, "who have we here?"

Alec quickly told the Scotsman their names, and the man gave a broad grin. "Mother," he called to his wife, who was seated at the pianoforte in preparation to play a musical accompaniment to the ceremony. "We've got ourselves a Romeo and Juliet!"

"Then I shall have to play sommat special for them," she said, flipping quickly through her stack of sheet music.

"Now then, Romeo," Mr. Elliot instructed, "you stand here, just so. And you, Juliet, will walk down this short aisle to meet your groom at the altar."

It was indeed a very short aisle, but Juliet, a posy of violets that had cost Alec an exorbitent amount clutched in one hand and her walking stick in the other, waited in the rear of the shop while Alec followed the blacksmith/minister to the front.

"He's a handsome laddie," Mrs. Elliot said to Juliet as they waited for the signal from Mr. Elliot. "It's plain to see yours is a love match, and no mistaking."

Before Juliet could correct the woman, she launched into a wretched performance of a popular ballad based on the story of Romeo and Juliet. As neither Mr. Elliot nor his wife seemed to mind the unhappy end that those famous lovers met, Juliet supposed she shouldn't either.

Her head held high, she walked carefully down the short aisle toward a smiling Alec, and was relieved when Mrs. Elliot brought her song to a premature end.

The ceremony itself borrowed much from the Church of England service—or as far as Juliet could tell it did. When Elliot joined their hands together and Alec slipped his signet ring onto Juliet's finger and pronounced them married, she felt as much emotion as she might have done had they gone through all the pomp and circumstance of a fancy London wedding. And when Mr. Elliot slipped up and referred to her bridegroom as Romeo, she felt a giggle escape her.

"Och, man, kiss yer bonnie bride!" Mr. Elliot said with a beatific smile. And he didn't need to say it twice. As Alec touched his lips to hers, Juliet silently vowed to keep him from ever regretting this marriage made in haste.

"Let's go back to the inn and order luncheon," Alec said with a crooked grin. "Getting married makes me hungry."

Juliet's cheeks heated as she caught the possible double meaning of his words. But he seemed not to notice the entendre. Deciding to go along with the jovial mood, Juliet smiled up at her new husband. "Me too." And they walked in companionable silence to the inn.

Twelve

Seated across from Alec in the private dining room he'd arranged for their wedding luncheon, Juliet felt the return of her old nervousness around him. After their extended trip to Scotland, she'd thought her anxiety was gone forever. But the weight of his emerald on her finger, coupled with the knowledge that they were now bound to one another, till death did them part, made it impossible for her to eat more than a few bites of the excellent venison pie.

Whereas they'd found plenty to talk about on the journey to Scotland, now the ease between them had been replaced by a tension that had everything to do with the ring now snugly fitted to her ring finger. As if sensing her thoughts, Alec reached across the small table and took her hand in his.

"It's all right to feel nervous," he said softly, his thumb caressing the back of her gloveless hand. "New experiences are always a little terrifying, don't you think?"

She looked up at him from beneath her lashes to see the now familiar crooked smile that gave his perfectly formed features a boyish quality that made him even more handsome.

"But you aren't anxious," she couldn't help pointing out, a shiver running through her at the light touch of his skin on hers. It was hard to imagine this handsome, perfectly mannered gentleman, who seemed to be at ease with everyone he met, feeling out of his depth at all, ever.

"What makes you say that?" he asked, in mock surprise. He raised his left hand as if taking an oath. "I am utterly terrified, I assure you."

Juliet sighed. "I find it difficult to believe that you've never done this before." She waved a hand in the air to indicate she was speaking of the private parlor, the meal, and not necessarily the circumstances.

"But I've never done this with a wife," he said, his blue eyes serious. "Never with you."

Her chest constricted, and she looked away lest he see just how much she'd been affected by his words.

"Juliet," he continued, "you are not alone in any of this. We are partners now. Partners look after one another."

She fought a laugh. "You need the least looking after of anyone I've ever met."

"I think you have me confused with some other paragon of perfection," he said with a shake of his head. "I am just a man, my dear. Just like any other. And I shall need your support just as you'll need mine."

"Is that how marriage works?" she asked, really wanting to know his opinion on the matter. "I've only had my parents' union as a model," she said, "and they can hardly stand to be in the same room with one another. I find it difficult to believe that they managed to—" She broke off, a blush stealing into her cheeks.

"Quite," Alec said. "My own parents were much the same."

Remembering his father's reputation for brutality, Juliet felt a stab of sympathy for her new husband. She was going to change the subject but he surprised her by continuing. "Their marriage was arranged, so I don't believe there was any promise of love between them. But when he wished to be, my father could be quite charming. I have little doubt he worked his wiles on my mother until she adored him. It was his way, you see. I saw it happen enough over the years, and not only with my mother. He would entice her with gifts and kind words and wooing. Then once she was in his thrall, he'd become controlling and cruel. I can't count the number of times Mama attempted to leave him. In the end, she only found her escape through death."

"It was a carriage accident?" Juliet asked carefully, not wanting to endanger their rapport, but sensing that he needed to speak of the only parent who had shown him any affection.

Alec blinked, and seemed startled by the question, but then recovered his aplomb. "Yes, a carriage accident. My sisters were still in the nursery. And I was preparing to go up to school. It was . . ."

There was something about his mother's death that he wasn't telling her. Juliet knew this as well as she knew her own soul. But she also knew that pressing him for an answer before he was ready to tell her would only make him loath to speak to her about such things. Taking his hand in hers, she let the moment pass.

"I don't think Mama and Papa would ever actually live apart," Juliet said. "They are both too concerned with appearances to do anything so public. Papa has his diplomatic reputation, after all. And Mama enjoys the status his position gives her. They make the occasional public foray to keep the gossips at bay, but for the most part they keep to themselves."

"The very fact that neither of us has been sent to Bedlam is a miracle, is it not?" Alec asked. He seemed grateful that she hadn't pressed for more information about his mother. "Between the two of us, we have seen enough of unhappy families to write a slew of Greek tragedies."

"At least you are a man," she said with more vehemence than she'd intended. "For ladies, I think there is very little to recommend the married state. Even now that there are fewer arranged marriages, men still have the advantage in most situations."

"How so?" He leaned back in his chair, seeming genuinely interested to hear her opinion on the matter.

"Well, what options are there for a woman who does not wish to marry? Unless she has an independent fortune, she will need to have some occupation to provide funds to live on. And there are precious few options. Especially for a gentlewoman. There is governessing, which pays precious little, and entails teaching someone else's children while fending off advances from the gentlemen of the house. Mrs. Turner says that . . ."

She paused, remembering her friend was still missing. A wave of guilt washed over her as she realized she'd forgotten the search for her friend in the tumult of their elopement and escape from her mother and Turlington.

"We'll find her," Alec said, correctly interpreting her silence. "I promise you. And hopefully we will learn from Mr. MacEwan that he has heard from her."

"Thank you," she said with relief. "I was wondering just how to remind you in a way that was not too terribly bothersome."

"Already trying to figure out how to turn me up sweet?" He raised one blond brow. "I am shocked, madam!"

At her guilty expression, he shook his head. "I am only teasing, Juliet," he said with a reassuring smile. "Though you needn't cozen me. Simply ask and if it is a reasonable request, I'll be more than happy to comply."

"Thank you," she said again, this time more subdued. "Though I cannot help but worry at the time we've lost by coming here."

"You must take care of yourself." He reached for her hand again, squeezing it in sympathy. "If Mrs. Turner is your friend, she will understand the need to keep you safe from Turlington. No matter how unusual her opinions on marriage."

"You are kind," she said quietly, thinking of the secret she'd yet to share with him. "Perhaps more than I deserve."

But strangely, he was the one who seemed ill at ease now. "Do not put me on a pedestal, Juliet," he said. "I am just a man, and certainly not a perfect one. Though I suspect my next request will do well enough to show my clay feet."

She turned her head, looking at him more closely. She had little doubt that he was uncomfortable now, but why?

"What's amiss?"

Alec ran a finger beneath his neck cloth, as if it had suddenly become unbearably tight. "First, know that what I am about to ask is not out of any sort of . . . I mean to say that the irregularity of our marriage . . . or rather, the haste with which we . . ."

Juliet stared as the most suave and sophisticated man she'd ever met stammered out an unintelligible explanation. Of what she had no idea.

"Dammit," Alec said finally, "what I'm trying to say is that I think it would be best if we consummate this marriage and sooner rather than later."

As he watched his new bride's mouth drop open, Alec cursed himself for a fool. He was not a stripling trying to woo his first woman, for God's sake. If the fellows at his club were privy to this conversation he'd be laughed out of London.

"Not because I am overly eager," he said hastily, then seeing the hurt in her eyes, he pinched the bridge of his nose. "That came out wrong."

"No, I think you were perfectly clear," Juliet said, her face set as she struggled up from the table. "If you'll excuse me, my lord, I feel a headache coming on. You will no doubt feel relief at your reprieve."

"Dammit," he said in frustration, "no I don't!"

"So, your sense of duty has overcome your lack of eagerness? Well, pardon me if I do not feel sympathy for your dire circumstances."

Her back ramrod straight as she turned it to him, she limped to the door.

Before he could think better of it, Alec stalked past her to block the door. Unable to stop in time, Juliet pitched forward until he caught her by the shoulders. For a split second they stared into one another's eyes. But Juliet's anger was strong and she broke the contact first.

"Will you please stay here and listen to me?" He dipped his head so that he could regain that connection. "Please."

"What is there to listen to?" Juliet demanded, her hurt showing in her eyes despite her proud bearing as she tried to push him away from the door. "Protestations that you find me lovely despite my physical flaws? Denials that you just complained about the fact that your duty to consummate this marriage conflicts with your lack of desire for me?"

Tired of her nonsense, he allowed her to move him away from the door, but played the moment to his advantage, using his grip on her shoulders to reverse their positions.

"Lack of desire?" he demanded, stepping close enough to press her back to the door. "Are you mad? I spent the entire drive from London trying not to fall on you like a ravening beast. Are you aware that I will never be able to smell roses again without my body rising to the occasion like a kite in a strong wind?"

He dipped his head to her neck, inhaling, gratified to see the pulse point there speed up. He leaned in and scraped his teeth against the soft skin there.

"Do you know," he said in a low voice, kissing his way up the curve of her jaw, "that you've got this way of nibbling your lower lip when you're nervous that makes me want to worship your sweet mouth like a pagan?"

Alec's mouth hovered over hers, their breaths mingling before he covered her mouth with his, rejoicing at the feel of her lips parting under his to allow the intrusion of his tongue. He tried to be gentle, but after so many days of holding himself back, the leash he'd kept on his desire snapped.

The loud clang of a tray clattering to the floor in the next room recalled him to his senses. With reluctance, he pulled back from her, reached out and tucked a stray curl behind her ear. Her expression of wonder was nearly his undoing.

"You see now how wrong you were, don't you?" he asked, his voice husky.

At her mute nod, he continued. "What I was trying to say, and managed to botch at every turn, was that I think it best if we consummate the marriage now so that there is no question of an annulment."

He braced himself for her refusal, but even so could not deny he'd be disappointed by it. Especially given how his body even now cried out to complete what they'd just started. Still, he thought wryly, they were in Scotland, where there was no shortage of icy water to dampen his ardor.

To his relief, however, she agreed with him.

"I think it is the only sensible thing to do," she said, still a little breathless from their kiss.

The tiny furrow between her dark auburn brows, however, made his heart sink. *She's going to change her mind. It is only to be expected. Indeed, it's a credit to her sensibilities.*

"Can one . . . ?" she began. "That is to say, is it quite *normal* to do . . ." She swallowed, her fair skin turning deep pink, then finished her thought in a rush. "*That?* In the daytime, I mean?"

Thank you, God!

To Alec's credit, he did not laugh at her question. Of course, it was mostly due to his vast relief, but that was beside the point.

"It is quite normal," he assured her.

"In fact, daylight can be a bonus since it . . ." Realizing that it was probably best not to elaborate on just how much visual stimulation affected the male of the species, lest he frighten her away, he coughed. "It's perfectly normal," he repeated.

At her nod, he decided it was probably best to stop while he was ahead.

"Why don't you go upstairs and have a bath and rest a bit while I go see to the horses?"

Juliet's relief was evident as she nodded.

They walked in silence up the stairs as Alec escorted her to their rooms. At the door, she turned to face him.

"Thank you," she said, her expression grave. "For everything."

He did her the courtesy of not misunderstanding her words. By marrying her, he'd saved her from an almost certain life of misery tied to Turlington.

"The pleasure is mine, Lady Deveril," he said sincerely. "Always."

With a short nod, she turned and entered their rooms, her walking stick making a faint tattoo as she went.

Because she'd been unable to bring her maid with her, Juliet had to have one of the maids on staff at the inn assist her with her gown. But, mindful of keeping her foot a secret, she dismissed the girl as soon as her gown was unbuttoned, and asked for a bath to be brought to their room so that she might soak away the aches their journey had caused her.

"You can go back down, Weston," she told the maid once the steaming water had been emptied into the hip bath. "I can see to myself from here."

Once the door closed behind the maid, Juliet felt the anxiety and stress of the past several days descend upon her like a blanket of chain mail.

Preparing for her bath, she removed her gown, and sat in her chemise and stockings upon the small chair she'd asked the maid to bring her. Bending forward, she unlaced her left boot and removed it. Then moving to her left she unlaced the corset that held the upper portion of her prosthetic lower leg and foot in place and removed the device, lowering it to the ground on its side. Breathing a sigh of relief at being able to rub some feeling back into the stump of her calf, she removed her garter and stocking from her left leg, and finally slipped out of her chemise. Bracing one hand on the chair, and one on the rim of the tub, she transferred her weight from the chair to the tub's side, and lowered herself into the steaming water, fragrant with lavender oil.

Alone and relaxed for the first time in two days, Juliet had thought she'd be more traumatized by the scenes with her mother and Turlington, but instead of dwelling on her mother's betrayal, her mind instead kept returning to the scene here in this inn, with Alec.

Dipping the sponge into the water, she lathered it with a bar of lavender soap that Cecily had insisted she pack in her suitcase of borrowed clothing, and washed the dirt of the road from her body. Slowly, she moved the sponge over the soft skin of her arms, wondering what it would feel like if Alec's hands were sliding over her. The thought made her heartbeat quicken.

That kiss downstairs had been nothing like she'd imagined embraces between married people to be. It had been wild, and raw, and unsettling. It was hard to imagine elegant, urbane Alec behaving in such a manner. But when he'd pressed her against the door, and brought her hand down to feel the evidence of his desire for her, she'd known instinctively that this man, the one who was not afraid to show how desperate he was to have her, was the real one. The sophisticate who set the fashion and entertained the *ton* with his wit, she now knew, was a façade. How ironic, that the two people who did their utmost to hide themselves from the *ton* were now married to each other.

As she worked her way down her body with the sponge, she wondered what he would say when he discovered her secret. A part of her had felt guilt at not informing him of her deformity as soon as he'd proposed. He had a right to know that his wife was more crippled than he had guessed. And yet, now that her goal of escaping from her mother had been accomplished, she knew that she could not have risked his rejection.

No, she knew she'd done the right thing in not telling him. But as the moment when she would reveal her secret drew near, she could not help the shudder that ran through her at the thought of how angry he would be. She'd convinced him to buy a pig in a poke. And though she might think the ends had justified the means, that did not mean that she relished his anger. In the weeks she'd come to know him, one of the things she'd most appreciated about his personality was his innate sense of fairness. She could only hope that that quality would prevent him from abandoning her.

Leaning back in the tub, she lifted both her legs to rest the backs of her calves on the edge of the tub. Critically, she looked at her right foot, as ordinary and serviceable as anyone else's. Then she turned her gaze to the empty space where her left foot used to be. Leaning forward, she touched the rounded end of her calf. Once upon a time such a light touch would have brought excruciating pain, but she had worked to desensitize the skin there, to ensure that she'd be able to wear the wooden foot her mother had insisted upon.

"Does it still pain you?" Alec asked.

Juliet gave a little cry of surprise and brought her legs back into the tub with a splash.

"I . . . I didn't hear you come in, my lord." She was mortified that he'd learned of her secret this way. And that he'd seen her ugly stump before she'd been able to prepare him for the sight of it.

"I didn't mean for you to," was his calm response as he moved farther into the dressing room. "I was sitting down in the taproom wondering just how much time to give you when it occurred to me that you were likely up here worrying about how to reveal your secret to me."

Hugging her knees to her chest, Juliet could not respond. Of course he was right, but that did nothing to assuage her distress at having him learn the true extent of her injury in such a manner. Not to mention the fact that she was stark naked.

"I apologize for interrupting your bath, but you cannot stay in there forever," he said, sitting on the chair she'd used earlier to get into the bath.

"I wasn't planning to," she said, disliking the defensive tone in her voice.

The little dressing room seemed even smaller with him in it. Sneaking a look at him, she saw that he was in his shirtsleeves, and had removed his cravat and boots. His attire was so much an element of his personality; it was odd to see him thus, as if she were seeing a medieval knight without his armor.

"It's been over an hour," he said with a raised brow. "Too much longer and you'd be as wrinkled as Prinny's neck cloth after a debauch."

Juliet gazed down at her knees. The water had grown cold, and his nearness sent a shiver down her spine that had nothing to do with the temperature of the water.

"How much did you see?" she asked finally. She'd need to know before she could begin to explain just why she hadn't told him.

"Enough," was his maddening reply. What did that even mean? Enough that he knew he did not want to consummate the marriage? Enough to know he was disgusted by her? Though, a little voice in her head informed her, that look in his eyes was not one of disgust. Nor was it the other emotion she'd dreaded from him: pity.

"So," she said, not daring to look him in the eye just yet, "you know my secret now. I won't blame you if you wish to wait to consummate the marriage. It is reasonable for you to feel some diffidence now that you've seen the extent of my infirmity. I apologize for deceiving you, of course, but I could not stay with my parents. And . . ."

And she had wanted him. It was as simple as that.

She only hoped he would leave quickly so that she'd be able to weep in private.

"Juliet," he said firmly. "Juliet, look at me."

Gently, he took her chin in his hand and turned her so that she faced him.

"I already knew," Alec said, his blue eyes intense, so compelling she could not look away. "I've known since the first dance lesson."

Thirteen

$\mathcal{A}$lec fought to keep from gathering her up, dripping from the bath, and kissing her senseless. If only to prove to her that her injury had changed nothing between them.

He told the truth. He *had* known since the dance lesson. His great-aunt Augusta had walked on a peg leg, and once he actually began to watch the way that Juliet walked he'd seen the similarities in their gaits. It had explained much about her. Why she kept herself at such a distance from the rest of the *ton,* why she made such an effort to stay on the fringes of society. She, and more likely her mother, did not wish for anyone to know she suffered from a deformity more usually afflicting war heroes and factory workers. His great-aunt Augusta had certainly remained sequestered in the country after her own injury as a girl.

"There is no question of not consummating the marriage," he said firmly. "If we do not, then there is a chance that your mother will protest the marriage. And our flight to Gretna will have been in vain."

And I want you, he said silently, trying and failing not to notice the curve of her breasts as they pressed against her knees.

As if hearing a death sentence, Juliet nodded. "If you'll just give me a moment," she said, "I'll dry off and ready myself for bed."

"I've got a better idea," Alec said, leaning down and lifting her by the arms.

"What? What are you doing?" Juliet stammered, resisting his grasp. "I cannot simply stand up, my lord."

"Alec," he said with a frown, "and you aren't going to stand up."

Before she could protest further, he scooped her up beneath her knees and lifted her bodily from the tub. Water sloshed over the sides of the tub.

"But you're getting all wet," she said, brows furrowed, as he sat with her in the chair beside the tub.

Taking the towel the maid had left for her, he unfolded it and wrapped it around her dripping body.

"There," he said, gathering her against him once more and rising to carry her through the connecting door into the bedroom. "Better?"

She sighed. "Well, you're still wet." But he could tell she was no longer worried about the dampness of his clothing.

The fire burned brightly in the hearth, and the room was warm and cozy, but that did not compare to the heat Alec felt at the press of Juliet's curves against him.

"You worry too much," he said, leaning his forehead against hers as he stopped next to the bed and gently lowered her onto the cool white sheets.

Stepping back, he drank in the sight of her as she tried and failed to keep the towel tight around her body. When she scrambled to hide beneath the covers, he stopped her with a word.

"Don't," he said, surprised at the note of supplication in his voice. "I want to see you, Juliet. All of you."

At that, she frowned, but removed her foot, and the remnant of her right leg from beneath the sheet, then slowly unwrapped the towel and dropped it to the floor. Her chin lifted a fraction, as if she were daring him to reject her.

Her mother had much to answer for, Alec thought, lowering himself to sit on the bed beside her. Leaning forward, he gathered her upper body in his arms and covered her mouth with his. At first she resisted the intrusion, but after he gently nipped her lower lip between his teeth, she opened to him. Slowly, carefully, he stroked his tongue into her mouth, feeling her relax against him. He'd meant this to be a careful seduction, but as soon as Juliet began to return the kiss, to slide her tongue tentatively against his, he was lost.

The heat between them surprised him. He had known there was attraction between them of course. He would not have dared the marriage otherwise. But he'd underestimated the effect her untutored caress would have on him.

Her mouth was hot against his, and wet, the sensation sending a jolt through his body, all of the blood in his head rushing downward. Through the linen of his shirt, he felt her breasts harden against him. With a curse, he slipped a hand down to cup her, sliding his thumb over the pebbled peak of her nipple. Pulling back from her mouth, he slipped his mouth down, nipping her lower lip, and kissing down over her chin to her neck.

Juliet's hands clenched reflexively over his shoulders, as he moved his mouth over her skin. With a murmur of pleasure, she slipped her hands up into the hair at the nape of his neck.

"So sweet," he murmured against the soft skin of her shoulder, kissing a path toward the soft flesh he'd been kneading with his fingers. At the scrape of his teeth upon the sensitive skin of her nipple, she let out a moan and pulled him closer to her. "Easy," he whispered against her, soothing her with his voice. "Just feel me."

Moving his mouth to her other breast, he slid his right hand down over the soft skin of her belly and into the reddish curls at her center. She was still wet from the bath, but when he dipped his finger against her soft folds he found what he was looking for.

"You see?" he asked, sliding up her body, kissing his way back up to her ear even as he kept his hand between her thighs. "You're ready for me," he whispered, taking her ear between his teeth. "Your body is preparing for me to make you mine."

As he slid his index finger into her, Juliet arched into him. "Alec," she whispered.

"That's right," he said, adding another finger to the first, reveling in the way her body clenched against him. "Alec. I'm the one who is giving you this pleasure. I'm the one whose name will be on your lips again and again."

He stroked in and out, bringing another moan from her. "You're mine, Juliet," he told her, his voice hoarse with emotion as she raised her hips to meet his hand. "Mine. And I want you, Juliet," he said harshly, pressing harder and faster into her. "Never doubt it. I want all of you. Every inch of flesh, every luscious curve, every scar, every blemish. All of you is mine."

She worked her hips against him, and at his words, she went over the edge, crying out as she spasmed uncontrollably around his fingers.

Juliet was still recovering her breath in the aftermath of her release when she felt Alec slip back into the bed. She'd heard him hastily removing his clothes, but had been too overcome with weariness to watch. Next time, she told herself.

When she felt him kiss her, she opened her eyes to find him watching her.

"Thank you," she said, against his mouth.

"For what?"

"For not running as fast as you could back to London?" She smiled crookedly, though the sentiment was deadly serious. She'd known he wouldn't run, of course, but there were few men who would have reacted to the news that they'd married an aberration with equanimity.

His expression darkened. "There was never any question of me running," he told her, his blue eyes serious. "I told you before. I already knew before we were wed about your secret. And I have no regrets."

"Even so . . ." She looked away from his intense gaze. "You were kind to marry me despite the—"

He dipped his head so that she had no choice but to look into his eyes.

"For the last time, kindness had nothing to do with it. Did I want you removed from your parents' household? Absolutely. But I married you . . ."—he caressed her jaw— "because I wanted you. And if I have to prove that to you by fucking you senseless every day for the rest of our lives I will do it."

At the crudity, she blushed, but did not break his gaze. "How would that work, exactly?" she asked wryly. "Would we have a set time every day? Like the dinner hour, only we'd call it the f—"

He stopped her words with his mouth and, setting Juliet's senses afire, rolled on top of her.

"Nothing so regimented," he said, bracing his arms over her and sliding his body against hers so that she shuddered at the feeling of skin sliding upon skin. "We'll do it whenever we please. In every room of the house."

"Even the butler's pantry?" she asked, her breath short as she felt the press of his erection against her stomach.

"Especially," Alec said, widening her legs so that he could rest his hips between them, "especially the butler's pantry."

Juliet felt a bubble of laughter rise in her chest at the absurdity. Unable to keep it in, she laughed.

"Wench," Alec said with mock severity. "It is wretched bad form to giggle while I'm making love to you."

"I am sorry," she said even as she laughed. "I cannot help it. These whole few days have been so dreadful at times, but now, here with you, I'm just so h—"

She stopped, just in time to keep herself from blurting

out the truth. That being here with him, in the circle of his arms, made her . . .

"Happy?" he asked softly, against her ear. Juliet was grateful that he wasn't looking into her eyes. Because just as quickly as the laughter had come upon her, now she felt the odd urge to weep.

But her relief was short-lived. Nuzzling over her face, he kissed her on the end of her nose.

"Juliet," he said, curving a hand over her hip, "I want to make you happy. There's no shame in feeling it."

His face was serious now, deadly serious, as he guided himself to her center. She should have felt embarrassed, but she could not look away from him.

"This may hurt a bit," he said, pressing forward into her wetness.

"I don't care," she whispered, opening her legs wider and allowing him to move forward in the process. And it was true. She welcomed whatever feelings this man, her husband, could give her.

They were both silent as he pushed relentlessly forward, breaching the barrier of her virginity that had marked her as untouched.

It was not pain per se. She felt instead a sharp tug and a bit of a sting. Then it was simply the foreignness of being filled beyond her capacity. She did not feel the same kind of urgency as before when he'd worked her with his fingers, but if he could be persuaded to do that before actually joining with her every time, she would not be opposed to doing this once a day.

"Did I hurt you?" Alec asked, worry in his eyes, his voice strangely breathless.

"No," she responded, still trying to figure out how it felt to have him inside her.

"Thank God," he said, exhaling. "I'm sorry, but this is going to be much faster than I'd planned."

She was about to tell him it was no matter, but then he began to slide back out of her. "But I thought—"

Her words were stopped as he pressed back in again, which felt very much like the euphoria that had filled her earlier with his fingers, only . . . more.

In and out, he slid his body deeper and harder each time he came back into her, and Juliet closed her eyes and let the urgency overtake her.

God, Alec thought, thrusting into her, this was progressing much more quickly than he'd anticipated, but he'd underestimated his own response to the feel of her wet heat gripping his cock. He hadn't been this overwhelmed since he'd lost his virginity. Again and again he moved in her, reveling in the clasp of her body around him, each gasp she uttered making him grow harder.

"Sweet," he said against her neck, feeling the grip of her hands pulling him by the buttocks back against her. "All mine."

"Oh, yes," she breathed, tilting her hips so that he gained a precious inch more.

Unable to control himself, he moved faster. He was on fire for her. It was nothing like the careful, gentle seduction he'd planned for her. Juliet deserved every bit of control he could muster. And yet, from the first moment of skin upon skin he'd been lost against the primitive drive to mark her, to take her with his body so that no other man would mistake her for an available mate. God, he sounded like an animal, but he felt like one. As if to prove it to himself, he lightly bit her neck as he drove into her. She must not have minded, because Juliet gave a little cry and moved in an uncontrolled frenzy against him. Her sheath gripped him in pulse after pulse of release as she trembled with the orgasm overtaking her.

The exquisite pleasure of it was too much and Alec followed her over the precipice into his own release. Thrusting into her again and again, he finally gave a hoarse cry and spilled himself into her welcoming body and collapsed.

They lay like that for several minutes, gulping in breaths as they tried to recover themselves, neither able to form a coherent thought.

When Alec realized he was probably crushing her under his weight, he rolled over onto his back, disengaging himself from her. He flung an arm over his eyes to block the light from the windows.

"Perhaps we could have a twice-daily time for that," Juliet said finally, curling her body against his. He slipped his other arm around her, pulling her closer. "Just until I become proficient."

"That would take lots of practice," he said, smiling, "are you sure you're willing to devote that much time to it?"

"It's how I learned the pianoforte," she said. And from the shift of her body, he knew she'd remembered about Anna's disappearance.

He sighed, and took the hand that had been on his chest and kissed her knuckles.

"We'll find her," he said quietly. "Have no fear of that."

"I just know how it is to be alone. And afraid. I do not want that for her."

He kissed the top of her head, thinking of just how familiar she must be with feeling alone and afraid.

"Juliet," he said. "I need you to tell me how it happened." He didn't need to say just what he was speaking of. They both knew what he spoke of.

She stiffened against him, and for a moment he feared she might refuse. But finally, she pulled the sheet up around her, as if she needed a shield to speak about it. He wanted to protest, but knew better than most how essential one's armor was when going into battle.

As she had done in the bath, she pulled her knees to her

chest. With her hair tumbling down over her shoulders, the morning sun lending it a reddish-gold glow, she had the look of a fallen angel, or Eve suddenly wary of her nakedness.

Hating the distance she'd put between them, but knowing it was what she needed to tell her story, Alec loosened his grip, giving her the freedom to pull away if she wished. To his relief, she stayed.

Staring out into the room, she began to tell her story.

Fourteen

*W*hen Napoleon was defeated for the first time in '14," Juliet began, thinking back to that late summer four years ago when her life had changed forever, "Papa was dispatched from India to Vienna to assist in the negotiations for the peace. Mama and I had been in England, rusticating as she termed it, but as soon as she heard that there was to be a gathering in Vienna she began making preparations. I believe she was just as pleased with Napoleon's defeat for her own reasons as she was for the sake of peace."

She remembered the energy her mother had expended preparing them for the trip, the gowns she'd ordered, the boxes and boxes of belongings she'd had put into the traveling carriages to go with them on the ship from Dover.

"I was not so eager to travel to the Continent as she was," she said with a wry smile. "She had insisted I remain in the schoolroom until my debut the next year, but for Vienna, she was willing to make an exception. I think she had some mad dream that I'd meet a German prince and become the queen of some small nation where she could rule through me."

"But you did not wish to go." It was more statement than question.

"Not at all," she agreed. "I wanted to stay in the country and continue my lessons. And when autumn came, I had plans to travel to London and teach pianoforte at the Salon for the Edification of Ladies that Madeline and Cecily were forming."

"But that seems a bit too . . . ladylike for your salon," Alec interrupted. "Isn't that something that most ladies learn before their come-out?"

"You have forgotten that I write my own compositions, as well as play," Juliet reminded him.

It was to be expected that young ladies preparing for their debut would receive a modicum of training in various ladylike arts: needlework, watercolors, and if she had the aptitude, voice and the pianoforte. But composition was, as yet, a man's purview.

"Ah, yes," he said with a grin. "I *had* forgotten. What a multitalented lady I have married."

Though Juliet had hoped to divert his attention to some other subject, he was not to be so easily led. "Vienna," he prompted, steering her back to her original story.

"Well, I was not interested in going to Vienna, but Mama insisted, and by the time we arrived the congress was in full whirl. Because many of the diplomats had brought their families with them there were any number of entertainments. Only these were headier somehow. As if we knew even then that more war was on the horizon."

She thought back to those first few weeks of testing the social waters. Of her mother introducing her to every unattached member of the Continental nobility she could scrounge up. She was not allowed to dance of course since she wasn't officially "out," but that did not prevent her from taking turns around the room on the arms of the young gentlemen who were seeking frivolity after the seriousness of their days in negotiations.

"We'd been there a few weeks," Juliet went on, "when I had had enough. Mama was particularly insistent upon my paying more attention to an aging archduke. He was nearly my father's age, and he smelled of patchouli. Of course I tried to tell her that I had no interest in the man, but as she often is when she's got the bit between her teeth, she was having none of my protests. Indeed, she used the same sort of strategy with Archduke von Weber as she did with Turlington. If Mama cannot get someone to assent of their own free will she maneuvers them into a corner from which there is no escape."

Alec squeezed her hand, and Juliet was glad again to have escaped her mother's plans this time.

"I told no one my plans, of course," she said. "But I packed a valise and waited for the household to settle. Finally, when I was sure no one would catch me, I slipped out and made my way through the streets of Vienna. Since Napoleon had been vanquished, people were eager to travel across Europe once more, so I had no doubt I'd find someone willing to transport me to the coast. I had saved my pin money for months, and was willing to pay whatever it took."

She remembered the mix of fear and excitement that had rushed through her as she made her way to the nearest coaching inn. She'd always been cautioned by her parents not to wander the streets of whichever country they happened to reside in. As an English young lady she would seem particularly vulnerable to anyone wishing to harm her. But there was no help for it. She had needed to get out of Vienna before her mother forced her into a match that would make the rest of her life a misery.

"I was nearing the coaching inn where I'd hoped to find transport when I stopped to let a man pass," she said. "He was limping badly and as he got by me, he instinctively reached out for support. Only it took me off guard and I was pushed into the path of an oncoming carriage."

Alec swore.

"I was able to swing my upper body away and protect my head, but my right foot was trampled by the horses," she said, her voice sounding far away to her own ears, as if someone else were telling the story. "I didn't know it at the time, but Mama had suspected I'd try to run so she'd sent one of the servants, a man who has been with our family since Papa's first journey to India. I had been pulled from the street by a group of men who had been loitering outside the inn when I heard Mr. Sankoori ordering one of them to return to our house and inform my parents. The pain was—"

She stopped, swallowing at the memory of pain so excruciating it had made her swoon.

Wordlessly, Alec pulled her against his chest. Needing the support of his body, she did not protest. Somehow the comforting circle of his arms made the telling of the tale less horrific than it had been in the past.

"Mr. Sankoori had them get a litter, and the men who had seen me fall lifted me onto it and moved me to the inn. By the time Mama and Papa arrived I had been given laudanum to dull the pain. Though I could still feel it, it seemed farther away somehow. As if it were happening to someone else."

"Your parents must have been frantic," Alec said.

"Oh, they were appalled. Not only by what had happened to me, but also because I think they wondered how it would affect them. Would what had happened to an English citizen on the streets of Vienna affect the negotiations? At least that's what I imagined Papa considered. Mama was simply crushed that her dreams of running a German principality were shattered."

She felt Alec's grip tighten, but he remained silent. "When the physician came and announced that my foot would need to be removed, I think you could have heard Mama's screams all the way back in London. As I learned later she was given a strong sleeping agent. And as Papa needed to go make arrangements to control just what bits of the tale he wished to have told to the public, he left. I was there with my maid, Weston, and Mr. Sankoori.

"The doctor was the personal physician of the Duke of Richmond, who was in Vienna for the talks. And as Papa had lined his pockets with enough gilt to ensure his silence and his best work, he made sure that the removal itself was as comfortable as it could be."

Odd how she felt the need to describe the amputation in a way that lessened the horror of it. Perhaps because she sensed that Alec would suffer for her if she told just how awful it had been. What she could remember of it, that is. She had fainted not long after the procedure began.

"When it was finished, the problem became blood loss. I have since learned more about the way physicians often perform such surgeries, and it's appalling how many people die from the removal alone. I was fortunate to have an experienced surgeon to treat me. But even he was powerless to stop the bleeding of my wound."

"Thank God you were in Vienna and not in some battlefield hospital," Alec murmured against her hair. "Though I do not think I will ever be able to forgive your parents for leaving you to suffer through it alone."

His ire on her behalf warmed her. "I had Mr. Sankoori. He has been closer to me in his way than my parents have been. He has been with my family since my father's first trip to India.

"Indeed," she continued, "it was Mr. Sankoori who saved my life."

"If he hadn't been trailing you, there's no telling what might have happened to you," Alec agreed.

"No," she corrected him, "I mean he is the one who suggested the treatment that finally stemmed my blood loss. Without Mr. Sankoori, I would have died there in Vienna."

"What did he suggest that a trained physician could not?" Alec asked, his tone puzzled.

This was the part of her treatment that Juliet had been dreading telling him about. It wasn't so much that it had been awful, though it had been. It wasn't even that it was something that was not widely practiced in England. It was the very sound of it, which made everyone who heard the tale recoil in horror.

"He had them cauterize the wound," she said carefully.

Then, as if he did not know just what that meant, she added, "With hot iron."

It was a credit to Alec's self-restraint that he did not reveal through his expression just how disturbing it was to imagine Juliet undergoing the cauterization process. He had spoken to several men from his estate who had lost limbs in the campaign against Napoleon and they had been tight-lipped about what they'd undergone to heal their wounds. And these were large strapping men, used to hardship. The image of Juliet going through those same trials made him want to strike out at something. Instead, he simply held her and let her tell her tale.

"Dr. Jones was loath to perform the same sort of procedures on me that he employed on the battlefield," she said, echoing Alec's thoughts. "Though I suppose amputation was something he judged could not be helped."

"And this Sankoori was the one who insisted on cautery?"

"Yes," she said, her voice matter-of-fact, as if she were not speaking of the day that had changed her life forever. "Dr. Jones was unused to caring for women, and ladies in particular. He had some chivalrous notion that there were some procedures that were simply not appropriate for the fairer sex. Mr. Sankoori convinced him that if I died from blood loss there would be much more for the fine doctor to worry about when he was without a position and left alone with his scruples."

"Where were your parents while this was going on?" Alec demanded, though he had a fair idea of what her response would be. Lord and Lady Shelby had never struck him as overly concerned about their daughter's welfare. Lady Shelby's plot to marry Juliet off to Turlington was proof enough of that. And Lord Shelby had doubtless been busy with some diplomatic business that ranked higher in his cares than an injured daughter.

"Well, as I told you before, Mama was given a sleeping agent, and she remained insensible during my stay at the inn," Juliet said. "After he ensured that word of my injury hadn't spread to the rest of the congress, Papa returned to his duties with the diplomatic corps. At least that is what I understand happened. I was in no condition to know, of course."

The wistful note in her voice made Alec's gut clench. He knew what it was to long for a parent's approval. How bittersweet it could be to have them take notice of you and then withdraw that notice soon after.

"With neither of my parents there, it was Mr. Sankoori who insisted upon cauterizing the wound. By that point I was insensible. So you mustn't imagine I harbor nightmarish scenes of unspeakable pain in my memory. I do remember some of that wretched scene, but it's in fits and starts. Mostly I recall the feel of my father's hand in mine."

He could tell from her insistently upbeat tone that she did remember more than she let on, but he let her have her polite fiction. He wasn't sure he'd be all that willing to reveal his thoughts during such an ordeal either.

"And then it was done," she continued. "We stayed on in Vienna for many months while I healed. Papa put it about that I'd been injured in a riding accident and insisted that I needed my rest to keep the more intrusive gossips away. And then Napoleon escaped from Elba and Waterloo happened. The city was in chaos, but I was focused on my own recovery at the time. And then Mama found Herr Bock, who fashioned a false foot for me. And a deception was born."

"Did you not have visitors during your time in Vienna? Someone who knew your secret?"

"Mama was quite insistent that no one know the full extent of my injuries," Juliet said. "Then by the time I had recovered enough to contemplate visitors, war had broken out again. It was perfect timing for Mama's scheme. At the time I remember thinking that even warfare suited itself to her wishes rather than the other way around. Then, of course, the casualties began pouring into the city and there was no need to hide."

"So you returned to London with a limp and a deception," Alec said, marveling at just how successful his mother-in-law's plot had been. Even the royal family had been less successful at keeping King George's madness under wraps.

"Yes," Juliet ceded. Seeming to suddenly remember her nakedness, she pulled away from him. "I hope you are not . . ." she began, not meeting his gaze. "I hope you are not terribly disappointed with my infirmity," she said quickly, as if by saying the words quickly they would negate the necessity of a response.

Unable to take another minute of her apologies, he wordlessly pulled the sheet from her body and flipped her beneath him.

"No more apologies about this," he said against her neck, his hand resting proprietarily on her hip. "I told you before that I already knew about your amputation. I married you because I wished to do so."

She was not distracted enough, however. "But . . ." she began to say. Alec stopped her words with his mouth, and the intrusion of his very intrigued cock into her moist heat.

"This," he said, thrusting against her, "this is how much I am bothered by your deception."

Her sharp intake of breath as he came into her robbed her of the ability to argue further. But even as he set out to distract her from her fears by making thorough love to her, Alec knew that he'd not heard the last of Juliet's apologies on the matter.

Lady Shelby, he thought, had much to answer for.

Fifteen

They left early the next morning, and as is often the case, the journey back seemed to pass more quickly. Perhaps because Juliet felt easier in Alec's company. Marital intimacies had a way of dissolving some of the awkwardness that had dogged their interactions before the wedding night. Or day, as it were.

Seated next to her husband, tucked into the curve of his arm as the carriage swayed, Juliet marveled anew at just how understanding he'd been about her fatal flaw. She wasn't sure what she'd expected, of course. She had no experience in revealing the extent of her injury to bedfellows, after all. And her mama had seen to it that no one outside the tiny circle of herself, Mr. Sankoori, Mr. Bock, and Juliet's maid Weston knew of it. Even her cousins had been kept in the dark, only being informed that the injury was a permanent one, just not what the injury had entailed.

Though Juliet had little doubt that the news would shock most of the *ton,* she also suspected that her mother's insistence that anyone who knew of it would hold Juliet in contempt was an exaggeration. Certainly her insinuation that no one would wish to marry her as she was had proved false. She still wasn't sure what had persuaded Alec to rescue her from Turlington's clutches, but she was grateful to him. Even more so because instead of being angry with her for her deception, he'd focused his wrath instead on Lady Shelby.

His tenderness of the day before, coupled with his lack of disgust upon learning her secret, had endeared him to Juliet in a way that she had seldom felt for another person, let alone a man. If she were not careful, she'd find herself losing her heart to her own husband. Though on a certain level, she knew gratitude to him simply for accepting her, flaws and all, was understandable, Juliet was also aware that allowing herself to fall too much under her husband's spell would be a recipe for disaster. They had both entered into this marriage without any illusions about it being a love match, after all. And she sensed that asking Alec for more than he was willing to give would place him in an untenable position. It had only been a few weeks ago that he'd seemed uninterested in marriage at all. Not that she was worried he would be unfaithful to her. He'd promised her his fidelity, and though many gentlemen of the *ton* made such promises with no intention of keeping them, Juliet knew that for Alec his word was his bond. No matter how he might be tempted, she knew instinctively that he would not betray her trust.

"What's amiss?" the object of her speculation asked, frowning down at her.

She shook her head to clear it. She was being missish in the extreme.

"I was just wondering about Mrs. Turner," she said, regretting the lie, but knowing that to reveal her true thoughts would be begging a discussion she simply was not ready to have. "Do you suppose she's been in touch with Mr. MacEwan at all? I almost daren't hope for it, given how disappointing each setback has been thus far in our search for her."

"I have no idea," Alec said thoughtfully. "It did seem to me from what her landlady said that he was much in your friend's company. And if they were engaged to marry I cannot think that she would go so long without contacting him."

"That is what I thought about myself, though," Juliet said glumly. "I thought we were close enough for her to trust me with such news. Though I suppose there were quite a few things she didn't trust me with. Alice's parentage, her engagement, her need for funds."

"I have no doubt that she trusts you," Alec said firmly. "But sometimes circumstances make it difficult to tell those we love the truth."

"That is certainly something I am familiar with," she said wryly. "The only people we informed about my injury were those who absolutely had to know. I did not like prevaricating, but circumstances made it imperative. Or so I thought."

"From what we've learned so far," Alec said, "it seems very likely that Mrs. Turner is in a very difficult position. And has been for some time. If she is indeed your friend, I think it's quite likely that she felt she had no choice but to hide the truth regarding any number of things from you."

"I fear you are correct." Juliet sighed. "I do so hate to think of Anna so isolated and alone. I hope that she was able to take Mr. MacEwan at least into her confidence. I think the most disturbing aspect of this entire business has been the fact that we've found no one whom she felt safe enough to confide in."

A shout from the outriders indicated that they'd entered the grounds of the Mounthaven estate, and within the hour Juliet and Alec were waiting in the Earl of Mounthaven's best parlor for his personal secretary, Mr. Alistair MacEwan. The earl himself was out of the country at the moment, and the house was quiet in its master's absence.

They were joined presently by a ginger-haired young man of sensible dress, who seemed puzzled by their visit.

"My lord," he greeted them, "my lady, is there something I can assist you with?"

"I believe you will not know of me by my married name,

Mr. MacEwan," Juliet said, disliking to ruin his calm, but knowing there was no help for it. "I am the former Miss Shelby."

His quizzical expression turned into one of genuine pleasure. "Miss Shelby! Or rather, Lady Deveril, it is a delight to finally make your acquaintance. Mrs. Turner has nothing but good things to say of you!"

"It is on Mrs. Turner's behalf that we are here," Alec informed him baldly. "I don't suppose you've heard that your friend has been missing for the past several weeks?"

The shock on the young man's face told them everything they needed to know.

"I . . ." MacEwan's agitation was evident. "What happened?"

"We are unsure," Juliet told him. "I received a note from her informing me that she was leaving town for a bit, but she didn't say why. When Lord Deveril visited her apartments the next day upon my behest it was apparent that she had left in a hurry."

"And the child?" Mrs. Turner's fiancé asked. "Is she gone too?"

"No, and that is what troubles me," she said. "Little Alice is being cared for at our house until we learn what's happened to Anna."

"What we need to know from you," Alec said briskly, "is do you have any notion of where she might be, or whether there might be some reason to suspect foul play?"

MacEwan shook his head in disbelief.

"I beg your pardon, but I must sit down," he said, collapsing into a wingback chair.

Juliet waved his apology aside. "Have you heard from her, Mr. MacEwan? Anything at all?"

"Just a brief note last week, telling me that she was quite busy and would be unable to write again for a few weeks." He paused. "But wait, I thought you said she's been missing for several weeks."

"Then how could she have written you only last week?" Juliet asked aloud.

"That's just it," MacEwan said, "I've heard from her several times over the past few weeks. There was no mention of being unable to write to me until last week."

"Some of this we can attribute to the slowness of the mail, but if you have letters from Mrs. Turner dating back several weeks, then I think we have proof that she is alive and well somewhere."

MacEwan's eyes widened, as if he'd realized for the first time just how serious the situation was.

"I can't believe it," he said. "After what that bastard did to her before, I thought she was finally through with hardship. I am planning to return home to my brother's estate at the end of the year to become steward for him. We were going to be married then."

"Do not give up hope, Mr. MacEwan," Juliet said firmly.

"I'm not. Anna is as strong a woman as I've ever met. Whatever has happened to her, she will come through it."

"Might we see these letters you've received from her recently, MacEwan?" Alec interjected. "There might be some clue in them that will give us an idea as to where she's being held. Or who is holding her."

MacEwan nodded, and excused himself to search out the letters.

"This is wretched," Juliet said once the man had gone. "How on earth will I ever face that man again if we don't find her?"

Alec squeezed her shoulder. "It is not your doing," he assured her, "any of it. If you hadn't insisted that we begin looking for her, I doubt anyone would even know Mrs. Turner was missing at all. You cannot berate yourself for being unable to work miracles."

"I just feel so helpless," Juliet said, appreciating his support in more ways than she could say. "When the issue is something to do with me, like my injury or my troubles with Mama, at least I have some measure of control. With this, I have no way of controlling any of it."

He was about to respond, when MacEwan returned bearing the letters.

"There are only three," he said, handing them to Juliet. "And I've checked the handwriting and it is definitely Anna's."

With Alec reading over her shoulder, Juliet scanned the missives, which chronicled fictitious anecdotes about the baby, Anna's students, and various other daily minutiae. In truth, they were rather dull as love letters went, though there were heartfelt farewells at the end of each. In fact, it was the conclusions that had Juliet frowning.

"Please know that no matter what happens, no matter what separates us, I will always love you."

"Does she always end her letters with such declarations?" Juliet asked, disliking to embarrass the man, but needing to know his answer.

"We both . . . that is to say," MacEwan stammered.

"I do not ask because I don't believe them, Mr. MacEwan," Juliet told him, gently. "I ask because it sounds very much like something she would say if she feared never seeing you again."

MacEwan blanched. "Not as such," he said. "We do speak of our affection, of course, but this is more . . . dramatic than she is normally wont to write."

Juliet exchanged a look with Alec, who said, "What's this here about an artist wishing to paint her portrait?"

Anna had mentioned it in all three of the letters. In the first, she'd spoken of how flattered she'd been by the artist's request, and how much she regretted having to deny him. Then in the second, she'd spoken of how she admired the man's work, which she'd seen in the National Gallery hanging "among England's finest artists."

But it was the mention in the third letter that made Juliet's heart clench with fear.

"I regret not agreeing to the request by this fine and gifted artist to allow him to capture my likeness on canvas. What a satisfaction to know that I might serve to warn other women away from the same mistakes I've made."

"Did this not strike you as odd?" Alec asked the other man.

The secretary thrust a hand through his now thoroughly disheveled hair. "She is always teasing me about my having taken up with a fallen woman. She knows I don't blame her for what that bastard did to her. How could I? I think the joking is her way of dealing with society's condemnation."

Since he did not appear to know about Anna's earlier encounter with Squire Ramsey's son, Juliet did not tell Mr. MacEwan of it. But given the fact that she'd been victimized not once but twice by men she trusted, Anna's references to herself as a fallen woman were even more disturbing. "She has always had a dark sense of humor," she said aloud. "I doubt anyone who has endured what she has could emerge without a healthy sense of the absurd."

"But about this artist," Alec interjected. "Who is he? And why has Mrs. Turner mentioned the fellow in only the letters she's written since she went missing? If I were to hazard a guess, this artist sounds suspiciously like *Il Maestro*."

Juliet bit back a gasp. The idea that Anna was being pursued by *Il Maestro* was at once believable and disturbing. Though she had never considered Anna to be a fallen woman, or the like, the more she learned about her friend the more she wondered if her friend thought of herself in those terms. Accepting the offer to pose for the artist who had made a name for himself by painting history's most notorious fallen women might be empowering for someone like Anna. But it also might be a means of punishing herself in the most public manner possible. The notion sent a chill of fear through Juliet. A chill that no amount of hot tea could warm.

"Anna told me she'd been approached in the park by a

man claiming to be an artist," MacEwan said. "She never told me his name, but she said that he wished to paint her portrait as part of his next exhibit. But when she told him no, he kept coming back and pestering her to agree. I never heard what came of it, though. I assumed she'd gotten rid of him because the next mention of him was in the letter where she regrets sending him away."

"Did you believe her?" Juliet asked.

MacEwan shrugged. "I have three sisters and I know how apt to change their minds ladies can be," he said. "I assumed she'd thought more about it and decided she'd made a mistake. So, yes, I suppose I did believe her."

"Whether she decided to pose for *Il Maestro* or not," Alec said gravely, "I believe this mysterious artist might be the last person to have seen Mrs. Turner before she disappeared."

Their journey back to London was overshadowed by Juliet's increased fears regarding Anna's whereabouts. Her disappearance had been troubling, of course, but behind the worry there had always been a hope, however false, that she had simply taken a trip to see some relative or friend who was heretofore unknown to them. But the interview with Mr. MacEwan, and his revelation about the mysterious artist, had made that scenario seem more and more unlikely.

They arrived at the Deveril town house in the falling London twilight. And with a prescience known only to superior servants, Alec's butler, Mr. Hamilton, had the entire household staff assembled almost as soon as his master assisted his new bride from the carriage.

Though she had known her position as Alec's wife would involve any number of such formalities, Juliet couldn't help the knot of anxiety forming in her belly as she took in the assembled men and women to whom she would serve as mistress for the duration of her marriage.

Her sentiments must have communicated themselves to Alec, because he leaned down and said softly, "We don't have to do this now, if you don't wish to. They will all still be here in the morning."

But Juliet knew from her years of traveling from post to post with her parents that it was best to establish oneself with the servants from the beginning. If only to ensure that they respected her as their new mistress. Her pride also prompted her to do whatever she could to counterbalance any weakness her physical infirmity might convey to them. Though her will was strong enough, she had found that many assumed her to be a shrinking violet simply by dint of her limp.

So she gave her new husband a brief shake of the head, and allowed Mr. Hamilton to introduce her to the men and women standing before her. She made sure to repeat each one's name, and to commit to memory some little detail that would help her remember each of them tomorrow.

As she moved closer toward the end of the line, Juliet noticed Alec's sisters, waiting for them just inside the entryway.

"I am so pleased you're home," the shorter of the two, Katherine, an ash blonde with her brother's blue eyes, said. "Congratulations to both of you. And welcome home, Juliet."

And before she knew what to say, Juliet was clasped in an impulsive hug.

"You might give her a moment to catch her breath, Kat," Lydia said wryly. "Apologies for my sister, Juliet, but she has the manners of a barn cat."

Looking from one to the other of her new sisters-in-law, Juliet found herself surprised but pleased by their warm welcome. They'd known one another for some years since they were both out and active in the social whirl. But even so, they might not have been best happy at their brother's marriage.

They were at once recognizable as Deveril's sisters. Not only did they share their brother's eye color, but there was something about the underlying bone structure of their countenances that just seemed . . . Deverilish. Though neither was as pretty as their brother might be called handsome, they were each attractive in their ways. And there was an animation about their mannerisms that gave Juliet the impression of barely restrained energy. She had little doubt that their brother had been led on a merry dance once he'd assumed their guardianship.

"Neither of you is particularly well mannered, Lydia," their brother said with an affectionate grin. "Though it isn't as if I haven't spent good money to see it drummed into your featherbrained heads."

"Fie on both of you," Kat responded with a decidedly unladylike snort. "I have been waiting this age to welcome Juliet into the family and there is nothing either of you can do to dampen my enthusiasm."

"It is Lady Deveril now, kitten," her brother returned, "and no one is trying to dampen your enthusiasm. We are simply urging you to restrain yourself a bit. You'll scare her off, if you aren't careful."

Juliet took in their familiar banter with interest. Her own relationship with her brother was nowhere near as easy as Alec's with his sisters seemed to be. And since she'd been dreading this meeting given the haste with which she and Alec had been married, she found the scene to be reassuring.

"Do not scold them on my account, Alec," she said, holding out her hands to each of her new sisters. "I am grateful that they aren't scandalized beyond repair at our elopement. In fact, I find their enthusiasm refreshing."

She felt him wrap a reassuring arm about her waist as he said wryly, "You say they are refreshing now, but you've not been faced with it across the breakfast table before you've had your morning tea."

"Don't listen to him, Lady Deveril," Lydia told her with a grin. "He only teases us so because he is jealous that we command more attention than he does these days. There was a time when our brother was quite the talk of the town."

"But no more," Kat added lightly. "He is become an old sobersides in his dotage."

"I suppose I'd best hire some footmen to carry me about in a sedan chair, and begin taking the cure for my gout," Alec returned with a mock sigh. "Do you see what abuse I am forced to take from them, my dear?"

Juliet colored at the endearment though it was innocent enough. "I hope you will both leave off calling me Lady Deveril and continue calling me Juliet. We are still friends, after all."

"Of course," said Kat warmly, squeezing her hand.

"We are truly pleased to welcome you to our home," Lydia said, her eyes crinkling at the corners in just the same manner that her brother's did. "Already I can see that you've managed to lighten Alec's mood. He's been so serious since our father—"

But Alec broke in before she could complete her thought. "Warm though your welcome has been, it was a long trip home from Gretna and I for one am exhausted."

"Of course!" Katherine said with a guilty start. "We hadn't meant to keep you here chattering in the entryway! I am so sorry, Juliet. What beasts you must think us!"

"I'll have cook send something up for you both at once. We have already dined, and we have that . . ."—Lydia paused as if searching for a word—"that thing that we were doing. Don't we, Kat?"

"Huh?" Katherine asked, looking askance at her sister. "What thing? What are you . . . ?"

Juliet saw Lydia's elbow make contact with her sister's ribs. "The *thing* . . ." she said meaningfully.

Catching the slight nod in Alec and Juliet's direction, realization dawned on Kat's face. "Oh!" she exclaimed. "The *thing*! Of course, how could I have forgotten it?"

Both sisters grinned at their brother and his new bride.

"We'll just leave you to it then," Alec said with a slight roll of his eyes. "I'll show you to your rooms, my dear."

As she allowed him to lead her toward the staircase, Juliet heard giggles behind them. "I believe they haven't got a thing to do at all," she said with a shake of her head.

"Of course they haven't," her husband replied, with a laugh. "That was their oh-so-subtle way of excusing themselves so that we might be alone together."

"Because we are newly wed?" Juliet asked, with a frown. "Or because we are just returned from a long trip?"

"Both, I would imagine," he replied thoughtfully. "Since they are not long out of the schoolroom, I don't suppose they know exactly what married couples *do* with one another. At least I certainly hope they don't."

"I don't know," Juliet said with a grin. "Cecily and Madeline and I had some very informative discussions about it. Maddie even found a book that—" She broke off. "Well, let us just say that it cleared up some misunderstandings we'd had."

"About what?" Alec asked, as they reached the second landing, his gaze fascinated.

Juliet felt herself turning red, and refused to meet his eyes. "I'd rather not say."

"Oh, that is no fair at all," Alec said, pulling her along toward what she supposed were the master and mistress's rooms. "You can't tease me like that and then refuse to tell the whole story."

Juliet looked one way, then the other, to make sure they wouldn't be overheard. "If you must know, I was not convinced that the . . . er . . . male part could grow to such a prodigious size."

"Prodigious, eh? So this book convinced you of it?"

"Well, no, it was only after Cecily and Winterson married that we had confirmation."

Alec bit back a howl of laughter. "Does Winterson know Cecily told you two about the size of his . . . part?"

Juliet gasped. "Dear Lord, I hope not! I don't think I'd ever be able to be in the same room with him again!"

She shook her head in horror at the thought, then continued, following her new husband into the sitting room adjoining their bedchambers. "And of course I had my own confirmation of it on our wedding day."

Shutting the door firmly behind them, Alec pulled her against him and nuzzled her ear. "Did you indeed?" he asked, his voice still tinged with amusement. "And was it as *prodigious* as you expected?"

Juliet closed her eyes as he tugged on her earlobe with his teeth. "Oh, yes," she said on a sigh. "Very impressive, indeed."

"Dashed right," Alec murmured against her neck just before he reached down and lifted her into his arms.

She gave a startled laugh. "What are you doing, you madman?"

"I am carrying my bride to bed," he said firmly.

"It's the middle of the afternoon!" she protested, bending her knees so that they could make it through the door into his bedchamber.

"I thought we'd settled that in Gretna. It's perfectly normal for married people to engage in—"

He stopped upon seeing his valet in his room, engaged in unpacking his traveling things.

One look from Deveril was enough to make the man drop the task at hand and leave with a murmured apology.

"Deveril, you frightened the poor man to death," Juliet protested, blushing.

"I am sure Thompson will recover," her husband said,

depositing her upon his very large bed. "Now, where were we?"

Juliet had no trouble at all reminding him where they'd left off. She'd always been a quick study.

The next morning, after a long visit with Baby Alice—who seemed perfectly content in the Deveril nurseries—Juliet had the carriage brought round so that she might visit Herr Bock's establishment in Bloomsbury. She had waited until Alec left for his club to do so because though she had told him her secret, she still was reluctant to discuss the day-to-day aspects of life as an amputee. Perhaps it was silly for her to be so circumspect considering the intimacies she'd allowed him, but she had no wish to see him turn from passionate lover to pitying husband. In fact, she could think of nothing she feared more.

The trip to Herr Bock's was necessitated by her elevated status. She had no wish to shame Alec by appearing in public as his viscountess in anything less than her most fashionable ensembles. And that meant she would need new slippers as well as new gowns. The shoes she'd worn during her days attempting to blend into the background would simply not do.

Like many Harley Street physicians, Herr Bock saw patients in a small office attached to his home. Though he would never presume to make the comparison himself, he also was just as professional and meticulous as a physician, always ensuring that his patients were well cared for.

"Good morning, miss," Mr. Stephens, Bock's assistant greeted her, taking her coat and hat. "Mr. Bock is waiting for you."

From the moment he'd arrived in England three years ago with Lord Shelby's other staff, the craftsman had insisted on taking on the customs and mannerisms of his new home.

And when barely a year into his time there, he'd insisted upon setting up an establishment for himself. "For it seems to me, Miss Shelby," he'd said, "that there are others here who might need my help learning to walk again."

And though Lady Shelby had been livid, her husband had reminded her that the man was hardly an indentured servant and was free to come and go as he wished. Even in the face of a promise to increase his fees exponentially, Bock had stood firm. A few weeks later he'd found this little house in Bloomsbury and to Juliet's delight had set about bringing his skill to those who needed it.

"Miss Shelby," the burly German said, opening his arms wide as he welcomed her into his examining room. "How good it is to see you. You are having no trouble with the leg, I hope?"

Basking in the friendship she'd shared with this man who had saved her from life at the margins of society, where she would be kept completely out of sight, Juliet took his outstretched hands. "No," she assured him. "No trouble at all. Indeed I am here because of a happy occasion. I've married."

"Married! But you are not old enough for such a thing, surely?"

"I certainly am," Juliet said with a grin. "And I am no longer Miss Shelby but the Viscountess Deveril."

If he was surprised to learn she'd married so well, Herr Bock did not show it. He simply took her in a bear hug and wished her happy.

"Now," he said when they'd chatted a bit about her new circumstances, "you did not come here to tell me your news. Let me guess. You have need of the new slippers and shoes, yes?"

Though most amputees made do with a single prosthesis onto which they fitted shoes themselves, in order to keep her infirmity a secret, Juliet's mother had insisted from the start that Herr Bock make her as many legs as she had slippers. Which Juliet and Herr Bock had sensibly decided to limit to four. One with a half-boot, one with a dancing slipper, one with a riding boot, and one with a sturdy walking boot. Because it was nearly impossible to keep a shoe on her prosthetic foot without some sort of lacing or adhesive, Juliet would send the left shoe to Herr Bock and he would affix the shoe with glue. This allowed him to adjust the balance of the socket, which fitted around her calf, so that if there were a hill Juliet would not be pitched forward or backward by the change in angle.

When they had discussed her need for two more legs to go with her newer gowns, Herr Bock left the room so that Juliet might change into the short breeches she wore only to these fittings. Since even physicians thought it unseemly to see their female patients unclothed, it was highly irregular for Herr Bock to see Juliet in such attire, but she had long since become desensitized to their interactions. It was simply a necessary part of her life now, and she'd long ago become inured to the multiple ways in which someone with her particular injury had to give up any pretense of modesty. And besides that, her maid, Weston, was with her, so there was no real danger.

Quickly, she let Weston help her remove her gown and donned the short breeches and the shirtwaist that she wore on such occasions. Her legs were bare, and taking a seat on the stiff-backed chair put there for her use, she began to unlace the tightly tied corset that wrapped around her calf.

When she'd first seen the contraption four years ago, when Herr Bock had persuaded one of his other patients to demonstrate how it worked, Juliet had been astonished. It had only been a few months since the accident that had taken her leg mid-calf, and she was deep in the depression that the trauma had left in its wake. It had been her mother's insistence, one of the only times in Juliet's life when her mother had acted in a manner that met both their interests, that had brought Herr Bock to them. Lord Shelby had been posted to the conference of Vienna, and Herr Bock had come highly recommended by the war office. And watching that young woman, who had lost her leg in a carriage accident, walk about the room on her wooden prosthesis, Juliet had thought for the first time since her own accident that there might be some hope for her yet, and she had been grateful for once for her mother's domineering nature. Only later that evening had she realized that Lady Shelby's plan had been less about seeing that Juliet could lead a normal life than ensuring that Lady Shelby would not be embarrassed for the rest of society to know she had a crippled daughter. Still, motives aside, her mother's shame had brought Juliet into contact with Herr Bock, and that at least was something to celebrate.

The leg itself was simple enough. To put it on, Juliet would don the mechanism like a stocking, placing the stump of her calf through the unlaced corset, and down to rest on top of the wooden lower leg and foot, which had been padded for her comfort.

When Herr Bock returned, he knelt before her and examined her residual limb, ensuring that there were no skin abrasions or irritations that would indicate the prosthesis was not fitting properly. Then he asked Juliet to don the prosthesis, and when that was done, he directed her to the parallel bars in the next room, where he could watch her gait. Back and forth she walked as he instructed her to speed up, slow down, and try kneeling. She'd just reached the end of the bars when the toe of her false foot caught on the edge of the bar and she pitched forward.

Sixteen

When he'd finished his meeting with his man of business, where he made provisions for Juliet in the event that something should happen to him, Alec had asked his coachman to take him to White's so that he could seek out Winterson for advice on the matter of Mrs. Turner and *Il Maestro*.

As his carriage drove through the city, he spied a familiar-looking figure descending from a hack and hurrying up the steps, walking stick in hand, of an unremarkable row house. Who the devil was she going to meet in this part of town? he wondered, rapping on the ceiling to indicate that he wanted to stop.

Leaping down from the carriage, he doubled back to the door he'd seen his wife disappear through a few moments before. A small plaque next to the door simply read Otto Bock. No explanation of what type of service the man offered.

Frowning, Alec raised the knocker and gave a couple of sharp raps, which were answered by a clean-cut young servant. A footman of some sort, he assumed.

"I'm sorry, sir," the man said with a frown. "You're early. Mr. Bock is in with a patient still."

He opened the door and indicated that Alec should follow him. "If you'll just wait here it will be some time before he can see you."

A patient? A frisson of alarm ran through him. Was Juliet still suffering from the aftereffects of her accident? He remembered what she'd told him on their wedding night about the accident that had taken her foot and nearly taken her life. "I rarely even have phantom pain anymore," she'd told him. Could their journey to and from Scotland in such a brief period of time have aggravated her wound? Worse, could she be suffering from some other ailment in addition to her infirmity?

"I don't think you understand," he told the young man, pushing past him. "That patient your master is with now is my wife. I'll just step in and—"

He brushed past the servant and hurried forward to the door the young man had indicated with a nod when he'd informed Alec that Mr. Bock was with another patient.

"Wait!" the man said, trying to grasp Alec's arm and prevent him from interrupting his employer. "Sir, you can't go in there! Sir!"

But it was too late. Alec had turned the knob and stepped into the examining room. And what he saw made his jaw and fists clench with fury. Juliet was on the floor, and a man he didn't recognize was on the floor next to her, his hands caressing her exposed limbs.

"Get the hell off my wife!" he shouted, taking Juliet's assailant by the collar, and, despite the awkwardness of their location at the end of some strange railed contraption, tossing him to the side. "My God, Juliet! Are you all right?"

He didn't for a moment think that she welcomed the man's caress. There was no way that she would have left his bed earlier that morning and gone straight to another man. He'd heard of some unscrupulous physicians who had no qualms about taking advantage of their female patients, and he assumed this must be one of them.

But while she might not have intentionally sought out the other man, his wife was not pleased with her husband's interference. He reached down to help her up, but she slapped his hand away.

"Alec!" his wife asked, not in the least grateful for his intervention. "What are you doing here? And what have you done with Herr Bock?"

To his surprise, she used the rails to pull herself to her feet and moved quickly to her assailant's side. "Mr. Bock! Are you all right?"

"I am well, Miss . . . that is, Lady Deveril," the black-guard told her, straightening his spectacles. "I believe I have the pleasure of meeting your new husband, yes?"

"Yes," she said sourly, shaking her head in exasperation at her husband. "Though at this particular moment I am unsure why I consented to the match."

"I tried to keep him out, Mr. Bock," the man who had answered the door said apologetically, moving forward as if to remove Alec from the room.

"It is all right, William," Mr. Bock told his servant. "This is Miss Shelby's new husband. I believe he misunderstood the situation."

Looking from Juliet, to Bock, to his servant, Alec felt the ire that had propelled him through the door of the little room seep out of him. For the first time he took in his surroundings. It was a simply furnished room, with a couple of upholstered chairs, but what sent his finger to pull on his suddenly too tight cravat was the set of shelves set against the wall. On each shelf there sat a perfectly crafted, art-fully realistic artificial limb.

He closed his eyes at his stupidity.

"Oh," he said with a grimace.

"Yes," Juliet said, annoyance in her tone, "oh."

"So, this is the man who makes your feet?"

"If he will continue to do so after being so thoroughly insulted by my husband!" she said, hands on hips.

"Of course I will, Miss Shelby," Mr. Bock said with a

broad grin. He gave a slight bow toward Alec. "It is a pleasure to meet you, Lord Deveril," he said.

Alec shook his head at his own stupidity, but returned the other man's bow. "I hope you will forgive me, Mr. Bock," he said sheepishly. "I'm afraid I saw Juliet on the floor and jumped to the wrong conclusion."

"It is of no consequence, my lord," Bock said. "If I were to see my Frauke in such a position I too would jump to the wrong conclusion. Your jealousy over your pretty young wife does you credit. I have waited these many years for some fellow to notice Miss Shelby's . . . that is, Lady Deveril's beauty."

"I am lucky they did not," Alec said with a grin. "Otherwise I would not have been able to snap her up."

Juliet looked from one to the other of them and frowned. "If you two are finished speaking of me as if I were a valuable *objet d'art,* I would like to continue with my fitting, please."

Looking slightly abashed, Alec nodded. He was relieved to his core that she was safe, and that she did not have to endure the trauma of an assault in addition to her leg injury. He would have liked to stay and watch the fitting process, but assumed since he was now in her black books that she would prefer him to wait outside.

"Would you like to stay, my lord?" Mr. Bock asked before Alec could turn to go. "If it is agreeable to Lady Deveril, that is."

Alec looked to his wife, whose annoyance with him was still evident. But she must have seen something that placated her in his expression, because she gave a brisk nod. "Yes, that would be agreeable to me," she said, her face carefully devoid of emotion. Alec wondered if she were bracing herself for him to reject her offer. He could not imagine her parents had ever been particularly interested in the process by which her injury was rendered palatable to the judgmental *haut ton*. Indeed, he doubted they'd even done more than obtain Mr. Bock's services initially. Neither Lord nor Lady Shelby struck him as particularly concerned with seeing to their daughter's comfort or welfare.

"I'd like that," he said aloud, stepping forward to take his wife's hand in his. "I am sorry, my dear," he said softly, so that only she could hear.

Mr. Bock, perhaps sensing that they needed a moment, discreetly excused himself to attend to some no doubt fictitious task. At Juliet's nod Weston followed, leaving them alone.

"I suppose I can forgive you since you were attempting to protect my virtue," she said reluctantly. "How did you even know I was here?"

"Why did you feel the need to keep your appointment a secret from me?" he asked, answering her question with a question. "I would hardly forbid you to see the man who ensures that you are able to walk on your own."

She colored at the reminder of her own culpability in the debacle. "I wasn't keeping it a secret precisely," she said, her eyes troubled. "Though I will admit to not volunteering the information."

He searched her face, trying to discern what bothered her.

"I . . ." She paused, as if the words were hard to come by. "I suppose I didn't want to remind you that I am so very different from other ladies. That rather than shopping in Bond Street for slippers I am forced to have them affixed to a false foot. That I am just as much of a fraud as my mother is."

Her refusal to meet his gaze was nearly his undoing. He could cheerfully have run Lady Shelby through with Juliet's walking stick just then. The manner in which she'd reinforced Juliet's insecurities was simply cruel. It was a wonder her daughter had managed to emerge from her upbringing with any part of her soul intact. Not caring that Mr. Bock might return at any minute, he gathered Juliet into his arms and held her close enough to feel the slight tremor that ran through her.

"I would never accuse you of being a fraud, Juliet," he said against her hair. "And what makes you different from other ladies has nothing to do with where you obtain your footwear."

Juliet raised her brows. "Don't you mean calf-wear?" she asked wryly.

Alec barked a laugh. "You see? No other lady would laugh about such a thing," he told her, kissing her on the nose. "You are an original, Lady Deveril," he continued, "and worth a hundred of those other ladies."

He would have gone on, but a discreet knock at the door heralded Mr. Bock's return, and since they'd already wasted much of the man's morning, Alec did not wish to further discommode him so stepped back.

"Ah," Mr. Bock said with a broad smile, "you are reconciled, yes? Then let us continue."

Juliet arrived back at the town house in Berkeley Square to find that Cecily and Maddie had called and were awaiting her in the morning room.

"I hope you don't mind that we waited, Juliet," Maddie said without preamble as her cousin came into the room. "But we simply had to see you to assure ourselves that you were all right. And though your very starchy butler did tell us so, I'm afraid we don't know the man well enough yet to trust his word."

"She wouldn't believe me when I told her that you'd gone with Alec of your own free will," Cecily said with an exasperated shake of her head. "Though we both wished to welcome you back to town of course, and to assure ourselves of your good health."

The new Lady Deveril hurried forward to give each of them an impulsive hug. "I am perfectly well as you can both see," she told them, taking the seat they'd left her beside the tea tray. "Though there was certainly a point where I wondered if I would stay this way."

Maddie frowned. "What happened?" she demanded. "Was it Deveril?"

"Certainly not," Juliet assured her, pouring herself a cup of tea. "Alec . . . that is, Deveril, has been lovely. But Mama and Turlington made an appearance on the journey north and tried to kidnap me."

"No!" Cecily took her hand. "Though I suppose the fact that you are here and that the announcement ran in the papers this morning indicated that they were not successful."

Juliet told them about what had happened when Lady Shelby and Lord Turlington met up with them near Scotland. "And I have no doubt that if Alec had been less insistent they would have succeeded in forcing me to wed Turlington. He saved me and there is no other way to say it."

Her eyes troubled, Maddie took a bite of ginger biscuit. "I cannot say that I am displeased with how things turned out. It is much more acceptable to see you married to Lord Deveril than to Turlington. Or should I call him Churlington?"

Juliet laughed at the pun, then sobered. "My only regret is that some other girl will doubtless find herself married to the man soon. Now that I am no longer available, I fear there are enough cits willing to buy a title for their daughters that Turlington will have no trouble finding himself another bride."

"Not with the rumors that are circulating about the man," Cecily said. "Of course Winterson refused to give me the details, but it involves some very nasty dealings in the demimonde."

Maddie snorted. "I'm surprised that the gentlemen of the *ton* have become so nice in their sensibilities. Especially for the sake of the demimonde."

"Well, if they are so bothered by it, then you know it must be something quite disturbing."

Juliet thought about the way Turlington's attentions had always made her feel and she had little doubt that the rumors, whatever they were, were true. She fought back a shiver at her lucky escape.

"So, tell us about the wedding," Maddie said, as if sensing her cousin's discomfort. "Was it very romantic? I've always wondered just what Gretna is like."

So she launched into the tale of her whirlwind wedding, complete with humorous details about Mr. Elliot's insistence upon calling Alec "Romeo" and his wife's terrible playing on the pianoforte.

"It certainly won't be something you'll ever forget," Cecily said with a grin. "Plus you did not have to meet every obscure relative in the Deveril family tree. I swear Winterson's mama invited people even Debrett's had no knowledge of."

"True," Juliet said. "But I do wish you both had been there. It seemed wrong to celebrate such a momentous occasion without having my best friends there to share it with me."

Cecily squeezed her hand. "I wish we had too, but we'll be there for other important events."

"Like the birth of your first child," Maddie added, taking her other hand.

But their words sent a lash of panic running through Juliet, and she pulled her hands away. "I'm not sure we should start planning for that just yet. We've only been married a few days."

"You say that now," Cecily said with a grin, "but it will happen before you know it." She rubbed a hand over her growing belly. "I certainly didn't expect to find myself *enceinte* so soon. But here I am."

"Surely it doesn't happen that quickly for everyone,"

Juliet asked, a little desperate. "I mean, you are probably an exception."

"Juliet," Maddie said, exchanging a troubled look with Cecily, "you sound as if you don't wish to have children."

The room felt exceedingly close all of a sudden, and Juliet pulled slightly at the neckline of her gown. "It's not that I don't wish to have children," she said, knowing that her tone was a bit strident. "I simply don't know if I will be able to. Or if I should."

"Don't worry about it now," Cecily soothed, rubbing her cousin's hand. "There is plenty of time for you. Though I personally think you'd be an excellent mother."

Juliet smiled wanly at her cousin. "Thank you, dearest. I'm sorry I reacted so strongly. It's just that I've been worrying over the matter and I simply don't know if I'll be able to do it. Or rather, I worry what will happen once I have a babe. What if I turn out to be as terrible at mothering as my own mother is? The idea of inflicting such heartache on my own flesh and blood is horrifying."

"I think the fact that you are concerned about such a thing means that there is little danger you'll do so," Maddie said, reassuring her. "I sincerely doubt that Lady Shelby wondered for a moment about her ability to be even a passable parent. I think together you and Deveril will be an excellent team. With his gregarious personality, and your quiet observation, you're a perfect match."

Her cousin's words, and her succinct assessment of hers and Alec's personalities, were so astute that Juliet wondered whether others would have come to the same conclusion. She hoped so, because when news of the way she'd snagged one of the *ton*'s most popular bachelors got out she'd be facing some serious scrutiny from all the young ladies who'd had their eye on him. It would go a great deal in her favor if their marriage was thought to be a love match.

"Thank you both," she told Cecily and Maddie. "I know

I sound like a peagoose, but it's always been something I've worried about. Especially given how easy it is for harm to come to children even from the outside world. Look at poor little Alice and what she endured at the hands of that horrid Mrs. Parks!"

"How goes the search for Mrs. Turner?" Maddie asked, pouring each of them another cup of tea. "As far as I know there have been no developments here. Or," she added with a grin, "not that I've been able to winkle out of Lord Monteith."

Juliet explained to them their encounter with Mr. MacEwan and his mention of the artist who wished to paint Mrs. Turner.

"That is awful," Cecily said, giving a shudder. "Especially the way she seemed to be sending a covert message through her letters." Cecily had been integral in the decoding of messages left by Winterson's brother earlier in the year.

"I know," Juliet said, frowning. "I thought for a bit that Turlington might be the artist, but Alec seems convinced that it's *Il Maestro*. And I cannot say that I disagree. Which is troubling. The man's paintings are so . . . disturbing."

"Agreed," Cecily said with a shiver. "But how will you question *Il Maestro* if you have no notion of who he is?"

Maddie's eyes lit up, in that manner that always heralded an idea that would get them into a wealth of trouble.

"What if," she mused, "we put it about that we wished to commission a painting by *Il Maestro*?"

"Does he even take commissions?" Juliet asked. "I thought he only did them for his own amusement."

"I noticed a few weeks ago that the Wallingfords have a painting of Saint Joan in their morning room that has all the hallmarks of being one of *Il Maestro*'s works. And since Lord Wallingford spends all of his time gambling there can be no danger that he himself is *Il Maestro*."

"So, you're just going to ask Lady Wallingford where she got it?" Cecily asked, skeptical.

"No," Maddie said with a grin. "Juliet is."

"I reckon you are right that we need to find out who this *Il Maestro* is and then perhaps he'll lead us to Mrs. Turner." Thomas Greenshaw, Bow Street runner, took a gulp from his tankard of ale. Alec had sent round a note first thing that morning requesting a meeting with the man. Though he hadn't been comfortable saying so to Juliet, the tale that MacEwan had told them about Mrs. Turner's encounter with the artist had bothered him. There was something about the story that struck him as odd, though he couldn't quite pinpoint what that was. Either way, he was intelligent enough to know when to call in expert advice. And that time was now.

Though Greenshaw projected an air of idleness, with his slow movements and bored expression, Winterson had assured him that the man was one of the brightest men who'd served with him in the Peninsula. And thus far his assessment had proved correct. The runner had quickly grasped the importance of finding Mrs. Turner, and finding her quickly. Not only for her own sake, but also because her connection to Juliet made things dangerous for the new viscountess as well.

"I checked with every one o' my connections in the East End for word of a lady matching your Mrs. Turner's description, but no luck." Greenshaw wiped a large hand over his mouth. "If she's being held anywhere in the rookeries, I haven't heard about it. Nor have me contacts. So this bloke must be hiding her in plain sight."

"You may be right about that, but where?" Alec tapped his fingers impatiently on the rickety table he and Greenshaw occupied in the Cat and Pickle, a rather dismal little establishment on the edge of Whitechapel. "The gossips have long guessed that *Il Maestro* is a member of the *ton* but if so, he could have her hidden anywhere.

"What I need you to do, Greenshaw," he told the man, "is to make a thorough investigation of anyone who might be soliciting young women for the purposes of painting them. I do realize that there are any number of artists who take their models from the servant class, but this feels different. And there's an artist in particular I wish you to seek out. Actually there are two."

Greenshaw's gaze sharpened, and though Alec couldn't quite put his finger on what changed, something about the other man's posture communicated his attention.

"First I want you to learn as much as you can about the affairs of Lord Philip Turlington." Though Greenshaw didn't take notes, Alec knew he was making a mental note of everything he said. "My wife's mother was, until our marriage put paid to the notion, extremely intent upon having Turlington marry Juliet. I wouldn't be surprised if the man spirited Mrs. Turner away as a means of capturing Juliet's notice. Or even with the intention of using Mrs. Turner's freedom as a bargaining chip to control her."

"And this Turlington is an artist, my lord?"

"Yes." Alec's jaw hardened. "He is known for his society portraits. Which is how he met Lady Shelby. And his style is quite similar to that of *Il Maestro,* our other suspect. In fact, I wonder if *Il Maestro* and Lord Turlington might even be the same person. Their styles are quite similar. And *Il Maestro*'s exhibits are fast becoming the only art London can talk about."

"Aye." Greenshaw nodded. "Even I've heard o' the feller and I ain't what ye'd call an art lover. This is the bloke what paints the suffering ladies, right?"

"That's right," Alec confirmed, pleased that he wouldn't need to explain the importance of *Il Maestro* to the runner. "So far, no one knows the identity of the artist. Or, for that matter, his models. And, as you say, they are all suffering."

"I ain't exactly the type wot will blend into the crowd wot normally moves in such circles," Greenshaw said with a frown, and another gulp of ale, as if emphasizing his point. "But I reckon I can get some information from Turlington's servants and the people who work in the galleries where this *Maestro* shows 'is paintings. Most people are clumsy about hiding their secret identities. It just wants someone with a sharp eye to follow the threads."

And according to Winterson, Greenshaw had a very sharp eye indeed.

Still, all it took was one missed clue for the trail to go cold.

"Be careful not to disclose whom you're working for," Alec warned. "I do not wish for any of this to lead back to my wife. She's had enough difficulty of late."

"Don't you worry, my lord," the runner said with a cheeky grin. "I can be right discreet when I sets me mind to it."

"Excellent." Alec stood, and watched as Greenshaw unfolded his long-limbed form, and rose, his head almost reaching the tavern's low ceiling. The two men wended their way through the taproom toward the entrance, the smell of sweat, ale, and plain cooking enveloping them as they walked. Just outside the door, they shook hands.

"Don't you worry, my lord," Greenshaw said, his eyes serious. "We'll find your wife's Mrs. Turner. There's nothing I 'ate more than a man wot takes advantage of a woman alone."

With that assurance, the Bow Street runner left the tavern yard, and Alec swung up onto his horse and headed back toward St. James Street, where he was to meet Monteith and Winterson at White's.

Seventeen

*S*o Turlington and *Il Maestro* might be the same person?" Monteith demanded from his corner seat in the reading room at White's.

"That's what we need to find out," Alec admitted. He and Juliet had gone over and over the possibilities of the artist's identity, but aside from Turlington, whom they both agreed might be at the head of their list simply because they disliked the man, they could come up with no other possibilities.

"Couldn't we simply inquire at the Royal Academy for a list of members? Though the fellow has moved to other venues since then, his first exhibition took place there so he must have been a member at some point." Winterson leaned back in his chair and stretched.

"It's a good suggestion." Alec ran a hand over his face in weariness. He felt as if they were talking in circles. "Though I'm not sure they'll simply turn over their membership list to us without question. You saw yourself how closemouthed these societies can be when you dealt with the Egyptian Club. They are hardly welcoming to nonmembers."

"True enough," Winterson said. "But we can at least try."

"I suppose it might be easier for us to find something than for your runner to do so, Deveril," Monteith said thoughtfully. "If the society is reluctant to speak to peers of the realm then they'll be downright closemouthed with someone like Greenshaw. Especially with his Bow Street credentials."

"We all know it matters who you know and who will vouch for you," Alec said grimly. "Which is why Juliet is so worried about her Mrs. Turner. Though I cannot say I trust the woman as much as Juliet seems to. There have simply been too many instances where what Mrs. Turner has claimed and what was the truth have been two very different things."

"Speaking of your lovely wife," Winterson said, "I hope she is getting on well."

There was an unspoken question there, one that both irritated and impressed Alec. He was grateful for Winterson's help in their elopement of course, but Juliet was Alec's responsibility now.

"She is well enough," he answered mildly. "She seems to be getting on well with my sisters, and if I am right she is even now enjoying a coze with the Duchess and Lady Madeline."

"Good God," Monteith grumbled. "If those three are plotting then no man in London is safe."

At the suddenly intense glares Alec and Winterson leveled at him, Monteith threw up his hands in surrender. "No offense to either of your wives, but even you must admit that mischief seems to follow those three wherever they go."

"Still haven't forgiven Cecily for that incident in the park, eh?" Winterson asked dryly.

"No, and I doubt I ever will. I'd rather fight an entire battalion of French soldiers than attempt to come up with ways to tell my best friend that I've accidentally gotten his wife killed."

At the reminder of the incident, all three men frowned. Danger did seem to be something that followed the three women wherever they went. But Alec suspected it had less to do with their propensity for mischief than with the fact that none of them was content to simply accept the roles that society dictated they adhere to. While Juliet might be the most retiring of the three, even she had shown herself to be dedicated to throwing off the societal yoke when it was necessary to doing what she thought was right. She'd already proved that with her refusal to marry as her parents wished.

"Thankfully," Winterson said, interrupting Alec's thoughts, "that incident is behind us and unlikely to be repeated."

"Since we are still speaking of our wives," Alec said, "I would ask that both of you keep your ears open to any gossip that might circulate about Juliet. I know her mother and Turlington were quite angered at being thwarted, and I would not be surprised to learn that they were attempting to make her pay with her reputation."

As if conjured by the very mention of his name, Turlington entered the room, and to Alec's disgust made a beeline for their table.

As always, Turlington had dressed with a colorful disregard for current fashion. The man's waistcoat was a gaudy striped affair, which he wore beneath a bright blue coat. His shirt points were so high that it was doubtful he'd be able to turn his head with any degree of comfort. For an artist, he had shamefully bad taste in clothing.

"Deveril," he said, apparently ignoring the viscount's companions. "I could not help but see the notice in the papers this morning. May I wish you happy of your new bride?"

Inclining his head, Deveril said, "You may indeed. I hope now that you will leave us to our conversation."

"You wound me, my lord!" Turlington said with mock affront. "I should think you'd be more welcoming to the man who has information about your wife's beloved friend and teacher."

"The only reason I don't lift you up by that frightful

cravat and toss you from this room, Turlington," Alec growled, "is that I don't wish to cause my wife distress. If you really have information about Mrs. Turner, then spit it out and leave. Otherwise, just leave."

Turlington, like most bullies, was taken aback to find his prey fighting back. But the glint of humor in his eyes showed that he enjoyed provoking Deveril. "I had supposed that since you cost me a fortune by stealing the little cripple from me that you would be more receptive to my overtures. Funny how ungrateful some people can be."

Alec clenched his teeth so hard he feared cracking them. But he'd vowed long ago that he would not become the kind of man his father had been, brawling and dueling over every provocation. Still, he wanted the man out of his sight before he lost his temper. "State. Your. Business."

Seeing that he would be unable to goad Deveril into a fight, Turlington dropped his languid pose. "Fine. I am leaving for the Continent soon, and thought you might like to know that Lady Shelby has been boasting that she got rid of Mrs. Turner. She was afraid that the pianoforte teacher had too much influence over Miss Shelby . . . that is, Lady Deveril, and she told me she'd hidden her away before she could talk her former charge out of marrying me." The man frowned. "Not that she was ever disposed to do so."

"Why are you telling me this?" Alec demanded. He might have spent a hundred years prognosticating about what Turlington would do next, but he would never have arrived at the scenario going on before him.

Turlington shrugged. "Lady Shelby is a cold bitch. And she owes me a substantial debt. Which is why she was attempting to sell me her daughter's dowry. Her continued nonpayment has forced me to retrench to the Continent."

"So you're giving her back a bit of her own?" Deveril asked, frowning.

"With interest." Turlington nodded. "Now, gentlemen, if you'll excuse me?"

When the man was gone, Alec turned to his companions. "What the hell was that?"

"Then you don't think his explanation was sincere?" Winterson asked.

"No, I do not," the viscount said frankly. "That's what disturbs me. Turlington must already know I hold Lady Shelby in little esteem given her attempt to force Juliet to marry him. So why is he trying to stir up even more enmity between us? It isn't as if I can think less of her."

"So you don't think Lady Shelby has anything to do with Mrs. Turner's disappearance?" Monteith asked, his expression troubled.

"I don't know. What bothers me more is Turlington's sudden decision to throw Lady Shelby to the wolves." Alec pinched the bridge of his nose. "Why do I get the feeling that he is trying to protect someone else by doing so?"

"They really are lovely," Juliet told her husband as they rode in their carriage the short distance between their town house and the Wallingfords'. She reached up a hand to stroke the emeralds at her throat, unable to believe that such beautiful gems were hanging on her neck. "Thank you again."

Alec had surprised her with them that evening as she dressed for the Wallingfords' ball. Since it was to be the first *ton* entertainment they would attend as a married couple, Juliet had taken great care with her appearance, donning one of her new gowns from Madame Celeste's establishment, a deep green silk that set off her creamy complexion and contrasted beautifully with her auburn hair. Her maid, Weston, had been about to fasten her pearls, when Alec had appeared in the connecting door between their rooms.

"Perhaps you would wish to wear these instead, Juliet," he said, approaching her dressing table with the jeweler's box in hand. "I believe they will go well with your gown."

And he, who was known throughout the *ton* for his fault-less taste, would know.

Juliet turned just in time to see the warmth in his eyes as he drank in the sight of her. Warmth that sent memories and a jolt of desire coursing through her as she remembered just what it had been like to feel his strong body against hers, to feel his hands on her body, and his groans of pleasure vi-brating through her chest. As if he knew exactly what she was thinking, his gaze darkened, and for a moment, Juliet wanted to dismiss Weston and suggest to her husband that they stay home this evening.

But when she remembered just why it was so important for them to go to the Wallingfords' tonight, she got control of herself, and to her relief, or sorrow, Alec appeared to do the same. Though there was still a lingering hint of desire in his eyes.

Turning her attention to the jewelry box, she bit back a gasp as she saw the emerald parure in the box he held out to her. "Oh, Alec," she breathed. "I couldn't."

"Of course you can," he said, nodding to dismiss Weston from the room, while he placed the box on the surface of the dressing table. Lifting the necklace from its case, he brought it up to her neck, both of them watching the stones sparkle against her pale skin in the mirror. "You see," he said, with a half grin, "they are perfect for you."

Juliet bowed her head as he brought the two ends of the necklace together behind her neck and fastened the clasp. With a speed that almost made Juliet suspect she'd imag-ined it, he kissed her once just above where the clasp rested against her skin, and stepped back.

"There are earrings and a bracelet in the box as well," he told her, moving to stand in front of her again, folding his arms across his chest, as if he were unable to keep his hands from her. She inwardly chided herself at the thought. He was hardly overcome by desire. Still, he did feel something for her. Something besides simple friendship, that is.

"I don't know how to thank you," she said, careful not to show just how overwhelmed she was by his gift. She had no wish to be in the unhappy situation of falling in love with a husband who did not feel the same way about her. Especially given just how sought after Lord Deveril had been by the ladies of the *ton* before their marriage. Indeed, she had little doubt that there were any number of his past admirers who would not see his marriage as a deterrent to their pursuit, but who would instead see it as an incentive for them to renew their attentions. Especially those married ladies who would see his marriage to a plain spinster as a sign that he would now need someone more exciting to warm his bed.

"You can thank me by wearing them," he said simply. "They belonged to my mother. Indeed they were the only jewels she owned that my father didn't manage to pawn or sell when he attempted to rid the house of all reminders of her."

"Oh," Juliet said softly, touching the jewels at her throat. "Then they are too precious for me to wear to a silly ball." She reached around her neck to unfasten them, but Alec stopped her with a touch to her hand.

"No," he said softly. "I want you to wear them. I think . . . I know she would have liked you. And I wish for you to have them."

Juliet looked up at him; his eyes were now dark with sincerity. "If you are sure . . ." she said carefully.

"I am." Alec reached down to take her hand and assisted her to rise from the dressing table.

"You realize," he said, tucking her hand into the crook of his elbow, "that this is our first entertainment as a married couple."

"Yes. I had noticed," she said with a smile. "I do hope we don't cause too much of a stir. It's not quite the thing to marry in Gretna, is it?"

"Nonsense," he said, leading her from her bedchamber and into the hallway. "All the best in society are doing it."

Now, as they moved inch by inch through the streets of Mayfair, as the rest of the *haut ton* tried to get as close as they could to the Wallingfords' town house, Juliet marveled again at how generous her husband had been to give her the emeralds that had once belonged to his beloved mother.

"I don't suppose you have heard anything about my mother since we returned to London," she said gingerly, wanting to be prepared should her mother be in attendance tonight. "I know I must steel myself for the possibility of seeing her again of course," she added. "But I do wish that there were some way to avoid it."

"Don't worry," Alec said and reached across the carriage to take her gloved hand in his. "Even if she does attend tonight, I think my threat to expose her to the rest of the *ton* should prove incentive enough to keep her from carrying tales about our elopement. Indeed, if I am not mistaken your mother will do everything necessary to prevent the tale of how her attempt to make you marry Turlington was foiled from getting out. It does not paint her in a very sympathetic light. And she does seem to thrive on her reputation as a leader of the *ton*."

"I hope you are right."

"I know I am right," Alec said with a cynical lift of his brows. "Your mother and my father, for all that their reputations in polite society differ, are not all that different. They both thrive (or in my father's case 'thrived') on controlling those around them. My father used brute force, and your mother uses guile, but they are both bullies just the same."

It was one of the only times that he had spoken of his notorious father. Juliet had understood from his earlier comments about him that there had been no love lost between father and son, of course. But something in his tone tonight sent a shiver down her back as she thought about just what "brute force" might entail.

"Let us hope then that my mother chose to attend some

other entertainment tonight," she said with a brightness she did not feel.

"Do not worry so," he told her. "I will be there with you. And so will your cousins and Winterson and Monteith. And your aunts. Your mama will be outnumbered. And outgunned. Always."

She was spared a reply by the halting of the carriage.

Within twenty minutes she was going through the receiving line with Alec, being introduced as his viscountess. For someone who had spent the years since her come-out languishing with the other wallflowers, the approbation in Lady Wallingford's eyes before she welcomed Juliet to her ball was supremely satisfying. Any scandal that might have attached to their hasty wedding had been overridden by society's curiosity about seeing the newlyweds for themselves, as Lady Wallingford's less than discreet glance at Juliet's midriff confirmed.

"I hope you will grace us with your presence at the dinner party we are having next week," Lady Wallingford added. "I know I sent an invitation to your husband."

"I'm afraid we'll be unable to attend, my lady," Alec said, before Juliet could respond, his hand resting in solidarity on the small of her back. "We are otherwise engaged."

With that, Alec led her to where the butler stood announcing the guests to the room at large. Any sense of annoyance at his high-handedness was overcome by awe as a hush fell over the crowd as he proclaimed them to be the Viscount and Viscountess Deveril. But the quiet lasted only a moment before the room erupted into a cacophony of whispers and chattering.

"You two have certainly set the cat among the pigeons," Cecily said as she and Winterson approached them. "I don't think there's been this much excitement at one of Lady Wallingford's balls since Freddie Tipton put Blue Ruin in the punch bowl."

"I take it the dancing hasn't started yet?" Juliet asked,

surveying the chattering masses on the periphery of the ballroom. She could hear the orchestra tuning their instruments in the balcony.

"I think they were waiting for you two to arrive," Winterson said with a roll of his eyes. "The *ton* is nothing if not curious."

"Well, we will just have to give them something to talk about," Alec said firmly. "Do you feel up to dancing, Lady Deveril?"

Juliet glanced around the roomful of guests, not quite managing to mask their looks of curiosity. She had not danced publicly since that first heady dance lesson in Cecily and Winterson's best parlor. She had thought to sit tonight's dancing out, thinking that it was scandal enough for her to appear as Alec's wife, much less to engage in an activity she had heretofore eschewed. Still, there was something about the energy of the room, a sense of hushed expectation hovering in the air, that told her there was no better time to reveal her newfound dancing skills.

"In for a penny, in for a pound," she told Alec, with a wry smile. "Honestly, I do not think we could inspire more talk if we stripped naked and played piquet in the middle of the ballroom."

"It's a good thing I brought this, then," Cecily said with a grin, removing Amelia Snowe's pilfered dance card from where it hung around her wrist, and slipping it over Juliet's hand. "You left it that night. Let us think of it as a Duckling good-luck charm."

"Speak of the devil," Winterson said in a low voice, as Amelia and her boon companion, Felicia, came toward them.

"Let the games begin," Alec said, tightening his hold around Juliet's waist.

The blond beauty was, as always, exquisitely attired, this time in a pale blue satin gown that brought out the blue of her eyes, which were narrowed in speculation for a flicker of a moment before she switched to her normal, deceptively friendly smile.

"My dear Lady Deveril," she said with a catlike smile, "how lovely to see you now that you are returned from Gretna. I hope you found the blacksmith to be worthy of officiating at the marriage of a couple of your station?"

"I'm afraid our wedding was performed by a rather prosaic minister, Miss Snowe," Alec informed her, lying through his teeth. "I could not, in good conscience, allow my impetuosity in spiriting Juliet, that is Lady Deveril, off to Gretna to rob her of the respectable marriage she deserved."

"It was really quite a lovely ceremony," Juliet added, enjoying the way Amelia's eyes narrowed at their show of solidarity. "Of course, now my parents wish they had given their consent, but at the time they were quite adamant that Deveril wait the requisite period for the banns to be called."

"And I simply could not wait that long," Alec said with a rueful grin.

Like Lady Wallingford had done, Amelia allowed her gaze to rest on Juliet's midsection a bit longer than was polite. Part of Juliet resented the notion that they'd married because they had to. But another, more selfish part, loved that people actually thought someone like Alec would be so overcome by passion for her to anticipate their vows.

"Well, I certainly hope you will not regret your impulsiveness," Felicia said with a solicitous smile that was counteracted by the hard glint in her eyes. "The *ton* can be very unforgiving about such things."

"I thank you for your concern, Lady Felicia," Juliet said with an equally false smile. "Though I do not see how you would be in any position to know."

"I hope you will excuse us," Alec said cheerfully, "but I would like to dance with my bride now."

"Cecily," Juliet said, turning to her cousin who had been watching their exchange with Amelia and Felicia with undisguised interest. "Will you and Winterson take my walking stick, please?"

"Of course, my lady," Winterson said with a grin.

"With pleasure," Cecily said, taking the ebony stick from her. "Enjoy your dance."

When Deveril and Juliet moved out onto the ballroom floor to take their places in the set that was forming, Amelia and Felicia stared after them, stunned.

"Juliet cannot dance!" Amelia said, her mouth hanging open in shock.

"She is cri—" Felicia began, then upon Winterson's clearing his throat, continued, "that is, she is . . . er . . . injured."

"I think you'll find, ladies," Cecily said with satisfaction at seeing the gossips, who had made hers and Juliet's and Madeline's social lives unbearable for the past few years, so taken aback, "that when my cousin is determined to do something there is very little that can stop her."

"She's going to make a fool of herself," Amelia said harshly, her eyes never leaving Juliet as she and Deveril stood waiting for the dance to begin. "More than she already has after that silly elopement."

"I will thank you to keep your opinions about my daughter to yourself, Miss Snowe," Lady Shelby said as she stepped up to the group. "How is your mama? Still keeping company with Bertie Knighton?"

It was well known in the *ton* that Mrs. Snowe was engaged in a torrid affair with the much younger Bertie Knighton. And that Amelia disapproved, heartily.

As Lady Shelby had intended, Amelia held her tongue about Juliet and Deveril. "I believe we should go have some lemonade, Felicia," she said, pulling her friend along behind her as they left the small group

"Malicious cat," Lady Shelby said with a scowl. "Her family might be rich as Croesus but they are only two generations from the shop."

That she herself was only one generation from the shop didn't seem to bother Lady Shelby.

"What brings you to Juliet's defense, Aunt Rose?" Cecily asked cynically. "Are you the only one allowed to speak ill of your daughter?"

"Don't be melodramatic, Cecily." Lady Shelby waved away her niece's remark. "I am trying to ensure that the talk caused by their elopement is not compounded by spiteful cats like Amelia and Felicia.

"And make no mistake, I blame you for this dancing nonsense," she continued, her accusing gaze firmly on Cecily. "If you hadn't married Winterson so precipitately, Juliet wouldn't have become so determined to remove herself from the ranks of the wallflowers. I have worked so hard to ensure that she blends in to society without drawing attention to her deformity, but you had to ruin things by compromising yourself with Winterson."

Cecily was all too grateful that Winterson had stepped away to chat with Monteith. "My actions aside, aunt, I should think that you would wish for your daughter to find happiness. Which she clearly has."

"I wished for my daughter to do her duty and marry as her father and I saw fit. Since she chose to defy me and elope with Devil Deveril's son, then I am forced to ensure that she does not embarrass herself further. Though it would appear that I am too late for that."

She gazed grimly at the dance floor where Juliet and Deveril went through the motions of the set, Juliet perhaps more careful about her movements than the other dancers, but acquitting herself better than some without her handicap.

"What is so terrible about Juliet dancing?" Cecily asked, truly puzzled. "I do not understand why it threatens you so much. There are any number of dancers who are clumsy and lack all coordination. Which she certainly does not. She might have been dancing all this time, but was not allowed to do so simply because you feared her inability to perform some of the steps would embarrass you."

"Don't be a widgeon, Cecily!" Lady Shelby said hotly. "I do not wish for her to dance because there is a danger that she will reveal the true extent of her injury in doing so. I was doing it to save her embarrassment as much as for myself."

"If it is a matter of her tripping . . ." Cecily said.

"It is a matter of her false foot falling off," Lady Shelby said in a low voice. "She is missing her right foot. That is her injury."

The words were no sooner out of Lady Shelby's mouth, than Cecily heard a gasp from behind them. Her mouth agape, her eyes wide, Lady Felicia stood stock still, as if Lady Shelby's words had paralyzed her. Then, realizing what she'd just heard, her paralysis turned to glee. Cecily could all but hear Felicia's thoughts. *Wait until I tell Amelia,* foremost among them.

"Felicia, I beg you will not . . ." She had barely spoken the words before Felicia was pushing away from them, through the crowds, no doubt to where Amelia waited.

"Dash it," Cecily said as Felicia disappeared into the crowd. "I do not know which to be angrier about," she told her aunt, whose complexion had turned pale, "the fact that you made Juliet keep her true infirmity a secret for all these years, or that you were so rash as to announce it in the middle of a crowded ballroom."

"Oh, stubble it, Cecily," Lady Shelby said with an unusual burst of vulgarity. "I certainly did not mean to tell you in the hearing of that ill-tempered harpy."

"And the secrecy?" Cecily demanded, thinking back to all of the times that she had sat alongside Juliet with the other wallflowers, never knowing what kind of ordeals she must have endured every day since she'd returned from that fateful trip where she'd lost her foot. Her heart ached for her cousin.

"Look around you, niece." Lady Shelby gestured to a cluster of dowagers glancing back at them and out toward the set where Juliet and Deveril danced on, unaware that Juliet's secret was out. "Do you really believe that the *ton* would embrace Juliet knowing how deformed she is? How she must have a false foot fashioned for her out of wood? She is hardly a war hero who can blame her problem on the French. I made her keep her injury a secret for her own good."

"Somehow, I doubt that, aunt," Cecily returned. Knowing that Juliet and Deveril would be deluged by curiosity seekers as soon as their dance ended, she turned and went to find Winterson and Maddie in hopes that they could offset some of the more insistent gossips.

It wasn't long into the set that Juliet began to feel the eyes of many of her fellow ballgoers on her. She knew that her dancing was not as energetic or proficient as some other dancers, but she was hardly the worst on the floor.

"What is going on?" she asked Alec as the figure brought them together. "Am I really that awful?"

"I have no idea," Alec whispered back. "I think you're doing wonderfully well. But something has certainly set them agog, and I somehow doubt it's the brilliance of my Mathematical. Do you wish to sit down? I will take the blame if you wish to save your pride."

"No," she said as they promenaded down the row of dancers. "I won't let them shame me."

"Good girl." His smile sent a little thrill through her. He really was a handsome man, her husband.

But by the time the dance was concluded, the whispers in the ballroom were almost as loud as the orchestra.

"What's happened?" Juliet asked Cecily, who waited with Winterson, Maddie, and Monteith by the side of the dance floor. Though she had tried to tell herself that it was foolish to think that the talk could have been caused by her dancing alone, she secretly feared that her opinion of her dancing abilities was overly inflated. Perhaps she'd wished so hard to be a proficient dancer that she'd fooled herself into thinking she was better than she actually was. And she so disliked the idea of bringing shame upon Alec in such a way. Perhaps she should not have allowed him to talk her into the marriage after all. He deserved a wife who would make him proud, not cause talk everywhere she ventured.

But Cecily's words told her that the situation was much direr than she could possibly have imagined.

"They know about your foot," Cecily said, her lips pressed together in anger. "Your mother was haranguing me about our dance lessons and she let the truth slip out."

"Which wouldn't have been such a bad thing," Maddie added, "but Felicia overheard her."

Oh.

Juliet closed her eyes, and heard bits and pieces of the chatter around her.

". . . in a carriage accident . . ."

". . . can't imagine what possessed Lady Shelby . . ."

". . . Deveril got himself a pig in a poke . . ."

"There's a servants' hall just off the card room," Winterson said in a low voice. "No one will think less of you for leaving before they begin approaching you with questions."

Juliet bit her lip. She did not wish to give them, or her mother, the satisfaction of knowing she was bothered by their talk, but she also knew that sometimes it was best to retrench and rally one's forces for the next battle.

Thinking back to all the work she'd done over the years to bring herself back from her accident, how she'd struggled to regain her ability to walk, how she'd been kept from fully participating in the world around her by her mother, who feared just this kind of public shaming, Juliet felt something inside her snap.

She would not allow her peers to make her feel like

some kind of undesirable because of an accident that had been no fault of her own.

"I'm glad the truth is finally out," she said firmly, steeling her spine so that the gawking spectators would see that she was not intimidated by their talk. "I've been begging Mama to let me reveal the truth for years now. You can have no idea how awful it has been to keep such a secret from the world for all this time."

"I wonder, Lady Deveril," Amelia asked from her position next to Felicia as the two of them approached Juliet's party. "Did your husband learn about your missing foot before or after the hasty wedding? What a surprise that must have been."

Juliet felt Alec stiffen next to her, and realized that even if she did wish to stand her ground, it would perhaps be better for her husband's safety if they took Winterson's suggestion and left via the servants' hall. All they needed to compound the revelation about her foot was for Alec to challenge some loose-tongued looby to a duel.

Before he could speak, she tugged on Alec's arm and said, "Please, may we leave, my lord?"

His expression granite hard, Alec gave a brisk nod and hurried her through the still staring and whispering crowd to the long gallery off which the servants' hall lay.

They had just entered the gallery when Juliet looked up at a row of paintings decorating the walls and stopped abruptly.

"What is it?" Alec demanded. "Is it your injury?"

Juliet shook her head, and lifted her gloved hand to point at the first painting. It was a depiction of Desdemona, dead from strangulation at Othello's hands, lying on a mussed bed. It was a skillfully done work, with brush strokes so delicate that one could barely make them out on the canvas. But it wasn't the technique of the artistry that made Juliet stop. It was instead Desdemona herself.

"Good God," Alec exhaled.

"It's the missing steamstress, Jane Pettigrew." Juliet's embarrassment at having her secret revealed was replaced by dread. "She had only met the young woman a couple of times, but there was no mistaking her in the painting before them. This must be the *Il Maestro* painting that Lady Wallingford boasted of." And an inspection of the lower right-hand corner of the canvas revealed his telltale signature.

"I hope this doesn't mean that *Il Maestro* has disposed of Miss Pettigrew," Alec said grimly.

"I hope this doesn't mean that *Il Maestro* has moved on to painting Mrs. Turner," Juliet responded. "If so, we've got to find her as soon as possible."

Nodding, Alec pulled her closer to his side, giving her the protection of his body as they slipped down the servants' hall and out of the Wallingford town house.

Eighteen

When they returned home from the Wallingford ball, Alec refused to let Juliet retreat into the solitude of her room.

"It changes nothing between us," he told her, pulling her by the hand through the connecting door into his room.

As sometimes happened, Juliet was struck anew at just how beautiful he was. She knew that he would not wish to be described so, but his fallen-angel looks were much too gorgeous to be called simply handsome. The way his golden hair curled just over his brow, the fine lines of his facial features, even the fullness of his lashes, would have made him a lovely woman. But the strength of his jawline and the hard muscles that filled out his clothing marked him as deliciously male. A shiver ran through her as Juliet allowed him to pull her to him, even as she fretted about what effect her newfound notoriety would have upon him.

"Stop worrying," he ordered, kissing her just below her earlobe, even as his hand slid down to cup her breast through her clothing. "The *ton* have the attention span of a flea. They will be on to some other scandal by tomorrow."

But the next day came and went and still all the gossips could speak about was Juliet and her shameful secret. Her distress at being ridiculed at the Wallingford ball, however, was greatly diminished by the relief she felt at finally knowing that her secret was a secret no more.

She had known of course that maintaining her deception was difficult on a practical level. But never had she realized just how great a toll lying about the extent of her injuries had taken on her soul. No one, not her cousins, not her aunts, not even her dear friend Anna, had been allowed to know about her amputation. Only Alec, and he only recently, had shared in her burden.

"I hope this will not affect your standing in society," she told him that night as they lay together in his bed. "It is unfair that you should suffer because I failed to disclose the extent of my injury before we wed. I should have told you."

But he would have none of it, and tucked her against his shoulder with a proprietary air. "Don't be a goose. I told you before that I knew, or guessed, your secret before we wed. It makes no difference."

She began to argue, but he silenced her with a kiss and Juliet was forced to let the matter rest.

But it was difficult to ignore her situation the next day when her drawing room was filled with society ladies intent upon ensuring that she knew very well just how lucky she was.

"For I heard he was on the verge of offering for Caroline Simpson," the Countess Downes, and the mother of Lady Felicia Downes, informed her. "You did well to keep your . . ." she paused, whether for effect or because she was trying to find a polite way to say "amputation," Juliet couldn't tell.

"Your foot trouble," Mrs. Snowe, a buxom social climber who also happened to be the mother of the Ugly Ducklings' arch nemesis, finished for her friend. "You did well to hide it from him, my dear," she continued, her approval rankling with Juliet in a way her disapproval would not have. "For gentlemen do seem to be concerned about appearances, don't they?"

Juliet could think of no polite response, and she was saved from giving one by the appearance of Hamilton.

"My lady," he said quietly, "you have a visitor in the small sitting room."

Desperate for any reason to escape her present company, she excused herself and gave a nod to her sisters-in-law who were chatting with friends on the opposite side of the room. When she reached the hallway, however, Hamilton paused.

"His lordship has refused his uncle admittance more than once, but Mr. Devenish pushed past me and refuses to leave. I can have him removed by the footmen but I wished to inform you first."

Juliet frowned. She had met Alec's uncle many times when he had been an intimate of her father's but it had been some years since she'd had any contact with the man. Unlike Alec, Roderick Devenish bore a striking resemblance to the previous viscount, in both manner and looks. He also rivaled his late brother's reputation as a reprobate.

It would be unwise for her to meet with him without having her husband present, but curiosity, and a reluctance to return to the drawing room, made her say, "I will see him, Hamilton. But please remain nearby lest we need to employ the footmen in his removal."

At the butler's nod, she gripped her walking stick and walked calmly into the sitting room.

Her new uncle by marriage was staring up at the portrait of Lady Sophia Deveril, which hung in the room that was once that lady's sitting room.

"Her beauty still takes my breath away," Roderick said as she entered the room. "It's a shame what happened. A damned shame."

Ignoring his epithet, Juliet squared her shoulders and said, "Mr. Devenish, I am afraid my husband is not here to receive you. If you will return later this evening I feel sure he will see you then."

"I wouldn't wager on that, my lady," her husband's uncle said with a bitter laugh. "My nephew and I are not currently on speaking terms. But you knew that already, didn't you, my dear?"

The way he murmured the endearment sent a shiver of disgust down Juliet's spine. "Then I will have to ask you to leave, Mr. Devenish," she said firmly. "I have guests in the drawing room. If you'll excuse me?"

She began to turn but before she could make it to the door, Devenish stopped her with a hand on her upper arm. He wore gloves, but she flinched at the touch nonetheless.

"But it is you I've come to speak with, Viscountess Deveril," he said sharply. "There are some things I believe you should know about your darling husband."

Unwilling to show him just how unsettled she was by him, and curious about what the man had to say, Juliet waved him back into the room and took a seat herself on the settee.

"You have my attention, sir."

Satisfaction flickered across Devenish's face. "Then I will be to the point. I spoke earlier about the late Lady Deveril's death. I wonder if your husband has ever told you just how his mother died?"

He was like a cat toying with a mouse, Juliet thought grimly. He threw out questions in the hope that she'd rise to his bait.

"He has said little about his mother," she admitted. "I believe she died in a carriage accident."

As soon as she said the words she knew it was untrue. She also knew she was about to hear something she did not wish to.

"What if I were to tell you that Lady Elizabeth Deveril died in this very room. By her husband's hand."

She opened her mouth to refute the claim, but Devenish

wasn't finished. "What if I told you that your husband watched and did nothing?"

Juliet instinctively gasped. She'd expected Devenish to implicate his late brother. From everything she'd heard, the previous Lord Deveril had been a drunk and a brute. She had little doubt that the man would have been capable of killing his own wife.

But that Alec had witnessed the murder? It was too much to be borne. She stood, prepared to order the man from the house, but a voice behind her stopped her cold.

"Get out," Alec said from the doorway. "Get the hell out of this house."

Alec had returned home from White's with the shushed whispers of his peers ringing in his ears. Gentlemen were not so overt in their gossip as ladies, but they were not immune to the lure of a good story. And the tale of how the Viscount Deveril had been trapped into marriage with a cripple was a compelling one. Never mind that it had been obvious before the marriage that she had some sort of injury to her leg, and never mind that Juliet was lovely and one of the finest musicians in London. And, most importantly, never mind that he told more than one man that he'd known the true nature of her injury *before* they'd married.

There was also the fact that the *ton* felt betrayed by the fact that they themselves had been tricked into thinking Juliet was merely injured instead of maimed. The distinction was laughable to Alec, who felt only admiration for the fact that Juliet had managed to pass for so long without having anyone suspect her of hiding the true extent of her injuries. But society's pique could not have been greater if Juliet had revealed herself to be an Amazon princess rather than a gently bred young lady. And it would take some time for them to recover from the upset.

He returned home hoping to learn that Juliet's morning

calls had been more successful, only to be informed by Hamilton that she was in the small sitting room with his uncle of all people.

Angered because he'd informed the older man that he was no longer welcome in Deveril House, and worried that his uncle would reveal secrets he had no right to betray, he stalked into the small sitting room.

The room was silent, save for Juliet's sharp intake of breath at something his uncle had just said. From the look on Roderick's face it was not something particularly pleasant.

"Get out," he ordered, his anger rising as he saw Juliet's stricken face. Damn it, if Roderick had told her anything about what had happened in this room . . .

"Get the hell out of this house," he repeated, unable to stop himself from raising his voice even as he saw his uncle's pleased expression.

"Ask him, my dear," his father's brother said with a cryptic smile. "Ask him about what happened here in this room."

His poisonous work done, Roderick left the room, and Hamilton and the footmen were waiting for him just outside the door to escort him from the house.

"Alec," Juliet said, hurrying toward him.

"So, I suppose you have guessed my own little secret now," he said bitterly. "That makes us even, does it not, wife?"

As he had intended, her expression changed from concern to hurt. But, resilient as ever, Juliet quickly hid her pain. "I had not thought of it in those terms, my lord," she said calmly. "And whatever secret you harbor, I know we can get past it. After all—"

"There is no need to 'get past it' as you so eloquently phrase it," he said, knowing he was behaving like an ass, but unable to stop himself. "We are well and truly wed, and no amount of secrets and lies can put that asunder."

"That is true," Juliet said, ever reasonable, "so—"

"Do you not understand it, my lady?" he interrupted her. "I have duped you! *I* have duped *you*. All of London is atwitter with the news that the *ton*'s most eligible bachelor was tricked into marriage, but the joke is on them. For I'm the one who tricked you."

"How?" she demanded, her voice remarkably calm despite her pallor. "How have you tricked me?"

Stepping closer, he lifted her chin with a finger, and said quietly, "I let you think that I am a decent man. I let you think I am worthy of you."

She shook her head, as if trying to keep the words from worming their way into her ears. But the truth, as Alec well knew, was more insidious than the deadliest poison.

"I let you think . . ." he told her, kissing her gently, then stepping away from her, dropping his hands as if she were a hot coal.

"I let you think," he continued, backing from the room, "that I am not the son of a murderer."

Unable to watch the confusion on her face turn to loathing, he turned and fled the room.

When Alec finally stumbled home that night, in the wee hours of the coming day, it was to find his bed empty, and the connecting door between their rooms very firmly closed.

Just as well, he told himself. Now that she knew just what kind of stock he hailed from, Juliet would do well to protect herself from him.

He unwound the woefully wilted cravat from around his neck and closed his eyes against the memory of Juliet's face just before he turned and left the room. He had hoped to explain the most awful day of his life to her, but in his own time. After he'd assured her that he had done everything in his power to prevent himself from becoming the same kind of man his father had been. The same kind of man his uncle now was.

His uncle's revelation had put paid to that hope. He'd spent his whole life trying to atone for his own role in his mother's death. And when he'd seen the opportunity to save Juliet from her own hellish existence in her mother's house, he had, foolishly he now knew, hoped that he would at last have a chance to settle the score with fate.

But now that hope was gone. And he would have to find some other way to make his peace with fate. To prove to himself and the world that he was not just like his father. To show every member of the *ton* who whispered in hushed tones when he passed that though he bore Devil Deveril's blood in his veins, he would not, could not, turn into the kind of rage-filled monster who could beat a helpless woman to death in front of her child.

Yet the very urge to prove them all wrong was a kind of rage, he thought bitterly as he struggled to remove his boots without the help of his valet.

"Damn it," he said through gritted teeth as he tugged. The sound of the connecting door between their two chambers alerted him to Juliet's presence, which perversely made him tug harder.

"Let me help," she said, moving toward him, the thin fabric of her nightgown and peignoir shushing against itself as she walked.

Kneeling, she gripped the leather of his boot and tugged, her fingers brushing against his. He could not fail to notice that her lips were pursed in pique. Her auburn hair, neatly done up in the braid she wore to bed, hung down her back, giving her the look of an outraged schoolmarm. Unable to go in bare feet, or even the kind of night slippers worn by other ladies of quality, she wore the simplest of her prosthetic feet with a pair of lace-up half-boots. It was a sign of her agitation that she had ventured out of her own room in such attire, for she was as yet still worried about revealing her infirmity to anyone but him. He wanted to fold her into his arms and protect her from the world. But it was, it seemed, too late for that.

Still he could not resist questioning her.

"So you aren't afraid of me?" he asked, even to himself sounding like a petulant child.

"No," came her calm reply as she turned her attention to his other boot. "I am annoyed, of course. You didn't send word that you would be absent from dinner. And I was forced to send our regrets to Cecily and Winterson.

"I was somewhat worried as well," she added, pulling harder than strictly necessary on his boot.

Once she'd removed them, he took his boots from her and stood. "If that is the entirety of your scold," he said harshly, "I would like to go to sleep now. In case you haven't noticed, it's been a long day for me."

Turning his back on her, Alec shrugged out of his coat, and unbuttoned his waistcoat, his dismissal of her as obvious as he could make it.

But it would seem that Juliet was made of sterner stuff.

"Your uncle revealed nothing outside of telling me that your mother died at your father's hand," she said with a frown. "Which, incidentally, is something I already knew before he told me."

That brought him up short. "What do you mean, 'you already knew'?"

"Oh, come, Alec," she said wryly. "You have spoken of your father's brutality again and again. It is not such a far reach to suspect the carriage accident you blamed for your mother's death was a polite fiction invented to protect your sisters from the truth."

He stared at her as if she'd gone mad. Had he really been so transparent? Was it so obvious that his sisters had figured out the truth? He dragged a hand over his face, feeling the prickle of stubble on his chin.

"What I do not believe," Juliet continued, stepping closer to him, "is that you had anything to do with it."

"Your championship is laudable, my dear," he told her, holding her at arm's length. "But you do not know what you are saying. I am reminded every day of just how much of my father's blood runs through my veins. And through his brother's as well. Indeed, you would do well to avoid being in company with either of us from now on. You should have a care for your own safety lest you suffer my mother's fate."

"Do not be absurd," she argued. "You are nothing like either of them."

Pushing away from her, he strode over to stare out the window into the darkened garden below. "I suppose you will not be content with simply taking my word for it?" he asked without much hope. Juliet was turning out to be more tenacious than he could ever have imagined when they'd first met.

"Not at all," she snapped. "You have made some strong accusations against my husband. I cannot let that stand without some sort of proof."

"You are relentless, do you know that?" he asked, turning to find her, not surprisingly, just behind him.

Tilting her chin, she nodded. "Yes, I am. So you'd better tell me the truth."

Without a word, he took her arm and led her to the chairs before the fire. He would have preferred to drag her to bed and ravish her, but he could see from her expression that there would be no intimacy between them until he'd revealed all. Though, as luck would have it, he very much doubted there would be any further intimacies between them after he told his sordid story. With a pang of regret for what had been shaping up into a workable marriage, he began to tell her his story.

Nineteen

$\mathcal{M}$y parents' was an arranged marriage," he began, leaning forward with his elbows on his knees, as if resisting the urge to curl in on himself and hide his soft underbelly from predators.

Juliet resisted the urge to take him into her arms and soothe him. He looked so brittle. And she sensed that the slightest touch would shatter him. The planes of his face, so finely wrought, were made harsh in the firelight. As if the very act of revealing his secret had transformed his angelic countenance into something devilish.

"I believe at first that they were happy enough," he continued. "My father was able to restrain himself a bit more in those days, I think. Or perhaps he was afraid of angering my mother's family, from whom she received an annuity in addition to the bride gift she'd brought to the marriage. Whatever the case, they got along well enough and within two years I had come along, and with my birth my mother's main duty of providing an heir had been fulfilled."

Juliet ached to hear him describe himself in such terms. It might be true that as the heir he had been a duty, but no child should be made to think of himself as such. At least, she did not believe so.

"I was four when Kat was born, and it was then that I became aware of my mother's fragility. She had Nanny bring us both down to her in the parlor one afternoon, and when Nanny was called away for a few moments, Kat began to fret, as babies sometimes do. And when Mama could not quiet her, I began to feel true panic from her. I was only a child of course but her anxiety . . ." He stopped, searching for the words. "It frightened me. I tried myself to convince Kat to stop crying. I don't know how I knew it, but I did somehow, that her cries were distressing to Mama in a way that was more than the situation warranted."

She had little trouble imagining Alec as a small child, his gilded curls shining in the sunlight, trying to entertain his baby sister from her tantrum.

"This was when my father arrived," he continued, and Juliet felt her heart sink, knowing without words where this tale was heading. "He was foxed, though I only realized that later, and was annoyed at having his good mood spoiled by Kat's wailing. He ordered Mama to make the crying stop. And already overset by the situation, and I think annoyed at her own failure, she said something sharp to him. I do not even recall what it was. All I know is that the next thing I saw was my father's hand striking her face."

Alec closed his eyes, as if to erase the memory. "I can still hear the sound of his palm against her cheek. And the way that Kat's cries stopped suddenly as if she too were surprised at the blow. Of course she started up again almost immediately, this time with a wail fit to wake the dead, and by this time Nanny had returned and she hurried us from the room. But not before I looked back, and saw my mother cowering before his raised hand."

"That must have been dreadful for you," Juliet said quietly, trying to keep her tone measured and not reveal too much of her anger at both his parents for their handling of the situation.

"It was hardly the worst I saw between them," he said with a shrug. "Over the years they fought again and again. Though as time dragged on my mother's defiance became more muted. I believe there was something about pregnancy, or childbirth, that brought her low in some way. For she seemed to be at her most vulnerable point just after Kat, and later Lydia, were born. And there was something about her very fragility that seemed to bring out the worst in my father. As if he scented blood and knew it was time to go for the throat."

To hear him describe his parents so hurt Juliet's heart on his behalf. Still, she needed to hear it all. "Tell me the rest," she said quietly.

With a slight nod, he continued. "Something happened to Mama after Lydia's birth. Though she'd been vulnerable before, I believe there was something about her experience with Lydia that . . . broke her, for want of a better word. Though she'd never been a particularly social person she'd at least attended some society functions and events, but after Lydia's birth, she became almost entirely housebound. Whereas she'd made some effort to spend time with us for a little while every day, she became distant. Barely looking up when Nanny brought us in to see her. Or worse, ignoring us altogether. It was as if the very life had drained out of her."

What Alec described sounded very similar to something her own aunt, her father's sister, had undergone following the birth of her child. It was a sort of ill humor that descended upon one following childbirth, and often led to megrims, a decline, and in some severe cases, death. She shuddered to think of what Lady Deveril's children must have suffered on her behalf.

"I was around eleven, and preparing to go up to Harrow," he said, his expression bleak, "and Mama was begging my father not to send me away. It was an old argument. And to my shame, I was desperate to get away from them both. I loved my mother, of course, but she was smothering at times and I was ready to go off and become a young man without having her coddle me."

"Which is perfectly natural," Juliet interjected with a

smile. "I believe all children go through that stage at some point."

"Well, as careful as I was not to hurt her feelings, Mama was determined to paint my wish to go to school as a betrayal. And of course, simply to thwart her wishes, my father took my side in the matter." His eyes shadowed. "I do admit to feeling some discomfort at having him as my champion, but I was a selfish child and was willing to do whatever it took to get my way."

Juliet would have argued, but she could see that he had made up his mind on the matter. Though she doubted he'd taken into account the fact that he was a child at the time, despite his description of himself as such. Her heart constricted to think of the too-serious, wary little boy he must have been.

"That day, she was more overset than usual about the situation. They had been bickering about it all morning, and I could see that she was growing more and more upset. I tried to calm her but nothing was working. Finally, my father said something particularly cruel, something about it being better for me to be away at school with other boys than chained to my bitch of a mother."

He exhaled. "I don't recall the exact words. But they were the last straw for Mama. She rose from the chaise, and slapped him full across the face."

Juliet covered her mouth to catch her own gasp.

"I think in all the years he'd been hitting her it never occurred to my father that she could or would strike back. The silence that fell over the room was deafening. It was unlike anything I've heard or seen since. But when he returned the blow, I could almost hear the bones snap in her neck. Of course that's impossible, but I thought I heard them all the same."

"What did you do?" Juliet asked, her stomach in knots as she thought of how awful it must have been for him to watch such scenes play out before him.

"I didn't launch myself at him to protect her, if that's what you're asking," Alec said harshly. Though Juliet knew his anger was directed inward, she still felt the sting of it.

"I cowered in the corner, hoping he would forget I was even in the room," he said, a bit more softly. "Which he did."

"Thank God," Juliet murmured. "Else he'd have attacked you too."

"Possibly," he said. "But unfortunately for my mother, who had taken many beatings from her husband since the early days of their marriage, this time when she fell, she broke her fall in such a way that she hit her head on a table."

His eyes were bleak now, distant.

"So, I may not have killed her myself," he explained. "I may not have delivered that final crushing blow, but I did nothing to save her." He wiped a hand over his eyes, which were suspiciously damp. "I did not kill her, but I am just as guilty of her death as the man who did the killing."

But Juliet had had enough. "Don't you think for one moment, Alec Devenish, that you are anything like the man who fathered you." She stood up from her chair and put her fists against her hips. "You were a child! A child! Can you possibly think that you bear the same sort of culpability in her death as he did?"

"It's no use, Juliet," he said wearily. "I've thought and thought about this and I always come up with the same conclusion. Yes, I was a child, but hardly a baby. I could have stepped in between them but I was too worried about my own hide to do anything to save her."

"For bloody good reason!" Juliet nearly shouted. "You were a little boy. You'd seen him beat your mother time and time again. Simple experience would tell you that you could not go against him expecting a different outcome."

If he was shocked by her profanity he did not say so. "I

appreciate your championship, my dear," he said gently. "Truly, I do, but I long ago resigned myself to the role I played that day. I had, selfishly, hoped that you would never hear of it, but now that you have, I am grateful that, however misguided, you have chosen to take my part."

"Foolish man!" she hissed. "Can you not see the logical fallacy of your own argument?"

"I don't know what you—"

"Are you not the same man who told me I was not to blame for my mother's cruelty to me?"

He frowned. "Yes, but I don't see . . ."

Juliet bit back a curse. "Do you not see the difference between a small boy cowering from the father who had beaten his mother before him, and the grown woman who cowers from the mother who has browbeaten her all her life?"

"Don't be absurd," Alec said curtly. "You were hardly able to defend yourself and—"

"If you finish that sentence by saying that I was a cripple I will scream this house down."

His blush indicated that she'd guessed exactly what he was going to say. Damn him.

"So, am I really so incapacitated that as an adult female I am more powerless than a little boy?" she demanded.

"You're trying to trick me," Alec said finally, crossing his arms over his chest. "Into saying that we were equally powerless."

A sigh pushed from her. "I am trying to make you see that you are no more responsible for your mother's death than I am responsible for my mother's manipulation of me."

"But the situations . . ." he began.

Knowing she'd won, despite the fact that he was still making a token attempt to argue with her, Juliet moved closer to him.

"The situations both involved bullies bending their

children to do their bidding," she finished for him, unwrapping his arms from his chest and inserting herself between them. Reluctantly, he pulled her into them.

"You've nothing to be ashamed of, Alec," she whispered, caressing his face before she wrapped him in an embrace that was meant to comfort this man who had lived with a guilt that was as much a fiction created in the mind of a child as an actual culpability. To Juliet's mind, Alec was no more responsible for his mother's death than baby Lydia had been. The real culprit in Lady Deveril's death had been the husband who had met her low spirits after the birth of her daughters with violence.

"You were a child, darling," she told Alec against his temple, holding him to her breast as if he were the child he had been all those years ago. "You can have done nothing to stop your father from hurting her. If you had intervened he would likely have hurt you too."

She felt him tremble against her, his grief over his memory of that awful day, coupled with the absolution she offered, seeming to draw a response that was at once sorrowful and cathartic. He took her mouth in a kiss that was none too gentle. And she welcomed it.

"Juliet," he murmured against her mouth, stroking his tongue between the seam of her lips, "Sweet, combative Juliet."

She might have objected to being characterized as thus, but she was too overcome by the feel of his strong arms surrounding her, his hard body pressed insistently against hers. Her need to comfort him with words was swiftly transformed into a desperation to comfort him with her body, to give him everything he asked of her now.

Wanting to feel his skin against hers, she pulled his shirt from where it was tucked into his breeches, even as he pulled the sash of her dressing gown and bared her to his gaze.

"Beautiful," Alec said, lifting her into his arms. All Ju-

liet's worries of how to surreptitiously remove her prosthetic foot were forgotten in the heady sensation of skin
against skin as Alec swept her against his strong chest and
carried her to the bed.

He pulled the counterpane down, along with the top
sheet, and laid her down on the mattress.

"You are so lovely," he whispered, climbing up after her,
stroking a reverent hand over the skin of her breasts, her
belly, her legs. He paused just above the place on her right
calf where her wooden foot was fastened to her with a small
corset that wound round her just below the knee. Juliet had
laced it with a red ribbon, a touch of whimsy and prettiness
for the utilitarian instrument that was at once a shoe and
not a shoe at all.

Just as he had done with the sash of her dressing gown,
Alec pulled the red ribbon, untying it and unlacing the
contraption from where it held the false foot in place. Before Juliet could stop him, before she even knew what he
was about, her husband hovered over her newly liberated
lower leg, pressing his lips against the indentations in
her skin where the ribbon and canvas had pressed into her
skin.

To her shock, he ran his tongue over the seamlike scar
that ran down and around the bottom of her leg, where
once her ankle had been.

"Don't," she said, instinctively pulling her leg away
from him. But Alec's grip was firm, and strong.

"Juliet," he said, even as he worked his way up her leg
toward her knee, "your leg is nothing to be ashamed of. It
is a part of you. And I am determined to worship," he said
against her thigh, "every . . ."

He kissed her inner thigh. "Last . . ."

He moved up her body toward that part of her that cried
out to feel his mouth close over it. "Part."

With that last word, he slipped her knees over his shoulders and kissed her extravagantly at the apex of her thighs,

his lips, teeth, and tongue working against the sensitive skin of her molten core in a way that robbed her of breath.

Her every objection to such an intimate position was forgotten in the sheer overwhelming pleasure of his mouth on her. Before long she was moving involuntarily against him, and when he added his fingers into the mix, she had little choice but to succumb to the onslaught of sensation overtaking her.

She was still trembling with her release when she felt him move up her body, felt him take her mouth with a tenderness that nearly moved her to tears, her own flavor still present on his lips.

"Thank you," he said against her mouth, settling his body between her thighs.

"For what?" she asked dreamily, her body's languor from her earlier release being quickly replaced with a growing excitement at the feel of him pressed against her.

"For letting me in," he said simply. And before she could ask just what that meant, he lifted her hips and pressed himself into her, and thoughts were no longer possible.

Twenty

Unwilling to subject herself to another day of sitting in her own drawing room and being ogled like the unfortunate creatures in the London Zoo, Juliet informed Hamilton the next morning that she was not at home to callers.

Alec had gone out before breakfast, but not before a very satisfactory good morning that had left them both thoroughly sated. After his confidences of the night before, she felt closer to him than she had since their hasty marriage. It had been difficult to lower the defenses she'd spent the past several years putting solidly into place, but the more she came to know Alec—not the fashionable creature who led the *ton* about by the ear, but the real man beneath the costume—the more she simply liked him. He was funny and self-deprecating, but what she appreciated most of all was that he did not treat her like some wounded bird who needed to be rescued or mended.

Even when they had not known the true reason for her limp, the gentlemen she had interacted with since her injury had always made her consciously aware that they knew. It went beyond mere consideration—she would not have minded a discreetly offered arm to lean on—but instead was an emphasis on the fact that she was *other*. That they even condescended to speak to her was always held up, albeit without direct acknowledgment of the fact, as an act worthy of accolades. She should be grateful for their attention, they seemed to say.

But with Alec, there had never been the least hint that he considered himself her superior. Always, even when they had hardly known one another, he had treated her as a woman, not a person, worthy of his attention. It was a heady thing to be noticed by a man as charismatic as Lord Deveril. But it was the notice of Alec Devenish that truly made her heart sing. And that was what terrified her most of all.

After a leisurely breakfast in her room, Juliet headed for the music room to practice. The tumult of her life these past weeks had left her with little time for the things she had done as a matter of routine in her old life. Now, having been so long away from the music that she loved, Juliet sat down at the perfectly tuned instrument and to her pleasure found that her own sheet music had been installed there. Taking the new sonata by Beethoven she had purchased just before her escape from her parents' home, she applied herself to it, taking out all the frustrations and angst of the past weeks on the highly polished keys of the pianoforte.

She had just mastered a particularly difficult passage halfway through the work when she heard an apologetic throat clearing behind her.

"I beg your pardon, my lady," Hamilton said from the doorway, "but you have visitors and they insisted upon seeing you."

Before he could step forward to give her the card, Juliet saw her father and a gentleman she did not know pressing into the room.

"Daughter," Lord Shelby said, his voice clipped, "tell this fellow that you will see us and send him away at once."

Juliet opened her mouth to protest, but her father continued. "I know you have little reason to welcome a visit from either of your parents, but I promise you that what I have to tell you is of import. Not only for you but for your husband as well."

Since this was the most her father had spoken to her in some years, Juliet found herself nonplussed. Why on earth would he be so insistent upon speaking to her unless what he had to say was truly important? Deciding to let her curiosity rule her in this instance, she waved Hamilton away and led her visitors to the arrangement of seats on the opposite side of the room.

"Father," she said, her tone imperious, much to her secret pleasure, "I see that you have returned from Paris. Pray continue with what you have to say."

Now that he'd gained entry, Lord Shelby had the decency to look abashed. As she gazed upon him, Juliet realized that this was the most haggard she'd ever seen him. Gone was the elegant, controlled diplomat she'd become accustomed to. In his place she saw a man who got too little rest and who had pushed himself beyond his limits.

"I do not believe you have met Admiral Frye," Lord Shelby said, gesturing to the man next to him.

As her father's companion bowed, Juliet noticed for the first time that his coat sleeve was pinned up where his right arm should be.

"My lady," the admiral said with what appeared to be genuine pleasure, "I am delighted to make the acquaintance of the young lady who has set the *haut ton* on its ear."

Juliet looked from one to the other of the two men. "I do not understand, Papa," she said carefully. Could her father actually have brought this man who had clearly lost his arm in battle to give her some sort of encouragement about her own injury? The idea was so foreign as to be laughable.

Perhaps sensing the tension between the father and daughter, the naval man stepped into the breach. "Lady Deveril, I requested that your father, whom I have known since we were both in short coats, bring me to see you as soon as I learned of your courage the other evening at the Wallingford ball."

"But there was nothing courageous about what I did," Juliet said, shaking her head. "My secret was revealed and I took the soonest opportunity to make my escape. It hardly compares with what you must have endured in the war." She paused, and color suffused her cheeks. "Unless your injury was not received during the war. I simply assumed with your naval background that . . ."

Frye laughed heartily. "No, indeed," he assured her, "you are perfectly correct. I lost my arm at Trafalgar, make no mistake on it. And I wasn't the only one that day either. Though I was lucky enough not to have perished like Nelson did." He sobered at the thought of the great hero of the maritime war against Napoleon.

"Still," he continued, "though I don't say that it's exactly the same as what we went through, I do know how difficult it is to face a room full of folk staring at you like you've just waltzed out onto the dance floor without a stitch of clothes on."

Lord Shelby glared at his friend, who had the grace to blush. "Begging your pardon, of course, my lady."

Since she was unaccustomed to her father's notice of her at all, his protection of her delicate sensibilities came as a surprise. The whole meeting was extraordinary.

"I didn't know," Lord Shelby said, so quickly upon the heels of his friend's apology that at first Juliet thought he meant that he did not know the admiral would be forced to beg her pardon. But as he went on, her father's meaning became clear.

"I knew of course that you were injured in Vienna," he continued, his shoulders slumped in defeat. "But I was always inclined to believe that the sickroom was a lady's purview. I did check in on you, of course. And received daily updates from your mother upon your progress, but I did not know the . . ." He paused, the lines around his eyes and mouth making him seem older than his years. "For God's sake, I did not know you lost your foot! And your mother never informed me of the fact."

The anguish in her father's voice was genuine.

As if unable to remain still, Lord Shelby rose from his chair and stood before the fireplace, his hands clasped behind his back.

So unexpected was her father's confession it sent a jolt of surprise through Juliet that shook her to her core. "You did not know?" she echoed. "How is that possible? You were in the same house. You came to visit me in my sickroom afterward."

But as she cast her mind back to those terrible days when she lay burning up with fever after the amputation, and the subsequent cauterization, Juliet realized that she remembered little of that time. Aside from the pain of course. Hours and hours of unrelenting pain.

"No," her father said, "I didn't visit you." His eyes burned with remorse. "You must remember that those were the weeks leading up to Waterloo, and the entire diplomatic corps was working night and day to secure an agreement, which we did manage in those few days before the battle. Your mother assured me that you were being well cared for, and to my shame, I believed her."

And Juliet realized he told the truth. Strange that even now she could be disappointed in her father's lack of interest in her. She had thought she'd eradicated that need to please him long ago. But it would appear that some habits were nearly impossible to break.

"So you are here for what, exactly?" she asked him with a coolness that should please her but only made her stomach ache. "Apologies? Redemption?"

Lord Shelby stepped away from the mantel and knelt before her, like a supplicant. Taking her hands in his, he looked up into her eyes, and Juliet was surprised, and to her shame, moved, to see tears in them.

"Juliet," he said softly, "I am so utterly sorry that I was not there for you during what must have been the most dreadful weeks of your life." He shook his head. "My God, you were a girl, a child, really, and you endured more than many men who have been through battle."

She wanted to punish him for his selfishness, but Juliet knew that the blame did not lie with Lord Shelby. He had been embroiled in difficult diplomatic negotiations at the time. And he had relied upon his wife to let him know of anything he might need to be aware of. No, the real blame lay upon Lady Shelby's head, though it was doubtful that she would ever be punished for her misdeeds.

"I forgive you, Papa," she told him, squeezing his hands, and before she could say more, she found herself gathered to him in a hug, something she had not experienced since she was a small child.

"Thank you, daughter," Lord Shelby said against her hair. "Thank you."

The sound of a cough alerted father and daughter to the continued presence of Admiral Frye in the room. "Don't mean to break up the happy reunion," the older man said, "but I do have another appointment this afternoon."

"Of course." Lord Shelby drew back at once, and smiled ruefully at his friend. "Apologies, Frye. I forgot you were there."

"Don't mention it," Frye said. "It does my heart good to see the two of you mending fences. A daughter should be able to rely on her father's protection."

Juliet wasn't sure she'd go so far as to say that, but she was glad to have finally come to an understanding with Lord Shelby. She did not think she would need his support now that she had Alec to turn to, but she looked forward to renewing her acquaintance with the one parent she did not hold in contempt.

"That recalls me to our reason for calling upon you in the first place," Lord Shelby said, resuming his seat. "I have brought Frye here because he wishes to assist you in reconciling yourself with the *ton*."

"Aye," the admiral said with a grin, "when I heard what those cats had done to you at the Wallingfords' I told my wife that I was going to seek out my old friend Shelby and offer my assistance. And here you find us."

Juliet was flummoxed. Of all the reasons she had suspected her father had called today, this had been as far from her suspicions as one could get.

"Your assistance?" she asked carefully. "I don't understand."

"Come now, Juliet," Lord Shelby said, "even with Deveril's social standing behind you and society's insatiable curiosity, it will be difficult to rehabilitate your reputation without some assistance."

"It is not simply Deveril's standing that I rely upon," Juliet countered. "I also have my cousins and their parents who are willing to lend me support." But even as she said the words she knew that even that might not be enough.

"How much stronger would you be, then," Admiral Frye said, "If you had every man who wore a uniform on England's behalf in the war standing behind you?"

"But how could you possibly arrange such a thing?" Juliet asked, dumbfounded.

"You leave that to me," the admiral said with a grin. Then, seeing her doubts, he sobered. "Lady Deveril, you have no idea how many of our boys came home far different men than they were when they left. And they told themselves that it was worth it, because they were fighting for the country they loved. They know what it's like to face the stares, the cruelty, the taunts of those who won't tolerate those who are different. And when I tell them there's a young lady who suffered their same sort of injury, a young lady the likes of which they thought they were fighting for? Well, let's just say that I have little doubt that I'll find enough men willing to come to your aid."

He grinned. "Even if it means they'll have to wrangle themselves into fancy togs and pay a visit to the theatre."

Alec fought back a growl as yet another handsome ex-military man entered their box at the Theatre Royale to pay his respects to Juliet. When she had explained her father and Admiral Frye's scheme to him earlier that day, he somehow hadn't imagined that the men who would offer her their support would be so damned charming. Even the elderly ones seemed intent upon captivating her attention.

"Easy, friend," Winterson said at his elbow. "This was all part of the plan. It would hardly repair your wife's reputation if you were to call out the majority of His Majesty's war heroes for smiling at her."

"But it would make me feel better," Alec muttered through clenched teeth as he watched Juliet smile at the darkly handsome Earl of Rickarby, who had distinguished himself at Talavera and lost a leg in the process.

"Yes, well, it would not make Juliet feel better." Winterson seemed to be amused by Alec's discomfort.

And Deveril could hardly blame him. He was behaving like the worst sort of jealous lout. But he had grown accustomed in the brief weeks of their marriage to being the focus of Juliet's smiles. And he was having a dashed difficult time remembering just why he thought it was a bad idea to declare his affection for her.

Of course there was his fear of succumbing to the sort of passionate brutality that his father had fallen prey to. But Juliet had seemed to think that such fears were unfounded. And upon reflection, so did he. Once, he had been given to believe that such things were a part of one's makeup. But as he had managed in some thirty years to avoid falling into the same traps as his father and uncle, he somehow thought that the danger had passed. After all, hadn't his father been prone to deep play and womanizing from his days at Eton?

Still, something within him feared that if he were to reveal his feelings to Juliet, she would be forced to tell him she harbored nothing but gratitude for him. And that possibility alone was enough to keep him silent on the matter. Though at night, in the throes of a passion more powerful than any he had ever known, he might hope that it meant more to her than just physical release, he had no way of knowing whether his suspicions were true.

No, he would hold his tongue on the matter until both the disappearance of Mrs. Turner and Juliet's precarious position in the *ton* were resolved. It would be selfish of him to unburden his feelings to her while she was dealing with so much difficulty.

"I just hope this plot of Shelby's works," Alec said, returning his thoughts to the subject at hand. "She deserves to be able to move about in society without encountering hushed whispers and stares."

"Yes, she does," Winterson agreed, watching as yet another wounded military man entered the box. "It grieves Cecily that she has not been able to do more to rehabilitate her cousin's standing." He did not add that when Cecily was grieved so too was her husband, though it was evident enough to Alec what his friend implied.

"It grieves me as well," he said curtly. He had been a leader of the *ton* for so long that he had begun to take their acceptance and approval for granted, he was ashamed to admit. He had naïvely assumed that any scandal attached to their marriage, or anything else for that matter, would be short-lived thanks to the strength of his social connections. But not even Lord Alec Deveril's social cachet had been enough to prevent the talk when the extent of Juliet's disability had become known. It was not so much the fact of her amputation that riled the tabbies, but the masquerade she'd been perpetrating. That she'd pretended to be whole when she was not.

"But if the whispers and stares across the theatre are

anything to gauge by," Alec said, leaning his shoulders against the wall of his box, "then this gambit might be successful."

When the interval finally ended, there was yet a line of gentlemen waiting in the hallway beyond the Deveril box to gain entrance and an introduction to Juliet. Still, Alec could not help but feel some relief when they had their box back to themselves, with just the Duke and Duchess of Winterson, Monteith, and Alec's sister Lydia.

"The plan seems to have worked marvelously," Cecily said in a low voice from her seat next to Juliet. "I only regret that Maddie wasn't here to see it. She does love a spectacle."

Monteith snorted from his seat behind her. "She likes to create a spectacle, you mean."

"I am a great admirer of Lady Madeline," Lydia said with a toss of her blond hair. "She is loyal and always speaks her mind. Which I think is admirable."

"You are a good friend, Lydia," Cecily said. "And you, Monteith, should be ashamed. Poor Maddie is home with a sore throat and you are here impugning her when she cannot defend herself."

"Do not attempt to argue with her, Monteith," Winterson said with a laugh. "Cecily could argue the entire House of Lords into a stalemate."

"I am not so foolish," Monteith said, throwing up his hands in a gesture of surrender. "And I did not realize Lady Madeline was unwell. Apologies. I wish her a speedy recovery."

"I'll be sure to tell her," Cecily said. "I know she regrets not being here to support you, Juliet."

"I just hope that the admiral's efforts to repair my reputation have been successful," Juliet said. "I do hate to think of all his hard work having been for naught."

Alec resisted the urge to embrace his wife as she bit her lip, a sure sign of nerves.

"Are you well?" he asked as the curtains opened once more upon the performance of *The Tempest* that no one in the theatre seemed to be watching. "It would not be unusual for us to leave the performance early. People do it all the time."

"I am perfectly well, I assure you," Juliet whispered, reaching out to clasp his hand. "I am simply overwhelmed by the sudden attention. And I admit that I am reeling a bit to know just how very lucky I have been. Did you know that many of the soldiers who returned home from the war without legs are unable to afford even a rudimentary wooden peg leg? I had known of course that many veterans were unable to find work when they returned, but I am ashamed to admit that I had no idea just the sort of obstacles they faced once the victory parades ended."

"Ah, I see you've been speaking to the Earl of Leighton," he said with a grin. Leighton was a passionate advocate of veterans' affairs in the House of Lords, and as a hero of Vittoria himself, he took the welfare of his men, even these many years since he'd led them to victory, very seriously.

"Yes," Juliet said, "do you suppose we might do something to assist his work?"

"Of course," Alec assured her, and her shy smile and the wayward curl of auburn hair tickling her neck reminded him that it had been some hours since he'd kissed her last.

He'd spent the bulk of the day questioning purveyors of art supplies about their customers, in hopes of learning the identity of *Il Maestro*. But all he'd found out was that there were far more artists in London than he ever could have imagined, and that it was a damned expensive pastime. Now he was ready for the day to end so that he could make love to his wife. And if she was not amenable, then he planned to get some much-needed sleep.

Before he could rise so that they could take their leave, Alec felt a tap on his shoulder. Winterson nodded to the footman in Deveril livery standing just inside the box.

"What is it, John?" It was highly unusual for Hamilton to send for him unless the matter was serious indeed.

"My lord, Mr. Hamilton sent me to fetch you and her ladyship home," the young man said, still a little breathless. "Someone tried to get into the nursery and take Baby Alice. They didn't manage it, but Mr. Hamilton was sure you'd wish to know."

Not waiting to ask for more details, Alec went to Juliet and informed her that they needed to return home at once. Perhaps reading the worry on his face, Juliet did not question him, but informed her cousins and their escorts that there was a minor household crisis that required her help to unravel, and they were soon embarking upon a silent journey to Berkeley Square.

"I don't know what might have happened if I hadn't gone to check in on the poor lamb before I took to my bed," said Mrs. Pennyfeather, Alice's nurse. "But I did, and as soon as I entered the room I saw him climbing through the window."

That redoubtable lady had then screamed as loudly as she could, and in the ensuing din, the intruder had revised his desire to enter the nursery and made haste to climb back out the window he had been climbing into. By the time Hamilton had dispatched a footman to give chase the man was gone.

"You did the right thing, Mrs. Pennyfeather," Juliet assured the woman, handing her a cup of strong tea which cook herself had brought up to them as she, Alec, the nursemaid, and Hamilton discussed the break-in while Baby Alice continued to sleep like what she was—the proverbial baby.

"Hamilton," Alec told the butler, "you will post one of the footmen here with Baby Alice tonight, and tomorrow you'll see to it that the windows are all firmly locked against intruders."

"Of course, my lord," the older man assured his employer. "Shall I also see to it that the trellis that gave this blackguard a way into the house is moved?"

Juliet watched her husband over the top of her teacup. Alec seemed to be taking the invasion of his home rather badly. Though she supposed she understood why. It must be dreadful to be responsible for the safety and well-being of so many people. Though she knew as well as anyone that tonight's attempt to kidnap Baby Alice was not the fault of anyone but the man who had tried to climb into her window.

"Yes," he told the butler. "I will not hazard another risk to the child's safety."

Once the guard was stationed in the nursery, and Hamilton and Alec had assured themselves of the town house's security, Juliet and Alec mounted the stairs to their own chambers.

Juliet was tucked into bed waiting for Alec, who had become accustomed to sleeping in her chamber, even if only to sleep, when she heard a low murmur that did not sound like either her husband or his valet. Curious, she struggled to hear what they were saying, but finally gave up.

She was just drifting off to sleep when the snick of the connecting door woke her, and Alec, to her surprise, came into the room still fully clothed.

"I'm afraid I've got to go out," he said, leaning down to kiss her briskly. "I've just gotten a note from the runner, Greenshaw."

She propped herself up on her elbows. "What's happened?"

"He says they've found a body, and he thinks I should go have a look."

Juliet's heart constricted. "Not Anna!" she said, sitting upright.

Quickly, Alec reassured her, sitting down next to her on the bed. "No! I'm sorry. I didn't mean to startle you. It isn't Mrs. Turner, I assure you."

"Thank God." After all these weeks of searching for her friend, the one thing Juliet hadn't considered was that she might have taken her own life. It just seemed so out of character for the vibrant woman she knew Anna to be. "Who is it, then?"

"It's Turlington," Alec said. "Turlington is dead."

Twenty-one

Turlington's studio was bustling with activity given the late hour. Alec supposed such things were to be expected when a tenant was found dead.

He hadn't wished to tell Juliet exactly what Greenshaw had revealed in his note, but from what he'd been able to guess, Turlington's manner of death had been neither quick nor pleasant.

Before he could lift the brass knocker, the door was opened by one of Greenshaws men, who it appeared was expecting him. "My lord, Mr. Greenshaw is waiting for you in the study." Following the man through a long hallway, Alec idly wondered where Turlington had come up with the money for a rented room. Though he supposed that the fellow had been as behind with the rent as he'd been in paying his gambling debts.

The flat itself was unremarkable. Tastefully, if sparsely, furnished. The tiny room that must have served as Turlington's office contained little more than a desk scattered with papers and notebooks and ledgers. It was not the well-kept demesne of someone who valued order.

Greenshaw was seated behind the desk.

"Ah, my lord," he said, not looking up from the ledger he was scanning. "I'm glad you were able to come. It's a foul business this, make no mistake on't. Lord Turlington was a rough customer, but he died a painful death."

"I thought you wished me to see the body, Greenshaw." Alec pushed down his impatience with the investigator's casual manner. He might have been asleep in his own bed with Juliet if the Bow Street runner hadn't called for him.

"Yes, I do," Greenshaw said, finally looking up, and rising. "It will make more sense once you've seen him."

With that cryptic remark, Greenshaw stepped away from the desk and walked over to the shelf-lined wall. Reaching up to a red volume that stuck out just slightly from the shelf, he pressed the spine, and to Alec's surprise, the shelves swung out to reveal an open passageway.

"Follow me, my lord," Greenshaw said, not bothering to see if Alec followed him or not.

Shaking his head at the oddity of the man, Alec stepped through the doorway into a damp, stone-lined passage and walked toward the light. He emerged into a large room that had obviously served as an art studio for Turlington, and was greeted by the stench of death. Suppressing a shudder, he avoided looking into the corner that obviously held Turlington's body, and instead glanced around the room. Though it took a moment for his eyes to adjust to the dimness, he realized that the paintings that lined the walls were unlike any he had ever seen.

All of the paintings were excellently rendered. Clearly the artist—he supposed Turlington—was someone of considerable talent. The colors, the detail, the composition: all of it was as good as anything Alec had ever seen. But it was the subject matter of the art that chilled him. Each canvas depicted women in scenarios similar to those he'd already seen in the work of *Il Maestro*. Only these were more graphic, more disturbing.

The first to catch his eye was a portrait of Ophelia, her body naked and oddly vulnerable in death, her eyes open but lifeless as they gazed from the painting. There was something about the model that he recognized, as if he'd seen her somewhere before, in another context. One after the other, he scanned the artwork lining the walls: Desdemona dead by Othello's hand; Sappho, her broken body on the rocks; Cleopatra, dead from the bite of the asp. And each of the models was a different woman. There were six paintings in total, with a space near the end of the row which was clearly marked for another.

"What the devil is this?" he demanded of the runner, though he was very nearly sure what the answer would be.

"This," said Greenshaw dramatically, "is Lord Turlington's private studio. No one but his lordship's valet even knew of its existence, and he wouldn't have told me if he hadn't been afraid for his own neck. Especially given what happened to his master here tonight."

"So Turlington is *Il Maestro*?"

At that, the runner sighed. "It seems likely, my lord. Though I'm no judge of art or the like. We'll have to get someone from the Royal Academy in to say for sure. But at least three of these women in these pictures are dead. And I wouldn't be surprised if your wife's Mrs. Turner turns up the same way."

"How do you know they're the same women?" Alec demanded, turning from the eerie gaze of the woman guised as Cleopatra.

"I brought in one of the lads who fished one of them out of the Thames and he recognized the others," the big man said wearily. "The thing is that we might never know who the others are. If Turlington's main way to get rid of the bodies was to chuck them in the Thames then like as not the river did the work well enough on their faces even their own kin won't know 'em again."

Alec's heart sank. Juliet might never know what had happened to her friend. Still, there might be some clue here in Turlington's house that would lead them to Mrs. Turner.

As if he heard Alec's thoughts, Greenshaw gestured to the far corner of the chamber. "I suppose you'll want to see Turlington now."

When they reached the scene where Turlington had met his fate, Alec saw at once what Greenshaw had meant by the artist's manner of death being unpleasant. His head and upper torso visible over the rim of a hip bath, Turlington's face was contorted into a frozen expression of agony, his hands clasped round his own throat, as if he'd throttled himself. Alec had never made it a practice of studying the various ways in which someone might dispatch themselves, but there had been a housemaid at their country house—probably, in retrospect, one of his father's cast-off lovers—who had killed herself by taking rat poison, and she too had fallen into the sort of rictus Turlington exhibited.

"Did he die by his own hand?" he asked Greenshaw, noting the crystal decanter on the floor beside the tub, and the empty tumbler which had rolled away, spilling some of its contents onto the floor. But even as he spoke he knew it was unlikely. "It's hard to imagine a man choosing to die such an obviously painful death."

"Aye, it does seem an odd choice," the investigator agreed. "Especially when you take into account the note we found with him."

Alec turned to look at the man. "What note?"

Going to the mantelpiece, Greenshaw took down a marker, the sort that was used to display the title and artists of a particular work of art. In fact, it was much like the markers in Turlington's horrible gallery downstairs.

Alec took it from the runner's proffered hand.

A FALLEN MAN, FOUND DROWNED the placard read. But it was the artist's name that caught his attention. And the handwriting, which he knew so well from the letters he and Juliet had seen on their wedding journey, sent a chill down his spine.

LA MAESTRA.

Which in Italian translated to "the schoolmistress."

"This is Anna Turner's handwriting," Alec said.

"Aye," Greenshaw said. "I thought it might be. I'm afraid I've got no good news for you on that front."

"She staged her own disappearance then?" Alec had been suspecting something of the like for some time now. But he hadn't connected the dots between Anna Turner and Lord Turlington. His gut tightened as he thought what the news would do to Juliet.

"It looks likely, my lord." Greenshaw's homely face took on a hangdog expression.

"But what is her connection to Turlington?" Alec demanded. "Is he the father of her child?"

"I can't be sure. But what I do know is that Lord Turlington and Mrs. Turner have known each other for some time. Going back to her youth in some village in Kent."

"Little Wittington?"

"Aye, that's the one." Greenshaw nodded. "Seems Lord Turlington spent the summers with his uncle, a country squire by the name of Ramsey. And Mrs. Turner's father was the local vicar."

Alec remembered the tale that Signor Boccardo had told him and Juliet. "So Turlington and Mrs. Turner met again in London? And began a romance?"

"I think it more likely that Lord Turlington was holding a past indiscretion over the lady's head."

"Yes," Alec confirmed. "He would have known about her fall from grace at his cousin's hands."

"Whatever it was, she was afraid enough of it getting out that she was willing to do anything to stop him from revealing it," Greenshaw said.

"So Turlington is Alice's father?" Alec asked.

"I think it likely," the other man said. "Of course, we have no way of knowing what hand she had in these paintings. Did she help him lure these women to his studio? Did she help him do away with them? Who knows. There's no way of knowing for sure until we find Mrs. Turner and ask her."

And that, Alec knew, had just become more important than ever.

"I would suggest, my lord, that you not tell your lady about this just yet," Greenshaw said, his brow furrowed with worry. "For her own protection."

Thinking of how devastated Juliet would be to learn of her friend's perfidy, Alec silently agreed. He would put off the moment when she learned of Mrs. Turner's crimes for as long as he could. She deserved that much peace, at least.

When Alec had returned the night before, Juliet had been fast asleep, despite her attempts to stay awake. Then, to her frustration, he had risen earlier than usual, leaving her with a kiss and a promise to recount his meeting with Greenshaw as soon as he returned that evening.

She wanted to know whether there had been anything about Turlington's death that pointed toward Anna's whereabouts, but if there had been she knew Alec would have told her.

What had begun as a relationship based upon his desire to protect her from her mother and marriage to Turlington had developed into a marriage the likes of which she'd never dreamed of having. He was everything she could have wished for, if she had ever dared to dream of such a thing as a happy marriage. Not only was he a thoughtful and passionate lover, he had proved to her again and again that her infirmity was for him simply another facet of her, not something to be ashamed of. And with his help, she was coming to feel the same way. Oh, she still had her days of frustration at her inability to simply walk on her own, but no longer did she see herself as the flawed creature who had been bullied into living a lie by her mother.

Her one regret was that she could not share her happiness with Anna. Knowing just the sort of difficulties her friend had endured when she'd been seduced and discarded by Alice's father, she wanted to prove to her friend that not all men were callous blackguards. She even hoped that one day Anna would be able to settle down with Mr. MacEwan. That she could love him as Juliet loved Alec.

The truth of her feelings for him had only dawned, ironically, when he was nowhere to be found, she thought as she buttered her toast at the solitary breakfast table. Her sisters-in-law had already eaten and departed for a visit to Hatchard's, leaving Juliet alone with her tea and her thoughts.

Idly she sorted through the stack of invitations that had arrived that morning, no doubt as a result of her success last evening at the theatre. She made a mental note to send a thank-you note to Admiral Frye that afternoon.

Though she would much prefer to stay home tonight, she had set aside the three gatherings she thought Alec and his sisters might prefer when Hamilton entered the breakfast room with yet another missive.

"My lady, this just arrived," he said, offering the letter to her on the customary salver.

Taking up the note, Juliet bit back a cry of relief as she recognized the handwriting.

"Thank you, Hamilton," she said, "that will be all."

When the butler had gone, Juliet hastily opened the note but was disappointed to see only a few lines.

The Sydenhams' masked ball. Tonight. The portrait gallery. Eight o'clock. Tell no one. Please.
Your dear friend, Anna Turner

"Will I do?" Juliet asked her cousins as she performed a small twirl so that they could see her costume in all its glory.

"You are magnificent," Cecily breathed, her own gown marking her as an Amazon warrior princess. "Though I must say I'm a trifle jealous that you are attired as the most famous Egyptian of them all. I can't believe I didn't think of it."

"You've wished to be an Amazon princess since we were in the nursery, so do not try to cozen us," Maddie said with a dismissive wave of her hand. She herself wore the wide panniers and tall powdered wig of a lady of the previous century.

Though Anna's note had warned her to tell no one about the proposed meeting at the Sydenhams' ball, Juliet had seen nothing wrong with requesting her cousins to accompany her to the entertainment. She could hardly go unaccompanied, and inviting them along had not necessitated her telling them her reason for wishing to attend the party upon such short notice.

She had hoped to bring Alec, but he'd sent a note that afternoon informing her that he'd be dining with Winterson and Monteith at his club, so she had decided to make the evening a Ducklings' night out. Always ready for an entertainment that involved costumes, Cecily and Maddie had accepted her invitation with alacrity.

"Do you think anyone will guess that the asp curled round my staff is really a walking stick?" Juliet asked, nervously adjusting her wig. "I don't want anyone to guess it's me."

"No, it's perfect," Maddie assured her, "after all, you can hardly be Cleopatra after the asp has bitten her. That would be gruesome."

Juliet agreed, especially in light of the ghastly *Il Maestro* paintings they'd been forced to view in the search for Anna. Hopefully tonight's meeting would put an end to that search. And now that Turlington, who must surely have been *Il Maestro*, was dead, perhaps there would be no more of those horrid paintings either.

"We had best depart." Juliet pulled on her gloves. "The Sydenhams' ball is always a crush, so I have no doubt we'll spend more time than I would like simply waiting in the carriage to get to the door."

As it happened Juliet's prediction that the carriage line would be a long one proved correct. It was nearly eight when she made her way through the costumed throngs dancing and chattering in the Sydenhams' lushly decorated ballroom. Pushing past a satyr who seemed intent upon luring her into a secluded alcove, and a Roman centurion who claimed to know her from their previous acquaintance in an earlier century, she was nearly out of breath when she finally slipped into the gallery Anna had indicated.

Though the party was crowded, no amorous couples had yet sought out the wide room that ran the full length of the house for assignations yet, much to Juliet's relief. She had no idea just what sort of trauma Anna had endured during her disappearance, and her friend would doubtless prefer privacy to relate her story.

A little disappointed not to find her friend already there, she stepped farther into the gallery and made a desultory review of the Sydenham ancestors lining the walls as she waited. She was examining a compatriot of Henry VIII when a Grecian lady, complete with laurel threaded through her dark hair, entered. The mask she held to her face obscured her identity, but Juliet knew in a glance that it was Anna.

Twenty-two

*W*hat do you mean you don't know where they are?" Alec demanded, pacing up and down Winterson's study. "You were supposed to be keeping an eye on them."

When he had returned home from yet another meeting with Greenshaw, he had been unhappy to learn that Juliet had gone to spend the evening with her cousins. After what he'd learned today, he wanted to see with his own eyes that his wife was safe and well and, most importantly, out of harm's way.

"They are ladies, Deveril," the duke replied patiently, "not children in leading strings. I can hardly require my wife to ask my permission before she leaves the house. Besides that, I think it would just encourage her to defy me out of sheer principle."

"Well, you may do as you like with your own wife . . ."

"Thank you for that," Winterson muttered sotto voce.

". . . but Juliet is not as able to take care of herself as Cecily is and I dislike the idea of her being unprotected while her former friend is on the loose," Deveril finished, thrusting both hands through his hair, as if he were trying to keep his head from flying off his body.

"I think Lady Deveril has proven herself quite capable of taking care of herself," Monteith said from his chair before Winterson's desk. "You shouldn't underestimate her."

"That's all well and good for you to say, Monteith," Alec

said dismissively. "But Anna Turner, who spent the better part of a year luring young women to their deaths at the hands of Turlington, is out there and likely has my wife in mind for her next victim. And even Juliet would admit that she is not as physically able to escape danger as other ladies are."

"Good God," Winterson said, frowning. "So Juliet's Mrs. Turner was helping Turlington?"

"Yes." Alec continued to pace. "And she killed Turlington. And might very well be searching for Juliet even as we speak."

"How do you know this?" Winterson asked. "And why didn't you tell me so that I could act accordingly?"

"I only just learned of it this afternoon. Turlington left a letter with his solicitor confessing to all, but only to be opened in the event of his death." Alec paced the room. "I don't know when Mrs. Turner changed from unwilling participant to accomplice, but change she did. And she has nothing left to lose now, so I very much wish to know where my wife is!"

"What do you need from me?" Winterson stood, his hand going unconsciously to his side, as if looking for his sabre. "I can ask Cecily's dresser if she knows where her mistress has gone. I confess when she said she'd be spending the evening with her cousins I didn't think any more of it. I know those three can get up to mischief when they are together, but Cecily has shown herself to be quite levelheaded since we put to rest that business with her father and the Egyptian Club a few weeks ago."

"I have been guilty of the same," Alec said, shaking his head. "What troubles me most is that I knew of Mrs. Turner's involvement last night but did not tell Juliet. I was trying to protect her from the news for as long as I could. And now in doing so I have endangered her more."

"We'll find them," Monteith said firmly, laying a comforting hand on Alec's shoulder. Though grateful for his friend's assurance, Alec, remembering Turlington's twisted body, was not so sanguine.

"I'll go find Cecily's maid and see what she knows of her mistress's plans for the evening," Winterson said, striding from the room.

"Never thought I'd see the day," Monteith said, shaking his head as he watched his friend leave.

Trying not to let his anxiety take control of him, Alec made himself pay attention to Monteith's words. Anything to distract himself from his worry. "What?"

"You're just as bad." Monteith turned back to Deveril. "The two of you are being led about by the ear by your wives. Fortunately, I have no plans to become ensnared by the parson's mousetrap, so at least one of us will remain rational."

"Monteith," he told the other man, his heart constricting at the idea of the peril Juliet might be in, "you have no idea."

"Juliet." Mrs. Turner lifted her mask to show her face, which seemed thinner than it had when last Juliet had seen her. "You don't know how good it is to see you. I was afraid you would not get my note or, worse, that you would not come."

Rushing forward, Juliet hugged her friend. "I did get it. And of course I came! How could I not when I have been worried for you these past weeks? You've had me so worried! How on earth did you escape? Or was there even a need to escape?" The questions seemed to burst forth from her before she could stop them.

Seeing the impatience in her friend's face, Juliet broke off. "But of course you will tell me all of that later," she said, squeezing Anna's outstretched hands. "For now you must be desperate to see Baby Alice. We have her at Deveril House and . . . Lord, so much has changed since you left. I cannot even begin to tell you."

"I am eager to hear all of your news." Anna smiled and Juliet was reminded of how grateful she was to see her friend and mentor safe and alive. "But we must return to my captor's house at once to release the other women he is holding." Even as she spoke, she pulled Juliet toward the door of the chamber.

"Then it was not Turlington who held you?" Juliet asked, confused. She had been so sure that Turlington was *Il Maestro*. The knowledge that there was another such monster chilled her to the bone.

"No," Anna said gravely. "Though Turlington was a bad character, I was being held by someone else altogether. I do not even know the man's identity myself. But he has gone away for the evening so there is very little time for us to act."

"Let me send a note to Deveril," Juliet said. "He has been working with a Bow Street runner who will be able to help us as well."

She had turned, on her way to request paper and ink from Lady Sydenham, when Anna stopped her with a firm grip on her shoulder.

"No, Juliet," she said, her voice harsh, "there is no time. We must go now. Come with me. I have a coach and the footmen will be able to help us if we need assistance."

Troubled by the worry in her friend's voice, Juliet paused. "But Anna, I can hardly be of use to you in this instance. You know I have difficulty with my leg, and—"

"Darling Juliet," Anna said with a reassuring smile, "you underestimate your own strength as usual. I will be grateful to have you by my side when we rescue these poor girls. Now that I know how to get in and out of the secret chamber where he held me, it will take but a few moments to get back in. Please, Juliet, come with me. I cannot leave the other women there to suffer more abuse at his hands."

Grateful to have her friend back, Juliet gave a silent prayer of thanks for her return. "Then I will come with you, Anna. It will be a relief to do something to help these unfortunates if they've endured anything like what you've gone through."

Though she'd agreed to leave with Anna, knowing they'd worry at her disappearance, Juliet dropped the note that Anna had sent requesting her presence here. She had no idea where they were bound, but she hoped that knowing she was with Anna would assuage her cousins' worries for her safety.

Following Anna through the labyrinthine passageways that made up the Sydenhams' servants' quarters, before long they reached a door leading outside to the mews behind the town house. The smell of fresh hay and dirt from the back garden mixed with the sooty stench of London in spring. A hack, doubtless the one that Anna had used to get to the town house, waited just beyond the back gate.

Not waiting for the driver to assist them into the carriage, Anna climbed up inside, and reached back to offer Juliet her hand. It was difficult for Juliet to get into a carriage at the best of times, but tonight, in her thin dancing slippers without the strong arm of a coachman to help, it was particularly difficult. Feeling gawky and graceless, but telling herself it was for a good cause, she hoisted herself with her good leg, and braced her free arm against the carriage doorway into the interior. She was barely inside when Anna reached out and closed the door behind them and knocked on the roof to indicate that the driver should go on.

"So it was not Turlington who took you, then?" she asked once her breathing had returned to normal. "The runner, Greenshaw, sent word last night that they'd found his body in his house last night. Even if he wasn't responsible for your kidnapping, I cannot help but feel some relief at knowing he is no longer endangering young women."

Anna made a noncommittal noise, and continued to scan the scene outside the window, doubtless to ensure they were not being followed.

"I never liked him," Juliet continued. "Of course, I had thought it was because Mama spent so much time trying to convince me to marry him. I had wondered if he might be *Il Maestro,* but to be honest he never seemed to have the bottom for it. Even his attempt at stopping our elopement was a dismal failure."

"Yes," Anna said briskly, "well, you would be surprised just what someone will do if they are pushed hard enough. Take my situation for instance. Turned off without a reference from your parents. With child and nowhere to go. Some circumstances will drive a woman to take desperate measures."

Juliet frowned. "But your situation worked out well enough, did it not?" she asked. "You had your own little house, and were able to teach and keep Baby Alice close to you."

"If you call a dingy little house in a questionable area of town, saddled with a crying brat, well enough," Anna said with a scowl, "then yes, I suppose I did get on well enough."

At a loss for words, Juliet stared at her friend. It had occurred to her, of course, that Anna might resent her change in circumstances. After all, none of it was her fault. She had not sought out the addresses of her rapist after all. But she had thought Anna more resilient than she seemed to indicate just now.

"You are exhausted from your ordeal," she said carefully. "Of course you are. I do go on so, don't I. Just rest for a bit, dearest, and soon we'll have the others freed and you will be able to get the rest you need."

"But how can I rest when there is likely some other poor woman out there being subjected to the most hideous indignities imaginable at the hands of a loathsome man?"

Juliet couldn't see her friend's expression, but she knew from her tone of voice that Anna was genuinely distressed at the notion.

"I know you must feel such anguish over their fates,

dearest," she told her friend, "but for now we can only do what we must for these poor creatures who are being held by your captor. Then once that is done, we shall do what we can for the rest of the women you worry for."

To her relief, Anna seemed to calm down, and reached out to squeeze Juliet's hand. "I knew you would understand, Juliet. You have been such a comfort to me since my ordeal. And you yourself have had to endure such hardship as well. Yes, you will make an excellent sister in my new endeavor."

There was something about her friend's tone that bothered Juliet. Some note of zeal that made her uneasy. "What new endeavor?" she asked. "Do you mean to begin a charity for unwed mothers or the like? I believe I can use my new position as the Viscountess Deveril to—"

But Anna interrupted her before she could finish. "Oh, no, Juliet, you won't be going back to Deveril. Not after what you must have endured at his hands." Before Juliet could protest, her friend continued. "Goodness, given his father's reputation I can only imagine what the son is like. No, you'll be with me. In fact, we might even add Deveril to our list of quarries."

Stunned, Juliet felt a twist of fear in her gut. "What do you mean by quarries, Anna?"

"Oh, you know," her friend and mentor said, as if she were describing the alphabet to a child, "our victims. I dislike calling them victims, though. It sounds so sordid. When in reality they are the ones who are sordid."

Twenty-three

I got the idea," Anna continued, "from Turlington. I told you a little fib, dearest. There was no captor. Just Turlington. He is the one who had the idea of painting fallen women as fallen women. And he needed me to help him procure them. Anyway, at the time I thought it was a noble calling, warning young women through art to protect themselves from fates like mine. But I soon realized that Turlington was enjoying the women more than sending the warning messages. So I had to put a stop to that."

Juliet swallowed. Anna was ill. Whether because of what she'd endured at Turlington's hands, or from something that had happened to her earlier, she did not know. But clearly the friend she'd known and loved for all these years was ill and Juliet would need to do something to keep her from harming anyone else.

"How did you stop him, Anna?" she asked, trying to figure out what part of town they were in. She'd made the mistake of not paying attention when they'd first left the Sydenhams' and now she greatly feared that unless some telltale sound or scent made itself known she would be unable to ascertain their direction until they disembarked.

"Certainly nothing like *he* did to his models," Anna said, her tone censorious. "When I think of how hard I worked to convince some of those girls to come with me, I become furious at Turlington all over again. I had no idea, mind you, no idea that he planned to use them just as their original seducers had done before their downfalls. I thought I was leading them to die a noble death, and to serve as an example to other young women who might be in danger of following a similar path."

Closing her eyes against the idea of Anna's role in those young women's deaths, Juliet forced herself to make her keep talking in the hopes that Anna would tell her just where they were heading.

"So, did Turlington die in the place where we are going?" she asked, careful to keep her tone conversational.

But Anna had enough of her wits about her to guess Juliet's intention. "Now, Juliet," she chided, "you will learn soon enough where we are headed. You mustn't play guessing games. I cannot risk you escaping and telling that husband of yours where I am."

"But I thought I was coming to be your compatriot," Juliet said, wishing that the carriage ride would end so that she could do something to alert Alec. "Do you not trust me?"

Anna's laugh was sad, wistful. "I wish I could, Juliet," she said. "Truly I do, but I know how difficult it can be to disengage oneself from a man once he has one in his spell. I don't blame you, of course. I suspect Deveril, for all that he is the spawn of the Devil, can be quite charming. But until I am well and truly sure that you are no longer in his thrall, I'm afraid I cannot trust you."

To Juliet's relief she was saved a reply by the stopping of the carriage.

"Ah, excellent," Anna said. "Here we are at last."

Taking up her own mask, Anna folded it in half and bade Juliet to come closer. Guessing what she intended, Juliet cursed inwardly as Anna tied it around Juliet's eyes, like a blindfold.

"I apologize for this, Juliet," she said soothingly, "but it is the trust issue again, I'm afraid. I have no doubt you will prove yourself loyal to me soon enough. After all, I have had so many more years with you than Deveril has."

Praying that she would soon have many more years with Deveril, Juliet allowed herself to be led from the carriage. And prayed.

When Deveril, Winterson, and Monteith arrived at the Sydenhams', it was to find Cecily and Maddie waiting for their carriage in the entrance hall.

"Thank God you're here, Winterson," Cecily said with relief as she spied them. "Juliet is missing."

"Dammit," Alec said, his frustration making him curt. "What happened?"

"She didn't tell us why she wished to come tonight," Maddie said. "But we suspected she was coming to meet someone about Mrs. Turner."

"Why?" Winterson asked, his gaze on Cecily.

"She was never very good at keeping secrets," his wife explained. Then realizing that she was talking about the girl who had kept her amputation a secret for years, she shrugged. "Not this kind of secret, anyway."

"She has never liked attending balls before so we guessed she must have received word about Mrs. Turner, so we agreed to come with her," Maddie said. "Then when we found this, our suspicions were confirmed."

Maddie held out the note Juliet had dropped in the portrait gallery.

"I think she meant to leave this for us," she said, her brows drawn. "As a clue when she left with Mrs. Turner."

"How do you know she wasn't taken?" Alec asked, looking up from the note Anna had sent Juliet.

"We asked Lady Sydenham's footmen if they remembered seeing anyone in the gallery. And aside from Juliet, they described a lady in Grecian dress whom I assume was Mrs. Turner. And he said he saw them leave together. Juliet was walking on her own. With no prodding from Mrs. Turner."

Alec cursed again, and turned to leave.

"Wait, Deveril," Winterson said, hurrying after him. "You don't know where they've gone."

"I have a good idea," Alec said as Monteith, Cecily, and Maddie caught up to them. "Turlington kept some rented rooms in Cheapside where he painted and God knows what else. It's where his body was found. It will be empty still since the runners have requested they not be let again until they've finished their investigation. I have little doubt that Mrs. Turner will return there for whatever it is she means to do to Juliet."

Winterson nodded. "Here's our carriage," he said as the conveyance Cecily had called for earlier arrived. "Take it."

"Not without us," Cecily protested, pulling Maddie along behind her.

With a sigh, Alec handed them into the carriage, followed by Winterson and Monteith.

He was in a hurry, but he would doubtless need all the help he could get if he were going to get Juliet back unharmed.

Twenty-four

*J*uliet blinked against the candlelight when Anna removed the blindfold from her eyes. They were in what was clearly an artist's studio. Presumably Turlington's, or *Il Maestro*'s if the paintings were anything to judge by.

"I am sorry for that," Anna said, stepping back from where Juliet stood near the mantel. "As you can see, we are in the studio of the artist formerly known as *Il Maestro*. Of course he is known only as dead now."

The gallows humor was lost on Juliet, who was still trying to accustom herself to the idea that the woman she'd known as a dear friend was also a murderess. Still, it would not do to anger her. She didn't wish to end up like Turlington.

"So how did you dispatch him?" she asked, looking away from the macabre paintings lining the wall. "I can only hope that it was something befitting his crimes," she added, hoping to convince Anna that she was pleased to learn of Turlington's demise.

"Oh, have no fear of that," Anna assured her, gesturing that Juliet should take a seat before the fireplace. "I treated him like the rat he was."

The room was chilly, and Juliet couldn't help a little shiver as Anna knelt before the fire to light it. For a fleeting second, she considered using her walking stick to subdue her captor, but Anna turned just as Juliet thought of it.

"Excellent," she said, hoping she sounded as if she approved of her friend's murderous actions.

"You needn't placate me, Juliet," Mrs. Turner said with a rueful smile. "I know you are somewhat horrified by what I've become. But that's just because you are still under Deveril's thumb. You will see the sense in what I've done and what I plan before long. It will just take a bit of time for you to understand."

"Th-thank you for your understanding, Anna."

Taking the seat across from Juliet's, Anna smiled. "It isn't difficult. You were always my favorite pupil. Certainly the most talented. Once we have little Alice here with us, we will have a wonderful life here together. Without men to disturb us with their pawing and demands."

"Alice?" Juliet asked, remembering the man who had tried to get into the baby's room the other night. "Were you the one who tried to take her, then?"

"Of course," Anna said seriously. "I thought to bring her here just as soon as Turlington was dead, but I realize now that was foolish of me. I should not have tried to bring her here until I had you here too."

She reached across to grasp Juliet's hand. "It will be wonderful. Mark my words."

Just then, a light knock sounded on the door of the room, and a footman bearing a tea tray stepped inside.

"Here you are, madam," the man said, his face lowered so that Juliet had a difficult time seeing it.

They'd had the Winterson coachman stop several houses down from Turlington's house so as not to alert Mrs. Turner, should she indeed have Juliet there. The gentlemen left a protesting Cecily and Maddie behind with instructions to wait in the carriage. And when they walked the short distance to Turlington's house they saw that there were lights burning within.

"You were right, Dev," Winterson told him in an undertone. "Now how do we manage to get inside without endangering Juliet?"

"I suppose knocking on the door and paying a social call is out?" Monteith asked, only half joking. "Sometimes the easiest way is the most direct."

"In this case, I don't think so," Deveril said. "For all that she helped Turlington dispatch half a dozen women, her real enmity is for men. I think having the three of us show up on her doorstep would be met with the same welcome as Napoleon visiting Allied headquarters."

"Good point." Monteith nodded.

"There are certain men that she can't help but deal with," Winterson said suddenly.

At Deveril's and Monteith's questioning looks, he grinned, and indicated that they should follow him around to the mews.

"Servants," Winterson said. "Is Mrs. Turner about to acquire three new footmen?"

Alec nodded. "According to Greenshaw, Turlington's valet has remained to see that his master's possessions are properly distributed and disposed of. I do not see why he would not have brought some of the footmen from Turlington House to assist him."

It took but a few minutes to lure Turlington's elderly valet from the kitchens and subdue him. As the shortest of the three, Deveril was the one who was assessed to be the most likely to fit into the old man's clothes. It was a testament to his love for Juliet that he donned the filthy garments without once complaining at their ill fit.

The only other servant had been a cook, who was more than happy to take the princely sum given her by Monteith and embark for her sister's house in Yorkshire.

Alec was just buttoning up the coat when Cecily and Maddie slipped into the kitchen of the mean little house.

"Why are you here?" Winterson demanded. "You should

go back to the carriage." Then remembering that the carriage was likely a dark London street away, he amended, "You should go out into the garden."

"Juliet is our cousin and our friend," Cecily told him firmly, mindful of keeping her voice low lest Mrs. Turner hear them. "And I will not wait quietly while she is in danger."

"Besides that," Maddie added, her voice equally low, "you might need us. Especially since it appears that Mrs. Turner is not at all fond of gentlemen."

"She has a point," Monteith said quietly. "Maybe we should send one of them in with the tea tray."

"Absolutely not," Winterson and Deveril said at once. The two exchanged a look of equanimity.

"I am going," Alec said, pulling down the tail of his coat. "When I give the signal, come in. Do you remember which book?"

"Yes," Winterson said. "Good luck."

With a brisk nod, Alec took up the laden tea tray and made his way through the house and into Turlington's study, where he found the secret passageway already opened. Well, that was one less hoop Winterson and Monteith would need to jump through when he gave the signal.

Inside the studio, he saw to his relief that Juliet was well enough and seated before the fire talking with Mrs. Turner. "I don't recognize you," Mrs. Turner said curtly. "Where is Jones?"

"It's his 'alf day, madam," Alec said, a note of placation in his tone. "I'm 'is nephew, Thomas."

Juliet looked at the fellow; something about his voice made her heart beat faster. Careful not to let Anna notice, she looked the man over and was once again struck by a familiarity. She knew those wide shoulders, that nipped-in waist, even the boots polished to a high gloss.

That was no servant! That was her husband!

"Thank you so much," she said, her enthusiasm brighter than the situation warranted. "I am parched."

Daring to look up into her husband's face, Juliet was unaccountably reassured by his wink. "A nice cuppa is just the thing, me mam always says, miss," he said. "Especially when yer expectin' a crowd for supper."

"Well, we aren't expecting a crowd, young man," Anna snapped, "so you may take your platitudes and return to the kitchen."

Juliet stared at Alec, trying to figure out what he'd meant. "Expecting a crowd," he'd said. Could he mean that she should expect more help? Yes, that had to be what he meant.

"Aye, madam," he said to Anna. "I'll just go back to the kitchen and stir the pot. Don't you worry none. We'll take care of things right and tight."

Obviously the admonition not to worry meant Alec had some plan, Juliet thought. But what? Who had he brought with him? She had no concerns for herself, since Anna, though deranged, seemed willing enough to trust her. But Alec could be in real danger—especially given Anna's hatred of the entire male sex.

"No need to trouble yourself," she assured him, hoping that he understood her. "I am quite able to take care of myself."

"That I don't doubt, miss," he said, stepping back from Juliet's chair and backing toward the door.

Breathing a sigh of relief that Alec was out of danger, Juliet sipped her tea. "Anna," she ventured, hoping that if she kept Anna talking that Alec would have a chance to put whatever plan he had into effect. "How long have you known Lord Turlington?"

"I suppose there's no harm in telling you now," Mrs. Turner said with a laugh. "Now that you're away from that brute you married.

"I've known Turlington since I was in my teens," she continued. "He was visiting his uncle, Squire Ramsey, who owned the living at Little Wittington where my father was vicar. Unfortunately, Turlington was just as much of a brute then as he is now. Juliet, you have learned yourself by now, I'm sure. But I was a poor innocent girl then and though I thought Turlington was a gentleman he proved to be anything but."

"He raped you?" Juliet asked quietly.

"Oh, yes." Anna laughed bitterly. "And what should my darling papa do but accuse me of luring the young man to his doom? Always, always men stick together. Whenever there is anything that they might blame on us, they do."

"But Signor Boccardo was there to take care of you, was he not?"

"Yes. Thank goodness for the signore. Without him I don't know what I should have done. He has been more of a father to me than ever my own was. Though Papa paid for his sins in the end."

Her mentor's tone sent a chill down Juliet's spine. "What do you mean, Anna?"

"Well, I could not let him get away with it, could I?" Anna sipped her tea as if she and Juliet were two old friends discussing the weather. "It was for his own good. I did regret that my mother and sisters had to suffer as well. But they were in a better place. Certainly better than this nasty place."

Juliet marveled that she'd not been able to see just how damaged Anna was before tonight. Always, at every suggestion that Anna might be less than righteous, Juliet had given her friend the benefit of the doubt. How many people might have been saved if only Juliet had seen her friend for what she was?

"Madam." Alec had once more stepped into the parlor, this time carrying a heavy tray. "I thought perhaps you might like some biscuits to go with yer tea."

"Ah, excellent," Anna said, turning to look at him. "I am quite peckish."

Then, something flashed across her face and Juliet knew she'd realized Alec was not what he seemed.

"Wait," she said with a frown, pulling a dueling pistol from her pocket and standing. "I've just remembered. Jones doesn't have any nephews. Who are you?" Anna demanded, pointing the pistol at Alec.

Before Alec could respond, Juliet stood as well, grasping her walking stick. "Anna, no!"

"I am Lord Deveril, Mrs. Turner," he said. "I'm afraid we haven't been properly introduced."

"Of course you are," Anna said with disgust. "I might have known you'd come to get her back. Well, I am happy to tell you, Lord Deveril, that Juliet is quite happy without you."

"I somehow find that difficult to believe," Alec said, trying to figure out how to get the gun away from Mrs. Turner without harming Juliet in the process.

"No," Juliet said, to his surprise. "She's right, Alec. I do wish to stay here with her."

She turned and gave him a warning look before continuing. "You should go now before we are forced to make an example of you. Just as Mrs. Turner was forced to do to Lord Turlington."

Ah, so Juliet knew what her friend had done to Turlington. And she was now trying to get him away before he ended up in similar straits. Unfortunately, he was unwilling to leave his wife behind to save his own neck. He was stubborn that way.

"You see, Lord Deveril," Mrs. Turner said, still brandishing the pistol, "she does not wish to return with you. Though I'm afraid we will have to make an example of you anyway. I can hardly let you walk away now that Juliet has told you what I did to Turlington. A shame, really, because I know Juliet is fond of you, but we must all learn to live with the consequences of our actions."

"No, Anna." Juliet turned back to her former friend. "He will tell no one. He is quite trustworthy. You will see."

"I am sorry, dearest," Mrs. Turner said firmly, not even giving Juliet a glance as she aimed her weapon at Alec. "You haven't learned it yet, but men are simply not to be trusted. I am sure that you would have learned of it sooner or later if you had stayed much longer with Lord Deveril, but I'm afraid that I will have to ensure that he does not carry tales from what he's seen today."

Alec was preparing to duck as Mrs. Turner's finger got closer to the trigger, but before he could move, Juliet swung her walking stick upward with all her might, and Mrs. Turner, her gaze on Alec instead of her former pupil, was caught off guard. The blow caught her just where her hands were joined on the pistol, and instead of Anna pulling the trigger, the pistol itself flew across the room.

Taking the moment of mayhem for the gift it was, Alec launched himself at Mrs. Turner's middle, throwing her to the floor in a tangle of skirts.

At the sound of Mrs. Turner's screams and the cracking of the pistol misfiring as it hit the floor, Winterson, followed by Cecily, Madeline, and Monteith, burst into the room.

Together Alec and Juliet subdued Mrs. Turner, Juliet sacrificing the sash of her Cleopatra costume to bind her former teacher's hands behind her back.

"I should have known you would be untrustworthy," Anna said with disgust. "I thought I was doing you a kindness by letting you keep your walking stick."

"That was your first mistake, Mrs. Turner," Alec told her, holding Juliet in the circle of his arm. "You underestimated her as a foe. If you knew anything about my wife, you would know that she is entirely capable of taking care of herself."

And that, he realized, was the honest truth.

* * *

It was some time later before she and Alec were able to return home, and despite the lateness of the hour, Juliet was grateful to sink into a hot bath and wash what felt like a year's worth of grime from her exhausted body.

She was lying with her head back against the rim of the tub when she heard Alec come in.

"It seems like ages since I walked in on you in that tiny little dressing room in Gretna," he said, kneeling behind her and taking the weight of her head and shoulders against his chest. "Do you remember?"

"How could I forget?" Juliet asked, smiling at the memory. "I was mortified that you'd discovered my secret."

It did feel like lifetimes since they'd married. And they had certainly been through enough turmoil for a lifetime. She thought again of that moment when she'd seen that Anna intended to shoot Alec while she looked on. It had been one of the most awful moments of her life.

"Did you mean what you said tonight?" she asked Alec. "About me being able to take care of myself?"

She had never considered herself to be particularly capable or powerful. She had managed to keep her amputation a secret for so many years not through her own force of will, but instead through her mother's. And when she'd set out to find Anna, she had asked for assistance from Alec.

"Of course I meant it," he said against her damp hair. "Juliet, you are the strongest person I've ever known. Man or woman. You grew up in a household with your horrific mother and your neglectful father, yet managed to turn out with a compassionate and caring heart. You have gone through pain and hardship that would embitter a saint, yet manage to have compassion for those who haven't endured a fraction of what you'd endured."

"Stop," Juliet said with a laugh. "I have just dealt with things in the way anyone else would. You are the strong one. When I think of what your father put you through it makes me want to—"

He stopped her with a kiss, a passionate affair that allowed them to share all their mutual admiration in a manner that was both satisfying and just a little bit naughty.

"Thank you for saving me tonight, wife," he said into her ear, allowing his hands to dip down into the water of her bath and slide up and over her breasts.

Juliet bit back a moan at his touch. "Of course. I could hardly let my teacher shoot the man I love," she said breathlessly.

She realized what she'd said when Alec's hands stilled.

"What did you say?" he asked, almost as if he were afraid to hear her answer.

She'd been afraid of this. She hadn't intended to tell him of the change in her feelings at all, but she'd been caught up in the moment. And she *had* been unwilling to let her teacher harm him. Not only because he was a person who deserved to live, but also, and most especially, because she, Juliet, loved him.

"I believe you heard me," she said quietly, glad he was behind her so that she wouldn't need to look into his eyes as he told her how sorry he was to hear how she felt about him.

"Say it again," he said, a frisson of some unknown emotion in his voice. "Please, Juliet. Say it again."

She pulled away from him and clasped her knees to her chest. "You needn't humiliate me, Alec. I said I loved you."

She felt a burning in her nose that presaged tears, and prayed that he would leave before she embarrassed herself.

"Humiliate you?" he asked, his voice puzzled as he stood and walked around to the other side of the tub where he could see her face. When she refused to look up at him, he climbed, breeches and all, into the tub with her and fell to his knees before her. Annoyed at his persistence, Juliet childishly covered her face with her hands.

"Why should I wish to humiliate you, my dear?" he asked, pulling her hands away from her face. "Why would I do such a thing to the woman I love?"

Daring to open her eyes and look at his face, so dear to her now, she saw that he was utterly sincere.

"You . . . you love me?" she asked cautiously, watching with awe as his worried expression turned into a grin. "You love me."

"I love you," he said, kissing her on the nose. "And you love me?"

"I do," she confirmed, breathless as he somehow managed to adjust their positions so that she was sitting on his very eager lap.

"Then, Lady Deveril," he said against her ear, "I think we should set about engaging in an activity that is by many called a physical expression of that love."

"You wish to sing a duet?" Juliet asked guilelessly, moving shamelessly against his erection.

"Oh, I will have to punish you for that, wife," Alec growled, heedless of the water sloshing over the sides of the tub.

And it turned out to be a very pleasurable punishment, indeed.

Epilogue

So," Juliet told her cousins the next afternoon over the tea tray, "Anna helped Turlington by luring the fallen women to his studio, and when she realized that he was rather more interested in adding to their fallenness than in using them to warn others of the dangers of men, she poisoned him."

"I can hardly believe we simply allowed her to run tame among us for all those years without knowing what a danger she posed," Cecily said, sipping her tea. Taking another macaroon, she waved off Madeline's frown. "Hush, Maddie, the baby likes macaroons."

"I'm sure the baby does," Maddie said with a roll of her eyes, "but I suspect Cecily likes macaroons too."

Ignoring her cousin's teasing, Cecily turned back to Juliet. "But I want to know what is to become of Baby Alice. Did Mrs. Turner reveal who the poor darling's father is?"

"Alice will remain with us," Juliet said firmly. "Anna refuses to reveal who her father is and there is nothing we can do to make her. In the meantime, Alice will be looked after as if she were our own. If at some point we learn who her father is, then we will deal with it."

"So how are you, dearest?" Maddie asked, her eyes serious. "I know it cannot have been easy for you to learn that Mrs. Turner was so willing to sacrifice you for her cause."

Juliet considered the question. "If I were in the same position I was in when Anna first disappeared," she said, "I have no doubt that her betrayal would have been soul-crushing."

"But . . . ?" Cecily asked, clearly waiting for more.

"But," Juliet continued, "I am no longer that same girl who relied upon her friends to prop her up. I am no longer at the mercy of my mother. And I am no longer burdened with keeping the secret of the true extent of my infirmity."

"And?" Maddie asked, her brows raised in expectation.

Juliet tilted her head and gave a moue of disgust. "I should have known better than to keep any detail of my personal life from the pair of you. I shouldn't be surprised if you listened at keyholes."

"Do not be foolish, Juliet," Cecily chided. "We would never listen at keyholes when there are servants to bribe."

"So, you might as well tell us, Juliet," Maddie added. "We'll find out somehow."

"Very well," Juliet said with ill grace. "If you must know, Deveril and I . . . that is to say, we—"

"Dear heavens, I've had faster head colds than this," Cecily complained.

"We are in love," Juliet said finally. Then against her will, because she was just so pleased with the news, she grinned. "There," she said with the happiest *humph* ever, "is that what you wished to hear?"

Cecily laughed, and Maddie clapped, before they each hugged their cousin heartily.

"This is the best news I've heard since Cecily told us she was *enceinte*," Maddie said with a grin.

"Oh!" Juliet said, sobering. "Speaking of that day . . ."

"Never say you are expecting too!" Maddie said, her eyes widening.

"No! No! Heavens, no!" Juliet said, real alarm in her face. "At least I don't think so."

She did some mental calculations. "No."

"So, what about that day?" Maddie asked, puzzled, looking to Cecily, who would not meet her eye.

"Well, if you will recall," Juliet said, reaching into her reticule, "it was on the day that she told us about the baby that Cecily gave me this."

She held out Amelia Snowe's dance card, which Maddie seemed reluctant to take.

"What's wrong?" she asked. "Don't you wish to take the *ton* by storm?"

As if drawn to the token against her better judgment, Madeline took it from Juliet's hand. "It's not that I don't wish to leave the ranks of the spinsters and the wallflowers," she said. "It is deadly dull."

"Then what bothers you?" Cecily asked, rubbing her arm in an effort to soothe her cousin's nerves.

"Well," Maddie said, her face unusually serious, "you both found husbands and fell in love when you used the dance card."

"Yes," Juliet agreed. "We did."

"I don't need the dance card for that," Maddie said.

"What do you mean?" Cecily demanded, her voice high. "Are you married?"

"Don't be absurd, Cecily," Maddie said, "of course I'm not married."

"Then what?" Juliet asked. "What is it?"

"Well," Maddie said with unaccustomed shyness, "it's just that I have another plan to distinguish myself. Something that doesn't involve dancing or balls or husbands or any of that. And I hope that it will do some good in the world."

"But what is it, Maddie?" Cecily asked, intrigued. "Whatever it is, I am sure that Juliet and I will be happy to help you."

"Of course we will," Juliet said with a nod.

But Maddie wondered. Now that Cecily was a duchess and Juliet a viscountess, perhaps they would not be so eager to support her plan. After all, they had their families to think of now. Still, she would give them the benefit of the doubt. Taking a deep breath, she said, "A novel. I am writing a novel."

There was a long silence as Cecily and Juliet took in the news. Followed by a loud series of squeals.

"Darling," Juliet said with a grin, "why didn't you say so? Of course we will support you! We love novels!"

"You goose," Cecily chided. "I was quite afraid that you were going to announce that you were going to take up driving coaches or smoking a pipe."

Maddie laughed at that. "I cannot stand the smell of tobacco, Cecily. You know that." She gave heartfelt sigh. "I am so glad you approve. I was terrified that you would both be less than pleased. I mean, all the fashionable people prefer poetry to novels. And the sort of novels I mean to write will not be the genteel sort like Miss Austen's. Instead mine will deal with real hardships. And vice."

"Then we shall love them all the more," Juliet said loyally. "Though I do adore Miss Austen's stories."

"I do too," Maddie said, squeezing her cousin's hand. "But I wish to tell stories about more than just courtship and love."

"So long as you do not give up on courtship and love all together, dearest," Cecily said, reaching out to grab her cousin's other hand. "I know that you mean to distinguish yourself with your writing, but I want you to take the dance card with you anyway."

When Maddie opened her mouth to object, Cecily held up a staying hand. "I know that you do not much care for the idea of it, but I cannot help but want the same kind of marital happiness for you that Juliet and I have found. Please, Maddie, will you take the dance card? For me? If for no other reason than that I suspect it is a lucky charm of sorts for us. And you will need luck as well as talent to become a successful novelist, won't you?"

Maddie looked down at the filigreed, fan-shaped dance card. "All right," she told her cousin. "I will take it."

"In all honesty," she admitted, "I cannot help but giggle remembering just where our great source of luck has come from. If only Amelia knew how much her dance card has helped us, she would terrify London with her screams of rage."

"A toast," Juliet said, raising her teacup in the air. "To Amelia!"

"To Amelia."

"May her dance card bring our Maddie as much luck as it's brought us," Cecily said.

"And may her novel writing career bring her many admirers," Juliet added.

Maddie rolled her eyes. "That is not what I am using the dance card for, Jules."

"There is no law that says you only have one wish upon the dance card," Juliet retorted. "Besides, admirers will surely make your books more popular."

Thinking of the reason she wished to write novels in the first place—to show her brother just how dangerous his choices had become—and just how much sway her popularity would hold with him, she relented. "To admirers then."

If admirers could make her brother reform his dangerous ways, then she would attract as many as she could get.

Historical Note

Unfortunately, most innovation in the field of prosthetics and orthotics has come about not because of disease, but in response to a man-made problem: war. As war has historically (with a few exceptions) been the purview of men, I could find no firsthand accounts of female lower-limb amputees in the early nineteenth century. I have little doubt that they existed, but their stories do not appear to have been recorded for posterity. And if they have, I was unable to find them.

What I do have, however, is an imagination, and because Juliet's injury took place around the time of Waterloo, I had little problem imagining that an upper-class English lady, whose father was a diplomat, would have access to a surgeon skilled at performing lower-limb amputations. And though there is no record of such a thing happening, I also imagined that a English nobleman, like Lord Shelby, would be able to pay enough money to bring a skilled craftsman back to England with them to see to it that his daughter was fitted with a proper series of wooden feet. I called this mythical prosthetist Otto Bock, after the Austrian company that makes my own hi-tech, above-the-knee prosthesis.

For the description of Juliet's prosthesis, I am indebted to *On Artificial Limbs: Their Construction and Application* by Henry Heather Biggs, 1855. And also, *A Manual of*

Artificial Limbs by George Edwin Marks, 1914, both of which are available in full from Google Books. For an account of England's most famous lower-limb amputee, hero of Waterloo, the Marquess of Anglesy, I recommend Paul Youngquist's *Monstrosities: Bodies and British Romanticism*, 2003.

Any errors are entirely my own.

Read on for an excerpt from the next book by
MANDA COLLINS

HOW TO ENTICE AN EARL

Coming soon from St. Martin's Paperbacks

*L*adies," Monteith said as he bowed to the cousins. "I hope you won't mind if I steal Lady Madeline for a word."

Yes, they do mind. Maddie didn't speak the words aloud, but she hoped that she conveyed the sentiment effectively. She wasn't ready to be in his company again. Last night's ordeal at Mrs. Bailey's gaming hell had been harrowing, and not only because of Mr. Tinker's murder. She'd seen Christian, or Monteith she corrected herself, in an entirely different light, and her newfound . . . awareness . . . was not at all comfortable or convenient.

"We don't mind a bit," Cecily said, breaking into Maddie's thoughts. Her sideways glance at Maddie indicated that she was ready to send her off with Monteith whether Maddie liked it or not. "I'm sure you both have much to discuss."

Maddie glared at her traitorous cousin. She'd deal with Cecily and her matchmaking schemes later.

Grudgingly she allowed Monteith to take her arm, and just as she had last night, she felt a thrill of excitement zing through her as she placed her hand on his arm. Trying to calm her senses, she realized that they were not headed toward the dance floor. But when she saw the direction in which he was headed, Maddie had to fight the impulse to balk like a mule.

"It is quite warm here," Monteith said, as if he hadn't

noticed his partner's reluctance to continue on. "Let's step outside for a breath of air, shall we?"

"Yes, let's," Maddie said, reconciling herself to the situation. Unable to stop herself, she reveled in the feel of hard muscle beneath his coat sleeve and leashed power as he walked beside her.

Before she could succumb to temptation and inhale the scent of him, they arrived at their destination. For which Maddie was grateful.

The terrace beyond the dance floor was blissfully cool after the closeness of the ballroom. And though several other couples had also sought out the openness of the balcony, their conversation was a far cry from the loud chatter inside the house.

A kinetic silence fell over them as they walked, arm in arm, toward a small alcove created by a bower of spring peonies trained to grow tall and tower over a bench. Reaching the secluded nook, Monteith stepped back and allowed Maddie to take a seat while he remained standing. Her independent nature didn't much care for the asymmetry of the arrangement, but some traitorous impulse within her did.

"You are recovered from last night's ordeal?" Monteith asked, his gaze boring into her.

There was an intensity in his question that puzzled her. He had seen her home last evening after all, and assured himself that she was well. She had lain awake long after arriving home, unable to get the image out of her mind of Mr. Tinker's face as he breathed his last. But eventually she'd drifted off. Not that she would reveal any of that to Monteith, of course.

"Yes," Maddie responded. "Thank you for asking, my lord."

His curt nod indicated that he'd expected as much. But it was Monteith's next words that indicated to Maddie that her welfare was not his only reason for asking her here.

"I have heard from more than one source that you are

claiming not to have witnessed anything about the man who killed Tinker last night," he said briskly. "Is that correct?"

Relieved, and a little disappointed that the charged atmosphere between them had disappeared, Maddie nodded. "It's nothing more than the truth. I didn't see the man who killed Tinker."

"How well did you know him?" Monteith asked. Then, perhaps realizing that it was an impertinent question, he added, "If you wish to tell me, that is." Though it was clear that the amendment was only for courtesy's sake.

Deciding that answering the question would harm no one, Maddie said, "I've known him as a friend of my brother for some years. Mama did not see him as the sort of person a young lady should spend a great deal of time with, however, so we were never in the same company above a dozen times."

"It's not like you to back down from a parental dictate," Monteith said with a raised brow. "Did you obey her?"

Maddie bit back a huff of annoyance. "Of course I obeyed her. To be perfectly truthful, I found him a bit of a bore. All he talked about was horseflesh and racing. Not a favorite interest of mine."

"What do you know of his friendship with your brother?"

This question stopped Maddie cold. "Why are you asking about James?" she demanded. "Surely you don't think he had something to do with Tinker's death."

Monteith looked as if he wished to evade the question, but said, "I don't know if he had anything to do with it. I was simply asking because there is a strong possibility that whoever killed the man was already acquainted with him."

Before Maddie could protest further, he lowered himself to the bench beside her. At eye level now, he said, "I didn't bring you out here to discuss your brother or his friends."

Maddie was disconcerted once more by those intense eyes. "I wanted to tell you," he went on, "that you are doing the right thing in telling everyone that you saw nothing last night."

He took her gloved hand in his. Maddie tried and failed to ignore the frisson of awareness that vibrated through her.

"The last thing you need is to draw the attention of a killer," Monteith said seriously.

"So you don't think James did it?" Maddie heard herself ask. It was a good thing, she told herself, that he didn't suspect James.

His lips tightened. "I didn't say that," Monteith admitted, making her stomach leap in fear for her brother. "I simply think that if the man who killed Tinker is not your brother, then you could do much worse than to let him know that you are not a threat."

"If?" Maddie demanded, pulling her hand from his grasp, looking Monteith boldly in the eye. "I know for a fact that my brother didn't kill his friend. He might be a gambler and an occasional drunkard, but he would never do something so reprehensible. Never."

"Easy," Monteith said, his voice soothing. "I know you love your brother. It does him credit. But I must tell you that this is a more complicated matter than it appears on the surface. And until the authorities can learn just why Tinker was killed, you must prepare yourself for the cloud of suspicion to hover over your brother for a bit. If he is innocent, as you claim, then it will just as quickly move on to implicate the real killer."

"I don't understand," Maddie said, frustrated by his lack of candor. What did Monteith know of the matter anyway? And why did he suddenly appear so grave. It was unlike him, she realized. He was always given to joking and laughing. She wasn't sure she'd ever seen him as serious as he'd been these past two days.

"I cannot tell you the full story," Monteith said, rubbing

the back of his neck. "But your brother is involved with some very bad characters. Men who would think nothing of killing a man for any number of reasons."

"Then they are the ones who killed Mr. Tinker," Maddie said with what she hoped was convincing authority. "Not James."

"It's too early to say," Monteith said, leaning forward to rest his elbows on his thighs. Maddie couldn't help but notice how the shift in position displayed his muscles beneath the fabric of his evening coat. "What I do know is that you are well out of the business. And I would suggest that when next you speak to your brother, that you caution him against the company he keeps."

"As if that would make a difference," she said before she could stop herself. Feeling disloyal, she went on, "That is not to say that James is stubborn, my lord."

Monteith laughed softly. "I'm afraid you won't fool me on that score. I know all too well that stubbornness runs in your family."

Since it was true, Maddie couldn't be too angry over the assessment. Even so, she wondered whether he was serious about her brother's intimates. "Do you really think that one of James's friends might have something to do with Tinker's death?"

"I do, indeed," Monteith said seriously. "And I would be pleased if you could find some way to keep out of the company of your brother and his friends until this matter is settled."

Christian watched as Maddie's brow furrowed with concern for her blackguard of a brother.

"Are you quite serious?" she asked, her color rising in her agitation. Feeling like a lecher for wondering, he speculated about whether the blush extended further down than the bodice of her gown revealed. He hadn't even allowed himself to entertain those kinds of thoughts for Maddie in the past, but once the barrier in his mind against them had crumbled at the Wexford ball, he'd had the devil of a time controlling them.

"I cannot simply abandon James to whatever it is that these people mean to do to him," Maddie went on. "He's my brother!"

Which was the trouble, Christian thought. She was loyal to a fault and it was unlikely that she'd consider her own safety as a reason for keeping out of the killer's way. Whoever he might turn out to be.

In an effort to smooth things over, and to remind her where his own loyalties lay, he said, "I do not mean that you should abandon him, Lady Madeline. I only wish for you to protect yourself. Your brother is a grown man and can fend for himself should it come to that, but you are . . ."

But that was clearly the wrong tactic, Christian thought with an inward curse. If she'd shouted at him, he'd have been less afraid than he was at hearing her softly angry tones.

"I am what?" Maddie asked with deceptive calm. "I am a weakling because I had the misfortune to be born a woman instead of a man? Is that what you're saying?"

"No, dammit!" Christian said, unable to keep the harassed tone, and the expletive, from his response. How did he manage to constantly be at verbal daggers drawn with her? "You're twisting my words," he went on in a calmer tone. "I only meant to say that James is his own person and shouldn't drag you into danger with him."

"I am already there," Maddie said vehemently. "I was there. I held that man in my arms as he drew his last breath. If you understand anything about anything, then you should know that such an occurrence has affected me deeply. And my brother's friendship with him only makes it more imperative that I do what I can to make sure that his killer is brought to justice."

Her words sent a jolt of terror through him. Lady Madeline Essex searching for Tinker's killer was the last thing he wanted to see. She'd already endangered herself enough with her visit to Mrs. Bailey's.

Careful to keep his fear from his tone, he said, "Lady Madeline, Maddie, you are not under any obligation to find this man's killer. Leave it to the authorities and I promise you that I will keep you apprised of any developments that might affect your brother."

He hoped the promise to keep her in the know would reassure her enough to let the matter go. He wasn't prepared for her next question, however.

"You just said that it should be left to the authorities," Maddie said, her eyes narrowed in suspicion. "And yet you say you will keep me apprised of things as they pertain to James. What do you know about the situation? Are you working for authorities now?"

"No, I misspoke," Monteith said quickly. *Dammit. Dammit. Dammit.* "I only meant to say that if I should hear anything about the business, I will share that information with you."

But it was too much to hope that she would be fobbed off with such a tale.

"I don't believe you."

Maddie's gaze was cool, self-assured. At any other time he'd have found it damned attractive. To be honest, he found it attractive now. But he also recognized that her expression spelled trouble for him one way or another for the next few weeks.

"I thought it was odd for you to be in such a place as Mrs. Bailey's last night," she said conversationally. "You aren't known for being much of a gamester. Even tonight you aren't haunting the card room like most gentlemen do to avoid the matchmakers."

"That doesn't mean that I can't have taken a recent interest in gaming," Christian said, though he knew she would not believe him. Her skepticism had shifted into certainty.

"You were there following my brother," Maddie continued, hammering another nail into the coffin of his peace of mind. "Or Mr. Tinker. It doesn't matter which, only that you were there when Mr. Tinker was murdered and now you're convinced that James had something to do with it."

"You can't know any of this," he said, still keeping up the pretense of denial. "I am a gentleman and as such am free to go wherever I choose. It is a mere coincidence that I happened to be there on the same night that Tinker was killed."

"You might even have killed him yourself," she said suddenly, standing up, her hands covering her mouth in dawning horror. "Oh, God. You didn't, did you?"

Leaping up from the bench, he took hold of her hands. "Maddie, you know that's not true. You know it. I cannot tell you why I was there, but I can assure you that I did not kill Tinker. For one thing, if I had someone would have noticed me disappearing from the card table long before he was found."

To his relief, she seemed to see the sense of what he said. Christian wasn't sure just why he'd panicked at her accusation, but panicked he had. Doubtless it was because he'd come to appreciate her good opinion and he did not wish to lose it. Of course that was it, he assured himself.

"I suppose you're right," Maddie said, clearly unaware of the inner battle her companion was fighting with himself. "Though I still don't believe it a coincidence that you were there last night. Nor do I believe your interest in James's presence there last night is mere curiosity."

"At least you don't think me a murderer," he said with more honesty than he'd intended. "I can live with your suspicion on the other matters, but not that."

Maddie's eyes softened as she looked up at him. "I don't," she said softly, reaching a hand up to touch him lightly on the cheek.

And all at once Christian became aware that they were all alone out on the Marchford's terrace.

He wasn't sure when Maddie had developed charms—the very idea would doubtless make her laugh—but ever since he'd held her in his arms last night, he'd had the devil's own time trying to erase the memory of just how right she'd felt there. Not to mention the memory of her soft, spicy, floral scent. He'd noticed it immediately when he'd greeted her earlier this evening as well, but he'd been able to file it away for later perusal. Apparently later was right now, he thought, as he leaned forward and brushed his lips against hers.